The Impassioned Choice

ETHERYA'S EARTH, BOOK 5
By
REBECCA HEFNER

Dear Mattie,
Enjoy!
Rebecca Hefner

Cover Design: Anthony O'Brien, BookCoverDesign.store
Editor: Megan McKeever
Proofreader: Bryony Leah, www.bryonyleah.com

Oh, Heden, how I love you—and I know everyone else does too. I'm so happy to finally give you the spotlight you deserve. Thanks for always making us laugh and for being such a sexy, warm-hearted geek.

Table of Contents

ETHERYA'S EARTH

The Passage

Purges of
Methesda

Cave of the
Sacred Prophecy

Strok Mountains

Portal of
Mithos

Deamon
Caves

Restia

Uteria

Valeria

Astaria

The River Thayne

Naria

Lynia

Human World

Prologue

Queen Calla groaned upon the bed, her shrill wail reminiscent of the screech owls that howled from the tall trees surrounding Astaria's castle. Clutching his bonded's hand, King Markdor whispered soothing words into the shell of her ear.

Her chapped lips formed an almost silent plea as she stared at him with her ice-blue eyes. "Why?"

"I don't know, sweetheart," Markdor said, touching his lips to her forehead. "The pain will be gone soon. I promise."

Vampyres, with their self-healing abilities, usually had seamless births, and the queen's struggles caused alarm to everyone in the anxiety-laden chamber.

"Here, my queen," one of the Slayera soothsayers said, approaching Calla and placing a fresh cloth upon her forehead. "This will help."

Several hours into the birth, Markdor had sent soldiers racing to the Slayera compound of Uteria in search of help. Slayera were prone to injury and did not possess self-healing abilities, and they had standard birth practices to alleviate a woman's suffering. The soldiers had returned with two midwives and two Slayera soothsayers, anxious to help their sister tribe's royals.

So far, their efforts were in vain.

Calla's battered body arched upon the bed. A scream tore from her throat by the fist of severe agony. One of the Slayera midwives yelled, "Push!" and a raven-haired baby began to crown. Markdor observed, stunned, as the child exited his bonded's body, blue veins stark under his pallid skin.

The midwife wrapped the child in a blanket, and one of the soothsayers rushed his body to the next room. Calla relaxed upon the bed, unaware of the commotion next door as her broken body attempted to recover.

"Where's my baby?" she called, lifting weak arms. "I need to hold him."

"He's with the caretakers, darling," Markdor soothed, swiping the wet strands of dark hair from her sweat-soaked temple.

"Please. He needs me. Bring him to me, Markdor."

With a sense of foreboding, Markdor reluctantly left the queen's side. In his heart, he knew. Every step toward the adjoining room was a step closer to learning of his child's death. Entering the room, he observed the flurry of activity as the midwives tried to resuscitate the baby.

Several agonizing minutes later, Markdor held up his hand. "Enough," he commanded softly. "We must let him go." Gently, he gathered the child in his arms and transported him to Calla. His wife held the newborn's small face to her breast, overcome with tears.

"Bakari," she whispered, pink lips against her baby's dark hair. "I will always love you."

Eventually, one of the soothsayers took Bakari from Calla's embrace, promising Markdor to prepare his body for the proper farewell to the Passage the young prince deserved. Once downstairs in the dark reaches of the castle, the Slayer soothsayers addressed the Vampyre archivists that had gathered around Bakari's body.

"He has the mark of the hidden prophecy," the eldest soothsayer said, his tone solemn and wary. With shaking hands, the man exposed the child's inner thigh where a deep pentagram was branded. A five-pointed star within a circle, the symbol elicited fear in the wise men.

"No one knows of the hidden prophecy," one of the Vampyre archivists said. "We chose to omit it from the manuals. Should we inform the king and queen?"

"No," the soothsayer said. "I will dispose of the body and rid it from this world. It is an abomination. We will prepare a coffin for the royals and let them believe the baby is inside. It is the only way."

"Treason," the youngest soothsayer whispered.

"Necessary," the eldest soothsayer replied. Wrapping the child in a blanket, he placed him in a wooden box.

Once all plans were cemented, the eldest soothsayer rode his horse, fast as the wind, to the ether at the edge of the immortal realm. Clutching the box to his treacherous body, he waded through the thick substance to the human world.

The soothsayer buried the child in a shallow grave at the base of an ancient oak tree. Beleaguered by guilt, he said a prayer to Etherya over the solemn site before reentering the immortal world. Upon returning to the soothsayer chambers at Uteria, he reached for a blank scroll and began to write:

Addition to the Hidden Prophecy of the Vampyre Offspring

Be it known that a prince was born to King Markdor and Queen Calla, third in line to the throne behind Prince Sathan and Prince Latimus. Prince Bakari bore the symbol of the hidden prophecy, which states that a marked child, born to a Vampyre royal, will bring death and destruction to Etherya's creatures. The child perished at birth and was transported to the human world, where he was buried with care. Through these actions, the realm is relieved of the burden of this prophecy.

Peace be to all of Etherya's creatures.

When the ink was dry, the soothsayer rolled the scroll tight and removed the loose stones in the wall. Crawling through the small, dark tunnel, he emerged on the other side into a cold, dry chamber. With finality, he deposited the scroll amongst the other secret prophecies and recordings.

Making sure to secure the rocks tightly back in the wall, the man exhaled a breath and let go of his nefarious deeds, for he knew soothsayers and archivists must only share the truths that would help Etherya's people. It was a sacred responsibility, of which few could comprehend the gravity. Secure in that belief, he returned to his life, the events pushed to the dark recesses of his memory.

Several days later, Markdor held Calla, grief emanating from her exhausted body.

"I don't know how to tell Sathan and Latimus about Bakari," she mumbled into Markdor's chest.

"We have time, sweetheart. We'll tell them when they're older."

"Okay," she whispered.

Only a few years later, the death of Markdor and Calla's third child would be lost to history when King Valktor struck down the Vampyre royals during the Awakening. All energy was dedicated to the War of the Species and the emerging threat of Crimeous. Bakari's presence in their world was a forgotten fairy tale, one that ceased to be told after several centuries. There were many other dark forces that took precedence in Etherya's realm.

Which is why no one in the immortal realm was aware that shortly after Bakari's burial, a woman found his shallow grave. She dug up the child and discovered the mark on his leg. Using powers that were enigmatic and potent, the woman brought the child to life.

But that is a story for another book...

4

Chapter 1

Six years after the immortals defeated Crimeous...

Sofia Morelli stood atop the old stone bridge, watching the river flow beneath. A narrow boat approached, slicing through the water, two men inside working in tandem to circulate the oars. Through the water they rotated, again and again, in a synchronized dance of skill and speed.

Neither of the men noticed her as they passed under the bridge, and that suited Sofia just fine. She'd learned long ago that being inconspicuous held great value. It was one of her more polished skills, helping her navigate through life on a journey with one singular purpose: to avenge her murdered grandfather.

She'd learned other skills along the way. Skills that made her invaluable in the Secret Society's quest to eradicate the immortals from the planet she called home. Before she exhaled her dying breath, she was determined to succeed.

The large man approached, his movements sure but unhurried. As she stared at the sunlit water glistening from the fresh morning sun, she waited.

"Everything is in place?" he asked, his baritone voice latent with assumed authority and the hint of arrogance that always slightly nagged her.

"Yes," Sofia said, nodding to the water. "Surveillance is embedded at all seven compounds including Takelia, although it wasn't easy. The red-haired bitch sees everything, and since that compound is new, it's extremely technologically secure."

"It's imperative that we're able to access the servers at all compounds. If you need more time—"

"I don't," Sofia said, turning to face him and sliding the hood of her sweatshirt to rest on her shoulders. Dark, springy curls bounced in its wake, falling just past her shoulder blades. Lifting her chin, she spoke with confidence. "I told you, I'm the most competent hacker you're going to find, human or immortal. The youngest Vampyre royal thinks he understands tech, but he has no idea. I'll run circles around him before he even understands what hit him. It's pretty late in the game for you to start doubting me, Bakari."

"I don't doubt you, Sofia," he said, his tone sincere. "We only have the element of surprise once. It's imperative we take advantage of it. The immortals are most powerful when they band together. We saw this when they defeated Crimeous. It's best for us to attack them separately, as they navigate their lives, before they become aware of us."

"And once they're aware?" she asked, arching a raven-dark brow.

"Then it will be all-out war," he said, solemn. "So, let's seize the opportunity of their ineptitude while we can."

"Agreed," she said, blinking up at him as she nodded.

"Once you gather the intel we need, we will contact the others to strategize our attack. You'll supply us with their schedules, daily routines and information regarding where we are likely to do the most damage."

Sofia's heart squeezed as it always did when she thought about the children of the immortal royals. Although she hated the red-haired Slayer-Deamon, the children of the immortal sovereigns were innocent. Bakari was intent on killing them as well—a part of his plan she vehemently disagreed with.

"The children aren't responsible for the sins of their parents," she said, knowing her argument would fall on deaf ears but determined to try. "Tordor is only seven, and Adelyn is barely six years old. Jack isn't even seventeen yet. Your sister has a young daughter and is pregnant. You really wish to kill her? Perhaps she can be turned."

"We've discussed this, Sofia," he said, his tone resigned. "Although Arderin lives in the human world and is less of a threat than the others, she chose to bond and procreate with a child of Crimeous. It's disgraceful. Etherya did not place us upon the Earth to denigrate bloodlines. There is an order to the world, and I will see it restored. This means innocents will perish. You must get over your childish wish to save those you deem worthy. Calinda and the spawn Arderin carries in her belly have Crimeous's malicious blood, the self-healing strength of my parents, and the power bestowed upon Valktor as Etherya's own child, created from her womb. They are abominations."

Sofia sighed, her strict Catholic upbringing precluding her from wanting to contemplate murdering a child, no matter how great the possibility of its future evil machinations. "It goes against everything I was taught."

"And what about your grandfather's murder?" he asked, a slight hint of anger lacing the words. "Did you forget that he was gutted in his own home and left for dead?"

Rage flared inside her, as it always did when she thought of the death of her beloved grandfather Francesco. Evie had squashed his light with her blood-soaked hands, and Sofia would ensure she paid for it...a thousand times over, until she begged for mercy.

"No," she snapped, feeling her nostrils flare. "I'll never forget. She destroyed the one person I had left in the world. There are consequences for that."

"Good," he said with a tilt of his head. "Clutch onto your hate. Use it to tamp down your feelings of mercy. They have no place in this mission."

"I will." Resolved, she pulled the folded papers from the large pouch in her sweatshirt, situated above her abdomen. "Here is the report on the human woman you asked me to investigate." When Bakari reached for the folder, Sofia held it back. "Tread lightly. She only *appears* human. I'm convinced she's something else entirely. Her blood runs thick with the secrets of her Native American and Creole ancestors. Tales of her presence have circulated through the parish where she lives for centuries, although she appears to only be in her thirties. If you go to Louisiana to surveil her, be careful."

"Thank you," he said, grasping the sheets and placing them into the black bag that sat upon his broad shoulder. "And where will you be over the next few months as you gather the intel we need?"

"I have a place here in Florence, but I also keep my flat in New York. Both are equipped with everything I need, but I believe Italy is where I'm supposed to be right now." Closing her eyes, she lifted her face to the blue sky. "I feel him here, as if he were by my side." Slowly, she exhaled a reverent breath.

"You will avenge him, Sofia." Bakari cupped her upper arm in a show of support. "We all will have our revenge. Stay firm in that knowledge. Call me when you have enough to move forward."

"I will."

With one last nod of ascent, the massive Vampyre drew his coat closed and turned, his loafered feet quiet against the stone walkway of the bridge.

Once he was out of sight, Sofia pivoted back toward the river, resting her forearms against the rocky surface of the bridge wall. Lacing her fingers, she prayed to God, asking for His help in avenging her grandfather, and asking His forgiveness for the carnage that would result from her quest to accomplish that goal.

Chapter 2

Two months later...

Heden sat in front of the menagerie of screens that lined his desk in the tech room. Absently clicking the mouse with his index finger, he studied the traffic analysis. He'd run the report this morning to ensure all of the compounds' servers were communicating effectively. Scanning the data, his eyes narrowed.

Nothing seemed out of the ordinary, but Heden had the distinct feeling something was awry. Scrolling through, he read the information that had been transmitted—mostly schedules of activities on the various compounds. Security trainings held by Kenden and Latimus, council meetings held by Sathan and Miranda, open health clinics run by Sadie and Nolan. All of it was very...*normal*.

And yet Heden felt the tiny hairs on the back of his neck prickle. Rubbing his bearded chin, his fastidious brain clicked into overdrive. He'd let his goatee grow into a beard a few years ago, wanting a change, although he kept it trim and groomed, noting the ladies seemed to appreciate his "manscaping." Directing the tiny arrow around the screen, he opened the task manager and catalogued the usage. The computer was running several tasks: Bluetooth applications, the webcam app he'd recently installed, a cybersecurity program, antivirus... The list went on and on. All seemed to be using the appropriate amount of CPU and memory.

Heden's finger froze above the scroll wheel of the mouse when the arrow stopped over a program he'd never seen and certainly hadn't installed: **SSHost.exe**. The program was using slightly more CPU and memory than the other programs, but nothing out of the ordinary. Opening his browser, Heden performed a search, which returned results for several other software constructs but nothing titled **SSHost.exe**. Not recognizing it, he highlighted the program and ended the task. It disappeared from the screen but not from Heden's busy brain.

Leaning back in the desk chair, he sucked in a large breath, staring at the ceiling as he threaded his hands behind his head. Heden knew Evie had installed some updates at Takelia recently. The Slayer-Deamon was more tech-savvy than the rest of the royal family due to her time spent in the human world, so perhaps she'd instituted something to help with cybersecurity there.

A slight bit of alarm gnawed at his gut. Deciding he wanted to speak to Evie himself, he grabbed his phone to shoot her a text.

Heden: Hey, Evie. I want to check out the computer systems at Takelia. You around tomorrow?

Three dots appeared, blinking as she responded.

Evie: Sure. One p.m. is good. Or you can attend the fundraising lunch Miranda's forcing on me. It's like death and torture rolled into one, but worse.

Heden breathed a laugh. The daughter of the Dark Lord Crimeous and Miranda's mother, Princess Rina, definitely had a biting sense of humor. Heden loved her for it, as he thought his two older brothers quite stuffy and serious. It was refreshing to have someone else with a sense of humor in their extended family.

Heden: Sounds fun, but I'll be painting my toenails. And washing my hair. And something else I haven't made up yet. See you at one p.m. at the main house at Takelia.

Evie: Yup. Bring a defibrillator to shock me awake from the boredom. See ya tomorrow.

Heden closed out the remaining programs and pulled up the open port checker application. It would run silently in the background while he headed to pick up Tordor from school. Sathan and Miranda were both occupied at Uteria, and Tordor attended the elementary school on the Vampyre compound of Astaria. Since Heden lived on the compound, he'd offered to pick up his nephew and hang with him until his parents returned that evening.

Tordor's schedule was also comprised of many weekend outings and activities with children at other immortal compounds. Miranda and Sathan wanted to ensure that as the first Slayer-Vampyre hybrid, the prince was immersed in all facets of the kingdom. The immortal king and queen wanted their son to represent a new era for their realm, where they shared one world and the compounds were united.

Unable to shake his unrest, Heden's mind churned as he traveled the paved walkway from Astaria's main castle where he resided and maintained his precious tech room. The school was several blocks away, giving him time to ponder as the afternoon sun wafted over his skin. By the goddess, the heat from the rays felt amazing. Now that Vampyres had been able to tolerate sunlight for several years, living in the daylight had become normal again, but Heden remembered darker days. Times when their world had been plagued by the War of the Species and the maliciousness of Crimeous. There had been so much destruction; so much death. The peace that enveloped their world now was blissful and serene. *And possibly dangerous*, a voice in his mind whispered.

Heden stared at the sidewalk, his sneakered feet soft on the concrete. Had they been existing under a false blanket of complacency? Were there still unforeseen threats to their world? Someone who wanted to hack their technology and attack them from within?

Wracking his brain, he tried to think of a possible enemy. Darkrip and Evie had burned Crimeous's body in the Purges of Methesda. The Dark Lord would never grace their world again. Perhaps one of his followers who was left behind? Latimus and Kenden appeared confident they had captured all of the Deamons loyal to Crimeous in the months following his death. Was it possible they had miscalculated?

His thoughts were interrupted by his nephew, who waved at him as he trailed over.

"Hi, Uncle Heden."

"Hey, buddy. How was school?"

"Fine," Tordor said, shrugging.

"Just fine?"

The kid stared up at him, squinting from the sun. Not wanting him to burn his eyes, Heden squatted down.

"Did you send her the note?"

"Yeah," Tordor said, clutching the straps of his backpack as he kicked the ground. "I saw her read it by the cubby, but she didn't say anything to me afterward."

Heden gave the boy a tender smile. "Well, you're a pretty intimidating suitor. The prince of our little realm. She might be scared to tell you she likes you back."

"Maybe," Tordor said, studying Heden with his forest-green irises, the same color as Miranda's. "Or she might like someone else."

"No way, buddy," Heden said, ruffling Tordor's thick black hair, a mirror image of his father's. "You just have to woo her. Women want to be pursued. One day, I'll tell you about your Uncle Latimus and how I helped him win over your Aunt Lila. They owe it all to me." He winked conspiratorially.

"You've already told me, Uncle Heden. Like, a thousand times. You tell the same stories over and over. I think you need to get some new ones."

"Out of the mouths of babes," Heden muttered, standing and placing his hand on Tordor's shoulder. "Thanks for reminding me how boring my life is."

"You're not boring. Just old."

Heden threw his head back, laughter bellowing from deep within. "That I am, kid."

Although his nephew was young, he spoke the truth. Heden had been living the same life for centuries now. Sometimes, he would study his siblings, all immersed in their loving families, and marvel at how much they'd changed. Sathan, Latimus, and Arderin were all parents now, with responsibilities beyond anything Heden had ever comprehended. They'd built something unbreakable and poignant with mates who were their equals and whom they loved with their entire souls.

Heden loved his siblings dearly, but lately, he'd begun to feel like a third wheel. On the nights he shared family dinners with Sathan or Latimus at their homes, he would sometimes sense they were ready for him to leave so they could begin their nightly rituals, in which he wasn't included. He would take the train back to Astaria, observe the empty seat beside him and wonder if there would ever come a time in his life when he would perform those rituals. Would there be a mate and children who needed him to give them a bath, read them a bedtime story, and hold them in his arms as they fell asleep? Or was he destined to be the perpetual outsider, always welcome in his siblings' lives but never truly belonging?

Realizing Tordor's comments had stirred up the errant thoughts, Heden tamped them down, wanting to focus on spending time with the tyke. They walked back to the castle, chatting along the way in the warm, breezy day.

Heden had a soft spot for Tordor, as he did all his nieces and nephews, but a lot rested on the shoulders of the little heir. He was the symbol of their combined kingdom. Heden was no parenting expert, and Miranda and Sathan did a great job with their son, but that was a lot of pressure for a seven-year-old. Heden felt it important the prince just got to be a kid once in a while.

"Let's have a mud fight outside the barracks. Yesterday's rain left an awesome puddle of sludge we can wrestle in."

Tordor seemed hesitant as they entered the large doors to the main house. "I don't know. Mom was really upset last time we mud-wrestled. She yelled for, like, a really long time."

"She doesn't scare me," Heden said, already anticipating how furious Miranda would be when she discovered them both covered in mud. Last time they'd taken advantage of the thick, wet dirt, they had trudged it all over the expensive carpets. Their sweet housekeeper Glarys almost had a heart attack, and Heden had offered to clean every last drop. Then, he'd hired the cleaning company run by old man Withers and his three stunning daughters. They'd giggled as they cleaned, Heden helping while he ogled their luscious backsides. It certainly hadn't seemed like punishment. He'd gotten to know them *very* well that day.

"C'mon, kid," he said, pulling off his shirt and tossing it on the tile of the foyer. "Race ya."

Tordor hesitated, gaze darting around the room, and then threw down his backpack and yanked off his shirt too. Their laughter echoed down the hallway as they ran toward the barracks.

* * * *

"Heden! I swear to god, you're freaking dead, you hear me?" Miranda's voice boomed throughout the castle, magnified by the acoustics of the foyer. "If my son is covered in so much as one *speck* of dirt, I'll strangle you myself!"

"Chill, Miranda," Heden said, strolling into the room as if he had all the time in the world and wasn't being stared down by an angry-as-hell woman. Rubbing the towel against his wet hair, he felt some drops land on the top of the clean t-shirt he'd just donned. "Tordor's in the bath and he's fine. We were wrestling. You know, something kids do? He can't save the kingdom if he doesn't learn to have a little fun."

Miranda's nostrils flared as she fisted her hands on her hips. Man, she was spitting mad. Heden waited for puffs of smoke to exit her ears.

"The hallway is covered in dirt."

"Is it?" He gave her his best expression of shock. "My goodness. It did rain yesterday..." Heden rubbed his chin and looked to the ceiling.

"I swear, you have the maturity of a ten-year-old." Reddened cheeks sat under her silky black bob, swishing as she crossed her arms over her chest. "He needs to be doing his homework."

"He will, Miranda," Heden said, grasping her forearm and pulling her into his firm embrace. "And how much homework can a first grader have anyway? Please, don't be mad at me." He pursed his lips and blinked rapidly, his face a mask of contrition.

"Damn it, you're hopeless," she said, breathing a laugh as she palmed his face. "Why can't I stay mad at you?"

"Because you love me to pieces. When are you leaving my idiot brother so I can properly court you and have you as my own?"

Miranda squeezed him, chuckling as she shook her head and detached from his embrace. "You couldn't handle me, buddy. Believe me."

Heden smiled as Sathan entered the room. "Thanks, bro. My son is behind on his homework, and my wife is livid. You're a real team player."

"I do what I can," Heden said, shrugging at his oldest brother. "I'll get the carpets cleaned, I promise. Tell Glarys I'll hire the cleaners again."

"I think we all know why you want to hire old man Withers' daughters again," Sathan muttered, placing his arm around Miranda's shoulders.

"I mean, if they find me irresistible, who am I to argue?"

Miranda gave one of her throaty laughs. "You're too much, Heden. Maybe you could actually settle down with one of them and stop the revolving door of endless women you seem to surround yourself with."

"I am not a one-woman man, Miranda. You should know that by now. Unless you leave Sathan, of course."

"I'm going to rip his throat out," Sathan growled to Miranda.

"Okay, boys. Enough. I've got to get my dirty kid clean, finished with homework and fed within the next two hours." She shot Heden a good-natured glare.

"Well, have fun with that. I'm out. See you old farts later." Heden snapped Sathan with his towel, causing his brother to charge him, and ran like hell from the foyer.

Once in his basement room, he finished toweling off his thick black hair and threw the cloth in the hamper. After toying around on his laptop for a while, he prepped for bed and relaxed into the soft sheets.

Placing his hands under his head, he stared at the darkened ceiling, recalling the program that had been running on the server. He hoped like hell it was something Evie had installed. Sighing, he rolled over. He'd know soon enough.

As he drifted off, Heden contemplated his earlier conversation with Miranda. She was always trying to get him to settle down and find a woman he could make a commitment to. The problem was, he'd never once met a woman who even came close to stoking that sentiment in him. His brothers' mates were amazing, both of them perfect matches for his strong, willful siblings. Heden couldn't begin to imagine finding a woman who came close to the magnificence of Miranda and Lila.

Having a reputation as a notorious flirt, Heden had always reveled in the attention he got from women. It was something that came easily to him, and he'd never lacked companionship. No, that was very easy to find.

What he had lacked all these centuries was *connection*. The sizzling spark of energy he observed between his brothers and their mates. The passion Miranda and Lila employed when challenging their husbands to be the best versions of themselves. The heat of their arguments, and the blazing desire when they forgave each other. Those feelings were so foreign to Heden.

It was as if it was all too...*easy* somehow. He couldn't recall a female who had turned him down once he'd truly set his sights on her. They would usually feign disinterest at first, in an attempt to appear coy, but he read people well. Once he gained their acquiescence and consent, Heden never felt guilty about not making a commitment. He was always sure to be completely honest with every woman he pursued that he was only looking for short-term fun. Perhaps some felt they could change his mind, but he knew that was unlikely. Heden enjoyed his freedom and the ease of his life.

Didn't he?

Gnawing on his bottom lip, he rotated onto his back, unable to sleep. Was the companionship enough without having the connection? It had been for so many centuries. What if he was ready for something more?

Deciding he needed to get laid, he huffed a breath and told himself to go to sleep. He'd hire the Withers girls tomorrow. Hanging with them would make him feel better. Perhaps if he convinced himself of that, it would stop feeling like a lie deep in his gut.

Chapter 3

The next day, Heden hopped on one of the trains that connected the seven compounds of the immortal realm and headed to Takelia. The new community had a more modern feel than the other compounds since it was built over the last few years. As he exited the train to the main town's square, he felt anxious under the early afternoon sun, ready to prove yesterday's unknown computer program was a benign anomaly that was probably mistakenly installed by Evie.

Children's laughter surrounded him as he bent to catch the ball that rolled to a stop by his sneakered feet. Picking it up, he threw it back to the kids.

"Thanks, mister," one of the girls called, the dark space between her two missing front teeth endearing.

"Sure thing, kid." A small waft of longing rushed over his skin, so slight he barely felt it. But it was there, gently coaxing him. Heden would love to have a few rugrats one day... *Many centuries down the road*, he reminded himself.

Two or three centuries at least.

Or maybe sooner...

The longing was replaced by a rush of anxiety.

Or...maybe some people were just destined to remain untethered and have lots sexy shenanigans along the way.

"Not you too," a sultry voice said behind him. "My husband has kids on the brain twenty-four-seven, and now I find you staring at the little beasts with stars in your eyes. They're not that cute. Believe me."

Chuckling, Heden tore his eyes from the children and turned to face Evie, enveloping her in a warm embrace. "Nah, they're little heathens. My bachelor card is firmly intact."

"Right," Evie muttered, studying him with her olive-green gaze. "You, my friend, are full of shit. Or did you forget I can read the thoughts flying through that ridiculously intelligent brain of yours?"

"Eh, I was just thinking about the future," he said, drawing back and shrugging. "The *very* distant future."

"Well, thank god," she said, linking her arm with his as they paced toward the castle on the corner of the main square. "You were my only holdout on the lovey-dovey shit. Let's keep it that way."

"*I'm* not the one who married Kenden," Heden said, ascending the marble stairs and grasping the golden handle attached to one of the large mahogany doors that led inside the mansion. "You knew what you were in for with that man. He's the poster child for commitment."

"I know," she sighed, lifting her hands in a defeated gesture. "I tried to fight it, but he's just so damn sexy, I was doomed from the start. It's extremely annoying. I still haven't forgiven myself for falling for him like a lovesick teenager." She waggled her auburn eyebrows. "But he's so good in bed. I mean, last night, we were trying this new thing—"

"Okay," Heden said, breathing an awkward laugh. "I think we're crossing the TMI line here."

She scrunched her features at him. "*Boring.* I thought you'd be one of the immortals who understood great sex. Oh well," she said flippantly, flicking her hair over her shoulder and entering the castle.

"How was the fundraising lunch with Miranda?"

"Fine," she said, rolling her eyes slightly. "She's so good at getting the old geezers to fork over their dough. It's not really my forte but, as governor of Takelia, I have to attend. I think I might have dozed off a time or two."

Heden chuckled. "The money will go to good use. Miranda and Sathan are dead set on creating a utopia for the realm. They won't stop until every subject is fat and happy."

"Seriously. My half-sister is a saint. I think she got all of our mother's good genes. And maybe Darkrip got a few, but he's still a bit salty."

"Arderin keeps him in check. He's so smitten with her. Our last visit was great. Your brother sure can chug a beer." Heden smiled as he recalled how he'd dragged Darkrip to a bar in the suburbs of Los Angeles, where Arderin was finishing up her medical residency training, and informed the Slayer-Deamon he needed a night off from playing "Mr. Mom." That comment hadn't gone over so well, and Darkrip had sullenly accompanied him to the establishment filled with a live DJ and blaring human music.

After a few beers, his sister's husband had loosened up and actually had some fun. Unfortunately, they'd lost track of time. Arderin was waiting for them at two a.m., hands fisted on her hips, shooting daggers from her ice-blue irises when they returned home. She'd seemed fine the next morning, so Heden assumed Darkrip had made it up to her with lots of apologies...and some other things he *definitely* didn't want to imagine in any context about his sister.

"What are you smiling about?" Evie asked.

"Just remembering the visit. Do you have any plans to go see them?"

"No, but I probably should before Ken knocks me up." Her full red lips formed a gorgeous smile. Although she professed that children annoyed her, her desire to add to their family was palpable. "I haven't been in the human world for a while and do miss it."

Evie had spent the last eight centuries of her life in the human realm, until she'd come back to the immortal world and fulfilled the prophecy by killing her father. Heden thought it an extremely brave decision and was thrilled she'd found love. Judging by the small snippets Miranda had told him, she'd had an extremely violent and painful start to her life. He was so happy she'd found a reason to stay in the immortal world.

Evie was an excellent governor and revered by the Deamons that now inhabited Takelia. The new compound was their most progressive yet, housing Deamons, Slayers and Vampyres. It was a beacon of hope for the future of an amalgamated immortal kingdom. There had been some concern the Deamons wouldn't be able to rehabilitate, but for the most part, they seamlessly blended into society. The ones that hadn't repented were now housed in the prison outside Takelia's walls, built by Latimus and Kenden to ensure they were kept away from the peaceful inhabitants of their world.

"Have a seat," she said, entering the tech room and motioning toward the chair in front of the plethora of screens.

Heden complied, marveling at the expansive room. He'd designed it with care, and since the compound was new, it had every gadget imaginable. Giddy with excitement at being surrounded by all of his hand-selected toys, he sat at the chair in front of several large monitors and began typing on the keyboard.

"So, what did you want to inspect?" Evie asked, leaning over his shoulder to observe the screen.

"You installed some updates recently, right?" he asked, fingers moving furiously over the keyboard.

"Yes. The antivirus needed updating, and I bought the new malware I ran by you last week. I installed that yesterday."

"Good," Heden said, lost in the various windows he'd pulled up on the monitor. Opening the task manager, he catalogued the programs that were running. Sure as day, about halfway down, it appeared: **SSHost.exe**.

"Is that something we should be worried about?" Evie asked, noticing he was hovering the arrow over the program.

"I'm not sure." Heden studied the CPU and memory used, noting it was identical to what appeared on his system yesterday. Nothing seemed out of the ordinary or alarming. "When you were in the human world, did you ever hear of a program called **SSHost.exe**?"

Her eyes narrowed as she looked toward the ceiling. "Not that I can recall. Usually, a host program indicates another server or VPN. Or spyware, but that would

16

be impossible, right? No one in our world can really write spyware code other than you."

"Yes," Heden said, the burn in his gut now a full-on blaze of anxiety. "No one in *our* world."

Evie blinked down at him, confused. "A human? But why? They don't even know we exist."

Heden leaned back in the chair, threading his fingers together behind his head. "I don't know. Arderin and Darkrip are there. Perhaps someone figured out they're not human and tracked them to the ether the last time they visited us. But still, I don't understand what they would gain from spying on our servers. They really only house basic, mundane information."

Evie pulled up a chair and sat. "Well, if I wanted to hurt someone, I'd study their movements and learn their habits. Are Miranda and Sathan's schedules kept on the servers?"

"Yes. As well as yours and all the governors of the compounds. It was always easier that way, so everyone can sync their activities on their smart watches."

Evie expelled a breath through puffed cheeks. "Son of a bitch. The most likely conclusion is that someone is surveilling us."

Heden nodded. "I've got to get this program off all our computers, stat. Then, we need to have a council meeting."

"Agreed. It's probably best you don't put the council meeting on the system-wide calendar. Having us all in one room is an opportunity for whoever is surveilling us. Better yet, I'd suggest a video conference from multiple locations, just to be safe."

"Good point. Thanks, Evie. Give me a few minutes to clean this up, delete the program, and do a basic check on everything else."

"Will do." Standing, she squeezed his shoulder. "Great job picking up on this. You're pretty smart for a Vampyre."

"I do what I can," he said, winking at her.

"I'll be in my office if you need me."

Once she exited, Heden turned to the screen, determined to rid the computers of every last trace of the bug. Then, he called the governors of each compound and logged in to their computers to remove the **SSHost.exe** from their respective servers. Wanting to get back to the tech room at Astaria, which he considered "home base," he boarded the train and spent the entire ride wondering who in the hell was watching them and what they could possibly want.

Chapter 4

Sofia propped her tablet on the desk in the tiny one-bedroom apartment she kept in Florence. Late-day drops of light filtered in through the white curtains that blew in the breeze from the open window. Double-clicking on the secure app, she opened the program and stared back at herself.

Spirals of black hair fell behind her shoulders, and her almost translucent green-blue eyes were filled with determination. They were a perfect blend of her parents' eyes—the green from her father, and the blue from her mother and grandfather Francesco.

She best remembered her parents' coloring from the photographs that adorned the withered albums her grandfather gifted her when she turned ten. Days earlier, her parents had died in a car accident in her native New York City, forcing her to leave the only home she'd ever known. He'd sat with her on the brown leather couch in his Italian cottage, holding her as she cried, heartbroken.

After her parents' death, Francesco had raised her and made efforts to keep their memories alive, reminding her of their love for each other. True love, which he assured her was precious and rare.

The idea was foreign to Sofia. What the hell was romantic love anyway? She'd always been awkward around boys, and then around men, never understanding why so many people made such a big deal about dating and sex. When she'd lost her virginity while in college in Pennsylvania, she'd done it to rid herself of yet another stigma: shy, unwanted virgin.

For some reason, Sofia just hadn't fit in anywhere. Perhaps it was losing her parents at such a young age and being raised in a rural Italian town by her much older grandfather. Never having kids to play with, she'd always gravitated toward tinkering with things that could occupy her busy mind...and that she could enjoy on her own. Being alone had never been a struggle for Sofia. She'd never felt lonely or craved the company of others. Instead, she found peace in it and mostly preferred spending her time that way. The one exception was her grandfather Francesco, whom she loved with her entire heart.

Sofia had made many mistakes in her twenties regarding Francesco. Now, she lived with the agony of his loss, and the weight of her regret was unbearable. Originally, she'd planned to attend college in Italy, wanting to stay close to her grandfather. But Francesco had been firm, urging her to go to America and experience college life there.

"I don't want to leave you, Grandfather," she'd said, grasping his wrists as he stood before her. "You need me here. I won't leave you all alone."

His blue eyes had sparkled with his ever-constant love for her. "I won't let you put your life on hold for me, Sof. I'll change the locks and throw away the key if I have to. You're going to America, and that's final."

Although she'd fought for months, eventually, she caved and attended college in Pennsylvania. After graduating, she moved to New York to attend the sommelier training course at the New York International Culinary Center. Much to her surprise, she loved the city. The hustle and bustle were the perfect speed for her fastidious mind, and New York was an easy place to function alone. It wasn't strange to go to a coffee shop, dinner or a movie on your own. Sofia thrived there, but in the back of her mind, she also felt quite guilty.

She'd left Francesco alone, in the twilight of his life, living in a remote Italian village. Many times, she'd offered to move back, but he insisted she stay in New York and not waste her life on a man who'd already lived his own.

"I'm thinking about moving home with you, Grandfather," she said one day as they spoke on the phone.

"I won't even hear of it, darling girl," Francesco said. "You are enjoying your life in New York and can come and visit me once things calm down at your fancy restaurant. Italy will always be here."

"But *you* won't always be here," she whispered fervently.

"None of us will, my dear. Time is more precious for you now than it is for me. You're in your thirties now, and I know you crave children of your own."

"I do, but I have time."

His sigh echoed through the phone. "Time is the one thing we all have until we realize it's gone. You'll understand this more as you age. You've done so well, crafting a career from everything I taught you about the vines. I'm so excited to see what you will become, Sofia."

Against her better judgement, Sofia decided she would stay in New York, but she did request some time off work and purchased a ticket to Italy. Sadly, one day before she was set to depart, she received the call informing her of Francesco's death.

Shock had pervaded her bones, followed quickly by grief, and she'd collapsed to the floor to drown in unending tears. Even though she'd known she shouldn't leave her grandfather, she'd done so anyway, and he had died alone, without anyone to comfort him. Self-revulsion swamped her as she blamed herself for abandoning him when he needed her most. She knew then, in that moment, she'd never forgive herself.

Francesco had always been the one constant in her life. The one person who loved her unconditionally, even though she was a bit withdrawn and awkward. When she'd received the call that he'd suffered a heart attack in his home, fallen and broken his neck, it didn't compute in her logical brain. Francesco was extremely healthy, ate well, and stayed in rather good shape for someone in his late eighties.

Sofia smiled when she remembered the tales he would recount from his "skirt-chasing days," as he liked to call them. Women seemed to find him irresistible, a fact he reveled in. There were always two he spoke of most frequently: her grandmother Maria, and a red-haired woman named Evie.

Evie had met him in his very early twenties, and they'd had a passionate love affair. A faraway look would enter his eyes as he smiled and told tales of their fiery courtship. But his stories were also laced with cryptic musings about how she seemed more than human. How she never seemed to age and had the power to cripple a man with a stare. Sofia had attributed those comments to her grandfather's dramatic temperament, which was quite rampant.

He'd told the story of how Evie had eventually left, ensuring him she wasn't the one he wanted to bestow his love upon. In the aftermath, his shattered heart longed for companionship, and he met Maria. Her family had purchased several acres of land adjoining his estate, and the rest was history. He'd taken one look at the raven-haired beauty and declared her his future wife.

Maria declined his advances for months, fearing he was still in love with Evie, but eventually, he proved to her his intentions were true. They married a few years later and became pregnant with Sofia's mother, Lorena, in a short time.

Sadly, Maria died during childbirth. With yet another broken heart, Francesco raised Lorena, deciding to never marry again. Although he dated many women, his Maria was the only woman who had secured his heart. Eventually, Lorena married Sofia's father, an American, and her grandfather spent his remaining days on the land he'd cultivated with his wife.

Upon learning of her grandfather's death, Sofia had flown from New York to Italy to arrange his funeral. She'd gone to identify the body in the hospital, holding back tears as she kissed his cold hand in the staid room. When she entered his small cottage atop the Italian hillside, a waft of cold air had enveloped her, and she'd felt a deep sense of foreboding. Telling herself it was just sadness that this was where he'd taken his last breaths, she set about cleaning the cottage.

As she tidied up the living room, she noticed something gleaming on the wooden tabletop, under the lamp. Grasping it with her fingers, she lifted it high, examining it in the light of the setting sun that filtered through the living room window. It was a long crimson hair. Sofia scrutinized it for hours, wondering who had visited her grandfather at his home. Were they there when he died? Worse, did they have something to do with his death?

Unable to push the suspicion away, she'd headed to the local police department the next morning, demanding to see the police report and autopsy. Her grandfather had broken his neck, which the police assured her was from hitting his head as he fell to the ground after his heart attack. Yet the break seemed to be clean and precise, as if controlled by something...or someone.

The report had also shown Francesco had cancer in several of his organs. Again, this was a shock to Sofia since she'd assumed him relatively healthy, and she railed against the fact she'd left him alone and unknowingly sick.

After the funeral, Sofia hired a private forensic investigator to study the break in Francesco's neck as well as the red hair she'd found. She could still remember the man giving her the results in his office in Rome.

"The break was definitely intentional and done by another person," the investigator told her. "I'm one hundred percent sure."

"Why wouldn't the police investigate this as a homicide?" Sofia asked, crushed by the news.

The man sighed. "The police forces in these small rural towns aren't equipped for large investigations, Sofia. Your grandfather was almost ninety years old and had cancer, according to the autopsy. Their explanation of what happened was plausible, given the circumstances."

"So, because someone's old and has cancer, it's okay to murder them?"

"Of course not. But I don't think there was any malice in the local authorities' actions. That's all I'm saying."

"And what about the hair?"

The investigator flipped through the file, turning it and showing it to her. "That one is a bit more complicated."

"Complicated how?" Sofia asked, looking over the report, which appeared as an unintelligible jumble of words and symbols to her.

"The hair has DNA, but it's not...*human*. It's a sequence of polynucleotides, but not anything remotely close to ours."

"That's not..." Sofia struggled to comprehend his words. "How is that possible?"

"The simplest answer is that it's not. I had the lab test it three times. The results came back the same. We seem to have a mystery on our hands, unless you know of a completely human-like species that exists separate and unknown to us."

"That's impossible."

"It is," he said with a nod. "The only explanation I can surmise is that the hair's structure has been compromised in some way. I'm sorry I can't help you more. I'll take a reduced rate to compensate for the lack of intelligible knowledge from the hair sequencing."

"Thank you," she said, standing. "Can I take this file? And the hair?"

"They're all yours," he said, ensuring she left with both.

Later that evening, in Francesco's living room, Sofia stood over the wooden table where she'd found the auburn tress. Lifting her hands, she mimicked snapping someone's neck. As she performed the action, a few strands of hair became dislodged from her scalp, one of them landing on the table. It was all the proof she needed. Her grandfather had been murdered. But by whom?

She stayed up all night, studying the hair through the plastic bag that encased it. As she pondered, her grandfather's voice filtered through her mind.

Evie was my first love, Sofia. She was such a beauty. She never seemed to age...

My Evie was a complicated woman, Sofia. She could silence a man with only a stare...

She had a mean streak as deep as her fiery red hair...

Tracing the plastic-laden tress with the pads of her fingers, Sofia accepted the truth. This woman, whom her grandfather had loved so very long ago, had murdered him.

Armed with that knowledge, Sofia began a quest to avenge her beloved grandfather. First, she had to track down the red-haired bitch. Difficult, since she was quite elusive and never stayed in one place for long.

Sofia embarked down a painstaking path of tracing Evie's steps from when she'd dated Francesco all those years ago in Italy. Since he inhabited a small town, Sofia was eventually able to speak to others who remembered her, and she discerned Evie had moved to France after she parted with Francesco.

Armed with the woman's description and the vast resources of the Internet, she tirelessly tracked her until she discovered her, living in Paris. She seemed to live a solitary life, mostly enjoying one-night stands with handsome men but otherwise untethered. Oh, and there was one other thing... The woman appeared to be in her late-twenties. Impossible, since Francesco had told her he and Evie were roughly the same age.

Sofia tracked her for a while, building up the confidence and fortitude to confront her. She also bought a gun, deciding if Evie confessed to the crime, she might have the urge to kill her. It went against her religious beliefs, but her grandfather deserved justice, and Sofia was determined he would get it. She believed that was the only way his soul could truly rest in peace. And perhaps it was the only way she could forgive herself for leaving him.

On the day that Sofia planned to confront her, she noticed Evie walking out of her condo building, inconspicuous in jeans, a t-shirt and a cap. The stunning woman walked to the nearby park, Sofia following a safe distance behind. Glancing around, Evie straightened her shoulders and headed into a densely wooded area that surrounded the park. Hiding behind a bush, Sofia observed the woman hold her palm up, facing out. Closing her eyes, a thick, clear plasma seemed to form in front of Evie's body. And then, she walked through the ether and disappeared.

"What the hell?" Sofia whispered, running to the spot where the woman had vanished. But her effort was futile—the ether had evaporated. Sofia rubbed her eyes, wondering if she was completely insane but also convinced she'd just experienced something magical...and dark...and not of this world.

Vowing to learn everything she could about the mysterious portal of dense plasma, Sofia began an exhaustive search. It was imperative to observe another creature travel through the barrier. Burying herself in online classes, she taught herself how to code and became an extremely proficient hacker. She'd inherited more than enough to live on from her parents' insurance policy, bestowed in a trust when she turned twenty-one, and her grandfather's estate, which had appreciated nicely over the decades. It meant she could dedicate all her time to exacting vengeance for Francesco.

With her newly cemented programming skills, she installed spyware that would alert her to any surveillance videos pinged as "unexplainable." There were many false alarms, people who thought they saw ghosts or spirits, but eventually, she hit the jackpot. Two people she now knew to be Arderin and Darkrip had broken into a lab in Houston. The dark-haired man seemed to freeze the security guard that discovered him just by holding up a hand. After they'd run outside, he placed his arms around the woman. The video from across the alley was grainy, but Sofia saw what she needed: the couple had vanished into thin air.

Sofia had taken the next flight to Houston, searching every hotel for a man with a short buzz cut and a woman with long, curly black hair, until she discovered where they were staying. Several days later, they left the hotel and headed to the nearby park. Away from the prying eyes of other passersby, she observed Darkrip hold his palm to the air, generate the ether and walk through with Arderin.

Collapsing forward, Sofia gripped her knees with both hands as she panted. Holy shit. This wasn't an anomaly. There was another world that coexisted with theirs.

For years, Sofia tried and failed to replicate what she had seen, finding it impossible to recreate the dense plasma. She kept an apartment in New York City, where she used the vast resources at the public library to research every historical account of other creatures that might exist in their world. Since her grandfather's estate was large, she decided to sell it, choosing to maintain a small flat in Florence instead. With her American and European homes set, she fell down the rabbit hole of searching for an answer.

Sofia became even more comfortable in her solitude, choosing not to date or socialize. After all, what would she say to someone she met on Bumble? *Hi, I'm Sofia. My life is consumed with avenging my dead grandfather by finding an alternate world full of otherworldly creatures and ensuring the demise of an ageless witch he dated over sixty years ago.* Good god, they'd think her insane.

Of course, her self-imposed isolation was detrimental to the other main goal she aspired to achieve. Having lost Francesco, Sofia desperately longed to have a biological child—or children, if possible. With her only living relative gone, she ached to have another being to connect with in the world. Someone who shared her DNA, whose face she could look upon and see reminders of her grandfather and parents. Along with her need for revenge, the desire to have a child grew and curled in her gut with each passing year.

Realizing she most likely needed to attain vengeance before she could blaze the trail of becoming a mother, she continued to research the enigmatic ether, determined to solve the mystery of how to traverse it. One day, as she stood in the French park where she'd seen Evie disappear into thin air, Sofia felt the tiny hairs on the back of her neck stand up. Surreptitiously sliding her hand across her hip, she reached for her gun.

"Would you like to know how they generate the ether?" a deep voice called behind her, causing her to pivot and gasp.

"Who are you?" Sofia asked the man, who was over a foot taller than her, with broad shoulders and raven-black, slick hair. Her fingers tensed on the handle of her weapon.

"You don't need to shoot me, Sofia. Besides, unless you use an eight-shooter, I'll self-heal in moments."

"Who. Are. You?" she repeated through gritted teeth.

"I'm someone who can give you the answers you seek. But only if you want to find them. My help is not offered as an act of generosity. It will require payment on your part."

Sofia studied the brooding man, his energy intense and pulsing. "What type of payment?"

His thick lips twitched. "I'm looking to start a war and I need soldiers. If you commit to supporting my cause, I will help you in return."

"What cause?"

"There are changes happening in the world beyond the ether. Changes detrimental to the ways of life that have existed for millennia. There was a powerful dark enemy whom I hoped would exterminate everyone in the immortal world, but sadly, they defeated him. They now rush to create a utopia that blurs the balance mandated by Etherya. I cannot allow that to happen. I must save them from themselves."

"Etherya?" Sofia asked.

"The goddess who created the realm beyond the ether."

Sofia had been raised a devout Catholic by Francesco, taught to believe there was only one true God. But with what she'd seen over the past few years, she couldn't dismiss any slice of knowledge. Even something that contradicted her faith.

"Will it require bloodshed?"

"Yes," he said, unwavering.

Sofia considered his words, curiosity from the small snippets of information he'd already imparted causing her facile mind to churn. "Will it lead to me killing the red-haired bitch who murdered my grandfather?"

He grinned and arched his dark brow. "Absolutely."

Chewing on her lip, Sofia contemplated his proposition.

"I have several other soldiers to recruit. During that time, I will teach you how to generate the ether, and you can study the world of the immortals. All will become clear to you eventually. Who I am, and how I'm connected to the leaders of Etherya's realm. All you have to do is join me, Sofia."

Sofia closed her eyes, inhaling deeply as emotion swirled within. Intertwining her fingers, she silently prayed to the Lord above, asking his forgiveness for her next words. Then, opening her eyes, she extended her hand.

"Deal."

She watched Bakari shake her hand, their pact filling her with equal parts dread and anticipation. She would finally be able to set things right and allow her grandfather's soul to rest in peace. *But at what cost?*

Yanking herself from the memories, Sofia saw the members of the Secret Society log on to the call, one by one. Once their faces were all visible in the miniature windows onscreen, Bakari spoke.

"Thank you all for joining the call. It is a blessing Sofia has armed us with tablets that are able to communicate between the human and immortal worlds. We all appreciate your efforts, Sofia."

She nodded as the group murmured their thanks.

Bakari continued. "Sofia has logged the schedules of the immortal royals, and everyone has been sent their tasks. Let's go around the group and confirm. We'll start with Diabolos."

"Thank you," the Slayer aristocrat said. His chestnut hair was coiffed and refined. Sofia thought him passably attractive but also an arrogant douche. He had a chip on his shoulder about his wife marrying his best friend after he'd perished. He was only alive now because of the drops of Crimeous's blood their society had cloned. It held many sacred powers, including resuscitating centuries-dead immortals.

"Miranda, Sathan, Aron and Tordor will be at Uteria's castle at the specified time. I will plant the explosive and have the eight-shooter loaded. I will enter the dining room as they're eating dinner and shoot Sathan first, since he will most likely recover from the explosion. Then, I will head into the hallway before the explosive detonates. Everyone will rush to Sathan to assess his wounds, and that is where they will die. I will exit through the servant's door to the vehicle outside."

"And do you still wish to kill your wife?" Bakari asked.

"Absolutely. She has a private showing at the gallery that evening, which is why Aron will be free to join the royals for dinner. I'll approach her as she leaves through the back door of the gallery. That bitch will die screaming my name. But not before I have some fun with her."

Sofia shivered, sickened by the man's evil plans. The woman he'd been married to was far from a royal and only related to an aristocrat by marriage. If only there was some way she could steer Diabolos away from hurting her...

"Thank you, Diabolos," Bakari said, ripping her from her musings. "Melania, please detail us of your strategy."

"Everything at Valeria is set," the woman said, her tone cold and calculating. "My husband Camron will be at Naria and will be unharmed. As you know, that was a term of my alliance."

"Understood," Bakari said.

"Latimus, Lila and their two young children will be picking up Jack from his private school at Valeria and heading to his uncle Sam's house to have dinner. As the governor's wife, I will approach all of the surrounding houses and inform the Vampyres we are having an impromptu surprise banquet at the main house. This will rid the area of any witnesses. I will arrange for their transport to Valeria's main house, allowing Vadik to complete his mission."

"I will set off an explosion outside the house, causing Latimus to exit. I will shoot him with the eight-shooter first and then proceed to kill the rest of them," Vadik's deep voice stated. "All will be dead within seconds. Of that, I am sure."

"I appreciate your willingness to take out so many of our enemies, Vadik. Ananda?"

"I know the main castle at Astaria well, as I frequented it often before the king banished me," the withered lady said, her tone filled with rage. Sofia noted she must've gone through her immortal change late in life, her body locked in its wrinkled shell. "Heden will be downstairs in the tech room. I will murder him with the eight-shooter before he detects my presence, and I will escape unnoticed."

"Excellent," Bakari said. "I will set several explosives around the main dining room at Takelia. Evie, Kenden and Larkin are all confirmed to have dinner there. I will also be armed in case she attempts to transport. She will perish, along with the others." Sofia could almost feel his gaze through the monitor.

"That just leaves me," Sofia said, huffing out a breath, trying not to let the gravity of their deeds dampen her resolve. "I will approach Darkrip and Arderin's house in L.A. once they sit down to dinner with Calinda. I will shoot Arderin first with the eight-shooter. Darkrip will be so distraught, especially since she's pregnant, that I should be able to kill him directly afterward."

"Then we all have our orders," Bakari said. "We strike one week from today, early evening. Are there any last-minute details we need to discuss?"

"What if we fail?" Melania asked. "I can't be outed as a conspirator. I'm the governor's wife after all."

Sofia wrinkled her nose at the entitled woman. She was quite nasty and extremely unlikeable. Someone she never would've spoken to if she hadn't been dragged into this life of vengeance and retribution.

"The meeting point is still the same," Bakari said, referencing the hidden cave located in the uncharted woods near the Purges of Methesda. "Whether you fail or succeed, the plan is to meet there after the attacks. I expect everyone to be there."

"Aye," they all concurred in unison.

"Very well. You all are free to go. Sofia, please hang back so we can speak privately."

The other members disconnected, and Sofia waited for the Vampyre to speak.

"I see the indecision and compassion in your eyes, Sofia," Bakari said. "It worries me. Will you be able to kill my pregnant sister? If not, I can send you to Takelia instead."

"I think you're physically better matched to take on Kenden and Larkin. I can do it. Darkrip is evil and must be vanquished."

"Very well," Bakari said, his body language emitting a wariness that relayed his doubt about her ability to complete her mission. "We're counting on you. Don't let us down."

"I won't," she said, ready to be done with the annoying lecture. "I'm available on my cell if you need me." With that, she closed the cover over her tablet, ending the transmission. She was pretty sure the arrogant Vampyre wasn't thrilled about being rudely cut off, but she was over him. In fact, she was over all of it. What in the hell had she gotten herself into?

After brushing her teeth, she threw on an old tank and shorts and slipped into bed. Closing her eyes, the faces of the children that would perish by their actions began drifting across her mind. Unable to stop her tears, Sofia buried her face in the pillow and cried herself to sleep.

Chapter 5

At Astaria, Heden was hosting a teleconference of his own from the tech room.

"Can everyone hear me?" he asked, checking to make sure his computer's microphone was at maximum volume.

"Loud and clear," Miranda said, sitting beside Sathan in the conference room at Uteria.

"Good. I'm sorry to schedule this meeting so late, but Evie and I discovered something earlier today that can't wait." Heden brought everyone up to speed, informing them of the surveillance program and its subsequent removal from the servers as well as the threat he foresaw. Once all the updates had been shared, he said, "The only conclusion I can surmise is that someone from the human world is spying on us."

"Wow," Miranda said, exhaling a puff of breath that fluttered her dark hair. "That's intense. Thanks for all the information, Heden, and for getting the program off the servers. Why would anyone from the human world want to spy on us?"

"We don't know," Evie said, Kenden at her side. "I can only deduce it's someone who figured out Arderin and Darkrip aren't one of their own."

"Could it be one of their governments? The Americans, Chinese or Russians?" Latimus asked.

"It's possible," Heden said. "I just don't know. At this point, I'm going to have to go to the human world to investigate."

"Oh, Heden," Lila said from her seat beside Latimus. "What if something happens to you? Lattie," she said, clutching her bonded's muscular forearm, "you should go with him."

"Do you want me to accompany you?" Latimus asked, placing his arm around Lila's shoulders in an absent, soothing gesture.

"As much as I'd love to spend twenty-four-seven with your ugly mug, I think I should go alone." Heden's lips curved as Latimus scowled.

"You're such a dick."

"From you, that's a compliment," Heden said, smiling as he chomped the gum he'd thrown in his mouth earlier. "Don't worry, buttercup," he said, addressing Lila. "I'll be safe. It will be easier for me to track down whoever installed the surveillance program on my own. Working solo means I can work quickly and efficiently. Also, I need to warn Darkrip and Arderin."

"Is there a way to create a device that can breach the ether?" Sathan asked, worried. "I don't want Arderin there without a way to contact us any longer. This cements the need to have the ability to communicate directly with her."

"I've just never dedicated any time to developing equipment that can communicate through the ether since our world is so separate. But I think I could figure it out if I tinkered long enough. I can make that a priority as soon as I get home from tracking down our spy."

"Good," Sathan said. "We need to keep her safe since she's pregnant."

"I know, Sathan," Heden said, reminded of how protective his oldest brother was of their sister. "Darkrip will keep her safe until I can figure something out. I don't want anything to happen to her either. She's my favorite sister."

It was a recurring joke he and Latimus used to drive Arderin crazy, since she was their only sister.

"I'm going to leave in the morning," Heden said. "I've already packed and have enough Slayer blood to last over a week. I'm going to leave our schedules in the system as they were. It will appear that I'm still here, and you all are still partaking in your daily activities that are on the books. It's a great opportunity to identify a threat if they were indeed looking to strike. Although I removed the **SSHost.exe** program from our servers, I'm not confident we're completely free of spyware. Remember that as you communicate."

"We'll stay sharp, Heden, and wish you luck on your journey," Miranda said. "Promise us you'll stay safe."

"I will, Miranda," he said, giving her a reassuring grin. "If I discover anything of note, I'll come back through the ether and contact you all immediately."

"We love you," Lila said in her sweet voice.

"I love you all too, even my man bun-toting brother," Heden said. That elicited a chuckle from everyone but Latimus, whose eyes narrowed with good-natured distain. "Chop that thing off while I'm gone, will ya, bro?"

"Lay off my bonded," Lila said, pecking Latimus on his cheek. "His man bun is sexy."

Latimus finally smiled and stole a kiss from her pink lips. "Do you want me to drive you to the ether in the morning?"

"That would be great, Latimus. I take it all back. You're a specimen of true masculinity, and don't let anyone tell you otherwise."

"Call me if you need me to come over," Evie said. "I'm extremely familiar with all facets of the human world and can be there in a snap. Safe travels, Heden." She and Kenden gave a wave and closed her laptop, ending the call.

"Bye, Heden," Miranda and Sathan called in unison.

A few seconds later, the transmission ended.

Heden spent the next few hours shoring up his kingdom-wide responsibilities as the tech guru of their world. After a few hours of fitful sleep, he rose with the sun and hopped in the four-wheeler with Latimus. Armed with his supplies, he waded through the thick wall of ether and entered the human world.

Chapter 6

Sofia sat in her rented car, parked across the street from Arderin and Darkrip's home in the suburbs of L.A. It was in an unassuming cul-de-sac surrounded by other homes of similar structure and size. None of their neighbors would suspect the truth: they were living in the presence of immortal beings posing as humans so Arderin could finish her medical residency.

Lifting her binoculars, Sofia studied the family in the soft morning light under the blue sky. Darkrip was sitting with Callie at the table while Arderin scrambled eggs at the stove. Grasping the pan's handle, she swiveled, scooping a fluffy pile onto her daughter's plate and then her husband's. He grabbed her wrist as she began to turn away and drew her down for a kiss. After giving him a peck, she placed the pan in the sink and opened the refrigerator. Pulling out a clear jug filled with red liquid, she poured some for Callie, then for herself, and sat down to join them.

Sofia observed, understanding now, after years of studying the immortals, that the hybrid children of Vampyres and Slayers needed both food and Slayer blood as sustenance. The combination in equal parts kept their young hearts beating.

Callie was a beauty, a mirror image of Arderin. She had a precocious nature, which made it challenging for her parents to control her remarkable powers. As the granddaughter of Crimeous, the Dark Lord's blood ran true in her veins, as it did her father's. It was a compelling reason to dispel her from the Earth.

And yet as Sofia watched them complete the mundane task of eating breakfast together, little bugs of anxiety crawled in her stomach. Through the large bay window, Arderin reached over and grabbed the fork out of Darkrip's hand, devouring the eggs he'd stacked upon it. In retaliation, he picked up a speck of egg from his plate and threw it at her. It landed on her face, causing Callie to break into a fit of giggles.

It was all so normal. All so right. How in the world was she going to murder these people who loved each other so much? Reaching for her bag in the passenger seat, she pulled out her phone and began scrolling through pictures of her grandfather. Every time she had doubts, Sofia reminded herself that she was doing this for him. So his soul could rest.

Her thumb froze over the screen, her favorite picture of Francesco smiling back at her, blue eyes sparkling. Would he truly want her to murder these immortals?

Knowing the answer deep in her soul, she whispered a curse, clicked the phone off and threw it on the seat.

Sofia had been so wracked with guilt after Francesco's death and so desperate for knowledge about the immortal world, she'd latched onto Bakari's offer without truly familiarizing herself with those she aligned against. She realized now that was a terrible misstep. If she'd taken the time to study how the immortals interacted, beyond just tracking their movements and habits, she would've observed flawed but righteous people, all of whom strived to act with morality and decency. They loved their families and children with the same ferocity she loved Francesco. Even Evie, whom she would always hate with a passion, had seemed to turn over a new leaf and saved so many immortals when she defeated Crimeous.

Refocusing on the house, Sofia emitted a soft gasp. Lifting the binoculars, she honed in on the front porch. A thick, emulsified band of air appeared beside the house. As if in a dream, she watched a body emerge. Tall and broad, the man exited the ether, a black bag strapped across his shoulders and back. The plasma disappeared, and the man headed toward the front door, lifting his hand to knock. There he stood, frozen, hand in the air. Was he waiting for something?

As if tethered to him by a thread of energy, Sofia *felt* him turn before he actually made the movement. Experiencing the moment in slow-motion, the man dropped his hand, slowly pivoted and latched onto her. Eyes clear and full of purpose narrowed, his expression grim. They spoke a thousand silent, unintelligible words in that fraction of a second. Sofia's heart slammed in her chest, and she struggled to breathe. Gathering her wits, she broke the intense eye contact, revved the car and sped down the street, away from the madness.

A few miles down the road, she pulled into an abandoned gas station, throwing the car in park. Grasping the wheel with white-knuckled hands, she rested her forehead against it as she drew heaving gasps of air into her lungs. Once she was able to regain her wits, Sofia acknowledged the truth: Heden was in the human world and he was onto her. She didn't know how much he knew, but it was evident he'd discovered her surveillance program.

She recognized the immortal world's gifted hacker from her reconnaissance. It had taken her weeks to develop a program that would go unnoticed unless he had reason to look for it. The Vampyre was extremely intelligent and close to his family. It was only a matter of time before the Secret Society was discovered.

Terror invaded her pores as she imagined relaying the news to Bakari. They were supposed to attack in a week, and he would be furious. Deciding she needed to assess how much Heden knew so she could formulate a solid plan, she headed to her hotel, dread pulsing through her shaking body.

Chapter 7

"Heden!" Arderin squealed, yanking open the door and clutching him in a smothering embrace. Drawing back, she palmed his cheeks.

"How are you here? Why are you here? Oh my god, is something wrong? Darkrip, come here! Heden's here!"

"I can see that, darling," Darkrip said, expression droll as he appeared behind her. "Perhaps he could tell us the purpose of his visit if you gave him some space."

Scowling at her husband, she grabbed Heden's wrist, tugging him into the house and closing the door. "Don't mind my extremely *rude* bonded," Arderin said, shooting a glare at Darkrip. "He's still adjusting to life outside the Deamon caves. Perhaps one day, he'll learn some manners."

"God forbid." Darkrip lifted a sardonic brow. "Hey, Heden," he said, extending his hand. "Good to see you. Why in the hell are you here?"

Heden shook his hand and heard a tiny gasp below. Looking down, he saw Calinda staring up at them.

"Daddy, you said a bad word," she whispered.

Darkrip shot Heden a grimace. "Fifty cents in the swear jar. I think the damn thing's worth about a million dollars at this point."

Arderin bent to pick up her daughter and balanced her on her hip, next to her several-months-pregnant belly. "Daddy is very sorry that he said *two* bad words, aren't you, Daddy?"

"Yes," Darkrip said, looking anything but. "I'll put an extra dollar in the swear jar today."

Callie looked at Heden, the girl's wide blue-green eyes almost melting his heart. "Can I tell you a secret, Uncle Heden?" she asked.

"Sure thing, chicken wing," he said, extending his arms to take her from Arderin. Holding her close, he rotated so his back was to her parents, seemingly giving them privacy. "Whisper it in my ear so they don't hear."

Cupping his ear with her small hand, she spoke into the shell. "I don't mind if he curses because Mommy says I get to keep all the money when I get older. As much as Daddy swears, I'll be rich!"

Heden laughed, resting his forehead against hers so he could gaze into her eyes. "You're brilliant, baby toad. Don't let anyone tell you otherwise, okay?"

"Okay," she said, nodding as she beamed.

"Oh, god, that stupid nickname," Arderin groaned. "Can you be more annoying?"

"What?" Heden said, facing her and trying his best to look innocent. "You're *little toad*, so she's *baby toad*. It only makes sense, sis."

"I hate that nickname," Arderin said, reaching for Callie's hand after she squirmed out of Heden's arms back to solid ground. "Let me get her ready for school, and then we'll talk, okay? In the meantime, go ahead and update Darkrip on why you're here. Be back in a few. C'mon, baby."

They trailed up the stairs, his sister and her mini-me, as Heden marveled at their likeness.

"I know," Darkrip said, shaking his head. "There are two of them now. It's exhausting."

Chuckling, Heden patted him on the shoulder. "You signed up for this, buddy. I told you she was difficult."

They strolled into the living room, Heden sitting on the couch while Darkrip eased into the leather reclining chair beside him. "Difficult and amazing and perfect," Darkrip sighed, relaxing into the seat. "She owns my soul." Smiling, as deeply as one like Darkrip allowed himself to, he studied Heden. "So, as much as I love the surprise, I'm guessing you're not here for shits and giggles."

"Unfortunately not," Heden said, rubbing his hands over the tops of his thighs. "First things first, you're being surveilled. Actually, we all are."

Darkrip's shoulders tensed, and he leaned forward, resting his elbows on his knees. "For how long? By whom?"

Heden held up a hand. "Let me start at the beginning. There's a lot." After expelling a breath through rounded cheeks, Heden updated his brother-in-law.

"Damn," Darkrip said, sitting back as the information washed over him. "We all thought we'd seen the last of our enemies when my father was defeated."

"Yes. It's frustrating and concerning. We have no idea who's surveilling us. However, I did recently gain a new lead."

"When?"

"About five minutes ago, outside your house. A dark-haired woman was staking you guys. Six-JRN-three-seven-two."

"What?" Darkrip asked, confused.

"The license plate of her car, which I assume is rented. I'll trace it and figure out who she is." Pulling out his phone, Heden jotted down the number in the notes section.

"You remember stuff like that automatically?" Darkrip asked, impressed.

Heden shrugged. "I've never claimed to be the smartest immortal, it's just a fact." Grinning, he acknowledged his teasing.

"He's always had a photographic memory," Arderin chimed in, floating down the stairs and into the room. "Which does *not* mean he's smarter than any of us. He just has the brain of an elephant. And about as much hot air as one." Scrunching her features at Heden, she sat beside him on the couch.

"Remind me why I love you again?" he asked, rubbing his beard.

"Because I beat you up when you were five, and you've been terrified of me ever since."

"True story," Heden murmured as Callie dashed toward them.

"I'm ready, Daddy! Can I wear my new coat today?"

Standing, Darkrip sighed and ran his hand over her raven-black curls. "It's eighty degrees outside, but you've broken me, so wear what you want."

"Stop it," Arderin scolded, lifting from the couch to swat his arm. Squatting down, she kissed Callie on the nose. "Have a good day at school, baby. We'll have fish sticks tonight, okay?"

"Yay!" Callie exclaimed, jumping up and down as if she'd won unlimited amounts of candy. "Bye, Mommy."

"Heden will update you while I drive her to school. Be back soon, princess." After squeezing Arderin's hand, Darkrip and Callie headed out the back, and the car engine sounded in the driveway.

"So, it's bad," Arderin said, sitting beside Heden.

"It's not good, sis," he said, placing his arm over her shoulder and drawing her close. "But I'll be damned if anyone hurts our family. We'll figure this out, no matter what."

"At least the timing is good," she said, snuggling into his side. "I'm working nights the rest of the week. Don't have to go in until eight o'clock tonight. It will give us time to have dinner, and you can read to Callie before she goes to sleep."

"Sounds perfect. I missed you."

"Missed you too," she said, burrowing into his broad chest.

Reveling in the joy of having her near, Heden told her everything while they waited for Darkrip to return.

Chapter 8

The next morning, Sofia sat in the coffee shop, earbuds blaring under the cloth of her sweatshirt's hood. Her fingers moved feverishly over the keyboard as she worked to restore the spyware she'd placed on the servers at the immortal compounds.

Cursing, she scowled at the error message that popped up. Although she'd completely reprogrammed the software, she hadn't been able to reinstall it. Heden was a competent hacker, and now that he was onto her, she had a feeling she was screwed. She'd always thought herself more proficient than him but also had the element of surprise. Now that he'd discovered her, he would go full force to protect his family. The Vampyre siblings were close and would sacrifice anything to safeguard each other.

Squinting at the screen, she began rewriting a section of code to see if it would allow her to infiltrate the immortals' computers through a different channel. Suddenly, a text box appeared on the laptop, the curser blinking.

Sitting up in her chair, Sofia popped the buds from her ears as the curser fully grabbed her attention. Then, three ominous words appeared: **I see you**.

Sofia's heart leapt into her throat, blood pulsing through her shocked body. Glancing around, she didn't see Heden anywhere in the café. It was pretty hard to miss a six-foot, six-inch man, so she surmised he was surveying her remotely. Understanding she was made, she began to type.

You've stumbled upon something you can't possibly understand. I suggest you leave me alone.

The curser blinked as Heden responded.

I know you're human, what you look like, and that you're spying on us. There is no way in hell you're going to hurt my family. Got it?

Air exited Sofia's nostrils as she exhaled. Sadly, the plan was already in motion. His family was already dead.

Antagonizing me is a wasted effort. I'm sorry. Things have been put into place that cannot be undone. Don't contact me again.

With shaking hands, Sofia closed her laptop. After gathering her things, she threw her empty cup in the trash, pulled her hoodie securely over her black curls and exited the shop.

Several footsteps later, she felt his presence. Even though her head was down and her sneakered soles set a steady pace, there was the unmistakable and unshakable intuition that someone was following her. Steeling herself, she clenched her jaw and pivoted.

Heden stood on the sidewalk, tall and broad under the blue sky. Cars whizzed past as their gazes held. Thick, firm lips sat in a straight line, surrounded by his beard. An austere nose led to full, dark eyebrows that bracketed ice-blue eyes. Murder swam in the clear orbs, causing Sofia to wonder if she'd ever seen anyone so angry. If so, she couldn't recall. No one had ever looked at her with such rage.

"Hello, Sofia Morelli." His deep baritone washed over her, sending chill bumps across her arms and causing the hairs on the back of her neck to straighten. "I think it's time we had a little chat."

Sofia swallowed, comprehending that she could never outrun this hulking Vampyre. He was at least a foot taller, and muscles seemed to bulge from his arms under the sleeves of his black t-shirt. Faded jeans encased the tree trunks that comprised his legs. The public setting alongside the road probably ensured her safety more than running from him anyway. Immortals were consumed with not being discovered by humans, so she doubted he'd hurt her in full view of others. Clutching the strap of her laptop bag, she faced him with every ounce of courage she could muster.

"Hello, Heden."

Those piercing eyes narrowed as he glowered down at her. "Why are you spying on the immortals? Why would one human go to all this trouble?"

Sofia blinked as she contemplated her answer. "You must know I'm not working alone."

His irises darted between hers, studying her. "Who hired you?"

She scoffed. "Oh, I'm not getting paid. In currency, at least. My restitution will come when the mission is complete."

Confusion lined his expression. "Are you seeking information on immortals? Perhaps from discovering Arderin and Darkrip aren't human? If you want data, I could supply it to you. It's natural for a human who discovers the immortal world to be curious."

She smiled although it held no amusement. "If only that were the case. Things are too far along. I'm sorry." Shaking her head, she turned and began walking again.

"Wait," he said, grabbing her bag and spinning her around. "Let me negotiate with you. Perhaps I can offer you something more valuable than whatever the person who hired you is offering."

Tears welled in Sofia's eyes as she stared up at him. The image of Francesco's smiling face filtered through her mind, sending a crack down her heart. "There is only one thing I want. One thing I've ever wanted. And I will have it, no matter the cost. The man I'm aligned with is the only one who can help me achieve it." A tear broke free, skating down her cheek, and she angrily swiped it away. "Goodbye."

"Sofia," he said, grabbing her upper arm before she could turn away.

Glaring at him, she shook him off. "Don't touch me!"

His hand fell to his side as a pleading expression lined his face. "Who hurt you, Sofia? Was it someone in my family? If so, I understand why you'd want to harm us. But please, at least give me the opportunity to make it right."

"There's no way to make it right," she said, wiping away another tear. "He's dead and never coming back! Gone, as if he never existed. Every person she loves will pay. I'm impressed you tracked me down, but your efforts are wasted. If you so much as follow me one more step, I'll send the video of your sister traveling through the ether to everyone in her residency program. Forget being a doctor—they'll think she's nuts and lock her up for decades. I could make your life a living hell and have videos ready to send to the authorities the second something happens to me. So, I'll say this one more time." Closing the distance between them, she said through gritted teeth, "Leave. Me. Alone."

Sparing him one last cursory glance, she turned on her heel and stalked away, hoping she appeared confident. But inside, she was a quivering mess.

* * * *

Heden watched the little human walk away as comprehension washed over him. Someone in his family had hurt her terribly. The waif of a woman had looked upon him with such pain in her translucent green-blue eyes. Never had he seen such anguish. Whoever she was trying to avenge had been someone extremely important to her.

Reaching to his back pocket, he pulled out his phone and entered the passcode. Clicking the app with the pad of his thumb, it opened onto a map. A blinking dot traveled down the street away from him, toward downtown L.A.

When Heden grabbed Sofia's bag, he'd surreptitiously planted a bug on it. The inconspicuous device would allow him to track her to whatever point she was using as home base. Once there, he would confront her.

In the meantime, he'd spend some time working on the patch he'd developed that would ensure their devices could communicate through the ether. Heden was on the right track, but it still wasn't working effectively. Now that he was beginning to fit the puzzle pieces of this bizarre mystery together, he wanted to be able to reach his family on the other side.

He sat in the coffee shop where Sofia had spent the morning. The charming café had fast Wi-Fi and strong coffee. Heden toyed for several hours but still couldn't come up with a working patch or the correct code to send messages to the immortal realm. Frustrated, he consulted his phone to see where Sofia was.

She was only a few blocks away, stationary near a hotel that was listed on the map. This must be where she was staying. After packing up his things, Heden slung his bag over his shoulder and headed to find her.

When he approached the hotel, the blinking dot appeared to be coming from the alleyway between the hotel and the strip mall next door. Moving slowly and discreetly, he slid up to the stone wall that comprised the back of the hotel. Shifting his head, he peeked around the corner.

Sofia was there, head tilted back, speaking to a man. One who was very tall and extremely broad-shouldered, with straight black hair the exact color and texture of Latimus's. His massive form was an almost exact replica of his brothers'...and his own. Feeling his eyes grow wide, Heden's brain struggled to make sense of the impossible: this man was a Vampyre.

Moreover, this man was a direct relative. The similarity of his appearance couldn't be explained any other way.

"What the hell?" he whispered.

Sofia's arms waved in the air as she spoke. The gestures were impatient and frustrated. The tone of her voice got louder with each sentence, and Heden struggled to hear their hushed words.

"No, Sofia," the man said. "We can't push off the attack. It's now or never. They might already know we're coming."

"Which is why I need more time. Give me one month. I swear, I'll hack back in again and figure out a way to get them all together so we can combine our efforts."

"I don't want them together!" he yelled, causing her to flinch. "I told you, they're strongest when they're united. We must kill them in small groups."

"Heden is on alert. There's no way I can kill Darkrip and his family now."

Rage marred the man's features. "I knew it would come to this. You're unable to kill them. Damn it, Sofia! He's an abomination, don't you see? So are his spawns. As long as Crimeous's blood flourishes, the immortals will never rise to true prominence. To their true potential!"

"I don't care about that," she snapped. "You know my reasons. And he wouldn't want me to murder them. I know that now."

"Traitor!" he screamed, grasping her around the neck with his large hand. "I'll fucking strangle you for crossing me!"

Sofia gasped, clutching at his hand and scraping it with her nails, attempting to pull it away.

It was all Heden needed to jump into action. Springing from his spot behind the wall, he jetted toward them. "Hey! Let her go!"

The man growled, his face snapping toward Heden. Replicas of his own eyes stared back at him, ice-blue and swarming with anger.

"No," the man said, the muscles of his forearm tightening as he choked Sofia. Heden reached behind and pulled a gun from his bag. Lifting it, he aimed it at the man who looked so much like Latimus. The situation was surreal.

"I won't ask again," Heden said, barrel pointed between the Vampyre's eyes where he stood two feet away. "I know this won't kill you, but it will hurt pretty fucking bad, dude. Let the human go."

He snarled, tossing Sofia aside. She crumpled to the ground, hands surrounding her throat as she gasped for air.

The Vampyre's shoulders straightened, and he turned to face Heden. "You've made a grave mistake here, *brother*. You cannot stop me!" Lifting his arms, he closed his eyes, palms facing the sky. "I will have my day. I am the one true ruler of Etherya's Earth. The one true heir. Enjoy your last days before I assume my throne."

He began to chant, the utterances a jumble of a language Heden had never heard. Clouds rushed in, darkening the sky above, as the Vampyre uttered the low-toned words. Lightening streaked overhead, booming as it illuminated the black clouds.

And then, the hulking man vanished.

Heden lowered the gun, unable to believe his eyes. The only beings he knew capable of dematerialization were Darkrip and Evie. Blood pulsed through his frame as he ran to Sofia, crouching down beside her. Deep red marks lined the pale skin of her throat, spurring a knee-jerk protective streak inside his gut. Unsure what to do with the unwanted feeling, he pushed it away to focus on the woman.

"Just breathe," he said, attempting to soothe Sofia. Those translucent eyes latched onto his as she panted, both hands resting above her collarbone.

"He shouldn't be able to dematerialize," she said, her voice hoarse. "I don't know how..." The words broke off as she began to cough. Heden rubbed her upper back, patting it gently until the coughing fit ceased.

Placing his fingers underneath her chin, he tilted her head so he could look into her soul. "Little human," he said, unconsciously running the pad of his thumb over her jawline, "what the hell have you gotten us into?"

Chapter 9

Heden helped Sofia to her feet, lifting her as if she were a feather. The woman was small, the top of her head barely cresting his collarbone. She eyed him warily, the scant freckles across her pert nose scrunching as her eyelids narrowed.

"Are you going to kill me?" she asked softly.

Heden realized he was still holding the gun in his left hand. "No," he said, engaging the trigger lock and stuffing the gun in the side pocket of his bag. "But I would like to go somewhere private, where we can talk."

She slid her teeth over her full bottom lip, gliding it back and forth as she gnawed. While she debated, Heden studied her. Never had he seen irises so clear. They swirled with shades of green and blue, magnificent as the jewels that sparkled on the fancy chandeliers at Astaria. Almond-shaped eyes under black-winged eyebrows led to a button nose and full lips. Springy dark hair sat atop her shoulders. His fist clenched involuntarily as he imagined grasping the strands in his hand. Would they be soft or coarse? Strange, but he felt compelled to discover the answer.

"I can't help you now," she said, dragging him from his musings. "Bakari will surely kill me for defecting. I thought I could do it, but I can't. I can't kill a pregnant woman."

"My sister," he said solemnly.

"Yes," she whispered.

"Who is Bakari?"

Her throat bobbed behind the smooth skin of her neck as she hesitated. "You already know."

"He called me brother and is a dead ringer for Latimus. How in the hell do I have a sibling I never knew about?"

Sofia sighed, rubbing a hand across her face. "I can't help you. I have to go into hiding. Otherwise, I'll be dead before morning. He's very powerful. More so now he's learned to transport."

Heden's eyes darted between hers. "I don't know you, Sofia, but I just saved your life. Not to be a dick, but you kinda owe me one here."

"I can't," she whispered, shaking her head.

"Um, yeah, you can," he said, picking up her bag, which had fallen off her shoulder during the tense exchange with Bakari. "I'll bet you have a room hooked up with all the fancy spyware you coded to hack into our servers. Nice job, by the way. I'll need you to show me everything. Come on." Extending the bag, he motioned for her to take it.

Sofia expelled a breath, grabbing the pack and swinging it over her shoulder. "I told you, it's too late—"

"I'll be the judge of that. Let's go. You can't fight me off, and you've lost your ally. It's time to help me, little human."

Rolling her eyes, she pivoted and began walking to the front of the hotel.

Heden's lips curved as he followed her, shoulders set and head held high. *Lots of thorns on this rose*, he thought as her hair bounced over her backpack. How many did a man have to navigate through to get to the petals? He wasn't sure, but it seemed like an interesting challenge.

They entered the lobby and elevator, Sofia pushing the button labeled "three." It whooshed to the floor, and she exited, turning left and holding the plastic card to the second door. Once inside, she threw her bag on one of the double beds.

"*Don't* touch anything," she said, holding up a finger in warning. "I need to use the bathroom, and then I'll decide what, if anything, I'm going to tell you. Give me a minute." Shooting him a glare, she entered the bathroom, clicking the lock behind her.

Heden didn't waste a moment, springing into action. Pulling the laptop from her bag, he set it on the desk and booted it up. When prompted for the password, he pulled his phone from his bag along with the USB cord. Opening the password hacking app, he plugged his phone into the computer, uncovering her credentials in three seconds flat. Once inside, he began clicking through the files.

There were so many, each labeled with names of his family and extended family. Accessing the folder named "Heden," he double-clicked the document titled "Notes." There, laid out before him, was a detailed account of the last year of his life. The spots he frequented, when he picked up his nieces and nephews from school, the women he'd dated. The Withers girls appeared on the list, reminding him of the monotony of his life. Wash, rinse, repeat.

The feeling his old existence had ended crashed over him. Enemies were detailing his every action and those of the people he loved. Peace was a beautiful illusion that was now shattered. How many unidentified foes were aligned with Bakari?

Heden clicked on another folder labeled "SS." Opening the first file, he read the name "Diabolos." It sounded familiar, as if he'd heard it somewhere before, but he couldn't place it. Was this person an immortal? If so, was he a Slayer, Vampyre or Deamon?

"Hey!" Sofia yelled, rushing over and closing the laptop. "I told you not to touch anything!"

Heden struggled to tamp down warring emotions: anger at being surveilled, and the deep, protective swell he felt toward this imp of a human. It was imperative he befriend her. She had valuable intelligence he was desperate to possess. The good news? He could be *very* charming when he needed to be, especially with women.

Pasting on what he knew to be a devastatingly handsome grin, he reached for her arm. "Sorry, I was just curious."

"Look," she said, shrugging him away, "I've monitored you for years. I get that you think you're god's gift to women. I couldn't give a damn about being seduced or getting laid or whatever you think you can accomplish with that shit-eating smile. Save it for someone else." Huffing, she began gathering her equipment to stuff inside her bag.

"Wait," he said, encircling her wrist.

"Touch me again, and I'll murder you."

Heden released her arm, unable to tamp down his smile. "You're feisty. I'm guessing by your last name, you're Italian. I've always heard Italians have a temper."

"You bet your ass we do. We definitely don't like having our computers hacked under our noses."

"Says the woman who put spyware on all my servers. Hypocritical, much?" he asked, arching an eyebrow.

"You immortals think you're so much better than us. If I hear one more person call me a stupid human, I'm going to freaking scream. I put the program on your servers because I knew I was a better hacker than you and you'd never find a trail. You'd only find it if you searched the task manager. And I was right." She crossed her arms over her chest, daring him to argue.

"Fine," he said, showing his palms. "You over-hacked me. Well done. What was it for? How did you meet Bakari, and why does he want to murder everyone on the damn planet?"

"I don't find I'm really in the helping mood right now. Sorry. Thank you for saving my life, but I have to get the hell out of here." She stuffed the laptop in her bag and began grabbing the few items in the drawers under the television, placing them in the suitcase resting on the luggage rack against the far wall.

Heden observed her furious movements, reminded of the profound pain he'd witnessed in her stunning eyes when he'd confronted her earlier that morning. She stalked into the bathroom, scooped up her toiletries and dumped them in the suitcase. When she closed it and started zipping it, he placed his hand over hers.

"I'm sorry," he said, making sure his touch was gentle. "Someone must've hurt you badly to motivate you to align with the creature I saw outside."

She stood frozen, breath slightly labored, as he held her hand.

"Whoever it was, I'm sorry. If you talk to me, I'll do my best to rectify it."

"You can't," she said, shaking her head, still staring at the felt suitcase. "It won't ever be right, and I'll never forgive myself. I should've been there with him. He was old, and I left him all alone. Now, he's gone."

"Who's gone, Sofia?" he asked, wanting to comfort her but sensing she needed space. Anguish vibrated from her body, surrounding Heden in the cloud of its pallor. It was heavy and dark, and he hurt for her.

She shook her head, a tear glistening on her cheek.

Emotion slammed his solar plexus. Unable to stop himself, he slid his palm across the back of her neck. "Who, Sofia?"

Suddenly, a rush of air washed over them, breaking the serenity of the moment. They both rotated toward the disturbance, but Heden's gaze was inexorably locked on Sofia's face. Her eyes widened, awash with fear and rage, and she whispered one shocked word: "No!"

* * * *

Sofia stood, stunned, as the woman she hated with all her heart materialized into the room. Fear closed her throat, and anger welled in her chest.

"No!" she screamed again, shaking her head.

"Francesco," Evie said, standing tall and still, her tone remorseful.

"Evie?" Heden asked. "What the hell—?"

"Her grandfather Francesco," Evie repeated, gaze never leaving Sofia's. "That's who she lost."

"How do you know this?" Heden asked, his voice sounding a thousand miles away to Sofia's ringing ears.

"Because I killed him," Evie said softly.

The confession broke Sofia, who'd waited so long to hear the words. A cry burst from her throat, and she said through clenched teeth, "Say it again, you horrible bitch."

"I killed him," Evie said, clear and morose. "It's the first time I've ever regretted killing someone, Sofia. Especially a man. I did it in anger but also in compassion. It's the only way I've been able to accept it. I'll never forgive myself, but at least I can accept I alleviated some of his suffering."

"What the hell are you talking about?" Sofia vibrated with indignation as she felt Heden struggle to make sense of their cryptic conversation beside her.

"He was sick, Sofia," she said, moving forward a few inches.

"No! Don't fucking move! I know about the cancer. I could've saved him!"

Evie held up her hands, conceding to Sofia's wish and remaining still. "There was nothing you could've done, Sofia. A creature such as I can see these things. I saved him months of tubes and hospitals, poking and prodding. Your grandfather was a proud man. Do you think he would've really wanted that?"

Sofia struggled to process her enemy's words, hating that she was robbed of the chance to help Francesco. "I could've tried to help—"

"No, Sofia. It was over for him. He lived a wonderful life. He rests with Maria in the Passage now—I can feel it with every bone in my body. Knowing he's happy helps me when I'm overcome with regret."

"How *dare* you say you regret anything! You murdered him!"

"I know he was all you had," she said. Sofia wanted to retch from the genuineness in her olive-green eyes. It couldn't be real. She was a monster. "I'm sorry I took him from you before you could say goodbye. It was very unfair, and I don't blame you for hating me. It's unforgivable."

Sofia inched toward the bed, consumed with the knowledge her gun rested inside her bag. She'd bought it for the sole purpose of killing the woman who now stood before her. Could she extricate it and shoot the Slayer-Deamon before she realized her intent?

"I know the gun is in your bag, Sofia," Evie said, her voice calm and undaunted. "You don't need to reach for it." Holding out her hand, palm up, she closed her eyes. Within seconds, a handgun appeared.

"Here," Evie said, slowly approaching Sofia, gun outstretched. "Take it. Shoot me, if you must. I denied you a goodbye, but I won't deny you your revenge. It's no less than I deserve." Ever so slowly, Evie grasped Sofia's forearm, placing the gun in her hand. "If you want to shoot me, I won't fight you."

As if in a dream, Sofia watched this person she'd spent countless hours tracking gingerly back away. Once a few feet were between them, she stopped. Resolve emanated from her unmoving body.

Hands trembling, Sofia grasped the butt of the gun with both hands. Lifting it slowly, she aimed between the red-haired bitch's arresting green eyes.

"Don't do this, Sofia," Heden's deep voice said beside her. "Evie has changed. She saved so many people in our world. She made a choice to be a better person. You have that same choice. Don't become what you profess to hate."

"I've waited so long to have you right here," Sofia said, wetness clouding her eyes as she held the gun, arms shaking and heavy. "So many years."

"I know," Evie said, her tone so sad it resonated in Sofia's deadened soul. "It's okay. Shoot me."

Breath shuddered through her quaking lungs as Sofia envisioned pulling the trigger. She wanted to so badly, but her fingers were frozen. Closing her eyes, she summoned the image of her beloved grandfather. His face beamed back, so full of love and hope; so proud of the woman she'd become.

Who would she be once she shot Evie? Would her heart finally be as black as the murderer who stood silent before her? Would her soul wither to be as dark as Bakari's, mired in violence and death?

Sofia.

The word whispered through her consciousness, Francesco's smiling face still in her mind's eye. It was said in his voice, as if from heaven.

Opening her eyes, Sofia admitted the truth. She would never be able to kill Evie. She would never be able to murder anyone. The capability just wasn't there. Feeling the failure consume her, she breathed a sob and collapsed backward, her knees giving out under her.

"Hey," Heden's firm voice said as he caught her, his broad arms sliding under her arms. "It's okay. I've got you."

Unable to control her sobs, she slid down his body, onto the floor, and buried her head in her knees, clutching her thighs to her chest. Wracked with pain, Sofia acknowledged she would never avenge her grandfather.

A steady hand stroked her hair as if from far away while she cried bucket upon bucket of tears into her dark-washed jeans. Eventually, the emotion evolved into numbness, causing the tears to abate. Sucking in deep breaths of air, she grasped her legs in a death grip, wanting to disappear though a hole in the floor.

"Shhhh..." someone soothed above her, and she realized it was Heden, comforting her as he caressed her hair. It was so long since she'd been touched by another, and it should've felt foreign since he was a stranger, but it felt...good. Right. Normal.

Thinking herself insane, she lifted her head. Focusing on Evie, she blinked her eyes to clear away the remaining moisture.

"Thank you for not shooting me," she said, her lips quirking into a sardonic smile. "I very much didn't want to bleed out today. Especially since my husband has finally knocked me up."

Out of the corner of her eye, Sofia observed Heden's wide grin as he still crouched beside her. "Yeah?" he asked, joy radiating from his large body.

"Yeah," she said with a nod. "I was going to tell you the other day, when you were ogling the kids on the playground, but decided to wait. I'm a mess. Ken's over the moon. I can't wait to see how I fuck this up. Just freaking great."

Lowering to the floor, she crossed her legs, now eye-level with Sofia. "I loved your grandfather, Sofia. I know that undoubtedly means nothing to you, but he was very special to me. This probably sounds insane but killing him was something I desperately needed to do in order to become the person I am today. I think he always knew he would help me realize my true potential. It doesn't make it right, but it's the only explanation I can give you. I will do my best to help you process your grief and ensure his soul rests in peace. What can I do to rectify this?"

"I don't want your help!" Sofia screamed, still hating this woman whom she didn't have the fortitude to destroy. "I want you to leave me the hell alone!"

"That's fair," Evie said, tilting her head in acknowledgment. "I'm pretty much the evil bitch you've always thought I would be, although my husband has tempered me slightly."

Anchoring on her arms, Evie stood, placing her hands in the pockets of her brown slacks. "When you're ready to cash in on the debt I owe you, both for killing Francesco and for not shooting me today, let me know. In the meantime, you're pretty much screwed. I came through the ether shortly after Heden. Somehow, I knew my past actions had a hand in whatever the hell was happening. I researched Bakari while Heden tracked you down. Because I'm able to transport, I discovered things about him from different pockets of the world. He's dangerous, Sofia, and now that you've crossed him, he'll be out for blood. You'd be smart to align with Heden and help his family, so they protect you in return. Otherwise, it will be your murder we're dealing with next."

With those ominous words, Evie shrugged. "I'm not trying to be dramatic but, *damn*, that was a great parting line." Red lips twitched in a smile. "See you guys later. I'll update the others on what I've learned until you can uncover the rest. Take care of her, Heden."

Air swirled around the room, and in a flash, she was gone.

Exhausted, Sofia tilted her head back to look at Heden. The Vampyre stared down at her, his palm still resting on her hair above her shoulder.

"So," he said, smiling. "You're into revenge. Cool, but heavy. Have you ever thought about knitting? Or tennis? Or maybe karaoke? There's got to be a better hobby that won't get you killed."

The gravity of the moment was so tense, so profound, that Sofia lost it. There, crouched on the floor, she broke into a fit of uncontrolled laughter.

Chapter 10

Sofia struggled to swipe the tears of mirth as her body convulsed with laughter. As the gasping abated, she shook her head at Heden.

"You like to joke," she observed.

"When the time's right," he said, flashing his teeth. His fangs sat slightly pointed above his full lower lip, and her stomach lurched into a somersault. Had he ever bitten anyone with them? Would it hurt?

"And in my opinion, the time is always right for a bit of humor." Lifting to his feet, he extended his hand. "Come on, little human. We've got a lot to discuss."

Staring up at him, she realized she trusted him. There was an air of calm sureness and relaxed openness that radiated from his hulking body. The feeling was so foreign to her, she hesitated.

"I'm not going to hurt you," he said, the words a soft rush against her suddenly heated skin. "Although I'm not thrilled you've put my family in danger, I need you. Come on." He motioned his hand, urging her to take it.

Placing her smaller hand in his, Sofia felt off-balance as he pulled her up. Planting her feet on the ground so she didn't sway, she grappled with what to say. Fortunately, her stomach growled, saving her from forming the words in her mouth that was suddenly dry as sandpaper.

"How long has it been since you ate?" he asked, concern in his deep baritone.

"I...I'm not sure," she said, running her fingers through the curls at her crown. "I was too busy trying to hack into the immortal servers this morning to grab anything at the coffee shop."

"Right. Well, your stomach's obviously not with the program. Let's get you some food while we chat."

Sofia blinked up at him. "It's fine. I need to figure out—"

"Nope," he interrupted. "I've learned from my sister and Miranda that nothing good comes from a hangry woman."

"Hangry?"

"Hungry and angry. That word's everywhere. Have you been living under a rock?"

Sofia shrugged. "There's not much time to keep up on pop culture when you're hunting your dead grandfather's immortal murderer."

"Eh, that's an okay excuse, I guess." He grinned, contorting his face into something so handsome. How many women had he given that smile to? Countless, if Sofia's research held true. She'd do well to remember he had incentive to charm her. The information she possessed was extremely valuable.

"Pack up your stuff, since your location's been made, and we'll head to my sister's house."

"They're not safe now shit's hit the fan. I don't know if that's a good idea."

"It's safer we're there so I can warn Darkrip. He's powerful and can better protect us there than anywhere."

Sofia hesitated, turning her head to glance at her suitcase.

"I've got it," Heden said, plodding over and zipping it before placing it on the floor and extending the handle. "Grab your laptop and bag, and let's go."

Realizing it was futile to argue, Sofia sighed, packed up the rest of her things and slung her bag over her shoulder. "I need to return the rental car. The less traceable I am, the better. I used a false name to rent it, but you found me, which means someone else can too."

"How long until Bakari attacks us?" he asked.

"Our plan was to attack in a few days," Sofia said, swallowing thickly.

"Then we need to get our crap together. Let's go."

He exited the room, Sofia reluctantly following, and they took care of checking out of the hotel and returning her rental car. After that, they hailed a cab to Darkrip and Arderin's suburban home.

Darkrip pulled open the wooden front door, a scowl on his face. He studied Sofia under the cover of the awning. "This one's got some really fucked-up images in her head," he muttered to Heden.

"I know," Heden said, placing his arm around Sofia's shoulders. The protective gesture made something swell in her chest. "But she's seen the errors of her ways. Right, Sof?"

Sof. It was the nickname her grandfather gave her. She'd always felt so loved when he held her and spoke the word. She wanted to tell Heden to fuck off, because no one called her that but Francesco, but she couldn't seem to form any words past the lump in her throat. Capitulating, she nodded.

"Who's the old man?" Darkrip asked. "The one plastered all over your memories?"

"My grandfather," Sofia said, her voice barely a whisper. "Your sister killed him."

Darkrip sucked in a deep breath. "We're going to need coffee. And whiskey. Come on." Stepping back, he gestured them both in.

Once the door was closed and locked, he herded them to the kitchen. Sofia thought it so surreal to sit at the table where she'd watched them yesterday, still planning to kill them. She realized now, she would've never been able to go through with it.

"First things first," Heden said, setting her suitcase in the corner before lowering beside her at the cedar table. "Darkrip's going to wrangle up some food for you since you look like you haven't eaten in days. And then you're going to tell me everything, so I can head to the realm and update Sathan."

"I didn't realize I was expected to play servant," Darkrip grumbled, opening the refrigerator to scan the contents.

"Don't worry about him," Heden said, giving her a conspiratorial wink. "He's grumpy but he totally digs this Mr. Mom stuff."

"I'm imagining disintegrating you into dust with a thought," Darkrip replied as he threw some ingredients into a pan and turned on the burner.

Sofia watched their interplay, understanding they were close. How did someone as evil as Darkrip learn to accept and love others without reservation?

"It wasn't easy," the Slayer-Deamon said, his back to her as he stirred the food atop the stove. "I'm not predisposed to feel emotion. But I've chosen to live by my Slayer side, mostly because my wife possesses my soul. It's extremely difficult but worth it. I have my daughter to think about."

"Do you always read others' thoughts?" Sofia asked. "It's pretty annoying."

"He'll stop if you ask him to," Arderin said, breezing into the room in a robe, toweling her long, wet hair. "But that depends. Are you the person who's been watching my family?"

Sofia felt a jolt of guilt, although she hadn't truly done anything to harm them. Yet.

"Yes," she said, thrusting her chin up. "You all have a sense of superiority that's ridiculous considering your past transgressions. Your husband and his sister have murdered countless people, and from what I understand, the Vampyres raided and stole the Slayers' blood for a thousand years in your world."

"The human has a bit of a chip on her shoulder," Heden chimed in when Arderin's eyes narrowed. "Sofia, meet Arderin, my pregnant sister you were planning to murder. Oh, wait...who's ridiculous now?" His eyes wandered to the ceiling as he rubbed his beard.

"Well, I'm here, and those plans are toast now, so I think the tally's still: human, not a murderer; and immortals, pretty fucking terrible."

"Here," Darkrip said, slamming the plate onto the placemat in front of her. "Chicken stir-fry. I'm pretty sure I didn't poison it. Eat up."

Sofia grasped the fork from his outstretched hand, deciding death by poisoned chicken might not be so bad. These people were pissed, and she didn't much like them either.

As she ate, she detailed her activities from the past few years. Darkrip and Arderin were shocked to learn she'd discovered them during their travels to Houston. Sofia brought them up to speed, recounting how she met Bakari and the other members of the Secret Society. She informed them of the immortals who'd been brought back to life by Crimeous's cloned blood, and the multiple-pronged attack that was scheduled only days away.

"Do you think they'll still try to carry out that plan?" Arderin asked, reaching over with her fork and scooping some food from Darkrip's plate into her mouth.

"She likes food even though she's a Vampyre," Darkrip said, answering the question floating in Sofia's mind. "Correction: She likes *my* food. I can't get a damn plate down before she's stolen it all."

"Thank you, husband," Arderin garbled, mouth full of food. She placed a loving kiss on his cheek as he glowered. "Your son likes it too. I need energy before I head to the hospital tonight." She rubbed her distended abdomen. "You were saying, Sofia?"

"I don't know," Sofia said, slowly shaking her head. "Bakari is determined to kill you all, and the plan was pretty flawless. But now that he's realized I can't complete my part, I don't know what he'll do."

"How did he learn to dematerialize?" Darkrip asked. "Did he inject my father's cloned blood?"

"From my understanding, it doesn't work that way," Sofia said. "It can bring an immortal back but it doesn't transfer the Dark Lord's powers."

"Then, how?" Heden asked. "Because the son of a bitch disappeared into thin air."

Sofia inhaled a breath. "He's been studying a woman who lives in New Orleans. She's...not of this world, but not of yours either. An anomaly I haven't spent enough time researching to figure out. She possesses the knowledge of the ancient Native American shamans and understands the complexities of dark magic, the occult and voodoo. I can only guess she concocted a spell or potion that allows him to transport."

Arderin sat back in her chair. "This is all so surreal. How can we have a brother we knew nothing about?" she asked Heden.

"I don't know," Heden said, lacing his fingers behind his head as he leaned back in his chair. Sofia noticed his biceps, straining and burly outside the tight sleeves of his shirt. "There's a five-year gap between you and Latimus. I just always figured Mom and Dad took a break from knocking boots, but it looks like they had another kid. Why wouldn't the archivists record it? Since it was before the Awakening, it should've been recorded by the Slayer soothsayers and the Vampyre archivists."

"Forget the archivists. Why in the hell didn't Mom and Dad tell us? Or at least tell Sathan and Latimus? It's bizarre."

Heden expelled a heavy breath. "The Awakening happened a few years later. Maybe they were waiting to tell us all when we were older and never got the chance. I just don't know, sis. It's mind boggling."

"He bears a mark," Sofia said, looking back and forth between them as they sat on each side of her. "I heard him discussing it with some of the others. Something about a prophecy and how the one who bore the mark would be evil. I think the soothsayers and archivists decided he was better off dead and decided not to record it. Unfortunately, someone found him and raised him in the human world. He's amassed wealth and status here that you wouldn't believe. He also likes to drink human blood. Bakari believes the legend of Count Dracula is based on him. He likens himself to a god and wants nothing more than to rule your realm."

"Wow," Heden said, unlacing his fingers and running a hand through his thick hair. "Sounds like our brother's an arrogant douche."

Sofia huffed a laugh. "Honestly, he is. His arrogance is one of the things I can't stand about him."

"Why did you align with him?" Arderin asked.

Exhaling a deep breath, Sofia rested her back on the chair and twisted her fingers together as she spoke. "My grandfather's murder was very difficult for me. He was the only family I had left. When I discovered someone had killed him, I became obsessed with avenging him to ensure his soul rests in peace. I'm Catholic and believe his soul can't live eternally in Heaven without retribution."

"And what does your god think about murdering innocent people to accomplish that goal?" Darkrip asked as he sat across from her.

Sofia shot him a sardonic glare. "Obviously, that was the part I was having problems with. I just couldn't bring myself to do it. All this time wasted, and I've failed miserably." Mortified she was getting emotional, she struggled to tamp down the moisture in her eyes.

"I get it," Heden said, reaching over to cover her clenched hands with his broad one.

Through her blurred gaze, Sofia witnessed the glance that passed between Arderin and Darkrip. They were as stunned by Heden's compassion toward her as she was.

"We believe in the Passage in our world, similar to your Heaven. One must have a proper send-off to the Passage to reunite with their family there. The sentiments are not so different."

"Yes, but Heaven is real."

"So is the Passage. In my mind, at least," Heden said softly. "I was only a baby when my parents were killed, so I don't remember them. I believe that one day, I'll meet them again in the Passage."

"But you're immortal and self-healing. The chances of death are slim to none for you," Sofia said.

"Not true," he said, squeezing her hand before he sat back, resting his palms flat on the table. "Many Vampyres have perished over the last ten centuries. We all have our time, immortal or not. When mine comes, I'll accept it."

"But for now, we'd like to stay alive if at all possible," Darkrip said, his expression derisive. "Heden, we need to get this information to the others as quickly as possible. As much as I like having you here, we need to get you back to the immortal world."

"Agreed. And I'm taking Sofia with me."

"Whoa," Arderin said, her dark eyebrows forming a V between her eyes. "No way. Etherya will crap herself if you take a human through the ether."

"We have to protect her, Arderin," Heden said. "Bakari and the others will be furious she defected."

"No fucking way!" his sister shouted. "Darkrip can transport her somewhere she can hide. I'm not pissing off the goddess. It's not happening—"

"I appreciate the two of you discussing me as if I'm invisible," Sofia said, jerking to her feet as her chair scraped the floor. "But I've taken care of myself my entire life and I certainly don't need help from a bunch of entitled creatures who aren't even human. Thanks, but I'm out." She stalked to the suitcase in the corner, pulled up the handle, stacked her bag on top and began wheeling it out of the kitchen toward the front door.

"Hey!" Heden said, grabbing her arm and bringing her to a halt in the hallway. "Sorry, but you're not going anywhere, Sofia."

She pivoted, yanking her arm out of his grasp. "I've told you what you want to know. Good luck saving your family. You don't need to keep me safe, and I'm done with this." Rotating, she resumed walking.

"Wait," he called. The plea in his tone caused her to pause. "I need your help enhancing our communication equipment. I haven't figured out how to transmit through the ether. How did you do it?"

Sofia scoffed, staring at the floor. "Years of coding. You'll figure it out eventually."

Her shoulders stiffened from his nearness as the heat from his large frame enveloped her backside. Ever so slowly, he slid his palms over the soft skin where her neck sloped.

"Please," he whispered, breath burning the shell of her ear. "If you help me, I'll repay you. Whatever you ask for. If I can make it happen, I will."

"I already told you," she said, turning to stare into his sky-blue eyes. One of his hands remained on the juncture of her neck and shoulder, the skin tingling underneath. "I've lost the one thing I want, and he's never coming back."

"You don't have any other family?" he asked softly.

Sofia wanted to drown in the sympathy that lined his handsome face. "No," she said, sadness flooding her as it always did when she took time to dwell on her solitary and isolated existence. "I really want to have kids one day, but I'm thirty-eight going on menopause, so my chances are about as good as winning the lottery while getting struck by lightning."

Broad lips curved into a smile. "You made a joke. Good one."

She rolled her eyes. "Yeah. I'm hilarious."

His eyes darted between hers as the silence stretched. "Don't go into hiding," he finally said. "Let me protect you. In exchange, you'll show me how to communicate through the ether. You helped get us into this mess, but you're stuck in it now too. Let's work together, Sof. Please."

"My grandfather called me Sof," she said, her voice thick and gravelly. "I liked it."

The pad of his thumb ran over her neck, back and forth, as the corner of his smile deepened. "Yeah? I like it too. But I won't call you that if it's too painful. I just think it's cute. Not as formal as Sofia."

She was sure he could feel her pulse thrumming under his thumb. "I'm not interested in being seduced. I'm not one of your stupid Vampyre women. It won't work on me."

"Thank god," he said, displaying a mock expression of relief. "Because you're hideous."

She couldn't control the laughter that sprung from her throat. "It wouldn't be right to let a stranger call me by the same nickname as the person who knew me best."

"Then I'll just have to get to know you."

"I'm also not interested in making friends."

"Great. I have enough of those. How about super-hackers on a mission?" Stepping back, he lowered his hand, extending it for her to shake.

"The last time I made a deal like that, it led me here."

"Then let's make sure this one's better. I promise not to force you to murder anyone. Deal?"

In spite of herself, she breathed a laugh. "Fine," she said, shaking his hand. "Let's see if I can stay alive long enough to teach you how to code. You're a pretty terrible hacker." Grasping his hand, she shook.

"I'll need a lot of instruction. We might end up becoming friends anyway."

"Lord, I hope not." Smiling into his gorgeous eyes, Sofia had the nagging feeling this wager was lined with conditions and complexities she couldn't begin to understand. It should have terrified her. Instead, against all odds, her heart felt free for the first time since her grandfather's death.

Chapter 11

Bakari drove the rental car down the dirt road that led to the wooden cottage. Long strands of willows stretched from the trees above, several of them brushing the top of the vehicle. Tupelo gum trees grew out of the murky water on either side of the road, their bases broad and ridged. They'd germinated decades ago, seeing much from their quiet, stable stumps.

Stopping a few feet from the red bicycle chained to the post by the front porch stairs, Bakari observed the shack. The wood had faded long ago, but it carried the charm of a home where life thrived. Smoke emanated from the chimney, forming a snake-like swirl that dissipated through the trees above to the blue sky.

Ascending the stairs, which were sturdier than they appeared, he waited. The door creaked open, and a woman emerged, her long yellow skirt flowing as she leaned her hip on the doorframe.

"Hello, Bakari," she said, stirring the contents of the small bowl she held in her hand. Whatever was inside smelled dank, as if she'd crushed up some acrid spices or perhaps a few wayward crawdads.

"Hello, Tatiana," he said, staring into her amber eyes, offset by thick, waist-length dark brown curls. Her umber-brown skin seemed to glow under the midday sun. He'd never seen her wear a stitch of makeup, nor did she need to. She was a stunning woman who betrayed an air of superiority and confidence that surpassed his own. Whereas many accused him of being arrogant and entitled, she would never be described with such words. Her power was intrinsic...understood...cultivated, so it wasn't a threat or a curse. It just *existed*.

"I need more of the potion," he said, not bothering with niceties so he could get straight to the point and push away the imbalance she made him feel. She was the only creature on the entire planet that had ever unnerved him. Intuition informed him this meant she was dangerous, but so far, she'd been an ally of sorts. Sometimes, he felt she was just toying with him, using him as a plaything to assuage the boredom of her mundane life. But she was a powerful ally, and with Sofia's defection, he needed her now more than ever.

An onyx eyebrow arched as she lazily stirred, her arm moving in an almost hypnotizing motion. "I felt the imbalance. You were able to dematerialize. I'm happy to see the concoction worked. I've been developing that one for some time."

Bakari nodded. "I ingested the potion and chanted the spell you taught me. I transported several miles. I would like to be able to travel further distances."

Dark pupils bore into him under her questioning stare. "You'd be wise to use ancient magic sparingly. The gods do not take well to those who do not respect their eminence."

"I have no wish to anger your gods. I believe they support my cause."

The stirring halted as she contemplated him through narrowed eyes. "The gods have a respect for the world of immortal creatures beyond the ether. Be wary you don't dredge up their protective nature. You have a great battle before you."

Bakari's own eyes tapered, becoming frustrated at her lecture. "I only wish to restore Etherya's realm to true prominence. To ensure the species remain separate and free of Crimeous's blood."

"Etherya herself once loved the creature Crimeous—"

"Enough," he interrupted, frustrated at how she always spoke in riddles and platitudes. "What will it cost me to get more of the potion? I'd like to purchase enough to last me several years. I can pay you whatever price you name."

Throaty laughter surrounded him as she scoffed. "Money has no value for me. You should know this by now."

Bakari felt his jaw clench. "Then, what? There must be something you want. Something you consider valuable."

Tatiana inhaled a full breath, her nostrils flaring as she pondered. Finally, she said, "I would like a lock of hair from a child of Crimeous. Anyone who shares his blood will suffice. It will be a potent addition to some of my more sinister spells."

Bakari quickly catalogued her request. Darkrip and Evie would be difficult to extricate such a sample from. "I will get one from Calinda," he said, referring to Darkrip and Arderin's daughter.

"That will be sufficient," she said with a nod. "Once I have it, I will repay you with enough of the concoction to last several decades."

Bakari wondered what dark spells she would use the tresses for.

"I have my own reasons," she said, somehow reading the question in his expression. "You don't see broadly enough to understand them. Your mind's eye is narrowed with hate and revenge."

"Says the woman who spends all day wielding black magic in a secluded cabin," he muttered.

The corner of her lip curved. "Go. Gather what I request. I will be here when you're ready to move forward." Stepping back, she sent him one last subtle and derisive nod before closing the door.

Sighing, Bakari headed to the car, annoyed he had to return to L.A. But first, he needed to contact the other members of the society. Angered that Tatiana wouldn't just supply him with the substance he needed to transport, he debated turning back and murdering her. Since that wouldn't help his cause, he drove to the airport, determined to stay focused on the end game.

* * * *

Moira turned the key in the lock on the front door of the gallery. Pulling the handle, she ensured it was secure. When the door didn't budge, she stuffed her keys in her purse and began walking home. The points of her heels made a clinking sound as she strolled upon the smooth sidewalk.

The night was clear under the full moon, allowing her to see her surroundings quite clearly. Passing the alleyway to her right, the blond hairs on her arms stiffened. Drawing her sweater tighter across her shoulders, she glanced toward the dark passageway.

A man stood back against the wall, shrouded in a dark coat and hat. For some reason, Moira froze, entranced. He lifted a cheroot to his lips, the tip glowing bright as he inhaled. The scent wafted toward Moira, and she gasped. It was the same brand of cigarettes her ex-husband always smoked. She would know the aroma anywhere, as it used to surround her battered body when he would light one after beating her.

Reminding herself Diabolos was long-dead, Moira tried to calm her pounding heart. The man's build was shadowed but reminded her so much of the man who'd caused her such intense pain.

The shrill chirp of the phone from her purse snapped her out of the nightmarish memories. Lifting the device, she held it to her ear. "Hello?"

"Moira," her current husband's voice called, "are you okay? You sound strange."

"I'm fine," she said, running her hand through her golden tresses. "Just thought I saw someone I knew."

"Are you on your way home?" Aron asked. "I'm leaving the castle now. I can meet up with you."

"I'm almost home. I can wait for you, if you like."

"No," he said, his tone warm. "Go on home so you can rest. You've been on your feet all day. I'll be there in about twenty minutes."

"Okay," she said, eyes narrowed as she watched the shadowed man throw his cheroot to the ground and stomp on it with his foot. Before sauntering away, she could've sworn he gave a slight tip of his hat. Was the action meant for her?

"Moira?" Aron called at her silence.

"Um, yeah, sounds good," she said, shaking her head to rid it of the madness. "See you at home."

"We're baby-making tonight, right?" he asked. Moira could almost see his smile through the phone.

"Oh, yeah," she said, feeling her own lips curve. "All night long, buster. Get ready."

57

Her regal aristocrat uttered a soft growl, causing her to chuckle. "I'm ready. See you soon, love."

Ending the call, she resumed her stroll, unnerved by how much the man in the alleyway reminded her of Diabolos. Unable to shake the morbid feeling, she kept her phone in her hand the entire way, finger near the call button, just in case.

Chapter 12

Heden decided to wait to return to the immortal world so he could spend some time with Callie before she went to bed. After Darkrip picked her up from school, they ate dinner together before Arderin went in for her shift that evening. Although Heden offered for Sofia to eat dinner with them, she declined, choosing to work on her laptop in the living room. Now she'd agreed to help the royal immortals, she wanted to disable the Secret Society's devices so they couldn't communicate through the ether.

After dinner was finished, Arderin pulled Heden outside, her grip firm on his wrist.

"Are you going to beat me up again?" he asked, letting her drag him into the back yard. "Because I'm pretty sure I can take you now that I'm fully grown."

His sister's features contorted with fury. "You're making a mistake, Heden. You can't take a human into the immortal world. What the hell are you thinking? She was planning to murder us about eight hours ago," she said, exasperated.

"Look," he said, holding his palms up, "I'm not happy about this situation either, but I can read people, sis. She's not a monster. She's a woman with a broken heart and an inflamed sense of revenge. Evie killed her grandfather, and we need to remember that."

"How do we know this isn't part of their plan? To have you witness Bakari attack her and gain your sympathy?"

Heden gave her a perplexed look. "Have you been watching human soap operas again?"

"For the love of the goddess," Arderin groaned, wrenching her hands at her sides. "This is not a fucking joke, Heden. Our family is under attack by a brother we knew nothing about and a bunch of other enemies, half of them brought back from the dead with Crimeous's blood."

"I know, Arderin," he said, placing his palms over her upper arms. "I get the gravity of the situation. We're going to fight it. Calm down. Your tantrum isn't good for the baby."

"Tantrum, my ass," she muttered, scowling as he rubbed her arms. Heden's heart splintered in tiny pieces when her bottom lip began to quiver. "I just love you," she said, shaking her head. "I love our family. I thought this was over when we killed Crimeous."

"Shhh…" Heden said, drawing her into an embrace. "It's okay, little toad. We're going to figure this out." He smoothed his hand over her dark curls.

"I don't trust her."

"I don't trust her either. But we need her, sis. She knows everything about our enemies. We have to work with her. She's also figured out how to communicate through the ether, and I want that technology implemented on all our devices." Pulling back, he lifted her chin with his fingers. "I mean, how awesome would it be to get to video chat with this handsome mug every day?" With his index finger, he pointed at his face.

She exhaled a laugh, shaking her head. "Sounds terrible."

"Blasphemy!" he teased.

Her ice-blue irises roamed between his. "You're compassionate toward her."

"Yes," he said, nodding. "I've rarely seen pain in someone's eyes as deep as hers. And yet she didn't have the heart to carry out the plan. She's all alone, and we need to help her."

"Why are you so good?" Arderin asked, cupping his cheeks.

"Being the youngest is hard," he said, answering honestly. "You all have found mates and built amazing lives for yourselves. I've always felt a bit overshadowed by how awesome the three of you are. I understand loneliness. Sofia is encompassed by it, and that makes me sympathetic toward her."

Love filled his sister's expression, spurring a warm burst of emotion in his chest. "Oh, Heden, I didn't realize you felt that way. You know I'm always here for you."

"I know," he said, affection for her swishing through his large frame. "You guys are my family, and I love you so much. It's just…I don't know," he said, releasing her and kicking the ground with the toe of his sneaker. "Sathan was always so protective of you, and you and Latimus have such a close bond. I just always felt like the fat kid left behind by the bus, running to catch up while my pants fell down around my ankles."

Arderin burst out laughing, causing Heden to giggle along with her. "It's a funny image, but now, I think I'm finally realizing why you developed the wicked sense of humor. It's a defense mechanism."

"Maybe," he said, shrugging. "It was a way to worm myself into conversation and get some attention. I mean, the three of you are pretty intense. It's hard out here for a pimp."

"Okay, Snoop," she snickered, rubbing the remaining wetness from her earlier tears off her cheek. "I get it. I'm sorry if I ever left you behind. I never meant to. I love you, Heden."

"I love you too," he said, smiling. "We're in uncharted waters here. I'm taking Sofia with me to help us. I'm determined to protect our family."

Her stunning eyes narrowed. "This had better not be about banging her. She's pretty cute for a human."

"Banging?" he asked, holding his hand to his chest in mock mortification. "I'm a virgin, dear sister. Didn't you know?"

"You're full of crap is what you are," she said, laughing as she regarded him. "Don't murk the waters, bro. We've got a lot on our plate here."

"I won't. Humans. Ew. Don't worry."

"Famous last words," she muttered. Huffing in a deep breath, she relented. "Fine. Take her to the realm. Figure out how to beat those bastards and how to contact us through the ether. I'm counting on you."

"Will do. I'd like to read to Callie before I go."

Arderin beamed at him, her white fangs glowing. "She'd love that."

After they headed inside, Arderin bathed Callie, stuffing her into pajamas with little giraffes on them that made her look insanely adorable. When Arderin left for the hospital, Heden read to Callie under the pink canopy of her small bed. Eventually, her eyelids began to droop, and he closed the book, placing a sweet peck on her forehead.

"Don't forget to give the picture to Jack," she said sleepily, looking so innocent as she gazed up at him.

"I won't," Heden said, sliding his fingers over her slick curls. Callie had drawn her favorite cousin a picture of them together, playing by the riverbank at Astaria.

"Mommy says Jack is super sweet to deliver us Slayer blood every month. Every time he visits, he tells me I'm special."

"You are special, baby toad," Heden said, already mourning that he had to leave her.

"Love you, Uncle Heden."

"Love you too." Placing a kiss on her forehead, he stood.

Once downstairs, he gave Darkrip a firm handshake. Gathering his things in his bag, he ensured Sofia had everything she needed in the pack slung across her back. They descended the wooden stairs to the back yard, and Heden held his palm to the air. Generating the ether, he guided Sofia in front of his large body. Pushing her toward the substance, they both trekked to the immortal world.

* * * *

Sofia waded through the ether, the thick substance threatening to choke her. Exiting the other side, she held her hand up to the blinding rays of the sun. As she gulped air into her starving lungs, Heden appeared beside her.

"It's still daytime here," she said, coughing as she struggled to breathe.

"Yep," Heden said, his breath also labored. Searching his bag, he located a cell phone. Booting it up, he consulted the screen. "About two o'clock in the afternoon. Traveling between realms creates some serious jet lag."

"I still haven't figured it out," Sofia said, swinging the pack from her shoulders and finding the water bottle inside. Unscrewing the top, she took a large swig. "When Bakari taught me how to travel through the ether, he didn't really explain the physics to me. He just showed me how to go back and forth. Sometimes, I came through at night. Others, during the day. How do you all know how to navigate it?"

"Honestly, it's still tough for me too. I had never been to the human world until my sister moved there. Kenden taught me how to generate the ether, but I'm still not a pro. Basically, you imagine where you want to emerge on the other side. The visualization creates a portal that takes you there, but the specific timing can be off. I imagined us returning to daylight, hence it's mid-afternoon. The potency of the mind is a powerful thing."

Sofia nodded. "I studied ancient religions in college. There are so many accounts of people being able to create things with just a thought. I think humans have only scraped the surface of our capabilities."

"Let's hope so. You guys are heathens."

Chuckling at her scowl, Heden pulled up his contacts and dialed Sathan.

"Hey," his brother said, "are you back?"

"Yes," Heden said. "Any chance you can send a four-wheeler to get us?"

"Us?"

"I brought Sofia back to help us. I'm sure Evie's updated everyone on the situation. The human has defected from our enemies and is now aligned with us."

Silence stretched through the phone.

"It's done, Sathan. Can you please send your favorite brother a ride?"

"I'm at Uteria," he said, his voice gruff. "Ken is here and will be there shortly in a four-wheeler. Are you sure we can trust the human?"

"No," Heden said, "but we need her. Tell Ken thanks. I'll ping him my location."

Lowering the phone, Sofia watched him send Kenden the pin.

"Well, little human, we have about twenty minutes before Kenden gets here. In the meantime, let's get to know each other better." He sat in the plushy grass, crossing his legs and leaning back on his outstretched arms. "Sofia Morelli, before you decided to murder my family, what the heck did you do with your life?"

Sofia couldn't stop the laugh from escaping. "I told you, I'm not here to make friends. I'll help you so we can stop Bakari, but then I'm heading back to New York."

"Tell me about New York," he said, undeterred.

Sighing, she figured it wouldn't hurt to chat with him about the city she loved. It was a neutral subject. She sat down, extolling the many virtues of the Big Apple until an engine roared on the horizon. As the four-wheeler approached, they gathered their bags, slinging them over their shoulders.

Kenden arrived, his chestnut hair tussled from the wind. Sofia recognized the handsome Slayer commander from her surveillance.

"Hey, Heden," he said, shaking the Vampyre's hand. "Glad you made it home safely." When he turned to her, Sofia noticed a deep swell of empathy in his deep brown eyes. "And you must be Sofia," he said, extending his hand. "It's really nice to meet you."

She swallowed, overcome by his kindness. He emanated a calm energy filled with caring and concern. "You must be the Slayer who married the red-haired bitch."

Kenden gave her a sad smile and shook her hand. "I understand you're not a big fan of my wife." Releasing her hand, his pupils roved over her face. "I met your grandfather Francesco in Italy several years ago. He was a kind and jovial man. I'm honored to have met him, and sadly, my actions spurred the events that led to his death. I'm so sorry, Sofia."

Tears burned her eyes as she struggled with emotion.

"I wish I had known Evie then," Kenden continued. "She wasn't ready to become the person she is today. I won't make excuses for her actions, and if you want to hate us both, I certainly don't blame you."

"I think I'll always hate her," Sofia said, shrugging. "But I've realized now that I'm just not capable of the things she is...or was in the past." She noticed Kenden open his mouth to argue. "Regardless, her actions led us down the path we're all on today. I've decided to help you all to prevent needless deaths, especially of immortal children. I hope I've made the right choice."

"It's a very brave choice," Kenden said, his tone reverent. "One that few would make. It shows your character, Sofia. Francesco would be proud."

Sofia blinked away the tears that culminated from the sentiment. "I hope so," she whispered.

"Come on, Sof," Heden said, placing a strong hand on her back. "Let's get you to Astaria. We need to set up in the tech room and have a video conference with everyone. Then, you can teach me all your super-spidey hacking skills."

"Miranda's called a council meeting for tomorrow, at ten a.m. at Astaria," Kenden said as they walked toward the vehicle. "She wants Sofia to attend. It's imperative we formulate a strategy to fight our new enemies. In the meantime, Latimus and I have assigned bodyguards to the children and people we deem as targets."

Heden nodded and gestured for her to climb in the four-wheeler. She strapped herself in the front seat, Heden doing the same in the back. Kenden drove them to the train at Uteria, and they rode the high-speed rail to Astaria. Once there, Heden led her to a room in the basement.

"This is Latimus's old room," he said, gesturing to the empty set of drawers along the wall and the entrance to the private bathroom. A king-size bed sat against the far wall. "The sheets are fresh, and you should have everything you need. My room is right next door," he said, pointing with his thumb. "Why don't you take a few minutes and then meet me in the tech room? It's three doors down on the left."

"Okay," Sofia said, wondering how she'd ended up here. A guest at the Vampyre compound, ready to align with those she'd recently been plotting to exterminate. If she'd had anyone remotely close to tell this story to, they'd be marveled by the excitement. Since she had no friends, she'd have to just revel in it herself. Man, her life was a real-life fairy tale. Or nightmare, if she was honest.

"Sofia?" Heden asked, yanking her from her musings.

"I'm good," she said, throwing her bag on the bed. "Let me brush my teeth and wash my face, and I'll be there. Thanks."

He closed the door behind him, and Sofia entered the bathroom. There, under the bright bulbs, she stared into her blue-green eyes.

"Good grief, Sofia," she muttered to herself. "What the hell are you doing? Your life is a mess."

Sadly, the bare walls of the staid bathroom had no answer for her.

Chapter 13

Sofia sat beside Heden in the tech room as he held a video conference with his family. He introduced her to everyone, and she awkwardly waved, wondering if she should say something. *Hi, I really enjoyed plotting to murder all of you with your long-lost brother?* Deciding that probably wouldn't go over well, she kept her mouth shut.

They ended the call with Miranda confirming the morning's council meeting. In the meantime, Heden would work with Sofia to configure devices that would communicate through the ether so Darkrip and Arderin could be contacted at all times.

Silence blanketed the room as she sat beside Heden's large frame. Struggling to fill the quiet, her eyes darted over the equipment.

"This is impressive," she said, jerking her head toward the plethora of screens and gadgets.

"Thanks," he said, his lips barely quirking into a grin. "Let's get to work. I'd like to start with the code you used. I've tinkered with some things, but they never work." Double-clicking to bring up a text box, he began typing, his thick fingers moving over the keyboard.

Sofia observed the jumble of letters, immediately identifying several mistakes.

"No," she said, encircling his wide wrist with her fingers. "You're already screwing it up. Here." Shooing his arms away, she placed the pads of her fingers on the keys. Eyes narrowed in concentration, she opened a new text box and began clicking the keys.

The letters flowed easily, and Sofia felt comfortable for the first time since entering the immortal realm. This was her territory, her comfort zone. In front of a screen, creating something from scratch. Usually, she was alone, but she didn't find Heden's presence stifling. Being that she didn't really relish the company of others, especially when coding, she figured she'd dissect that later.

Heden watched her with laser focus, his intensity spurring her to prove her proficiency. She wasn't an expert at many things, but, *damn*, she was a freaking great hacker.

"You're using C++ code," he murmured, chin in his hand, eyes glued to the screen.

"Yes. Video game developers use this in my world to develop code so gamers can play together live." Sofia glanced over, noticing how long his black eyelashes were as he blinked at the screen.

"I didn't even think of that," he said, frustration lining his face. "I was using Xcode."

"That's a good start," she said, nodding as her fingers continued tracking. "But it has lots of limitations. You can develop apps and possibly an application that can communicate across the ether, but it's Apple dependent. I use Objective-C. It works across multiple platforms, and Android devices are much more common in Europe and Africa."

"I'm not great at Objective-C. We don't use it a lot here, but I can get better. Honestly, I'm the only one in our world who's learned to code, to my knowledge. Our realm isn't as advanced or modern as the human world, and we prefer to maintain our sedentary lifestyle."

"That reminds me of my grandfather's home," Sofia said, smiling. "It sat atop a hill on the Italian countryside and was surrounded by tons of farmland and grape vines. He taught me how to make wine from the grapes that grew there. Even though I was too young to drink it, he let me anyway." Lost in the memory, she didn't realize her hands had stopped typing.

"So, you like wine," he said, eyebrow arching. "Putting that on the list." He tapped his temple with his finger.

"What list?" she asked, confused.

"The list of items I'm keeping in my head that will help me befriend you." White fangs glowed as he grinned.

Sofia's heart slammed in her chest as she wondered if a man had ever smiled at her so genuinely in such close proximity. "Why are you so nice to me?" she asked, slowly shaking her head. "I've put you and your family in immense danger. You should hate me."

"It takes a lot for me to hate someone, Sof. Someone in my family hurt you. I'd say that makes us even."

"I don't want to be even. I just want my grandfather back."

"I know," he said, his tone solemn as he absently tucked a black curl behind her ear.

Sofia stiffened. The act was foreign, and she wasn't used to being touched.

"Sorry," he said, shoulders straightening as he pulled back. "I'm a toucher. Drives Latimus crazy, especially when I pull him into a bear hug." Holding his hands high, palms out, his expression was contrite. "It's been a long day, and I'm beat. What do you say we pick this up early tomorrow morning, after we both get some sleep?"

"Okay," Sofia said, not understanding how her voice had turned to gravel.

"I'm going to begin perfecting my Objective-C skills as soon as I wake up. If you're not up by eight a.m., I'll knock on your door. Our housekeeper Glarys is an expert at cooking food. I've never had a taste for it, but she'll make you whatever you like. Darkrip used to rave about her food when he lived at Astaria. When you wake up in the morning, just head upstairs, and you'll find the kitchen down the hallway to the left. Make yourself at home."

"Thank you," she said, humbled by his hospitality.

"Sure," he said, standing and stretching his arms over his head.

Sofia thought his biceps might actually pop the sleeves of his shirt open. They were massive.

"C'mon," he said, extending his hand to her.

She let him pull her up and then quickly broke contact with his warm hand. They shuffled to their rooms, and he stopped in her doorway.

"Goodnight," she said, head tilted back as she stared up at him.

"Goodnight," he said. Giving her a nod, he headed toward his room.

Sofia closed the door and pulled the faded t-shirt and boxer shorts from the bag on her bed. Giving in to exhaustion, she cuddled under the covers and fell to sleep.

* * * *

Early the next morning, Sofia ambled up the stairs and found the kitchen. A woman with a head of curly white hair was humming as she scrambled eggs atop a stove. Sensing her presence, the woman tilted her head and smiled.

"You must be Sofia," she said, her tone warm.

Sofia nodded. "I assume you're Glarys."

"One and the same," she said, switching off the stove before pivoting to scoop the eggs onto a plate. "Sit down there at the island and let me pour you some juice. Or do you prefer coffee?"

"Coffee, please," Sofia mumbled, sliding onto the stool. The food smelled delicious, and she lifted a perfectly cooked piece of bacon to her lips. "Thank you."

"You're welcome." Glarys poured her a steaming-hot mug and set it in front of her. "I hear you're helping Heden develop technology to communicate through the ether. It will be wonderful to connect with Arderin and sweet Callie in the human world, and it's truly appreciated."

Sofia munched the crisp bacon. "Yeah, well, I don't have the best track record with immortals. Maybe this will be the beginning of a better path."

"Nothing I haven't seen before," Glarys said, waving a dismissive hand. "You should've been here when Darkrip appeared and got Arderin pregnant. Don't worry, we're used to reformed bad guys around here. I like your chances."

"We'll see," she mumbled, lifting a forkful of steaming eggs. Once finished with breakfast, she trekked downstairs to find Heden sitting in front of the screens in the tech room. His fingers flew over the keyboard, and as she approached, she noticed how broad his hands were. They could likely cup her most intimate place fully as he stared into her with those piercing eyes. Shivering, she pushed the image away. Unwanted desire had no place in the shit show she'd created.

"Hey," she said softly, not wanting to startle him.

"Hey," he said, eyes glued to the screen. "Have a seat." He gestured with his head to the chair beside him.

Sliding in, Sofia assessed his work. Realization swept over her as she comprehended he'd already written code that would allow cell phones to communicate through the ether.

"Holy shit," she said, eyes wide. "It took me years to figure out that code."

His fingers tapped with finality as he finished, hitting the Enter key with a blatant tap of his index finger. Facing her, he laced his hands behind his head, his thick lips curved into a grin. "Once you told me about C++ and Objective C, I couldn't get it out of my head. I barely slept and came in here to figure it out."

"Damn," she breathed, relaxing back in her chair. "I convinced myself I was a better hacker than you."

"Well, you figured it out first, so let's call it even." Ice-blue eyes sparkled as he regarded her. "Now that it's solved, I've got to program some phones and get them through the ether to Arderin and Darkrip. I want Jack to bring them when he delivers the Slayer blood today. Want to help me? If we work together, I think we can get it done before the meeting."

"Sure," she said, shrugging. "Since I'm here, might as well make myself useful."

They spent the next hour at the large conference table, plugging the code into various cell phones for each member of the royal family. As they toiled, they got to know each other, recounting past stories and favorite things.

"Wait," he said, eyebrow arched as his fingers stilled over the keypad of one of the phones. "You like the Jonas Brothers? Aren't you, like, way too old for that?"

Sofia rolled her eyes. "They were popular when I was younger and they've had a resurgence, okay? And who are you calling old anyway? Aren't you about a thousand or something?"

He chuckled. "Yeah, something like that. I was born right before the Awakening."

Sofia recalled what she knew of the calamitous night Slayer King Valktor killed Heden's parents, King Markdor and Queen Calla. "You never got to know your parents," she said softly.

"Nope," he said, shaking his head. "Neither I nor Arderin remember them. It's a bummer, for sure. I want so badly to meet them in the Passage one day. I hope they'll be proud of me. I've tried to do my best to live up to the reverence our people have for them."

Sofia swallowed, slow and thick. "I lost my parents when I was ten years old. It was devastating. My grandfather Francesco raised me after they died, and he was the only family I had left."

Heden lowered the phone to the table and reached across, sliding his palm over her wrist. Squeezing, his gaze bore into her. "I understand how that feels. I love my siblings so much, but they're...a *lot*. I've felt alone so many times over the centuries."

Her eyebrows drew together. "From my surveillance, you and your family seem really close."

"Don't get me wrong, we definitely are. But now they have families of their own, it just feels a little...different or something," he said, shrugging. "But I love my nieces and nephews so much. I try to spend as much time with them as I can while not imposing on their family unit or whatever. I don't know if that makes sense. It's just a different vibe now they've all settled down."

She felt her lips curve. "It makes sense. And you've certainly developed a rapport with the ladies to take up any spare time you would've spent with your siblings, no?"

Chuckling, he tightened his grip around her wrist once more before removing it. Sofia missed the feel of his warm skin immediately, sending pangs of warning through her belly.

"I might have figured out a way to charm a lady or two, but that's easy. Creating something meaningful isn't so seamless."

A black eyebrow arched. "Not even with one of your many suitors?"

His gaze roved over her as he contemplated. "Sex is one thing, but connection is another. And so is love. You must've been in love before."

"Nope," she said, shaking her head as she pretended to plug symbols into the phone. Maintaining his gaze was too uncomfortable. "I've always been a bit awkward and unconcerned with girly things like makeup and fashion. And I'm probably a contender for the 'Frizz of the Year' award," she said, pointing at her black, spiraled hair. "There have been a few men I've dated, but the sex wasn't really mind-blowing for me."

Mired in the silence, she lifted her head to find him thoughtfully staring at her. "What?" she asked, a bit exasperated.

"I just...I can't imagine how someone as fiery as you could have bad sex. Doesn't seem possible."

She shrugged. "Doesn't matter anyway. I haven't been with anyone in a long time. Revenge was much higher on my list than dating."

"Hmm..." he murmured. "Well, hopefully, we can free you up to find a nice human to settle down with once we defeat Bakari and his henchmen."

"Yeah, we need to get on that. I'm worried he's already forming a new plan now he's in possession of Tatiana's magic."

Nodding, Heden resumed tinkering with the cell. "Let's finish here and give these to Jack, and then we'll figure it out with the council."

Once finished, they gathered the menagerie of devices and headed to the foyer, where a tall, auburn-haired Vampyre was waiting. Lanky and lean, Sofia knew immediately it was Jack, Latimus and Lila's adopted seventeen-year-old son. He hadn't yet fully grown into his body but when he did, he would most likely be massive, as most Vampyres were.

"Hey, Uncle Heden," he said. "Did you figure it out?"

"Sure did, kid." Heden handed him a plastic bag. "Two phones ready to communicate through the ether. Thanks for getting them to Arderin and Darkrip."

"Sure thing," Jack said, his gaze trailing to Sofia. "Thanks for helping. I've never met a human before, except Nolan. It's really cool."

"Thanks," Sofia said, feeling a kinship with the kind teenager. "I've only met a few Vamps, but you seem nice."

Jack breathed a laugh. "I try. I've got the four-wheeler all loaded up. I'm heading to the ether now. Dad assigned a guard to accompany me, although I told him I didn't need one." He proudly puffed his chest. "I'm already outperforming soldiers in the part-time battalion who have been there years longer than me. Once I graduate, I'm going to join the army full-time. Can't wait."

"You're already an awesome soldier, kid, but better safe than sorry," Heden said, patting him on the shoulder. "Thanks for taking care of the delivery. I didn't even think to take the blood when I went a few days ago. I was rushing to get to Arderin and figure out what was happening."

"It's fine," Jack said, shrugging. "Plus, I get to see Callie. She's the cutest damn thing."

"Oh, wait," Heden said, reaching into his pocket. "Almost forgot to give this to you." He handed Jack the folded drawing. "She made me promise."

Smiling, Jack straightened the paper, expression filled with reverence as he gazed at it. "She's going to be as talented as Mom one day soon. These drawings get better and better."

"Lila's our world's da Vinci, for sure. I'd love it if Callie has her talent. I can't draw a straight line."

"But at least you're good at tech," Jack said, lifting the bag. "I'll make sure these get there safely. Want to hang and play Fortnite when I get back?"

"Only if you want to lose," Heden said, arching a brow.

"Psst," Jack said, waving his hand with the drawing in it. "I'll decimate you, old man. You've got it coming."

"Can't wait." Heden drew him into an embrace. "Be safe," he murmured in his nephew's ear.

"Will do." Drawing back, he saluted Sofia. "Nice to meet you, Sofia. Hope I get to hang with you too. You seem chill. Bye." Pivoting, he exited through the large front door, closing it firmly behind him.

Staring up at Heden, Sofia suddenly felt uncomfortable. She'd successfully helped him program the phones, which now lessened his need to align with her. Spearing her teeth into her bottom lip, she wondered what happened next.

"So...I think I should sit down and make a list of everyone who's on Bakari's team. I don't want to forget any details, and I'm sure the meeting will be uncomfortable. I can't imagine the council will be thrilled to hear how I plotted their eventual demise."

Heden grinned and extended his hand to her. "I'll protect you, little human." Shaking his hand, he urged her to take it. "Come on. I've got a notebook in the tech room with your name on it."

Against her better judgement, she slid her hand into his, heart pounding at the way it fit so perfectly. He tugged her toward the stairs, and she followed, clutching onto him although she already knew the way.

Chapter 14

Heden sat in the conference room at Astaria, observing Sofia as she stood at the head of the table meticulously describing each person on Bakari's team and their motivations. Every few seconds, his gaze would wander to the rest of the council members, searching their reactions and body language. Latimus was tense, his face marred with his ever-present scowl as Sofia recited the intel, but that was normal for his stoic brother. Lila sat beside him, her expression much more open and receptive.

Aron sat beside Moira, whom Miranda had asked to attend due to the fact her once-deceased husband, Diabolos, was a member of the Secret Society. Aron absently rubbed her stiff shoulders as she listened to Sofia's calm voice, her features slightly laced with fear.

After speaking for thirty minutes, Sofia gently laid the notebook on the table. Reaching for the plastic cup of water, she lifted it to her lips, her hand slightly shaking.

Empathy swelled in Heden's chest as he watched her. She was literally a world away from her own, endeavoring to help them even though many in the room were shooting her looks filled with anger and mistrust. Yes, she was partly responsible for their predicament, but she wasn't the leader and had only joined Bakari's cause due to her extreme grief following Evie's actions. No one was innocent here. They all had blood on their hands, and Heden felt the need to protect the human and remind everyone of that important fact.

"Thank you, Sofia," Heden said, straightening in his chair. Addressing the council from his seat, he intentionally made eye contact with each one as he spoke. "I want to remind everyone that Sofia is here of her own free will. She could've chosen to stay in the human world and left us to fight for ourselves without her intel. She also helped me write the code that allows the new phones I gave each of you to communicate through the ether," he said, gesturing his head toward the device resting on the table in front of Ken, who sat to his left. "She is our ally, and I expect her to be treated that way."

"And I killed her grandfather," Evie said, eyebrow arched. "She had every reason to join Bakari when he approached her. I can read the thoughts swirling in this room, and your distrust of her is misplaced. If there's anyone you should be angry at, it's me."

Miranda stood at the opposite end of the table from Sofia. "I suggest we let any residual anger go now. We've got bigger problems to tackle and must be united. If anyone has a problem with that, let's discuss it now."

Miranda's gaze traveled back and forth between Sathan and Latimus, both of whom sat with lips drawn into thin lines and muscled arms crossed over their chests. "I'm speaking to you two, in case you didn't get the memo."

Sathan's gaze traveled to Sofia's. "Can we trust you, Sofia Morelli?" he asked in his deep baritone.

Sofia sighed, sliding into the leather chair behind her. Resting her hands atop the table, she clasped them, her fingers fidgeting. "I realized recently that I just don't possess the will to end another being's life. Even if those beings are quite dismissive of humans and have committed some pretty terrible deeds." Eyes narrowed, she shot Evie a glare. "You all seem to have a distaste toward humans that baffles me, especially since we're certainly the most evolved species on the planet."

Latimus mumbled something under his breath, and Heden glowered at him, causing his brother's scowl to deepen.

"In the end, I'm pretty sure I'm insignificant to you, especially now that I've given you all my intelligence and you have nothing left to gain from me. So, I guess the question really is, can I trust *you*?"

Sathan inhaled a breath and straightened in his chair. "We appreciate your help, Sofia. I'm willing to move forward and cement an alliance with you. It would be unwise to turn away someone with your programming skills. As our plan to protect our families and subjects progresses, we might need your assistance after all."

"I second that motion," Miranda said.

"All in favor?"

A resounding "aye" reverberated through the room, with everyone in agreement—even Latimus, who seemed to have the most reservations. Miranda nodded and sat, training her gaze on Kenden.

"Ken, please update us on the heightened security measures you and Latimus have put in place."

"We've identified the threats based on Sofia's intel, which she supplied to me and Latimus last night," Kenden said, his tone firm and assured. "It seems Vadik and Melania are focused on attacking at Valeria, Diabolos at Uteria, Ananda at Astaria, and Bakari at Takelia. It's possible those plans have changed with Sofia's defection, but we've increased the number of soldiers at each compound and all are on high alert. Bodyguards have been assigned to the children of everyone in this room, and Larkin will be personally guarding Aron and Moira."

Moira clenched her hands atop the table as she spoke. "I saw a man the other evening who reminded me so much of Diabolos. I was so sure it was my mind playing tricks on me. I can't believe he's alive."

"He's not going to touch one hair on your head, Moira," Miranda said. "Take it from me. Larkin is a fantastic soldier, and I have utmost faith in his abilities to protect you and Aron."

"Thanks, Miranda," Larkin said, covering Moira's hands with his own as he sat beside her. "I've got you guys. I'll be moving into the downstairs bedroom as soon as we adjourn and won't leave your side until that bastard is dead for the second time."

Moira thanked the kind soldier, and the meeting changed direction so they could strategize and move forward. After a thorough discussion, it was decided Darkrip was capable of protecting Arderin and Callie in the human world, especially now their phones could communicate through the ether. Latimus and Kenden would work with their soldiers to beef up security first, then track down the enemies and systematically disable them until they were captured or killed.

"What should we do about Melania?" Miranda asked. "Being that she's the wife of Valeria's governor?"

"Sofia has assured us Camron has no idea his wife is involved. At this point, I think it's better to surveil her and see if we can gather some intel. She's not a trained soldier like some of the others and could end up leading us to Bakari."

"Okay, Ken, I'm on board with that. Hopefully she'll slip up and inadvertently give us a clue."

"We're forgetting one key player here," Sofia said once the plan to stop their enemies was set. "Tatiana Rousseau, who lives on the outskirts of New Orleans. She's been supplying Bakari with the dark magic that allows him to transport, but I don't think she's aligned with him in the cause."

"What leads you to believe that?" Miranda asked.

Sofia's eyes narrowed as she contemplated. "I spent some time surveilling her movements around her Louisiana home, gathering intel for Bakari. She doesn't really seem interested in forming an alliance with anyone, human or immortal. I get the feeling she's..."—she waved her hand, searching for words—"interested but detached, if that makes any sense. It would be helpful if we could discern her motivations and see if she's open to helping our cause instead of Bakari. She doesn't use electronic devices, so I can't hack her that way, but I could create some sort of surveillance system I could implant in and around her cabin. I'd obviously need help and would need to be inconspicuous."

"I can help you," Heden found himself saying before he realized the words had left his mouth. "We can create a surveillance program together, and I can protect you in the human world while we work."

Sofia's blue-green gaze studied him. "I've protected myself well enough on my own, thank you very much, but I could use your technical skills. It will cut the development time in half."

Heden nodded, feeling his lips curve at her dismissal of his protection offer. "Okay, let's do that. We can secure an Airbnb in the human world near Tatiana's home and work from there. As long as the Wi-Fi is strong, we'll be good to go."

"You'll need to carry some weapons through the ether, Heden," Lila's sweet voice chimed in. "I don't want anything to happen to you in the human world."

"Will do, buttercup," he said, giving her a wink. "Sofia and I will each carry a gun, and I'll strap an SSW to my belt as well. I'm not as well-trained as Latimus but I trust I can protect us there."

Lila nodded, concern lacing her gorgeous features.

"Okay, we all have our assignments," Miranda said as she rose, spine straight with resolve. "Ken and Latimus are running point, but we must all stay in constant communication. In the meantime, I'm going to go check on Tordor at school. The guards assigned to him are awesome, but I just need to hug my little man."

"I'll go with you," Sathan said, gripping her hand.

She smiled, squeezing as she stared down at him with love.

"I'm going to do the same with Adelyn and Symon," Lila said to Latimus, referencing their two youngest children.

"Okay, honey," Latimus said, brushing her pink lips with his. "I'll be home when it gets dark. Love you."

"One more thing," Evie said, standing and placing her hands in her back jeans pockets, her expression wary. "I was going to wait to tell you all but I'm currently ten weeks pregnant. It's important you all understand another child with my father's blood exists."

"Oh my god, Evie!" Miranda chimed, rushing around the table to give her a hug. "That's amazing! I'm so excited for you."

Evie pulled back and arched a brow. "That makes one of us. I hope the little bugger isn't as evil as my father. We'll see."

"Hey," Kenden said, pulling her to his side. "This baby is going to be filled with the blood of Valktor, Rina and my parents, who were wonderful people. Callie is such a sweet little girl, and I know our child will have the same qualities, sweetheart."

"I had to marry an optimist," Evie muttered under her breath.

"I think it's fantastic," Lila said, breezing toward Evie and enveloping her in a strong hug. "I'm here if you need anything, Evie."

"Thanks, guys," Evie said, wiping her palms on her jeans once she was free of Lila's embrace. "I'm going to do my best here. Thank the goddess I have Ken."

Her husband placed a kiss atop her crimson hair, and several others approached to congratulate Evie. Heden trailed to Sofia's side as she stood at the far end of the table, her expression impassive.

"Hey," he said, cupping her shoulder. "Thank you for helping us. I'm excited to create something with you in the human world. I've never collaborated with a programmer as competent as you."

She nodded, her gaze trailing to Evie. "Isn't anyone worried the child will be evil?" she asked softly.

"We all have our paths to chart, Sof. I believe in free will and choice. Hopefully, if Evie and Ken nurture the baby correctly, it will grow to be good and just. Callie is an amazing child, and I've never seen one speck of Crimeous's darkness in her."

"I guess," she said, kicking the carpet with the toe of her sneaker. "Only time will tell."

"Thank goodness we have a lot of time."

"Speak for yourself," she muttered. "I feel it slipping by so quickly, more and more as I age."

"Then let's not waste it," Heden said, squeezing her shoulder before releasing her. "Let's head to the tech room and find a place near Tatiana's where we can work."

Nodding, the human followed him from the conference room.

* * * *

Once he and Sofia were prepared for their journey into the human world, Heden went in search of his siblings. They'd agreed to meet that afternoon to discuss the almost unbelievable fact they had a brother they knew nothing about. Entering the conference room at Astaria, Heden smiled at Sathan.

"You need me to set up the video conference with Arderin?" he asked, sitting to Sathan's right while Latimus flanked him on the left of the large table.

"No," Sathan said, his face a mask of concentration as he fiddled with the laptop. "I think I've got it." Maneuvering the mouse, he smiled when Arderin's face appeared.

"Hey, guys," she said, waving. "This is so freaking cool. I'm so glad we can communicate through the ether now."

"It's all due to Sofia," Heden said. "She's a really valuable asset to our team."

"I give you a day before you bang her," Arderin said, rolling her eyes.

"Can we get to the discussion at hand?" Latimus asked, annoyed. "I have shit to do and a kingdom full of people to protect, and I really don't give a crap about who Heden is seducing at the moment."

"Chill, Latimus," Heden said, resting his chin on his hand. "I already told you, I won't use my seduction skills on Lila. You're welcome, by the way."

Latimus scowled while Sathan chuckled. "Okay, kids, let's get to it. I can't believe we have a brother. One who seems intent on destroying us and our kingdom. The way I see it, we need to figure out three things: why he wants to harm us, what powers he and his team possess, and if we can turn him back to our side."

"Agreed," Latimus said. "Sofia said he has a mark on his leg he discussed with the Secret Society. Supposedly, it represents his nefarious nature. I don't recall ever reading about that in the archives."

"Me neither," Sathan said. "We poured over the archives and soothsayer scrolls extensively when we were searching for Evie. There was no mention of another Vampyre royal child."

"How could they keep it from us?" Arderin asked. "Do you two remember her being pregnant before she was pregnant with me?"

"My memories are kind of mashed together," Sathan said. "I would've been about four or five when she was pregnant with Bakari. I think because I was so young, and she got pregnant with Arderin soon after she lost Bakari, the pregnancies just morphed together in my mind."

Heden nodded. "Maybe they were waiting to tell us until we were older. Telling young kids about a dead brother isn't an easy conversation."

"I think that's the most logical explanation," Sathan said. "Sadly, they didn't get to see us grow much older."

Silence pervaded the room as they contemplated. Finally, Heden said, "Well, Sofia and I will do our best to surveil Tatiana and figure out what powers she's bestowed upon Bakari. In the meantime, Sathan, I think you and Miranda should search the soothsayer manuals and Vampyre archives and see if there's any mention of Bakari."

"And Kenden and I will work on revamping the army. It's going to be a huge project. I was so sure we'd entered an era of peace. Now that we have kids and families, the stakes are even higher," Latimus said, running a hand over his face.

"We have to hold out hope we can eventually turn him," Arderin said. "After all, he's our brother. Blood means something to us, and perhaps one day, we'll be able to show him how important family is to us."

"Sofia said he's a purist," Heden said. "That he believes in true bloodlines and separation of the species. He absolutely hates the direction we've taken the immortal world, combining the species again and bearing hybrids."

"Where do those beliefs come from?" Latimus asked.

"I don't know," Heden said, shaking his head. "He's been in the human world for a thousand years. There are so many things he's been exposed to. It will be difficult to figure it out, but as we study him more, hopefully, we'll make some headway."

"I hope so," Sathan said, patting Heden on the back. "The first step is your journey with Sofia to perform reconnaissance on Tatiana. I wish you safe travels, brother."

"Thanks, Sathan," Heden said, determined to help his people.

"I love you guys," Arderin said, blowing them a kiss. "Stay safe."

Resolved to protect their realm, the royal siblings got to work.

Chapter 15

Bakari observed Callie as she played with the other children on the playground beside her school. She was a natural leader, directing her fellow classmates in a game of dodgeball before heading to the swings. Every student was given two minutes on the swing, monitored by Callie, before another could take their place. They followed her direction seamlessly, planting seeds in Bakari's mind as he watched the interplay. Once she was fully grown—if she stayed alive that long—her ability to guide and command others would be a huge asset. Filing that away, he waited.

The teacher announced recess was over, and Callie scowled, crossing her arms over her chest and asking for more time. Darkrip appeared, causing Bakari to sink further behind the tree. Now that Sofia had defected, Darkrip would be on high alert and was most likely volunteering at the school in order to protect Callie.

Fury for the stupid human filled Bakari's gut, and he cursed himself for ever approaching Sofia. He'd been able to sense her hate and thought it would make her a powerful ally in his quest to murder the immortal royals and set things right. Plus, he'd needed her hacking skills. It was a grave mistake and quite costly. Determined not to make another one, he watched the kids trail back inside the school.

Once the last bell rang and Darkrip loaded Callie into their SUV and drove away, Bakari approached the swing. There, tangled in the metal rings that hung from the base, were three dark, curly hairs. Absconding them, he placed them in his pocket. He would ensure they made it safely to Tatiana, so she would supply him with enough potion that he could transport as he wished in the land of humans and immortals.

Then, he would focus on killing his family.

Smiling at the thought, he ambled toward his rental car to begin the journey to LAX, confident it would be one of the last times he had to travel by such primitive methods.

* * * *

Jack was helping Arderin load the canisters of Slayer blood into the refrigerator when he heard excited footsteps pound up the wooden stairs of the back porch. The door slammed open, and Callie ran inside.

"Jack!" she called, giggling as he lifted her into his arms and swung her around.

"Hey, munchkin," he said, rubbing his nose against hers. "I missed you."

"Who's that?" she asked, eyeing the man who stood in the corner of the room.

"That's Bryan. He came along with me to make sure I'm safe. Did you have fun at school today?"

Nodding, she grasped his cheeks in her small hands. "I missed you so much. Did you bring me a present?"

"Hmm..." he said, squinting at the ceiling. "I think you're too old for presents."

"No way!" she said, shaking her head. "You can always get presents, even if you're a big girl. Mommy tells me that every time she makes Daddy buy her stuff."

"It's not *that* often," Arderin said, flicking her hair over her shoulder. "I mean, I have to keep up with these L.A. humans to blend in, and they have nice purses. What can I say?"

"Yes, I think I've bought each one featured on *Real Housewives*," Darkrip said, stalking over and placing his arm around Arderin's waist. "You're expensive, princess," he said, nipping at her lips.

"Don't make me bite you back, husband," she murmured.

Callie scrunched her nose. "They kiss all the time. It's so gross."

"They love each other. My mom and dad do the same thing, but I've gotten used to it, kid," Jack said. Although he was adopted by Lila and Latimus, several years ago, he'd begun calling them "Mom" and "Dad" as opposed to their formal names. He couldn't remember how it happened exactly, but it had naturally progressed. Jack could still remember his biological parents, both of whom passed years ago, and he felt extremely lucky to have been blessed with two sets of amazing parents.

"I love you," Callie said, placing a wet kiss on his lips.

"I love you too, munchkin," he said, smiling. Jack loved his family with his entire heart, but he had a connection with Callie that was unbreakable. It had always been there, since the moment he first laid eyes on her as a baby, and it coursed through him, so strong and true. "Uncle Heden gave me your drawing. It's really good. Thank you."

"You're welcome," she said, the tips of her incisors not quite as pointed as his since she was only half-Vampyre. "It was for your birthday last week. Now that you're seventeen, Mommy says you might break Aunt Lila's heart and live on your own."

"I don't have any plans to leave yet. Where else can I find the bangin' mac and cheese she makes?"

Her eyes roved over his face. "I got a new book. I can read most of the words. Can I read it to you before you go?"

"Heck yeah," he said, setting her on the floor. "In the living room?"

She nodded, black curls bouncing as she pulled him into the dim room. After turning on the lamp, Callie grabbed the book and settled into Jack's side. He held her as she read, so proud of how smart she was to already be reading so proficiently at six years old, although some of the words were stilted at points.

Eventually, Arderin headed to the hospital, and Callie's stomach growled. Jack left Callie to her dinner, promising to bring her a present next time he visited. With Bryan by his side, they reentered the immortal world, and Jack headed home to convince Lila to whip up some of the mac and cheese he was now craving.

Chapter 16

Heden strapped his bag over his shoulder and jumped out of the four-wheeler. Extending his hand, he helped Sofia hop down and walked to the edge of Etherya's Earth, where the wall of ether stood between them and the human world.

"Be careful," Latimus said. "And keep an eye on this one."

"I understand you don't like me," Sofia said, scowling. Heden admired her strength. Latimus towered over her, but she faced him like a champ. "I don't really give a crap. I'm not here to make friends."

"I don't really understand why you're here," Latimus said, crossing his arms over his chest. "You've got nothing to gain by helping us."

"I want to set things right," Sofia said, chin thrust high. "I don't want any harm to come to your pregnant sister or your children. Once I accomplish my goal, I promise, you'll never see me again. I've already spent too much time with arrogant immortals."

Latimus's lips drew into a thin line. "Damn it," he muttered.

"What?" Sofia asked, perplexed.

"I like your spunk, okay? It's annoying. I told myself I wasn't going to let you off the hook for putting my entire family in danger."

"She has a way of growing on you, bro," Heden said, patting Sofia on the back. She promptly swatted his hand away, causing him to chuckle. Man, he loved her fiery spirit. It was extremely attractive.

"Don't fuck this up, Heden," Latimus said. "We're counting on you."

"Love you too, bro. I know that's what you meant to say." With a wink, he turned to Sofia. "Ready?"

She nodded and walked toward the ether. Inhaling a deep breath, she began to wade through.

Heden took a step forward but was halted by his brother's firm grip on his arm.

"I've already lived through Sathan not being able to keep his dick in his pants. It almost ended in disaster. I see the way you look at the human. Be careful, Heden."

"Man, you are some kind of Debbie Downer, Latimus." Heden carefully extracted his brother's hand from his arm. "I'll kindly remind you that Sathan's intense need to be with Miranda is what eventually reunited our kingdoms. And I'm pretty sure I'm an adult and can do whatever the hell I want with my life."

Latimus's nostrils flared. "I just don't want your dick to get you into trouble."

Heden chuckled and rolled his eyes. "You're dramatic in your old age, bro. Go home to Lila and get laid. I'll be fine."

"Hey," Latimus called when Heden was almost to the ether, causing him to turn. "Call me if you need me. I mean it."

"Awww..." Heden said, lifting his hand to rub his heart. "I just got all warm and fuzzy inside. Thanks, Latimus. Now, tell me how much you love me and that I'm your favorite brother."

Latimus glowered. "Everything's a joke to you. I should've known." Pivoting, he stalked to the four-wheeler. Once he was behind the wheel, he lifted his hand in a wave, the gesture poignant.

Heden smiled, knowing that was his stoic brother's way of wishing him well. Straightening his spine, he entered the ether and waded through.

Sofia stood on the other side, pilfering through the bag she'd carried through. Pulling out a phone, she illuminated it under the rapidly darkening sky. "Should we call an Uber to the Airbnb?"

"Sure," he said, giving her a nod. Sofia had secured an Airbnb reservation in the human world for a small two-bedroom cottage a few miles from where Tatiana lived. It was on the outskirts of a rural bayou town and it would offer them the inconspicuous location they needed.

Her phone pinged as it confirmed the rideshare, and two minutes later, a woman in a black Camry pulled up. She chatted companionably with them on the ride, her Southern accent deep. Once they were at the house, Sofia punched the code into the keypad, and they entered.

After taking a small tour, Sofia took the room with the double bed, and he took the king since it would accommodate his larger frame. He quickly showered in the private bathroom and headed to the kitchen. The Slayer blood he'd deposited in the fridge would last weeks in the human world. Hopefully, it wouldn't take that long to study Tatiana and determine if they could recruit her to support their cause. They'd secured the rental home for a few days and would evaluate extending once they deciphered how difficult the surveillance would be.

Sofia padded out of her room, feet bare below smooth legs and thighs barely covered by cute, thin shorts. She wore a tank top that hugged her small frame, and Heden noticed her nipples were pebbled underneath the ribbed fabric. A black bra strap peeked out from underneath one of the tank's straps but the garment didn't offer much coverage. Blood coursed through his body as she approached, heading straight to the organ behind his fly.

"Hope you don't mind that I'm in my scrubs," she said, combing her fingers through her wet curls. "I work better if I'm comfortable."

Heden swallowed, feeling his throat bob. "Fine with me. I'm usually a jeans and t-shirt kind of guy."

"Whatever works," she said, shrugging. Reaching into the fridge, she pulled out one of the beers and popped it open. "What? The owner said we could have whatever the last guests left behind. Why waste perfectly good beer?"

His lips curved. "Excellent point. I'll take one too."

She grabbed one and extended it to him, and once he'd opened it, they clinked the bottles. "To a successful mission."

"Let's get to it then," she said, sipping the beer.

They set up her laptop on the desk in the main room, Sofia facing it as Heden pulled up a chair to sit behind her. She began typing, fingers moving furiously as she connected to the Wi-Fi. Once complete, she opened the internet browser.

"First things first, we need to download a secure VPN. I suggest Surfshark. I've used them extensively, and our work will be untraceable."

"I think NordVPN is better," Heden said, eyebrows drawing together. "I use that in the immortal world, and they have military grade encryption."

"That's just a marketing ploy," Sofia said, waving her hand. "All the major VPNs have top-notch encryption."

"Yes, but Nord has an anonymous payment structure."

"I can maneuver our Surfshark account to be anonymous, and it has much faster speeds than Nord."

Heden smiled at her, his gaze roving over her face. It shone with just the barest hint of freckles under the bulb of the overhead light, causing him to wonder if they got darker when she was out in the sun. Did they blend in with her smooth olive skin?

"Earth to Heden," she chimed.

He took a swig of his beer, slow and lazy, loving how the frustration on her face only increased. For some reason, stirring her ire was insanely enjoyable.

"Sofie?" he asked, arching an eyebrow.

"Yes?"

"Are you going to argue with me over every single thing we try to complete on this laptop? Because it's extremely cute, but I don't think we're going to get a lot accomplished."

Her features drew together. "I have no desire to be cute or anything remotely close. I just think you're wrong about the VPN."

"Fine. We'll use Surfshark, but just know, I'm only capitulating in this first battle. You won't win so easily next time."

"Whatever," she muttered, turning to face the laptop. She loaded the VPN and proceeded to set up an anonymous account as promised.

Watching her maneuver the various programs and text prompts with her agile fingers caused pangs of arousal to curl in his stomach. Heden had mostly spent time doing one thing with women: getting his groove on. Although that was extremely pleasurable, he never really took the time to get to know them on an intellectual level. It was most likely a defense mechanism, since he'd convinced himself he preferred to remain unattached, but it also led to him not forming the connection he'd begun to recently contemplate.

As he'd slowly opened himself to considering something more, this waif of a human had appeared in his path. Smart, adorable and feisty as hell, it was almost as if she was sent by divine intervention, if one believed in that sort of thing. Although he didn't yet know her well, Heden could see himself spending time with her, writing code and playing the video games she'd told him she loved when they'd chatted in the grass upon entering the immortal world.

Not only would she understand his need to decipher things and create new technology, she would be an asset in that undertaking. Heden wasn't too proud to admit she was a better programmer than he was. It was extremely sexy, and he found himself imagining what it would be like to whisper in her ear as he held her trembling body to his and asked her to code something just for him. Man, the image was so hot to a tech dork like him.

"What do you think?" she asked, looking at him over her shoulder.

"Sorry, what?" he asked, overcome by the smell of her damp hair.

"I think we should use the mini wireless cameras for inside the cabin, and the waterproof Nannday wireless cameras for outside. Thoughts?"

"Sounds good," he said, reminding himself to stay on task.

They proceeded to have several more discussions around the various technology to employ in surveilling Tatiana, and Heden reveled in each one. Sofia was extremely fun to argue with, although it was good-natured, and he sometimes would draw out the debate just to see her cheeks redden. Would her entire body flush like that as they made love?

Reminding himself he should probably keep it in his pants, they eventually finished the prep work. Tomorrow, they would head to the electronics store in the small town square and purchase the equipment they needed. Then, they would figure out how to install it in Tatiana's home—not easy, since Sofia had already observed she rarely ventured out.

Once they were both in their own beds, Heden turned out the light and stared at the darkened ceiling. He imagined having Sofia's body against his side, cuddling into him as her skin cooled. Smiling softly, he realized he wanted to seduce her. Latimus and Arderin's warnings be damned. Heden had never denied himself the opportunity to make love to a woman, and he wouldn't lie to himself about his desire for the human.

It was there, a latent pulsing through his entire body, and he meant to navigate around every thorn to get to her soft petals. Content in his resolution, he willed himself to sleep, wondering if he would dream of her in the balmy Louisiana night.

Chapter 17

Bakari sat at the makeshift table in the dirty cave, surrounded by the members of the Secret Society. As he brought them up to speed on Sofia's defection, he scanned their faces, judging their reactions. Ananda and Vadik were stoic, which was to be expected since both were usually emotionless. Diabolos' angular features were filled with rage, while Melania appeared terrified.

"It's unacceptable that you didn't tell us of her defection until now, Bakari," Diabolos said. "I had a perfect opportunity to kill my bitch wife a few days ago but didn't want to give up the element of surprise. Now, it's lost to us. What a waste."

"Sofia disabled the devices from communicating through the ether as soon as she defected, and I had other tasks to complete in the human world," Bakari replied, feeling his nostrils flare. "I delivered strands of Calinda's hair to Tatiana, and she supplied me with these." Pulling several vials from his bag, he sat straighter in his chair. "They will allow us to transport as Darkrip and Evie do. It's an invaluable asset. I will leave each of you with one container. You must place it on your tongue at least sixty seconds before you want to transport. Once you ingest it, the capability will last for several hours. There is a chant that will activate the serum, which I'll teach you before we leave today. Understood?"

The team nodded, and Bakari slipped the vials across the table, one to each of them.

"I have no idea what to do," Melania said, worry lining her pretty but cold features. "I saw Lila yesterday, and she said nothing to me, which means they're waiting for me to slip up. I can't let Camron discover my alliance with you. I think I have to defect as well."

Bakari sighed and ran his hand over his slick hair. "If you must, I won't object. I learned a lesson from Sofia. No one should be in this society unless they are one hundred percent on board with murdering the royal family and their offspring. There is no place for wavering."

Melania's eyes narrowed. "I want Lila, her vile bonded mate and her children exterminated from the planet, but I won't chance being caught. I'm sorry," she said, eying the other members. Standing, she placed the vial on the table. "I wish you all luck and will revel in the death of our enemies, but I must defect." With a nod of her head, she departed the cave.

"Anyone else?" Bakari asked once she was gone. "It's better if you leave now than wait until we've devised a new plan."

"I'm still committed," Vadik said. "I will avenge Crimeous until my dying breath."

"I'm not going anywhere," Diabolos said.

"Me neither," Ananda chimed.

"Good," Bakari said, standing and lifting the new tablet he'd secured so Sofia couldn't track his previous one. "I've formulated a new attack strategy. Now we've lost the element of surprise, we must change our tactics. I have secured samples of some deadly chemical toxins from the human world. They will poison any Slayer upon ingestion. Since they're rare, the immortal physicians will have trouble identifying them, which means they'll struggle to find a cure for anyone who consumes them.

"I'm giving you samples to have on hand in case you find yourself in the position to poison any of our targets. I don't foresee that happening, since Kenden and Latimus have increased security immensely around their families and across the realm, but it could happen. I have an appointment with a chemist next week to purchase a stockpile of chemicals so we can plan a full-scale attack." He slid a black baseball-sized pouch to each of the associates.

"Are you planning to attack the subjects of the kingdom now as well?" Ananda asked.

"That wasn't the plan initially, but I believe it will be required in order to exterminate the royals. If their efforts are divided across the realm, it will make it easier to find an opportunity to attack the family members. Chaos creates instability. The sovereigns will be so focused on protecting their people, it will create an opening for us."

"I thought you wanted to rule Etherya's realm for yourself. Will there be any subjects left to rule if you poison them all?" Ananda asked, eyebrow arched.

"Vampyres' self-healing bodies will not be harmed by the chemicals. I just need to make sure I leave enough Slayers alive to supply us with blood. I will build a better kingdom with the subjects that are left after the attack. The species will remain separate and pure, as the goddess intended."

"And what about the Deamon prison?" Vadik asked. "I still think our best option is to jailbreak the prisoners there and have them fight with us. They still worship Crimeous and will align with me as their commander."

"The security system is extensive there, thanks to Heden's programming and the well-trained troops. It's better if we poison the subjects first to create some diversions and hope they pull soldiers from the prison."

Vadik considered. "Being able to transport gives me the ability to get inside."

"Yes, but if you are caught, we'll have lost our most skilled combat warrior. I would rather wait until their resources have been stretched."

"I see the logic in that. I will wait, but I'm ready to move forward. I fear we've already squandered our best opportunities."

"Me too," Diabolos mumbled. "We're down to four members, and our chances of success diminish each day."

"This will not be a fast coup," Bakari said. "It is imperative we think each detail through. I know you all are anxious to prevail. I am as well. But it took centuries for the kingdom to devolve to this point. It will not be fixed in days or even weeks. I ask for your patience so we may form an infallible plan. It is better to toil a few weeks in caution than fail."

"I agree," Vadik said. "I don't want to come this far only to crumble at the end."

"All right," Diabolos said. "I will be patient, but you must stay in contact with us, Bakari. I want regular updates."

"Our new devices can't communicate through the ether but they also can't be tracked by Sofia. I will make sure to travel to the realm and update you as often as I can."

"I am determined to succeed," Ananda said, "and I will keep watch on my niece's children and look forward to your brief once you secure the chemicals from the scientist."

"Thank you," Bakari said, rising. "If there are no more questions, we can adjourn."

After the members all nodded with resolve, Bakari dismissed them, more determined than ever to prevail.

Chapter 18

The next day, Sofia and Heden traveled by rideshare to the electronics store, purchasing several wireless cameras and other various electronics they needed for their surveillance. Once they had everything, they instructed the driver to drop them off half a mile from Tatiana's property. After traversing the forest, they came upon the clearing where her house resided. Hiding behind a large willow tree, they observed the cottage.

A winding trail of smoke curled from the chimney even though it must've been eighty degrees outside. Heden thought it smelled quite rotten and wondered if the mysterious woman was cooking something nefarious in a cauldron in the fireplace. From what Sofia had told him, Tatiana liked to concoct different brews for her spells and chants.

"Should we go closer?" Sofia whispered, palm flat on the brown bark of the tree.

"Let's give it another few minutes," he murmured. "Maybe she'll give us an opening."

Sure enough, only a few moments later, the front door creaked open and a woman appeared. She had long, curly brown hair and smooth russet skin under a flowing blue dress. Flat sandals adorned her feet, and she trailed to an open-top Jeep in the driveway. Sitting behind the wheel, she started the car, revved the engine and pulled onto the gravel road.

Wanting to shield them, Heden gently pushed Sofia further behind the tree, crouching into her as the car drove off in the distance.

"Now's our chance," Sofia said, squirming against him in an effort to dislodge from his protective stance. Wriggling, she turned to face him, sending daggers of arousal through his veins. "Let's hang the inside cameras first."

Heden stared at her upturned face, unable to move as her small breasts jutted against his chest. His fingers tensed slightly on the rough bark of the tree as they bracketed her head. Frozen, his gaze roved over her pert nose, delectable freckles, and limitless eyes.

"Hey," she said, placing her palms against his pecs and pushing. Her features drew together when he didn't even budge. "She could come back any minute. Let's go!"

Desire coursed through him as he inched forward, aligning their bodies until he could feel her rampant heartbeat against his own. Unable to stop himself, he slid his hands behind her neck, placed his thumbs against her jaw and tilted her face to his.

"What the hell are you doing?" she rasped, lips shining from where her wet tongue darted to lather them.

Short breaths escaped his lungs. "I want to kiss you, Sofie."

"Now?" she almost squeaked. "We might only have minutes to infiltrate Tatiana's house, and you want to kiss me now?"

Exhaling a laugh, he nodded. "Now. I'll make it quick, I promise." He waggled his eyebrows.

Curious blue-green eyes darted between his.

He gently nudged her nose with his. "Please, Sof." Ever so gently, he ran his lips over hers. "By the goddess, your lips are so soft."

"*Heden—*"

Opening his mouth, he closed over hers, inhaling his own name from her lips.

A high-pitched mewl escaped her throat, causing his body to tighten further as he maneuvered his lips over hers. Needing to taste, he slipped his tongue inside her warm mouth, feeling her body tremble as he plundered the wet depths. She tasted like rose and honey, rolled into a flavor so sweet he craved more. Cupping her neck with his broad hand, he slid the other across her collarbone, over the side of her breast and around her trim waist before gliding it over her jean-clad ass. Undulating his hips into hers, he clenched the ripe globe, groaning into her mouth.

Her fingernails speared his chest through his black t-shirt, the pleasure-pain driving him wild. In retaliation for the sexy gesture, he softly sucked her bottom lip through his teeth, alternately flicking it with his tongue. Her eyes blasted open, staring into his as she panted beneath him. Gaze locked with hers, he swiped his tongue over her lips and rested his forehead on hers.

"Damn, Sof," he mumbled against her lips. "You taste like heaven."

Her eyes were so deep, Heden was sure he could see her soul. With two words, she ripped him open. "*Don't stop.*"

Growling with lust, his free hand fell to her rear. Clutching her ass with his palms, he lifted her as if she were a feather, loving how her legs instinctively wrapped around his waist. Seating his pulsing length into her core, he devoured her mouth.

His spunky human gave as good as she got, thrusting her fingers in his thick hair as she jabbed her tongue inside his mouth. Lifting to meet it, his tongue warred with hers...licking...sucking...sliding over each other until Heden thought he might die if he didn't bury himself inside her. Groaning in frustration, he broke the kiss and buried his face in her neck.

Her body trembled as she spoke in his ear. "Heden?"

"I'm sorry," he said, squeezing her with his burly arms. "It's just so much. Your taste and your smell. I have to stop."

Heden felt the doubt course through her gorgeous body. Lifting his head, he locked his gaze with hers. "Not because I want to stop, Sofie," he said, shaking his head. "Because if I don't stop now, I might not be able to. I want you very badly, little human."

Her tiny nostrils flared. "You do?"

The corners of his lips curved. "I do. But we have a job to do, and I'd rather get that out of the way so I can focus on you."

His ego swelled at her expression of extreme disappointment. She nodded.

Lowering her, he set her on her feet and straightened, running a hand over her ponytail. "I think I messed it up," he said.

Lifting her hands, she maneuvered the band and reformed a perfect ponytail in five seconds flat. "All good. Let's go."

With a tilt of his head, they began walking toward the cabin. Heden noticed how tightly she clutched the bag in her hand, her knuckles almost white. She seemed frazzled by their kiss, and he recalled their conversation in the tech room where she told him she didn't date often. Pursuing a pretty woman was second nature to Heden, but he reminded himself that not everyone was as comfortable with casual flings. Wanting to put her at ease, he slid his hand over the juncture of her neck and shoulder.

"Don't tense up, Sofie. It was just a kiss. I promise, I won't ravage you unless you beg me."

"Beg you, my ass," she muttered, swiping his hand away. Approaching the front door, she pulled some small tools and crouched, eyes narrowed as she began to pick the lock. "In your dreams, Vampyre."

Heden grinned, watching her deft fingers, loving how she'd slipped back into their jibing banter. It was comfortable for her and would put them back on even ground. The last thing he wanted was for her to shut down around him.

A click sounded, and she stood, triumphant. "Let's go," she said, pushing the door open and waving him inside. "Remember the plan?"

Heden nodded. Striding to Tatiana's bedroom, he secured the small camera to an inconspicuous location on her dresser, facing the bed. It would be impossible to notice it unless one knew to look for it. Heading back to the main room, he saw Sofia fastening the camera below the mantel above the fireplace.

"Done," she said, swinging her pack over her shoulders. "And I hung the one under the counter too. It has a clear view of the fireplace. Let's hang the outside cameras quickly."

They closed the door behind them, careful to reset the lock, and each trailed to a tree on opposite sides of the home. Once the cameras were secure, Sofia lifted the monitor from her bag. Observing the screen, she double-checked everything.

"Two outside cameras, one bedroom, and two main room. All are submitting signals. Let's go."

They trekked back through the woods, navigating the dense brush and overgrown bushes until they came to a gravel road almost a mile away from Tatiana's cottage. Sofia called the rideshare and showed him the screen. "Five minutes."

The car pulled up, and they hopped in back. Heden could sense her excitement at the seamlessness of the mission. For his part, he wasn't so convinced.

Upon walking into their rented house, Sofia threw her bag on the counter, triumphant.

"We did it! I'll run the feed to my laptop so we can watch from there."

Heden studied her. "Don't you think it was just a tad too easy? I'm wondering if she knows we're here."

Sofia inhaled a deep breath, pondering. "You could be right. She's wily and observant. What would she gain by letting us place the cameras?"

"Perhaps she wants to assess our capabilities. See what she's dealing with."

Sofia bit her lip, chewing thoughtfully. "Or maybe she wants the cameras in place so we only see what she wants to show us. It would be a way to manipulate our surveillance of her."

"True," Heden said, striding over to the laptop on the desk in the large room. "Let's bring up the feed."

Sofia trailed over and configured the laptop to show them the different angles. Locked on the feed from the fireplace image, their shoulders stiffened as the front door opened and Tatiana walked into the dim living room. Slow and meticulous, she searched the room, gaze traveling as she surveyed. Walking toward the mantel, she stopped in front, facing the camera.

Amber eyes glistened from the glow of the fire as Tatiana stared through the laptop monitor. Full red lips turned into a smile. Tipping her head, she nodded, acknowledging their surveillance.

"Shit," Sofia breathed. "She's onto us."

"Yes," Heden murmured as Tatiana trailed away, seeming to disregard the cameras as she began unloading the grocery bag on the counter. "But she didn't tamper with the camera or remove it. It's almost as if she wants us to watch her."

"Why?"

"I have no idea, but let's not squander it. I say we take turns. One hour each. Sound good?"

"Sure," Sofia said, glancing at her watch. "It's almost two o'clock. I'll take the two to three shift, and we can alternate from there."

Heden couldn't stop his grin, realizing she was now fully focused on their mission and avoiding acknowledging their earlier liplock. "Did you want to discuss the fact we were sucking face earlier? Because I don't think I'd mind revisiting that."

"I'm good," she said, her expression resolved. "I'm here for one purpose and would like to focus on that."

He studied her, deciding not to push it...for now. "Okay, Sof. You can take the first shift." Unable to help himself, he reached for the dark curl that had escaped her ponytail. It was soft under his fingers, and he reveled in her tiny shiver. "Come get me when you're ready to switch." Already missing the feel of her silky hair between his fingers, he gave her a nod before heading to his room.

Firm in their plan, they began to study the woman who, for unknown reasons, wanted to be observed.

* * * *

Ananda studied Lila as she picked up her two youngest children from school. Located a few blocks from Lynia's main square, the property was heavily protected by swarms of soldiers, undoubtedly placed there by the brute Latimus.

Ananda hated the Vampyre commander, not only because his bastard brother King Sathan had banished her from the royal compound of Astaria centuries ago, but because the man was a heathen. Shivering at the thought of his filthy, blood-soaked hands touching one inch of her niece's skin, Ananda scowled.

Lila was supposed to become queen. Ananda's aristocratic sister, Gwen, had ensured the betrothal when Lila and Sathan were babies. When Gwen and Theinos passed, Ananda proclaimed herself Lila's advisor, intent on molding her into the perfect aristocratic wife and queen. Despite her best efforts, Sathan had treated Lila like garbage and cast her aside when he fell for the Slayer whore Miranda.

When Bakari had resuscitated Ananda, she'd been distraught to learn the warmonger Latimus had bonded with her niece. Disparaging all of Ananda's training, Lila seemed to love the barbarian back even though it went against every natural order in the immortal world. Betrothals were sacred and traditions were revered, and Ananda would be damned if she stood by and let the immortal royals destroy centuries of evolution.

Bakari shared her beliefs: a sense Etherya created the species to be separate, and traditions should be upheld. Pledging her loyalty to him was effortless, and she felt he would set things right. Ananda would do everything in her power to help him.

Lila held her two-year-old adopted Vampyre son, Symon, giving him a kiss as she swung him through the air. Then, she lifted Adelyn, the little girl who shared Lila's violet-colored eyes even though she was a Slayer and Lila was a Vampyre. Ananda felt the bile bubble in her throat. How could her niece love a Slayer child as her own? It was an abomination, born of a disreputable Slayer mother who discarded the child without a thought. Ananda was determined to save these people from themselves. The level of desecration of their sacred customs was maddening.

From across the field, Ananda observed Lila grab the backpack that held the Slayer blood and food the children had carried to school. It had been tough with all the soldiers milling around, but Ananda had been able to sneak in and sprinkle the poison flecks Bakari had given her over the food that remained in the lunchbox. If ingested, it would kill Adelyn almost immediately since she didn't possess self-healing abilities.

Ananda hoped it would send a message to her niece and the rest of the royals, for she was tired of waiting to kill the ones who had so little disregard for the rules of Etherya's realm. The Secret Society had plotted extensively and had begun to fracture. The time to attack was upon them. Clutching her hands, Ananda sent a prayer to Etherya, hoping they would succeed in their quest.

* * * *

Darkness fell upon the small cottage, causing Sofia to straighten on her bed as she looked out the window. Upon defecting from Bakari's team, she'd disabled their communication devices, rendering them unable to transmit through the ether. Now, she was working to trace their devices and track them through the GPS settings. Unfortunately, she'd been unable to locate them and realized Bakari must've supplied them with new contrivances. That would make her task more difficult, but she was determined to find a way to surveil the Secret Society.

Rotating her neck, she squeezed the tension away from her shoulders. Feeling her stomach growl, she shut down her laptop and padded to the kitchen. Scowling at the meager contents of the fridge, she closed the door and reached for her phone.

"I need to order food," she said, approaching Heden as he sat at the desk watching the laptop screen. "Any update on Tatiana?"

He shook his head, and Sofia noticed the broad muscles of his back flex under his black t-shirt. Good lord, he was massive. Earlier, when he'd given her that earth-shattering kiss, Sofia had felt his body vibrate against hers, full of lust and desire. Not even understanding how someone as viscerally sexy as Heden could want her, she studied him.

Sofia had always considered herself awkward and a bit standoffish. She rarely put herself in situations where men hit on her, and if they did, her first instinct was to rebuff their advances. At first, it stemmed from her lack of understanding of intimacy. The idea of sex was complex to her, and she had a hard time imagining opening herself up to anyone. The few men she'd been with had often commented that she needed to relax. Frowning, Sofia wondered how in the hell you were supposed to relax when a man was spreading your legs open and doing all sorts of intimate things to your innermost place. How did you trust someone when you were that raw? For someone who'd lost her parents so young and only had her grandfather as a confidant, it was a foreign concept.

Discovering Evie and blazing a path of revenge had given Sofia a new excuse. After all, there wasn't really time to date when you were pursuing your grandfather's immortal murderer. It had blanketed her in purpose, and she'd convinced herself she didn't need sex, intimacy or love. Although she definitely wanted children, she was lucky to live in modern times and considered artificial insemination by an anonymous donor an acceptable option.

Heden mumbled an answer to her question, hand over his chin as his gaze stayed fixed to the screen, although the words didn't register to Sofia. Instead, she moved closer, as if pulled by an invisible tether, suddenly aching to touch the pale skin of his neck above those magnificent muscles.

How would it feel to have him loom over her, his hulking body tense and ready to claim her? Would it hurt? After all, he was colossal compared to her. Flashes of other lovers ran through her mind as she recalled the sometimes clumsy experiences. Men telling her to calm down and lamenting how hard they had to work to bring her to orgasm. Most times, they were unsuccessful, and she chalked it up to her just not being great at sex. The thought of disappointing Heden, whom she knew to be a prolific lover from her surveillance, made her inwardly cringe.

"Sofie?" he called, head turning as he stared up at her. "Did you hear me?"

She stared into his ice-blue irises, losing herself to their depths. When she'd first focused on them, on the bustling L.A. sidewalk, she'd felt her heart leap into her throat. He was one of the most handsome men she'd ever seen. When he'd kissed her earlier, her entire body had gone up in flames, and she'd been terribly disappointed when he'd ended the embrace. Perhaps it was for the best. She would never be able to please someone as experienced as Heden.

"Yeah," she said softly, clenching her fist at her side in an effort to control her desire to reach for him. When had the arousal taken hold? From that first moment in L.A.? When he'd shown her such kindness in front of his family, even though she'd put them all in such danger? When he'd stared at her with those gorgeous eyes as she trembled in his arms, his deep baritone telling her how much he wanted her?

Damn it. Her attraction to him was something she hadn't anticipated, and it worried her. They needed to work together and would be in close proximity for the foreseeable future. Now that she'd kissed him, the craving had taken hold deep in her gut, and she was unable to squelch it. Anxiety at the loss of control swamped her, and her heart began to pound in her chest.

"Hey," he said, reaching up to gently cup her cheek. "You okay, Sof?"

"I, uh..." She struggled to breathe against his warm palm. "Yeah, I'm fine. I need to order some food."

He nodded and stood, stretching his beefy arms above his head.

Sofia swallowed thickly as she gripped the phone in her free hand. "I'm thinking Chinese since it's easy. Do you want anything?"

"Nah," he said, shaking his head. "Wish I liked food. Just Slayer blood for me."

There must've been a question in her expression because the corner of his lip curled. "Go ahead and ask me, Sofie."

"Ask you what?" she rasped, hating that she couldn't control her breath.

He stepped closer and brushed a wayward tendril at her temple behind her ear. "If I've ever drank from a human. You're dying to know."

"I am not," she said, defiant even though his words were true. "I couldn't care less. Like I said, I know how many women you seduce and understand it's just a game to you."

Hurt flashed in his eyes, and guilt squeezed her heart. "It's not a game, little human. I'm honest with every woman I pursue."

"Honest that you're only looking for one thing. I'm not interested in that."

His eyebrow arched. "Your scent would indicate otherwise."

Sofia felt her cheeks enflame with embarrassment. "That's just a chemical reaction. I know Vampyres have heightened senses for arousal. It doesn't mean anything."

His tongue darted over his full lips, causing them to glisten under the pale light of the living room fixture. The action spurred a flush of moisture between her thighs, compounded by the heat emanating from his thick body.

"Honestly," he said, stepping forward so their bodies brushed, "it means something to me, Sofia. I don't play games, so let me make this clear. I want you, and judging by how your body is reacting to me, you want me too. I think it would be easier to work together if we relieved the sexual tension, but that's up to you. I'm not in the business of forcing women into something they say they don't want. So, why don't you think about it and let me know when you've decided? Until then, I've got plenty of things to keep me busy. I'm still tweaking the coding so I can improve the comm devices so Latimus and Ken can implement them to the soldiers throughout the realm. I'll let you take the next shift while you eat."

Lowering, he spoke softly in her ear. "I've always been taught that drinking from humans is a waste of effort, but I'd make an exception for you, Sofie. I'd start here," he said, placing his finger on her pulsing vein and slowly tracing the length. "Then, I'd suck you until you screamed in my arms. All you have to do is ask." Straightening, he gave her a wink. Lowering his hand, he stalked to the refrigerator, grabbed a thermos of Slayer blood and headed toward his room, closing the door behind him.

Sofia missed his touch immediately. Expelling a breath, she lifted her phone, noting how badly her hand was shaking. Would it truly sate the sexual tension if they made love? Or would it make things worse if they had a disastrous sexual encounter? How could she continue to work with him if she disappointed him in bed?

Annoyed at the questions swirling in her mind, she ordered food from the delivery app and sat down to watch the screen. Tatiana was stirring something in the cauldron above her fireplace, the movements slow and measured. Suspending her hand above the pot, she sprinkled in what looked to be hair, although Sofia couldn't be sure. Who was it from? An animal, or perhaps an immortal being?

Picking up the pen that sat atop the notebook, Sofia noted the occurrence. She and Heden had various notes they'd taken during their surveillance so far, and tomorrow, they would compile them and look for patterns. For now, Sofia sank into the chair to watch the mysterious woman as she waited for her food, determined to push a certain attractive Vampyre from her thoughts.

Chapter 19

The next morning, Heden emerged from his bedroom ready to study the notes they'd taken on Tatiana and report back to Sathan. Thanks to Sofia's shared coding knowledge, he could now video chat through the ether, which was invaluable. Not only that, it allowed him to check in with his family as well.

Noting the time, he pulled up the video call app on the laptop and rang Arderin. She answered on the second ring, propping the phone against the wall as she dressed Callie.

"Hey, baby toad," Heden said, grinning as his sister stuffed the tyke into a shirt. "Is Mommy being rough with you?"

"Mommy is overworked and pregnant, and Daddy should be doing this crap," Arderin said. "He's downstairs with Evie and Latimus. They're meeting this morning to discuss the heightened security measures across all the worlds. With Darkrip protecting us here, and Latimus and Ken on high alert in the realm, there's a lot going on."

"Mommy's grumpy," Callie said, frowning. "She says I can't go to school without Daddy anymore. I have to say he's a vault-a-neer."

"That's *volunteer*, baby toad, and it's what you need right now. We can't have anything happen to you."

"I told Mommy I can use my powers if I need to. They're really strong now, and I can hurt any of the bad men who try to get me."

"What's the rule about using your powers, baby?" Arderin asked, a warning in her tone.

Callie sighed and rolled her eyes. "Only in the house when you or Daddy are here. But that's so *boring*. My powers are special, and I want to use them."

Arderin's face fell as she smoothed her hand over her daughter's cheek. "Please don't argue with me today, baby. I'm tired, and your brother is kicking up a storm."

Callie touched Arderin's belly with her hand and gasped. "I can feel it."

"Yep, that's our little Creigen. He's going to do whatever his big sister does. I hope she can teach him to keep a secret."

"I can," she said, crossing an X over her heart. "I promise. I'm sorry, Mommy. I know you get mad when I use my powers."

"How can I get mad at you? Can you tell Uncle Heden to have a good day?"

Callie did as she was told, waving before her gaze trailed upward. "Hi, Sofia. Are you having fun with Uncle Heden?"

Heden smiled up at Sofia, who stood silently at his back. Her face was swollen with sleep, causing her to look innocent and unguarded. His throat tightened as he imagined her waking atop his chest, smiling into him, open and bare. By the goddess, he yearned for it.

"Hi, Callie," she said, waving at the phone. "You look pretty. Are you heading to school?"

Black curls bobbled as she nodded. "Daddy comes with me every day now. He says it's annoying but necessary. I think he gets annoyed a lot."

"Ain't that the truth," Arderin muttered. "I've gotta get this show on the road. Did you need to talk to Darkrip?"

"No," Heden said. "I'll call him later, once Sofia and I have compiled the notes, but he and the others should know Tatiana's aware of our surveillance. We don't understand why she's letting us observe her, but it must have some purpose."

"Strange," Arderin said, eyebrows drawing together. "Well, Sofia did say Tatiana didn't appear to have any alliances. Perhaps she's studying you guys too. Be careful, bro."

"I will. Kisses and hugs. Tell Darkrip and Latimus I'll call them later."

Callie blew him a kiss, and the screen went dark.

Sofia appeared slightly uncomfortable as she scratched her head under her mess of tight curls. "I need to shower, and then we can sit down and go over everything."

Heden nodded. "I walked into town and got some eggs, bread, chips—that kind of stuff. Want me to fry up some eggs while you shower?"

A dark eyebrow arched. "You know how to cook eggs?"

"I watched a YouTube video while you were sleeping. Seems pretty self-explanatory."

Chuckling, she shrugged. "Okay then. Fry away. I'll be out in a few."

Heden got to work in the kitchen while the pipes of the older house creaked overhead. Needing to create space on the small island, he accidentally knocked her purse off as he cleared everything. Bending down, he began stuffing everything back in and froze when he saw her license. Taking note of the information, he set the purse on the nearby chair and waited for her to enter.

"Perfect timing," he said, scooping the eggs onto a plate. "Salt and pepper?"

"Sure," she said, sitting on the island stool and taking the dish and shakers from him. Grabbing a container from the fridge, he sat beside her, joy coursing through him when she closed her eyes and smiled.

"These are delicious," she said, swallowing and scooping up another forkful. "Great job, Vampyre. You can officially cook eggs."

He took a swig of the Slayer blood, thrilled with her praise. "So, I figure it should take us about a few hours to go over the footage and summarize the notes. Then, I need to call everyone and update them. All in all, we'll be done by four or five. In the meantime, we'll continue to surveille Tatiana, but she goes to bed rather early. She was asleep by nine-thirty last night."

"Yep. Can't say I blame her for that. I've never been a night owl."

"You didn't party when you were younger?"

She scoffed. "Party? Um, yeah, no. I'm kind of a loner, in case you haven't noticed. I'm a huge geek who likes programming and video games. Doing that by myself is actually pretty fun."

"Maybe you just haven't met anyone who shares your interests. I like those things too, you know? Latimus could never understand why I'd hole myself up in my room to write code or play with virtual technology. You like what you like, nothing wrong with that. Still, it's nice to go out and enjoy life sometimes."

"I guess," she muttered.

"Especially on your birthday."

Her shoulders tensed. "Yep, I guess that would be a good day to go out and party."

"Great, then we'll do that tonight once Tatiana falls asleep."

"Oh, it's not my birthday."

Heden almost laughed at her lack of eye contact as she stared at the plate. "Wow, you're an awful liar. I accidentally knocked your purse over when I was cleaning the counter. Today's your thirty-ninth birthday. That's exciting, Sofie. We have to celebrate."

"I don't really celebrate my birthday, but thanks." Standing, she carried the plate over to the sink and began washing it.

"That's unacceptable, and I'm not taking 'no' for an answer, so you can give up that notion right now. I think it's time you had some fun, Sofia."

Heden could sense her frustration as she shut off the faucet and dried her hands. Leaning back against the sink, her features drew together. "First of all, we're in the middle of a shit show I had a hand in creating. Having fun is very low on my list. Secondly, I know you're not familiar with the human world, but thirty-nine isn't exactly a milestone birthday. I'm totally fine just hanging here and completing the multitude of tasks at hand. Thanks though."

"I love that you think you have a choice here," Heden said, reveling in the way her cheeks reddened as they continued to argue. "We'll go out once Tatiana's asleep. End of story. For now, let's get started on the footage."

"You can go out and have all the fun you want," she said, nose in the air as she trailed to the desk. Sitting down, she brought up yesterday's footage so they could study it.

"Oh, I plan to," Heden said, sitting beside her. "With you by my side. Can't wait."

A muscle clenched in her jaw. "You're infuriating."

"You love it," he whispered in her ear.

Planting a palm over his face, she pushed him away. Heden nipped at it, reveling in how fun it was to tease her. Her nostrils flared, and he damn near giggled.

"You have the maturity of an infant."

"Aw, that's so sweet. Miranda says the same thing. I assure you, I'm very mature when the situation calls for it."

"Sex," Sofia muttered. "Always sex with you. Give me the damn notebook. I want to compare the notes we took."

Heden grabbed it and handed it to her, pulling it back when she reached for it. Her frustrated grunt went straight to his dick, causing it to harden beneath his jeans.

"Give it to me, you heathen." Grasping the notebook, she roughly dragged it from his hands.

"Man, you're a tiger," he said, aching to carry her to bed and seduce her hesitancy into flames of need. "It's so fucking cute, Sof."

She shot him a glare from the corner of her eye, filled with restrained laughter. Nice. His gorgeous human was warming up to him after all.

"So," she said, ignoring his comment. "I've noticed she seems to be showing us what she puts in the cauldron, but why?"

Heden tucked a wayward raven-black curl behind her ear. The action was becoming a habit he never wanted to break, for it gave him a reason to touch her. "That she does. Let's try to discern what the items are, and then we can research them and find a pattern."

Sofia pulled up the footage, and they got to work, Heden deciding he'd give her a break from his teasing before turning on his full charm later that evening. It was his little human's birthday, and he was determined she'd loosen up and enjoy it.

* * * *

They toiled for hours, meticulously detailing the items Tatiana dropped into the steaming broth. Since some of the footage was grainy, considering she kept her cottage dim, they did their best to decipher the ingredients. Eventually, they came up with the following list:

- Dark, curly hairs (from Arderin or Callie perhaps?)
- Eyeballs of a small animal or rodent
- A frog's tongue
- Alligator skin
- Drops of a red unidentified substance (Sofia and Heden both feared it was Crimeous's cloned blood)
- Long leaves from the Cypress trees that lined the bayou

- Various herbs and spices that remained unknown

Once the list was compiled, they called Sathan and updated him so he was prepared for the evening's council meeting.

"Thanks, Heden," Sathan said, running his hand through his thick hair during their video chat. "This is good intel, but I don't like the unknowns. Sadie and Nolan are cataloguing the results from the apple Adelyn brought home from school with her yesterday."

"Why?" Heden asked, looking worried. "Did something happen?"

"Latimus has been sending all her uneaten food to the doctors to test, thinking our enemies might try to get to her that way. Sure enough, the apple she brought home yesterday was poisoned. Sadie and Nolan are identifying the various substances now. They could be some of the same ones Tatiana is using. Who knows? We're guessing here."

"We'll figure it out, bro," Heden said, features drawn together, "but I can't believe someone got past Latimus's guards at the school."

"A woman posing as one of the children's grandmothers seems to be the culprit. The soldier who let her in didn't deem her a threat because she appeared frail. It was most likely Ananda."

"Damn," he said, lacing his fingers behind his head. "Latimus's troops are slacking."

"We're years removed from the war. I think we've all become a bit complacent. If there's a silver lining in this situation, it's that we can identify weakness in our men and retrain them to be more effective."

"Ken and Latimus will be swamped, but it's for the best."

"Agreed. How's the human doing? She hasn't defected yet, right?"

"Still kicking, although your brother could drive a saint mad," Sofia said, batting her eyelashes.

"Honestly, I'm with you on that, Sofia. Keep him in check, okay?"

"Ten-four," she said, saluting the screen.

"I'll shoot you an update after the meeting wraps up tonight. In the meantime, how's the coding coming for the devices? I want all our soldiers equipped with the most up-to-date technology, just in case we need to quickly order a battalion to L.A. That's obviously a worst-case scenario, but I want to protect Arderin and Callie at all costs."

"Good," Heden said. "I just need to tweak a few more things and I should be able to roll it out to Ken and Latimus so they can install it on all the soldiers' devices."

Sathan nodded. "Thanks, Heden. You're actually pretty helpful when you're not focused on driving me or my wife insane."

"You're my favorite brother too, Sathan. Don't tell Latimus because I told him the same thing last week. Good luck at the meeting."

They signed off, and Heden turned to Sofia, fangs resting atop his bottom lip as it curved. "So, it looks like we're done here. There's a happy hour calling our name."

"We have to watch Tatiana," Sofia said, pointing to the laptop. "She won't go to bed for several hours."

"Not to state the obvious, but Tatiana's life is as boring as yours." Sofia glowered at him. "It's true. All that woman does is stir the pot. Literally. And not in any way remotely fun. Come on, Sof," he said, extending his hand to her. "Let's get ready. Throw on your heels and let your hair down."

"I hate heels," she said, rising from the chair. "They're extremely uncomfortable."

"Well then, throw on your sneakers, and let's go."

"I'd rather just stay and write some code to create a program that can help us catalog Tatiana's ingredients and movements. And I need to keep trying to locate Bakari."

"Nope," he said, grabbing her wrist and dragging her toward her bedroom door. "Coding will be here tomorrow. It's your birthday. Meet you back out here in ten minutes."

Sofia rolled her eyes and entered her room, locking the door behind her, showing him she had no intention of meeting him anywhere. Ten minutes later, he began pounding on her door.

She held firm.

Fifteen minutes later, he began singing "I Want It That Way" by the Backstreet Boys at the top of his lungs. Sitting on her bed, Sofia covered her ears. It was no use. Every time she thought he might stop, he began belting another tune. Sighing, she changed her clothes, questioning what the hell she was doing. After two verses of "Bohemian Rhapsody," she thought her eardrums might start bleeding.

"I can do this all night, Sofie," he called through the door. "I haven't even started on Madonna yet. Let's see, should I sing 'Like a Prayer' or 'Lucky Star'"?

Furious, she yanked open the door. "Stop. Fucking. Singing."

"Oh, sweet," he said, eyes roving over her frame. "You put on sandals. Much better than sneakers. You look hot. That shirt is silky." He slipped a finger under the thin strap of her tank top.

"It's comfortable, okay? It's hot as balls down here, and the fabric is cool."

"It's sexy," he said, waggling his eyebrows. "C'mon. Let's go. Unless you want to hear 'Toxic' by Britney. I'm awesome at that one."

Sofia groaned. "Fine. We'll go out for *one* drink." Closing the bedroom door, she grabbed her purse from the counter. "But that's it."

"Oh, yeah, totally," he said, making an X over his heart. "Promise."

"I think I saw your six-year-old niece make the same gesture today. Do you realize how ridiculous you are?"

"Who do you think taught it to her?" he asked, striding over and lacing his fingers through hers. "And I think you like that I'm completely ridiculous and make you laugh. Admit it. Just a little." He squeezed her hand.

"I hate it," she teased, scrunching her features at him.

"Not for long. Shots will make you love me. I get so much hotter after a few shots, and my sense of humor is off the charts. C'mon, Sof. Time's a wastin'."

She let him pull her through the door and onto the gravel sidewalk. Her hand swayed in his as they walked under the late afternoon sun. She should've pulled it away but found it impossible. Their palms seemed to fit together perfectly, and she begrudgingly admitted she liked the image of her smaller hand in his. It made her feel protected and...accepted somehow. Heden seemed to genuinely like being in her presence, and that melted something in her stoic heart.

Smiling, she let herself enjoy their time together as they trailed along. After all, it was temporary, and he would soon return to the immortal world and resume his life of being the realm's tech whiz and serial dater. For now, she would allow herself to be charmed by a handsome man who, despite their circumstances, was attracted to her. Sofia hadn't created any cherished memories since her grandfather died. Could she possibly create some with this affable Vampyre?

Forging ahead, she admitted there was only one way to find out. They approached a small bar that had a flashing "Beer" sign in the window. Heden held open the door and gestured to the darkened interior.

"After you, birthday girl."

Inhaling a deep breath, Sofia stepped inside.

Chapter 20

Hours later, Heden was onstage, karaoke mic in hand, belting a Garth Brooks tune at the top of his lungs. Sofia snickered from the bar as he motioned to her, begging her to join him.

"No way, buddy," she yelled, lifting the half-drunk tequila shot. "I'd need a thousand more of these to do karaoke."

"That's the love of my life, folks," he slurred into the microphone, causing Sofia to giggle. "She's the greatest human I've ever met."

"You're not so bad yourself," she called, thoroughly enjoying their exchange. The song finally ended to raucous applause from the patrons scattered throughout the bar, and Heden plodded toward her, sliding onto the bar stool.

"Two more tequila shots," he said to the bartender. "Have to get her drunk for her birthday."

"I'm good," she said, exchanging a look with the bartender. "We'll let you know if we need another."

"You still have half left. Who drinks half a shot? Come on, woman."

Sofia chugged the shot, grabbing the lime as her eyes watered. After sucking the juice, she threw it on the bar. "No more shots," she said, wiping her mouth. Heden stared at her, desire swimming in his eyes. "Don't look at me like that."

"Like what?" he asked, leaning closer. "Like I'd rather you suck me instead of the lime?"

Sofia laughed in spite of herself. It was difficult to act indifferent toward him after all the shots she'd imbibed. "Yes, exactly like that."

"But it's true," he growled, resting his forehead against hers. "You look adorable, all drunk and tipsy. Your cheeks are glowing. Let's blow this joint. I want to take you home and ravish you."

Fear flooded her as she slowly pulled away. Celebrating her birthday with Heden was one thing, but letting her guard down completely was another. She wasn't ready for that and doubted if she truly could be.

"We can go, but we're not hooking up."

His lips formed a pout. "Why do you hate me?"

She laughed, admiring his persistence. "I don't hate you. But you're really drunk, and I'm mostly drunk, and we need to sleep. I appreciate you celebrating with me, but it's time to go."

They paid the tab, Heden stuffing the bills she laid atop the bar back in her purse and insisting on paying from his stash of human currency. On the way home, they stopped to grab a slice of pizza for Sofia, and she scarfed it down as they stumbled under the full moon. Once back at the house, Heden kicked off his shoes and began undressing in the living room.

"No way," Sofia said, clutching his wrist and leading him into his bedroom. "You'll undress in your room like a civilized person and pass out on your bed, not the couch."

"I should be taking care of you," he said, sliding his hand behind her neck. "Why are you taking care of me?"

"Because you're drunker," she said, giggling. Man, he was wasted, but she was certainly tipsy.

"Help me undress," he said, lifting his arms. "I can't get it off."

"You're such a baby," she said, grasping the ends of his shirt. As soon as she pulled it off, she realized her mistake. His chest was a masterpiece, chiseled with a firm six-pack. Black, springy hairs covered his pecs and whirled around his nipples. Sofia's mouth began to water as she imagined sucking him there.

"Yesss," he hissed, reading her thoughts. "Please, Sofie. You're the perfect height to kiss me there. Please, baby. I want your mouth on me."

Emboldened by the liquor coursing through her veins, she lifted her hand and swirled her fingers through the prickly hairs. With her thumb and forefinger, she pinched the tiny nub and then flicked it with her fingernail.

"Fuck," he breathed, sliding his fingers to gently clench the hair at her nape. "Yes, Sofie. Please. I'm dying for you."

The words sent a rush of wetness to her core. Never had she heard such raw desire in a man's tone. Taking pity on him, she slowly eased toward him and rested her lips over his nipple. Extending her tongue, she licked the sensitive bud.

"Oh, god," he moaned, fist tightening in her hair, the possessive gesture causing pangs of desire to shoot low in her abdomen. Wanting to please him, she began lathering him fully, her wet tongue slathering his nipple with her saliva. His massive body shook against her, and she reveled in the knowledge she could make him shudder.

His free hand encircled her wrist, dragging it toward his fly. With deft fingers, he slid the zipper down and pulled his length through the hole in his boxer briefs. As she continued to lick his straining nipple, Sofia's eyes widened. His cock was massive, thick and throbbing, the veins pulsing under the purple head.

"Is this okay?" he whispered, bringing her hand to his shaft. "I don't want to pressure you, sweetheart."

She nodded, inching her fingers around his length, realizing she barely surrounded him fully. His girth was almost the span of her hand.

"Stroke me," he commanded, his voice gravelly.

She followed his directive while her tongue resumed its assault on his nipple. He spoke words of longing and desire, the vibration of his silky baritone at her temple causing her to body to shudder. Lifting her hand, she licked her palm, wanting to add a layer of lubrication against his sensitive skin. Encircling him again, his large frame quaked as he lifted her chin.

"Sofie," he murmured against her lips. "I'm about thirty seconds from coming in your hand. If you don't want that, let me go now."

"I want it," she whispered, stroking his bottom lip with her tongue. "I want you—"

His lips devoured the words, overtaking her mouth as he groaned against her. Broad hips jutted into her hand as she stroked him, his tongue sweeping every inch of her mouth. Never had Sofia been kissed so thoroughly—or so desperately—and it snapped something inside her soul.

Opening her eyes, she watched him through slitted lids, arousal evident in every inch of his gorgeous face.

Ending the kiss, he stared into her eyes. "Sofie," he cried softly, hand fisted in her hair.

"*Heden.*"

Suddenly, his huge frame began to jerk, and Sofia realized he was coming. Exulted that she could bestow such pleasure, she held tight as he climaxed in her embrace. He groaned her name and buried his face in her hair, his lips resting on her neck. Slowly, his body began to relax, and she felt a small sensation on the sensitive skin of her nape.

"Are you sucking me?" she asked, her voice husky.

"Mmm hmm," he said, chuckling softly. "I'm going to pierce this vein one day, little human. Get ready. But I'll ask you first." Lifting his head, he gazed at her, his eyes glassy. "Deal?"

"Deal," she said, shivering in anticipation.

He expelled a large breath. "Wow, I made a mess. Let me run to the bathroom and I'll return the favor, okay?"

"You don't have to," she said as the anxiety about being with him slowly began to creep back in. "I'm not sure if it's a good idea we have sex, Heden. Especially since we're drunk."

"My practical human. What would I do without you?" He placed a sweet peck on the tip of her nose.

"I'm serious," she said. "Sex is a big step for me. I'm not sure it would even work between us."

"Okay, sweetheart. I don't want to make you uncomfortable. Let me clean myself up in the bathroom, and then maybe I can just hold you for a while? I don't want tonight to be over yet."

She nodded and watched him trail to the bathroom. Wanting to freshen up, she headed toward her own room, where she washed her face and brushed her teeth before changing into her shorts and t-shirt. Or should she wear something else? She took a moment to pilfer through the meager contents she'd brought with her.

After agonizing for several minutes, she decided the shorts and t-shirt were fine. Heading back to his room, she approached him where he lay on his stomach on the bed. Lifting her hands to her mouth, she stifled the laugh. Her Vampyre was naked, stretched out on the bed, fast asleep.

Leaning over, she tapped his face with her finger. He didn't budge. Chalking it up to the fact they definitely weren't meant to have sex tonight, she turned to leave. A hand snaked around her wrist, fast as lightning. In two seconds flat, she was under his naked body, attempting to catch her breath.

"I can smell you when you're near, little human," he said drowsily, nuzzling her neck as he cuddled into her body. "Just give me five minutes, and I swear, I'll rock your world."

Sofia snickered, noticing his eyes were already cemented shut. "I think you're going to be asleep in five seconds, buddy."

"Then sleep with me," he said, throwing his leg over her thighs. His arm already encircled her waist, and he nudged further into the crease of her neck. She was wrapped up in his warmth so tightly, escape was impossible.

"Relax, Sofie," he warbled against her skin. "We're just sleeping. Let me hold you."

The cadence of his breath was calming as it washed over her, warm and intimate. His expression was open, and he looked extremely young. How old would he be if he were human? Sofia guessed twenty-seven or twenty-eight, max. He must've gone through his immortal change in his late twenties. Smiling, she realized that made her the "older woman" in a way, although in reality, he was many centuries older. What would people think if they saw them together? Would they think her a cradle robber?

Biting her lip, she traced her finger over his beard. It was scratchy under his soft lips, and she gave them a caress as well. Realizing she was trapped in the most delicious way, she gave in to the exhaustion and tequila. As her Vampyre held her close, she succumbed to her dreams.

Chapter 21

Sofia awoke to the most pleasurable sensation. A soft finger was tracing her face. It flitted over her brows, down her nose and stopped at her lips. Lifting her lids, she saw Heden looming above her, head resting on his hand, elbow propped on the bed.

"Hey," she said, her voice raspy from sleep.

"Hey," he said, his baritone causing every nerve ending in her waking skin to sizzle. "You look so pretty when you wake up, Sof."

She breathed a laugh. "I have morning breath, and my eyes are crusted over. Ew."

Chuckling, he placed a soft kiss on her lips. "Don't care. You're gorgeous. I loved holding you while I slept."

"Eh," she said, shrugging against the pillow, "it was okay."

"You spout lies, woman," he said, winking. "You adored sleeping in my arms. Admit it."

Heart thrumming in her chest, she searched his gaze. "Maybe a little."

His fingers continued their mesmerizing caress over her cheek. "I really blew it last night—literally and figuratively."

Sofia snickered. "You did. Everywhere."

His deep chuckle rumbled through his chest. "I'm so sorry. I was ready to show you what an amazing lover I am and I passed the fuck out. It's appalling, and I'm pretty embarrassed. I'd like to make it up to you."

"It's fine. Being intimate with someone is hard for me. It's probably good we just slept together."

Ice-blue eyes roamed over her face. "Do you want me to make love to you? We don't have to go all the way. I can make you come."

Cold daggers of fear shot through her heart. What if he couldn't make her come? She already felt awkward knowing she'd just woken up, which meant she definitely wasn't at her best. Would she close up with him? Worried, she chewed her lip, contemplating.

"It's okay, little human," he said, his smile so endearing her heart splintered. "I won't push you. We can accomplish what we need to today and try again tonight. What do you say?"

Sofia swallowed, terrified to disappoint him. "I might not be ready tonight. Or maybe I will. I don't know. I don't want to lead you on."

"I'm not worried about that at all. You're a straight shooter, Sof. If you feel ready, that's great, and if not, I'll just make out with you. For a reaaaaaally long time."

Her laugh surrounded them. "Deal."

"Come on then," he said, giving her one last poignant kiss. "I'm going to hop in the shower. You're welcome to join me."

"Um, yeah, I think I'll take my own, but thanks."

"Your loss. But I'll make it up to you one day." After waggling his brows, he disentangled from her and stood, stretching his arms above his head. Yawning, he smiled down at her, seemingly unconcerned with his nakedness. His shaft jutted up from the dark thatch of hair between his thighs as if it was searching for her.

Sofia let her eyes wander over his body, unable not to look at his magnificence.

"Like the merchandise?" he teased.

"Yep," she said, sitting up and rolling her neck. "It's not a bad view."

"My ego needed that. Keep it coming. See you in a few." He stalked to the bathroom and shut the door behind him.

Sofia plopped back down on the bed and gave a tiny squeal. It was so unlike her to be giddy, but she'd spent an extremely intimate night with a man and actually felt happy. Reveling in the unfamiliar feeling, she thanked the heavens for her good fortune and headed to her room to shower.

* * * *

Vadik observed Evie as she puked her guts up behind the newly planted oak tree on the outskirts of Takelia. She was visiting the Deamon prison with Latimus and Kenden to ensure the security was tight. It was a futile folly, and Vadik felt his lips curve in a sinister smile. Now that he had the ability to transport, his power was limitless.

He would never understand why the red-haired usurper denied her heritage. Crimeous had been his lord and king, and Vadik still worshiped him with unparalleled reverence. There had been a cold and systematic righteousness to the Dark Lord's actions. Through torture and murder, Crimeous had instilled fear in the land and upheld a sense of structured order. Vadik thought him the most valiant leader on all of Etherya's Earth.

When Evie had killed her father with the Blade of Pestilence, Vadik had screamed words of betrayal at the daughter who'd been deemed his successor. How could she toss aside her heritage and her unimaginable powers to live a squalid life amongst the Slayers and Vampyres? It was such a massive waste of resources and abilities.

Eyes narrowed, Vadik saw Kenden approach his wife and rub her back as she vomited into the grass. Crimeous's blood was malicious and it would cause Evie extreme sickness—not just in the morning, but all day, every day until she gave birth to the spawn. *Good.* The ungrateful bitch deserved to suffer. She might disparage the opportunity she'd been given, but Vadik never would. He would take her place and restore Crimeous's name to the prominence it deserved.

Pondering Bakari, Vadik admitted their goals were not the same. Bakari was arrogant and wanted power for himself. He didn't worship Crimeous as lord. But they were both aligned in their hatred of the immortal royals and both believed in a systematic approach for life in Etherya's realm. That shared goal would cement their alliance, at least until all the royals were dead. After that, Vadik wasn't so sure, but he would deal with that once their current objectives had been achieved.

He'd learned there was a value to living in the moment. He'd already waited years to take his revenge and understood it might take several more decades to fully achieve his purpose. That suited him just fine. There was a beauty in patience, as there was in so many things others deemed unnecessary.

Suddenly, Evie lifted her head, and Vadik froze. The bitch's green eyes locked onto him, and he stood his ground, refusing to sink further behind the tree. A voice wafted through his head: *You'll never succeed, Vadik. I'll always be one step ahead.*

Throwing back his head, he laughed, dark and sinister, denying her words. Lifting his hands in the air, he began chanting the phrases Bakari taught him from the human woman who wasn't so human after all. Black clouds whirled overhead, and he felt his body disintegrate into nothing.

Opening his eyes, he looked down on the burning lava of the Purges of Methesda. Staring into the glowing embers, he spoke to his king. "I promise, my lord Crimeous, I will avenge you until my last breath. Your eminence will reign once more!" Tilting his face to the sky, he prayed to Crimeous, hoping he would hear as he suffered in the Land of Lost Souls.

Chapter 22

Heden and Sofia trailed through the woods as they discussed next steps regarding Tatiana. The day was gorgeous, and Heden had suggested they take a hike to soak up the rays. Every time they reached a stump or dead log, Heden would reach over and offer to help her navigate over or around it. Sofia was an avid traveler and hiker and didn't really need his assistance, but she figured it wouldn't hurt to accept chivalry from her handsome companion. Plus, it added to his burgeoning ego, which should've been off-putting, but instead, Sofia found it rather endearing. His persistent efforts to seduce her were secretly thrilling, although she kept that info close to the vest.

"You must really enjoy being in the sun after all those centuries of darkness," she said.

"You have no idea, Sof," he said, stepping over a log and turning to lift her by the waist and place her on the other side as well. Damn, the gesture was so freaking charming. "It's absolutely amazing, although it took me a while not to burn. Now, I wear sunscreen. Most Vamps do."

"I'd imagine your skin was ill-prepared for the radiation, so that makes sense. Do you enjoy watching sunsets? If so, you have to visit Italy. The sunsets on the coast at Positano are so beautiful. You'd love them."

"I've never been," he said, shaking his head. "Maybe you can take me there one day."

"I'd like that."

"So, I think we've gathered all the intel Tatiana is going to give us. She's obviously controlling what we see. It's time to approach her. Should we just visit her when she's home?"

"That seems best," Sofia said, contemplating. "I mean, honestly, if she wanted to harm us, she could've done so by now. As you saw from Bakari's transportation, she has powers I don't even claim to understand. I have no idea how she's learned to wield powers that should only exist in the immortal realm."

Before Heden could answer, a possum scuttled out of the nearby bush and ran across their path, startling them both. As his hand gripped hers, a woman appeared to walk from the bush, although the clearing had been quiet moments earlier.

Standing tall, she crossed her hands in front of her abdomen, assessing them. Sofia clutched Heden's hand, and he squeezed back, assuring his protection.

"Hello, Tatiana," he said with a tilt of his head. "We were just strategizing on the best way to approach you. Thanks for saving us the hassle."

Her dark eyebrow arched. "Anytime. I find it's easier to eliminate unnecessary actions. Although you and I have much time left on the Earth, your human here only has decades."

"So, you're an immortal?" Sofia asked.

"I'm..." She hesitated, seeming to ponder her response. "Not of either world. Not completely. I don't mean to speak in riddles, but my heritage is not what I've come to discuss with you. There will be time for that later. For now, I'd like to see if I misjudged your intelligence. After all, you two seem to possess quick intellects. Tell me what I want to know."

"You let us surveil you because you wanted us to see what you put in the cauldron."

"Yes," she said with a nod. "Go on."

"Your main concoction enables transport, but that one was easy," Heden said. "Based upon your ingredients, we also believe you've created serums that can heal and also bring a corpse back to life. We're worried about that one because it requires Crimeous's cloned blood."

"Very good," she said. "You're correct, although you've only identified three of the several potions I created while you observed me. The other brews aren't important now, since the ones you named are the only ones I gave Bakari."

"We'd like to ask for your alliance," Heden said, releasing Sofia's hands to show Tatiana his open palms. "I would be forever grateful, and the royal immortal family would repay you with anything you request. We would leave no stone unturned to secure any restitution you desire."

Tatiana smiled, the action contorting her face into one more exquisite than Sofia had ever seen. Amber eyes glowed above her full lips, and her brown skin was luminous in the rays of the sun that filtered through the trees.

"I appreciate your request, son of Markdor, but I cannot honor it at this time. It is not yet time for us to align, although that day will come soon enough. For now, I have shown you what you need to fight Bakari and the Secret Society. Take the knowledge I've imparted and discern what he wishes to use the potions for. I have faith you and the human will figure it out."

"Please," Sofia said, unashamed at the pleading tone in her voice. "I know you have no allegiance to Bakari. Is there anything we can do to secure your help?"

Tatiana slowly approached and lifted Sofia's chin with her ring-clad fingers. Several inches taller, she spoke softly down to her. "I sense your guilt, Sofia. Know that you are absolved. I've spoken to your grandfather in the great beyond. He is so very proud of you. All humans make mistakes, but it's the choices they make in their darkest moments that count. You were quite brave to defect, and that decision will be rewarded. More than you can ever know now."

Sofia's eyes burned at the mention of her beloved grandfather, and a tear trailed down her cheek. "Does he know I tried to avenge him?"

"He doesn't need vengeance, my dear. He never did. Francesco lived a long life full of love and laughter. If we could all be so lucky. His only wish now is that you find the same."

"I don't care about that," she said, swiping away the tear. "I just need him to know I'm sorry."

"Apologies have no meaning in the great beyond," she said, gently shaking her head. "He only wishes for you to be happy."

"Please tell him I love him," Sofia whispered, barely able to speak.

"He knows, Sofia. With all his soul." Lowering her hand, she turned to face Heden. "And you, son of Markdor. You will have a great choice to make as well. Sofia has done her part. I am confident you will do yours."

Heden's fangs glistened as he grinned. "Not to squelch the melodrama, lady, but you sure do talk in some serious riddles."

Throwing her head back, Tatiana broke into a jubilant laugh, her entire body quaking under her flowing green dress. "That I do, Vampyre." Stepping back, she regarded them. "I let you into my home, but that is now over. Please do not enter my property again without permission. I don't take lightly to those who do, understood?"

"Yes," they said in unison, their tones contrite.

"The cameras have already been disabled. You have everything you need. Take the knowledge you have back to the immortal world and help your family defeat the Secret Society. Sofia will question whether she should accompany you, but you need her. Don't let her waver. She is invaluable to your future, Heden."

"Yes, ma'am, Ms. Tatiana," he said.

"I like that. 'Ms. Tatiana.' I believe I shall request to be called that more often. Best wishes, my new friends. May your goddess Etherya and your Catholic god work together to ensure your success. For now, goodbye, until we meet again."

Lifting her palms to the sky, Tatiana tilted her face and closed her eyes, chanting words indecipherable to Sofia but similar to those Bakari had chanted in the alley in L.A. Wind swirled as the clouds above darkened, and she vanished into thin air, leaving only a swirl of dead leaves behind.

"Wow," Sofia said, expelling a breath. "That was heavy." Heden stared at her, his gaze reverent. "What?"

"You're just really beautiful when you cry," he said, inching closer and cupping her jaw. Slowly, he wiped the wetness away. "I'm so damn sorry about your grandfather, Sofie. I wish I could bring him back for you."

She sighed, basking in the warmth of his caress. "Her words gave me comfort, and I hope they're true. Perhaps he really is content up there and wants me to move on and focus on my own happiness. I wonder what she meant by 'the great beyond.' I'm guessing it's Heaven."

"It's the Passage. Only barbaric humans believe in Heaven."

Sofia breathed a laugh and made the sign of the cross over her chest. "I'm pretty sure you just damned yourself to Hell."

"No way. In our lore, there's the Land of Lost Souls and the Passage, similar to your Hell and Heaven. Hell doesn't exist, so I can't end up there."

"Well, Heaven definitely exists," she said, loving their banter. "There's nowhere else my grandfather could possibly be."

"Only the Passage exists, little human. Everybody knows that."

"Well, I guess there's only one way to find out. We're both going to have to die."

"If it means winning an argument with you, I'm down," he teased.

Sofia's features scrunched as she stared up at him. "Do I really argue with you that much?"

"About every damn thing, Sof. It's fucking adorable. I get so hard when you insist you're right."

Sofia's eyes widened, and her gaze traveled to his fly.

"Yep, right now. Want to bang on the old log? I'll take the bottom so you don't scrape your delectable skin."

She pulled away and swatted his chest. "I'm not *banging* you on a dirty log in a forest. Good grief, you're annoying."

"I'll show you annoying, woman," he said, bending down to pick her up. Sofia yelped as he threw her over his shoulder and began walking back toward the house.

"Put me down," she squealed, lightly pounding his back with her fists.

Heden smacked her jean-clad ass with his broad palm, causing her to squirm atop his shoulder. His hand smoothed away the sting, and then he nipped the juicy globe. Sofia gushed so thoroughly in her panties she thought they might melt away.

"Holy shit," he murmured, inhaling as he walked. "I smell your arousal, honey. It smells so damn good."

"I'm not aroused at all," she lied, wriggling against him in the hopes he would do it again.

"Don't lie to me, Sof," he said, placing another playful slap on her ass. As he took measured steps, he soothed his palm over the sensitive cheek. God, she loved it. Relaxing into him, she realized how safe she felt in his arms.

"I'm going to carry you like this all the way home," he said, placing a kiss on her butt. "You feel so good against me."

Although hanging over his shoulder was quite uncomfortable, it did give her a great view of his magnificent backside. Sliding her palms over his ass, she squeezed, loving the feel of the tight muscles beneath as he walked.

"You squeeze mine, and I'll squeeze yours back," he growled, clutching her ass cheek in his hand.

"Is that supposed to deter me?" she asked, laughing.

They proceeded to honor that arrangement the entire way home, Sofia's delight echoing through the forest lined with withered trees and curious critters who came out of hiding to see what all the fuss was about.

* * * *

Once home, they logged onto the laptop to verify the feed had been cut. Sure enough, every camera angle was black and inactive. Sofia removed the program from the hard drive, thankful they had already saved the segments of video showing Tatiana adding the various ingredients to the cauldron.

After video chatting with his family and updating them on the meeting with Tatiana, Heden discussed next steps with Sathan as Sofia sat beside him.

"Great job, bro," Sathan said.

Heden appeared pleased by the praise, and Sofia realized Sathan was the only father figure he'd ever known. Although they were brothers, she could tell he looked up to the king and found it sweet that he basked in the acclaim.

"At this point, it's probably best for you to head back to Astaria. You can focus on updating the military devices to communicate through the ether and also work with Sadie and Nolan to identify the toxins we found in Adelyn's lunchbox. The chemicals are new to our realm, and we want to identify them so we can have a cure ready if someone accidentally ingests them."

"I could write a program that could help the docs catalog and analyze the results faster. Those two love to write things on paper. It's outdated as hell."

"Agreed," Sofia chimed in.

"You're welcome to accompany Heden, Sofia," Sathan said. "We could use another programmer with your skills. I don't want to detract from your life in the human world, but if you're willing to help us for a few weeks or months, I won't turn it down."

Sofia chewed her lip, contemplating. Was there anything tethering her to the human world? Not really. For years, there had been no purpose to her life except exacting revenge for Francesco. Sadly, no one would miss her if she left.

But there were other things to consider now that she was free of her quest for vengeance. She wanted to bear a child of her own and was pushing forty. There was only so much time left for her to conceive. Each moment she spent in the immortal world was one that lessened her chances of being a mother. After being alone for so long, she was ready to love and nurture a baby.

Glancing at Heden, she noticed his imploring smile. "Come on, Sof," he said, nudging her shoulder with his. "Come back with me for a few weeks at least. I'm not ready to let you go yet."

Sathan cleared his throat, acknowledging he understood their relationship was no longer purely platonic. "Why don't you two discuss tonight? You have the house for one more night, right?"

"Yep," Heden said. "Let me work on our girl here. I'll do my very best to charm her into coming home with me."

"I bet you will," Sathan muttered, although it was good-natured. "Sounds good. Text me before you come back through the ether. Sofia, I hope you choose to come to the realm. We're thankful to have you on our team."

"Thank you, Sathan," she said, swallowing over the lump that formed in her throat. She was honored to be accepted by the people she'd wronged not so long ago.

Heden clicked off the chat and turned to her, fingers laced behind his head. "So, little human, we have all night. What do you want to do?" He waggled his eyebrows.

"Well, I'm not just going to jump into bed with you. Good lord. Is it really that easy for you with women?"

He shrugged. "Most of the time, yeah. I like that you're difficult though. It keeps me on my toes."

"Difficult, my ass," she said, standing and placing her hands on her hips. "I'm one hundred percent sure *you* are the difficult one in this relationship, but I won't argue with you."

"That's a first," he said, standing and running his hand through his thick hair. "So, what should we do with our last night in Louisiana?"

"Well, I'm starving and could definitely eat. This might sound lame, but I saw on Yelp there's a bar in town that has a bunch of arcade games and yummy appetizers. Is that super dorky?"

"Fuck yes, and I love it," he said, inching closer. Cupping her jaw, he tilted her face. "Please tell me they have Ms. Pac-Man."

"And Galaga and Space Invaders..." she said in a sultry tone.

"Keep going..." He inched closer to her face.

"And Centipede and Street Fighter II..."

"Damn it, woman, I'm going to come in my pants. Tell me one more. It's all I can take."

Sofia licked her lips, the movement slow and deliberate. "They have..."—she lifted to her toes and whispered—"Mortal Kombat."

He captured her lips, his tongue consuming her as he groaned.

Sofia threaded her arms around his neck, thrusting her body into his. Their tongues warred with each other as small moans of desire escaped their throats. Clenching his hair with her fingers, she tugged and felt his resulting shudder.

"I've never heard anything as sexy as you spouting vintage arcade games to me," he whispered against her lips. "Fuck, Sofie, you're incredible."

She chuckled and shook her head. "I'm a huge geek."

"You're my geek, woman. Get used to it." He playfully slapped her butt. "Come on, let's get you fed so I can ravish you."

She nodded and gave him one last kiss. "Let's do it."

Armed with their wallets and Sofia's empty stomach, they headed out into the temperate evening for what Heden insisted on calling their "dork date." To her, that sounded just about perfect.

Chapter 23

Sofia proceeded to have the absolute, hands-down, best date of her life with Heden at the arcade bar. The games were plentiful, and the food was fantastic. After several hours of competition, they were tied at five wins per person on the various consoles. Now, they were playing a hot and heavy two-player game of Ms. Pac-Man for winner-takes-all bragging rights.

Heden's thick fingers deftly maneuvered the tiny joystick, causing Sofia to wonder how in the hell he could be so agile with hands so large.

"My hands are magic, Sof," he said, eyes never leaving the console. "Don't doubt me. You'll see soon enough."

"In your dreams," she said, rolling her eyes.

"It's my only dream," he said, glancing up to wink at her. He finished two more levels before being eaten by the yellow ghost and dying a quick but painless death.

Sofia took the seat and proceeded to handily defeat the next four levels, only losing her last life once she'd squarely beaten Heden.

"Damn, you're good," he said, shaking his head as she rose. "I admit defeat. You own my body for the next twenty-four hours. I'm your humble servant."

Sofia threw back her head and laughed. "I'm pretty sure that's *your* prize, not mine."

"Fuck yes," he said, pecking her on the lips. Threading his fingers through hers, he led her out of the bar and down the darkened sidewalk.

"This will probably sound strange, but you're the first person I've felt this free with since my grandfather." Slightly embarrassed by the admission, she awaited his response.

"That means so much, Sof," he said, squeezing her hand. "I feel the same. It's been hard for me since everyone and their damn mother started falling in love and having babies."

"How so?" she asked, glancing up at him.

"I've always been close with my siblings but still...*apart* from them in a way. Sathan always had his duties, Latimus had his army, and Arderin was always buried in a book studying medicine or driving Sathan crazy." He grinned. "That was always *really* fun to watch, by the way."

Sofia chuckled, and he continued. "We were tethered together because it was just the four of us, even if I was the most aloof. As they all bonded and had kids, the separateness I'd felt expanded even more. It's hard to explain because I still love them all so much, but I've just been kind of drifting, I guess. Then, one day, the craziest thing happened."

"You met the most gifted hacker you'd ever seen?" she teased, beaming up at him.

His features contorted playfully. "Do you even know how to turn on a laptop? I can show you. You're a pretty crappy programmer."

"Says the man who didn't even know C++ code," she mumbled.

"Anyway," he said, winking, "I met this really awful hacker, but she was so damn cute, and I felt this instant connection with her even though she was trying to murder my family. It's the love story every young man dreams about."

Sofia rolled her eyes at his teasing. "Even though you're making fun of me, I get it. I think you and I both see the world the same way. Like, we don't quite fit into a lot of the situations we're presented with, so we forge ahead and create ways to exist in our reality even if it isn't comfortable. Outwardly, we function really well, but we don't really feel connected to a lot of people."

Their hands swung as they clung to each other, digesting her words. "That's exactly how I feel, Sof. Damn. You get it."

"I get it," she said, squeezing his fingers. "It's nice to find someone else who does."

Blue eyes glimmered with reverence and emotion as he gazed down at her. They continued to trail along, talking about everything and nothing, and Sofia realized how much she would miss him when they did ultimately part. In such a short time, she'd become so comfortable with him. It was poignant, and she was extremely thankful he'd seen the goodness and pain warring within her, almost before she recognized it herself.

Their words tapered off as they trailed inside, each exhibiting a reverent shyness that was atypical of their personalities. A lamp shone atop the bedside table from Heden's open bedroom door, the lone light that permeated the otherwise dim house.

Heden slowly approached her. "Sofie," he whispered, palming her cheeks with his strong hands, "I want you so much."

She stared into his gorgeous clear irises, anxiety slamming inside her pounding heart. "Okay," she said, nodding hesitantly. "But I've never really been great at this, so go easy on me."

"Impossible," he breathed, lowering his lips to hers.

Enveloped by his strength and his musky scent, she clutched him closer, whimpering as his tongue invaded her mouth. It slid over hers, claiming it, warring with it, until she was breathless.

Gently breaking the kiss, his gaze, blazing with desire, bore into her. "You're absolutely perfect. I can't think of one thing you could do to my body that I wouldn't enjoy. I mean, you're not the greatest coder I've ever seen, but other than that—"

"Stop teasing me," she said, swatting his pecs as he grinned. "I'm so nervous."

"Don't be," he said, dropping his hand to clutch her wrist. Pulling it to his chest, he placed her palm over his pounding heart. "It always beats like this when I'm around you. I don't think I've ever wanted anyone more."

"That's a good line."

He lifted her hand from his chest to nip her palm. "I mean it, Sof. There are no lines with you. Just you and me and my insatiable desire for you. You ready?"

"I'm ready." She threaded her arms around his neck. "But I am a bit intimidated. You're freaking huge. What if it doesn't fit?"

His warm chuckle surrounded her, causing embarrassment to warm her cheeks.

"Stop laughing! It's a valid concern, especially with someone as massive as you."

"Oh, I'll fit, honey. I'm going to have you flowing for me before I even consider fucking you. When you're ready, we'll know."

"Should we use a condom?"

"It's impossible for humans and Vampyres to spread disease or impregnate one another, but I'll wear one if you want. I want you to feel safe with me, Sof."

The tender words almost shattered her heart. "I feel so safe with you. It's...liberating. And it's not every day you can have sex with no consequences, so...let's bareback the shit out of each other."

"Dude," he said, shaking his head. "That's the hottest sentence anyone's ever spoken to me."

"And yet being called 'dude' is incredibly disconcerting."

He breathed a laugh. "Let me make it up to you, dude. I swear, I'm good for it."

Sofia couldn't stop her laughter. "You're incorrigible." Emotion swirled through her, igniting a maelstrom of feeling as he lifted her. Instinctively, she wrapped her legs around his waist, crossing her ankles behind his back.

His mouth pillaged hers as he stumbled through the bedroom door, stopping beside his bed. Anchored by her legs, she drew back, yanking at his t-shirt and pulling it off his shoulders. In between kisses, he freed her of her shirt, and she pressed her torso to him, craving contact.

Heden's lips blazed a wet trail across the curve of her jaw and then down the sensitive skin of her neck, coming to rest at the juncture of her shoulder. Groaning, he sucked her there, and Sofia knew he was imagining drinking from her. The thought sent a rush of lust through her shaking body, and she gasped.

"You okay?" he asked, lifting his head to gaze into her eyes.

She nodded, desire causing her skin to flush.

"You want me to pierce you with my fangs right there on your pretty neck, don't you, honey?"

"Yes," she whispered.

"I will, but first, I need to make up for last night. Man, you must think I'm so lame. At this point, I'm lower on the sexiness scale than Screech from *Saved by the Bell*."

Sofia threw her head back, overcome with laughter. "How in the hell do you know about that show?"

"Come on, woman," he said, nipping her lips. "It's a classic. I pride myself on staying up-to-date on human pop culture."

She traced her fingers over his cheek, stopping at the soft hairs of his beard. "I have a feeling I'm going to be torn between laughing and climaxing over the next few hours. Of course you wouldn't be serious during sex. It would ruin your comedic reputation."

"Sofie, if you think I'm not serious about you, you haven't been paying attention."

The words threatened to rip her heart from her chest, and she told herself to calm down. If she wasn't careful, she'd end up falling for him. This man who wasn't a man, and someone she had no future with. Determined to stay in the moment, she focused on his handsome features.

"Let me set you down for a sec," he said. After she uncrossed her legs, he slid her down his body until her feet hit the floor.

Feeling wobbly, she gripped his biceps.

"Hold on to my shoulders," he said, slowly kneeling before her. When she complied, he removed her sneakers and socks, taking his time as he slowly divested her of the garments. Reaching for the button of her jeans, he grinned up at her, holding her gaze as he unclasped the button.

"Your bra is pretty," he said, his voice husky as his irises roved over the small mounds of her breasts covered in black lace. She didn't have many appealing undergarments, considering them impractical, but this bra was her favorite. She'd worn it tonight hoping he might see it and glowed at his compliment.

He slid the zipper of her jeans down, and she threaded her fingers though his thick, wavy hair. He growled, closing his eyes as she squeezed. "That feels so good," he said, lifting his lids to drill into her. "When I'm inside you, I want you to clutch my hair and anchor yourself that way. I love having my hair pulled and my scalp scratched."

"Okay," she said, digging the tips of her nails into his scalp and dragging them across.

"Fuck," he breathed, closing his eyes again. "Not right now, honey, or I'm going to blow my load in my pants. Later though. Don't forget."

"I won't." He commenced ridding her of her jeans, dragging them off each leg and tossing them to the floor. She was left standing before him in only her bra and red cotton underwear. His gaze darted over her hips and the intersection between her thighs as he grasped her hips. Pulling her toward him, he buried his nose in the cloth-covered juncture and inhaled deeply.

"*Heden.*"

"Shhh..." he said, nuzzling her with his nose. "You smell so good. Let me have this much of you. For just a minute...or maybe forever..."

There she stood, grasping his hair, his face buried in her most private place, more open to him than anyone she'd ever known. The moment felt special...reverent in some way...and she felt the sting of tears. Through the moisture, she smiled at the strong man who bowed before her.

After a small eternity, Heden lifted his head and ran his hand over her mound. As her flushed body trembled, he hooked his fingers over the top of her panties and slid them down, tossing them near her jeans. Standing, he gripped her hand and led her to the bed. Sitting on the side, he drew her in between his open legs.

"You still have your pants on," she said, feeling her lips curve into a slight frown.

"I want to take my time with you," he said, grasping her other hand and pulling her down to him. "Kiss me, Sofie."

She followed his command, opening her mouth over his and slipping her tongue inside. As he moaned, she straddled his thick thighs, sitting atop his jean-covered erection.

His hands caressed her back, flirting with the tips of her curly hair, as his tongue warred with hers. When he slid his hand down over her hip and thigh and rested his fingers atop the triangle of black hair covering her deepest place, she gave a high-pitched mewl.

His chuckle both aroused and frustrated her. Self-doubt rushed in, and she reminded herself to remain calm and open.

"I like to laugh during sex, Sofie," he said, gently fingering her soft curls down below. "It's something that's supposed to be *fun.* I'm never laughing at you, so don't tense up. If you relax enough, you might just laugh along with me."

"I've never really had fun while having sex."

"You poor, sheltered human. I can't wait to change that narrative. You're going to have so much fun with me, I'll ruin you for anyone else. Ready?"

Sofia stared at him, worried he was right. "Ready," she whispered.

Nuzzling the tip of her nose with his, he lowered his finger to her opening, circling it, testing.

"Fuck. You're so slick, baby. Feel that?" He rimmed the swollen lips of her core, causing her to purr, and slipped a thick finger inside. Instinctively, her body clenched him, his teeth gritting as he breathed against her lips. "God, Sofie, you're so tight."

"It's been a long time," she said, trying to remember the last time she'd had sex. Many years ago, for sure.

"I'm not sure I'll survive fucking you," he said, stealing a kiss from her lips as he pumped his finger in and out of her tight, wet channel. "But I don't think I'll give a damn. What a way to go."

Sofia giggled, taken with the intimacy of the moment and his gentle teasing.

"She's laughing," he said, mock surprise in his tone. "Look who's loosening up."

"In more ways than one," she said, snickering at the double entendre.

"Oh, man. Don't make me give you a 'that's what she said,'" he said, shaking his forehead against hers. "Once you get me started, I'll go on forever."

"That's what she said," Sofie chortled.

Heden laughed, overtaking her lips with his and consuming them in a heated kiss. "Don't steal my material," he murmured against her lips. "That will get you punished."

"Oh, yeah?" she taunted. "How?"

He inserted another finger, stretching her swollen folds. Sofia exhaled a groan, her head lolling back as she struggled to breathe. It was so intimate, so freeing, to straddle him while he explored her innermost spot. Gathering some of her silky moisture, he spread it to her clit, causing the skin there to become slippery. Reintroducing his thick fingers to her channel, he rubbed the heel of his hand against her sensitive nub. Sofia rocked against him, the back and forth motions of his fingers and hand causing bursts of pleasure to shoot through her body. They spiked from her core, connecting with every nerve ending in her straining frame, lifting her from her body to a place where only pleasure existed.

Grasping his shoulder with a vicelike grip, she reached behind, attempting to unhook her bra. Frustrated, she grappled with the hook until Heden lifted his free hand, snapping the garment open in seconds.

Sofia stilled, panting as she eyed him warily. "Should I be jealous that you know how to do that so well?"

"Yes," he teased, scrunching his features at her as he nipped her lips and tore the bra from her body. "I'm the greatest lover the immortal world has ever seen. In fact, I have several ladies you can ask for references—"

"Shut up," she said, swallowing his words as she kissed him.

"Mmmm..." he said, lifting his hand to her breast and cupping the small swell. "I like this dominant side of you. We need to get a whip for next time. I'll go first."

"You wish—" She broke off, gasping as he pinched her nipple.

His fingers resumed their pace below, the heel of his hand grinding against her. Heden's gaze lowered to her nipple, now firmly pressed between his fingers. "Look at that sweet little nipple," he growled, tugging on it as she moaned. "You like that."

"Yes," she whimpered, her head falling back as she arched toward him.

"Poor baby," he murmured, releasing her breast and gliding his hand up to fist her hair. Tugging her head back further, he grazed his lips across her collarbone, moving closer to the tip of her straining nipple. "You're so wound up. Let me help you."

Extending his tongue, he licked around the nub, leaving a wet trail that encircled her breast. Lifting her head, she cemented her eyes to his, pleading. As her hips gyrated over his hand pistoning into her deepest place, his gorgeous gaze held hers. Extending his tongue, he touched the tip to her nipple.

Sofia bucked, feeling the orgasm build, reaching ever higher toward the moment she would explode all over him in a fit of spent desire. Never had she seen anything as sexy as Heden flicking her nipple with his tongue as he stared up at her, silently begging her to come.

Out of nowhere, a slight fear began to choke her. She was mad for this man who was so intent on giving her pleasure. What if she became addicted to his touch? His friendship? His...*love*? Happy-ever-after with a Vampyre was impossible—Sofia knew this in her practical heart. What the hell was she doing, opening herself so thoroughly to someone she had no future with?

"Don't leave me, honey," he murmured against her breast. "Come back to me."

"What are we doing, Heden?" she cried, desire warring with the terror inside.

"Hey," he said, gaze locking with hers. "Don't bring that stuff in here. It's just you and me right now. Nothing else. Stay with me, baby." His fingers continued the madness below, threatening to shatter her.

Moving his lips to her ear, he spoke reverently in his low-toned voice, the deep timbre soothing. "You're mine, Sofie," he declared, clutching her to him as he loved her. "*Mine*. I've been searching for you for so long, I didn't even know it."

Lifting his head, he locked onto her eyes. "Now, I want you to take my fingers and move that sweet little clit against my hand."

Sofia whimpered as her hips gyrated.

"You're beautiful and perfect, and I want you to come for me."

Following his directive, she lowered her lids and called his name.

"I'm right here, baby. I'm so fucking turned on for you. I can't wait to claim you and make you mine." Grasping her hair, he drew her head back, lowering his head to her nipple. "*Let go*, Sofia." Closing his teeth around her nipple, he gently bit the delicate nub.

It was the jolt she needed, sending Sofia headfirst into a massive orgasm. Grasping Heden's firm shoulders, she lost control of her muscles, unable to restrain the violent spasms. Crying out, she clenched her eyes shut as prickles of pleasure and fire shot to every pore of her burning skin. Somewhere in her dazed mind, she remembered she was supposed to be scared of her feelings toward him, but she didn't have the ability to hold onto the fear. It flew away into the night, dispelled toward the stars and moon along with any lingering reservations about the intense intimacy. Her magnificent Vampyre had dissipated them all. Inhaling huge gulps of air, she buried her face in his neck and drew him close with her quivering arms.

He held her, quiet and serene, which was quite a feat for her talkative immortal.

Squeezing him, she laughed into his pecs and gave them a sloppy kiss. "Somebody's quiet," she mumbled into his slick skin. It warmed her to know he'd gotten sweaty and sticky just from making her come. The thought of him oozing sweat as he loomed over her, his thick cock inside her, sent a fresh round of shudders through her spent body.

When he didn't answer, she lifted her head and cupped his jaw. "Heden?"

Removing his fingers from her, he lifted them, palming her cheek. There was something so sexy about feeling her own wetness against her flushed skin. But even better was the way the handsome man stared at her. Sofia had never seen such pleasure swimming in another's eyes.

"You're happy," she said, rubbing his beard.

"So happy," he said, his expression one of wonder and affection. But there was something else too. Something she struggled to read.

"What's wrong?"

"I was worried there for a second," he said, running the pad of his thumb over her lower lip. "That you weren't going to trust me and let go."

"There are a lot of unsaid things between us, Heden, that's all. It shook me for a minute."

"I know," he said, his other hand stroking her back. "I wish we had more time. I want years with you, Sofie. Centuries. However long it takes until you get tired of me and tell me to go to hell. Which I don't believe in," he said, lifting a finger.

She laughed, her heart jolting at his touching words. "I don't have centuries. I wish I did. Time's a bitch."

"It sure is, little human." He stood, holding her in his arms as he turned down the bed. Placing her gently beneath the covers, he slipped off the rest of his clothes, gazing at her the entire time. Lowering beside her, he pulled her against him.

Sofia rubbed the scratchy hairs on his chest, needing to at least acknowledge the unknowns. "I'm afraid to come back with you to Astaria. I experience some pretty intense feelings around you."

"Same," he said, running his hand over her back. Her gaze rested on her fingers plucking at his chest hairs as he stared at the ceiling. "I feel so connected to you, Sofie. I know it's only been a short while, but there's just something about you."

Ever so slowly, she slid the silken skin of her leg over his thighs and glided to sprawl atop his massive chest. "There's something about you too. When you're not making fun of me."

He grinned, running his fingers through her hair. "Me? Never."

Sofia slithered up his body, aligning her lips with his. "Make love to me," she whispered.

Breathing her name, his palms ran down her back, stopping to clutch the globes of her ass in his hands. Maneuvering her over his frame, he aligned the tip of his cock with her wet opening.

"God, Sofie," he said against her mouth. "You're still so wet."

Anchoring on his pecs, she straddled him, attempting to push herself onto his cock. Feeling the thick head inch inside her sent shards of arousal though her still-flushed body. She worked her hips, becoming frustrated that he seemed to be holding back.

"You can push harder."

"I don't want to hurt you. And I'm not sure if this way is best for our first time."

"Want me to flip over?"

"Hold on." Grasping her in his arms, he flipped them, rolling atop her and stroking her hair as it fanned on the pillow. "I wasn't worried before, but I'm a bit worried now. You're really tight, honey."

"So stretch me open," she said, biting her lip.

His fingers found her opening and gathered her silken moisture. Lifting to her clit, he began to stimulate it. Sofia's hips gyrated against his ministrations, the pressure so intense as he circled her swollen nub. Gliding to her opening, he jutted two fingers inside. Sofia told herself to relax, wanting so badly to please him.

"You're fine, honey," he said, moving his fingers inside her deepest place. "The more you tell yourself to open up, the harder it will probably be."

"How do I turn my brain off?" she asked, only half-joking.

"Think about other fun stuff. What's your favorite color?'

"Blue," she moaned, hips undulating against his hand.

"Dogs or cats?"

"Dogs."

"Beach or mountains?" He inserted a third finger, the stretching sensation pleasurable and uncomfortable all at once.

"I, uh..." She mewled softly. "Beach. Positano or Greece."

"Good answer." Removing his fingers, he aligned the head of his shaft with her opening. His finger resumed circling her clit as he loomed over her. "Favorite Vampyre?"

"You," she cried, arms encircling his neck. "Oh, god, Heden. Please."

He began pushing inside, tiny juts that filled her so completely she thought she might burst.

"You with me, Sof?" he asked, eyes boring into her.

"Yes," she said, gliding her hands to his head. Remembering his earlier directive, she grabbed the thick strands.

"Yeah, baby," he said, increasing the pace of his thrusts. "Tug my hair hard. I love it. You won't hurt me."

Needing to please him, she clenched tight, alternating between pulling the strands and scratching his scalp with her nails. With every motion, he groaned and pumped further inside her. Opening herself up to him, she spread her legs as wide as they would go, showing him with her body how much she trusted him.

"I need to fuck you harder," he growled, fangs bared as he stared down at her. "If I hurt you, tell me right away, okay?"

She nodded, her hair swishing over the pillow.

Anchoring on his palm, he began thrusting into her, still rubbing her clit with his other hand. Sofia could feel the head of his shaft pounding her core, and she wanted to weep with joy. Seeing him so lost to desire filled every chasm of doubt she'd ever had.

"*Sofie...*" Beads of sweat lined his forehead as he moved above her, the sight visceral and raw. They began to drip over her skin, and she loved that he was as consumed by the experience as she was.

"Nothing has ever felt this good," he groaned, hammering her with his pulsing cock. "Do you know how good you feel, baby?"

Her engorged clit tingled under his fingers. "I'm going to come again," she wailed.

"Yes, honey. Come all over my cock. Damn it...I'm going to lose it."

Her body snapped, and she succumbed to the pleasure, closing her eyes as he hammered into her, screaming her name. The walls of her core convulsed around his silken length until she felt him start to shudder. Stuffed to the brim with his magnificent cock, she felt it begin to pulse and then jet his release into her deepest place. Spearing his scalp with her fingernails, his colossal frame jerked above her several times until he collapsed in a heap over her trembling body. Laughs of pure joy escaped her throat, and she clutched him tight, needing to hold every fragment of his skin to hers.

He groaned into the soft curve of her neck, subsequent quakes wracking his frame. "Good lord, Sof. You fucking strangled my cock to death."

Unable to control her sultry chuckle, she ran her nails over his scalp, reveling in his resulting shiver. "You asked for it, buddy."

"Hell yes, I did. Man, your pussy is amazing. Like, it deserves an award. An Oscar or an Emmy or something."

"You're such a tool," she teased. "And I'm glad it felt good."

Grunting, he lifted his head, resting it on his hand as he undulated his hips against hers. "It felt fucking amazing. I'm staying here forever. My cock has found its permanent home."

She giggled, jutting right back into him. "As fun as that sounds, I'll eventually have to get up to pee."

"Never," he said, smacking a wet kiss on her lips. "Sorry, but you're never allowed to move again."

"We'll see, Vampyre."

They lay there, sated and lazy, staring into each other as their bodies cooled. Sofia trailed her fingers over his back as he slowly combed his fingers though her hair on the pillow.

"You look so gorgeous right now," he whispered after a while.

"So do you."

Tracing his thumb over her lip, his expression grew serious. Sofia knew he was thinking of the future and the inevitable end of their relationship somewhere down the line. "Please come back to Astaria with me. Give me two months. After that, we'll sit down and reevaluate."

"Heden," she said softly, shaking her head atop the pillow.

"Please, Sof. I can't let you go yet. I mean, I physically can't. I'm still inside you."

The chuckle rumbled in her chest. "It's a big risk for me. I want to have kids, Heden, and I'm running out of time for that. Every day I spend there with you is a day in a future that isn't mine."

Sighing, he cupped her jaw. "I don't want to take anything away from you, but two months is nothing."

"Not to you—"

"I'm not trying to diminish your dreams, Sof. I just want so badly for you to make mine come true a little while longer."

"Damn," she said, trailing her fingers through his hair. "That was a good one."

"Yeah?" He squinted at the ceiling. "I was thinking maybe it was too heavy. Have to make sure the levity is just right."

"Your comedic timing is intact," she said, giving him an affable eye roll. Contemplating, her gaze roved over his attractive features. "Okay," she finally said. "Two months. And then we'll reevaluate."

"Yippee!" he said, sliding his arms around her and squeezing tightly. "I'm going to make you so happy, honey. I swear, these are going to be the best two months of your life."

Sofia hugged him back, knowing he spoke the truth while acknowledging how much harder that would make her eventual departure. Pledging to enjoy the moment, she lifted her lips to his and allowed him to kiss her fears away for now, knowing they would return in the not-so-distant future...

Chapter 24

After the sun rose, they packed up their bags and tidied up the house, ready to depart to Astaria. Once finished, Heden closed the door behind him with a firm thud.

"Ready?" he asked, extending his hand to Sofia.

Nodding, she placed her hand in his.

He led her to the soft grass beside the house and held his palm in the air, generating the ether. Placing a protective hand on her back, he urged her to walk through first.

They emerged on the other side, the sun blazing above. Kenden was waiting by a four-wheeler and lifted an arm in a wave. Hopping into the vehicle, he caught them up on Vadik's appearance at the Deamon prison and his subsequent vanishing act.

"I didn't sense any malice in Tatiana's demeanor when we met her," Heden said. "I can't understand why she supplied the potions to Bakari and, by proxy, his allies."

"I don't think she sees it as helping them," Sofia said. "There's an underlying control in playing nice with both sides. After all, she also gave us intel. Perhaps she's letting things play out and doing what she feels is right in her gut."

"Maybe," Heden said, "but I don't like it. Vadik's interest in the Deamon prison is worrisome. If he figures out a way to spring the prisoners there, we'll be thrust right back into war. There are almost a thousand Deamons housed there."

"Latimus and I are all over it," Kenden said. "The troop count there has been increased tenfold, and the security system you implemented when it was built is fantastic. In the meantime, Sadie and Nolan definitely need some sort of program to analyze and catalog the various chemicals we've been finding faster. Moira and Aron found traces in the tomatoes in their garden as well. I want cures developed as soon as possible. We don't know how many toxins they have stockpiled, and if they somehow begin poisoning subjects, we want to be prepared."

"Done. Sofia's pledged to help us for two months. The little human is going to save us all." He squeezed her shoulder as she sat in the front seat.

"Not sure about that, but I'm happy to help," Sofia said, sliding her hand over his and squeezing.

Heden noticed Kenden smile at the reverent gesture.

"Have they found any chemicals at Astaria?"

"No," Kenden said. "Etherya's protective wall around Astaria prevented Crimeous from transporting there. As far as we can tell, the same holds true for the transportation serum.   It can traverse them anywhere in the kingdom except Astaria."

"Good. That means I don't need to have a guard with me every time I want to steal kisses from Sofia by the river. I'm not down with the cockblock."

Kenden arched a brow. "Stealing kisses, huh?"

"Yep, we're totally banging," Heden said. "Don't tell Latimus. He's a stick in the mud."

Sofia pivoted and shot him a glare. "Did you think of maybe asking me before you told Kenden we're together? Sheesh."

"Come on, Sof," he said, tugging her ponytail and laughing when she batted his hand away. "Ken already knows I'm a stud. It would make sense you couldn't keep your hands off me."

"Well, I'm happy for you guys," Kenden said, white teeth flashing as he beamed. "I want you to find happiness, Sofia. I feel terrible at the pain you've experienced over the past few years, and Heden's pretty awesome."

"Thanks," she grumbled, arms crossed over her chest.

Once they made it to Astaria, Kenden jumped out and proceeded to the barracks. Sofia slung her pack over her shoulders and began stomping toward the castle. Judging by the set of her shoulders and overall energy output, she was *pissed*.

"Sofie," Heden said, grabbing her wrist once they'd entered the house through the back door.

Turning, she shook off his arm. "Don't look at me all cute and innocent!" She stomped her foot on the ground. "You had no right to tell Kenden we're together."

His brow furrowed. "I didn't think you'd care. Are you embarrassed to be with me?"

She expelled a breath and lifted her fingers to her forehead, rubbing harshly. "Of course not. But I don't want your family to think I just came here for some extended booty call or something. I came to help because I still feel bad I had a hand in creating this mess."

"I know," he said, inching closer and sliding a hesitant hand over the skin above her shoulder. "But I thought you also came to hang with me, maybe just a little bit. I'm so honored you're here and that you're with me. I want to tell everyone."

"You want to tell everyone you're with a human? Won't they think you're slumming or something?"

His lips curved. "Not with you. You're one of the good ones." Drawing her close, he cupped her cheek. "I'm sorry. I didn't mean to tell people if you weren't ready. But we're going to be working together a lot, and it's pretty obvious you're crazy about me."

She rolled her eyes. "You're infuriating."

"Tell me you're insane for me," he murmured, lowering his face to hers.

"No."

Brushing his lips over hers, he grinned at her resulting tremble. "I'm so crazy for you, Sof. I don't want to hide it. I should've asked you first, and I'm really sorry I didn't. I want to tell my family about us. Is that okay with you?"

Translucent blue-green eyes darted between his. "I'm just worried it will set them up to believe I might stay here for the long-term. I can't, Heden. We both know that."

"All they'll think is that I'm happy. I don't think I've ever dated anyone for two months. They'll most likely think it's a miracle."

A laugh escaped her throat. "Is that supposed to make me feel special or something?"

"You are special," he said, giving her a sweet kiss. "Please don't be mad at me, honey."

Sighing, she glared at him. "Fine. You can tell everyone, and I'm not mad. But don't expect my time here to be an all-out sexcapade. I have a job to do, and I plan on accomplishing my tasks before I leave."

"Ohhh, a sexcapade. I love that word. Let's do that instead," he teased.

"No way, buddy." She grabbed the straps of her pack. "Should I stay in Latimus's room again?"

"You can, but I'd really like you to stay with me, Sof." He grasped her hand. "I'll leave it up to you, but I can be pretty persuasive." He waggled his eyebrows.

She bit her lip. "What if you get tired of me?"

"No fucking way. Come on. Let's unpack and make a plan."

"I'm pretty much used to living alone," she said, trailing behind him as they walked through the foyer and down the carpeted stairs. "I might be really difficult."

Approaching the door to his room, he turned and gave her a brilliant smile. "Little human, I'd expect nothing less from you." Giving her a wink, he watched her walk into Latimus's room before he entered his own. He gave her twenty-four hours before she gave up and just moved everything into his room. After all, they only had so much time, and he was determined to make the most of it.

* * * *

Heden gave Sofia a proper tour of the castle, which was enormous, telling her to make herself at home. When they passed through the kitchen, Glarys looked up from the pot she was stirring atop the stove and gave Sofia a huge smile.

"Back for more, Ms. Sofia?" she asked, blue eyes twinkling under her short cap of white hair.

"Yep," Sofia said, biting her lip. "But I don't want to put you out. Honestly, I'd love to help you. My grandfather made a mean sauce, and I could whip it up anytime."

"Well, that's a lovely offer, dear. Jack and Lila love pasta. I'll have you make it next time we have a family dinner."

"Sure thing. Thanks for your hospitality, Glarys."

"I trust Heden is taking good care of you?" Glarys asked, hand propped on her hip.

"Oh, I'm taking very good care of her," he said, striding over to plant a smacking kiss on Glarys's forehead. "She's the second hottest babe in this joint after you, Glarys. I've got to treat her right."

The housekeeper's face turned an endearing shade of red. "You boys are all such flirts. Go on and let me work. I don't have time for your teasing."

"Oh, I'm not teasing. One day, you'll run away with me." Looking at Sofia, he lifted his hand to his mouth as if to hide his words from Glarys and whispered loudly, "She's mad for me."

"Get out of here, boy," Glarys said, swatting him with her dish towel. "Nolan and Sadie are in the infirmary waiting for you. Take this banana to Nolan, please. He only ate half his sandwich at lunch."

"Yes, ma'am," Heden said, taking the fruit. "You're too good to us."

"Oh, I know. Now, let me get back to work."

Heden led Sofia through a hallway and down a dim stone stairway. Once it bottomed out, she noticed cells on each side, lined with metal bars.

"It was our dungeon during the War of the Species," Heden said, trailing beside her. "Those were dark times. I'm so glad they're over."

"Hopefully, we can save your people from another round of darkness," Sofia said.

"By the goddess, I hope so."

They walked through a door that led to an infirmary, fluorescent lights shining above three stretchers and a back wall lined with drawers and cabinets. Two people stood at the counter, one furiously scribbling notes as the other gazed into a microscope.

"These are our realm's esteemed physicians. Sofia, meet Nolan and Sadie."

"Hello, Sofia," Nolan said, turning from the microscope and extending his hand. "It's so nice to meet you."

"Hi," she said, shaking his hand and then Sadie's, which she realized was missing the two smallest fingers.

"I was burned a long time ago, and they're gone forever," Sadie said, referencing her fingers. "Hope it doesn't freak you out."

"Not at all," Sofia said, "although you seem to have healed nicely. You aren't scarred around your hand."

Sadie grinned and glanced at Nolan. "That's because my amazing husband here, along with Arderin, created a serum that healed my skin. It's why Arderin came to Houston when you discovered her and Darkrip all those years ago."

"Life really is a series of strange coincidences, isn't it?" Nolan asked.

"It is," Sofia said. "Well, the serum seems to have worked. And Heden tells me you just had your first child. That's fantastic. Congratulations."

"Oh, can I show you some pictures?" Sadie asked, pulling her phone from the pocket of her white lab coat. "Yes, I'm one of those mothers. Daphne is with her nanny at Uteria today, and I miss her so much even though we'll head home and see her in a few hours. Want to see?"

Sofia nodded, stepping forward to look at the doting mother's pictures. The baby was adorable, with a swath of brown hair and large hazel eyes. "Wow, she's beautiful."

"I know," Sadie said, clutching the phone to her breast. "She's the love of my life—along with my husband, of course."

"Thank you for remembering me, darling," Nolan said, kissing her sweetly.

Sofia studied them, questions swirling in her mind.

"Sadie used a sperm donor," Nolan said, smiling. "Sadly, I can't give her children since I'm human, but we found an anonymous donor at Uteria who had an amazing profile."

"There's nothing sad about it," Sadie said, squeezing his hand. "Nolan is an incredible father, and Daphne loves him with all her heart."

"I'd love to hear about the process you went through to conceive sometime," Sofia said. "I've considered artificial insemination as an option in the future."

Sadie smiled. "We'll make a plan to hang one evening while you're here, and I'll answer any questions you have. Heden informed us you're staying for two months."

"Yep," Heden said, sliding his palm over Sofia's shoulder. "And we're going to create some software to get you two dinosaurs off paper and into the modern world. It's about time I created an EMR system for you anyway, so we'll create that along with a program to help you analyze the chemical test results."

"On that note," Nolan said, gesturing to the microscope, "we were just studying samples from the poisons found in Adelyn's lunchbox and Aron's garden. The chemicals are all combinations of extremely rare synthetic and naturally occurring toxins in the human world. Whoever put them together for Bakari is an expert chemist, and the multitude of combinations is staggering. Sadie and I can create several different antidotes but we need to catalog the probability of which chemicals will be used most. Does that make sense?"

"Yes," Sofia said, wheels already turning in her mind. "I can create a program where we log the quantities of each chemical and write an algorithm that determines which ones have the highest potency and ability to form stable bonds with the others. It should only take me a day or two at most."

"She's a pretty terrible programmer," Heden teased, shrugging affably, "so I'll help her, of course."

Sofia shot him a glare. "I run circles around him, and he's insanely jealous."

"Well, I'm sure you're better than I am at anything remotely involving computers, so I defer to you both," Nolan said.

"Let me look over your results so far and take some notes, so I can make sure I write the software to the specifications we need." Approaching the counter, Sofia pointed at the white papers lined with scribbled notes. "Can I have a look?"

Sadie nodded, and Sofia took multiple screenshots with her phone. After discussing specifics with the physicians for several minutes, she turned to Heden. "Can we head to the tech room? I want to start this while it's fresh in my mind."

He smiled and nodded. "Let's get crackin'."

Chapter 25

Several hours later, Heden sat beside Sofia as her fingers sped over the keyboard. They were both plugged into the same hard drive and adding to the code along the way.

"No," she said, squinting at the large screen hanging above them on the wall. "I don't like that. Let's do this instead." She erased the last lines of code Heden had written and replaced it with cleaner symbols to create a more seamless pathway.

"Damn, that's good. It will allow the docs to click through the various screens of the software without having to save along the way."

"Yes," she said, eyes glued to the monitor. "Although it seems small, automatic saves will create more efficiency as they catalog information."

Heden studied her, incredibly turned-on by her intellect. He'd rarely met someone whose mind fired as quickly as his, although his siblings were all quite intelligent in their own ways, especially Arderin. Desire pulsed in his veins as he watched Sofia code, blood surging to his shaft.

"How much longer do you think it will take before we have a working software program we can test?" he asked, his voice gravelly from the thrumming arousal.

She pursed her lips. "Two hours, tops. I'm killing it over here. You're slacking though." Gazing at him, she gave him a brilliant smile.

By the goddess, she was gorgeous. Heden had been lucky to be with many beautiful women over the centuries, but surface beauty only went so far. Not only was Sofia insanely stunning with her blue-green eyes, button nose and beaming smile, her astuteness was so damn sexy. Deciding he was going to seduce her right in front of the computers as soon as they had a functional prototype, he got to work.

"I'm on it," he said, focusing on the screen.

For the next two hours, they toiled, Heden's concentration so intense he coded like a damn genius.

"Crap, that's awesome," she said as they were finishing up. "You wrote that last section in record time. What's gotten into you?"

Finishing up the last line of code, Heden exported the program to the desktop and brought it up onscreen. "Done. Let's let it sit for a few minutes while we take a break."

"Okay," she said, shrugging. "Want to head outside and take a walk? We should probably get some fresh air."

"In a minute," he murmured, so aroused from watching her program for the past several hours he thought he might lose it in his pants. Standing, he padded over and closed the door, turning the lock before pivoting to face her.

"Or you could lock us in the tech room?" she teased, eyebrows arched.

"I've never seen this room as sexy, but now that I've seen you code here, all I can think about is seducing you in front of the computers."

Her throat bobbed as she swallowed. "Don't we need to get the program to the doctors for testing?"

"What I'm imagining won't take too long." Grinning, he placed his hands on his hips. "Do you want me, Sof? Because I'm burning for you right now."

White teeth toyed with her lip. "Yes," she whispered.

Focused on her, he bunched the bottom of his t-shirt in his hands and pulled it over his head, tossing it to the floor. Her eyes grew wide as he began to unbuckle his belt.

"Are you going to strip in front of me?" Her nervous snicker sent shivers along his spine.

His hands froze. "If that's what you want." He arched his brow, awaiting her reaction.

"It's definitely what I want," she said, her voice raspy.

After unfastening his pants and shucking them off along with the rest of his clothes, he sauntered toward her. Extending his hand, he said, "Stand up, little human."

She tentatively slipped her hand into his and stood, her upturned face flushing red.

"Lift your arms," he commanded softly.

Her tongue darted out to bathe her lips, and his knees almost buckled.

"Sofia. Lift your arms."

She complied, lifting them in the air, and Heden pulled the shirt from her body. Reaching behind, he unclasped her bra and tossed it to the ground.

"Now I know why you were coding like a bat out of hell," she said, sliding her palms over his pecs. "You had a reward in mind at the end."

"Fuck yes," he breathed, reaching to unbutton her jeans. Sliding the zipper down, he urged her to remove her sandals and quickly discarded her clothing. "I want you to write some code just for me."

"While I'm naked?"

"Holy shit. Yes, Sofia, while you're naked. Come here."

Sitting in the black office chair, he tugged her to sit on his lap so she faced the multitude of screens lining the desk and wall. The smooth skin of her back was warm against his chest, and she wriggled her ass over his straining cock.

Heden hissed, positioning her so she could sit still while she typed. Dragging the keyboard toward them, he spoke low into the shell of her ear, "Write something for me while I touch you."

She exhaled a ragged breath and placed her hands over the keyboard. Bringing up the text prompt window, she began to type.

"Mmmm..." he said, nuzzling her nape while his palm roved over her quivering abdomen. "You're using Java. Hot, but super easy."

She breathed a laugh. "I can't write complex code while you're doing that to my neck."

"This?" He lightly scraped his fangs over her pulsing vein. "I haven't drunk from you yet. Are you ready for that, honey?"

"Yes," she moaned, squirming against him.

Her fingers blazed over the keyboard, writing some generic code as he grew even harder beneath her. "Do you know how sexy you are when you're coding? It's so fucking hot, Sof."

"I've always seen it as pretty boring," she mumbled, head falling back on his shoulder to allow him better access.

"No way." His fingers trailed down her stomach to the springy patch of hair that covered her core. Searching, he found her folds, swollen and thick, and almost wept with joy. His tongue began sweeping over her neck, dousing the sensitive skin with his saliva so he wouldn't hurt her when he impaled her.

"Will it sting?" she asked, lids heavy as her hips undulated over his fingers.

"No, baby," he murmured. "My saliva will shield you from the pain. You ready?"

She purred in assent, her lithe body flushed and aroused. Sliding his finger to her clit, wet with her moisture, he began circling the enflamed nub as he aligned his fangs over her vein. Heart pounding in his chest, he sank his teeth into her tender nape.

Sofia cried his name, body arching as he growled against her. Blood flooded his mouth, thick and spicy, and he closed his eyes, overcome with pleasure. His sexy human writhed against him as he drank her essence, his need for her so intense he wondered if he would ever escape it. Although he couldn't read her thoughts from direct drinking as he could a Slayer's, her energy surrounded him, pure and clear. Heden felt her spirit, fiery and vibrant, and became drunk on the woman who'd consumed him.

Needing to connect with her in every possible way, he slid her over his thighs, aligning his shaft with her drenched opening. Holding her steady, he pushed into her from behind, sanity fleeing as the tight walls of her pussy squeezed him.

"Oh, god," she wailed, reaching behind to clutch his lower back as she searched for an anchor. "Yes, fuck me this way."

Listening to his woman, his hips jutted into her, spearing his shaft into her core, increasing the pace until he was drowning in ecstasy. Full with her lifeforce, he broke the connection with her neck and searched for her lips, moaning when she cemented them to his.

His tongue invaded her mouth, pumping in tandem with his cock as he hammered into her. Wanting to give her the immeasurable pleasure she was bestowing upon him, his fingers found her clit and flicked it mercilessly.

"Come all over me, baby," he growled against her mouth. "Fuck, this is so hot."

"You're so deep inside me...oh, *fuck*...I'm coming..."

Her body bowed, mouth open in a silent wail as she began to shudder atop his massive frame. Feeling her walls spasm around his shaft was mind-blowing, and he pumped into her, drawing out the pleasure until he was sure his balls would explode. Gritting his teeth, he buried his face in her neck and let go, releasing into her wet depths as she shattered against him.

They cried each other's names, quaking and raw, connected in the most primal way.

Heden slid his arms around her waist, drawing her close, craving every inch of her skin. Heaving large breaths into his lungs, he spurted the last drops of his release, unable to comprehend the intense pleasure. Making love to Sofia was his every dream come true. Passionate, intelligent, sexy...she was *everything,* and he was quickly becoming possessed by this waif of a human.

Wanting to heal her bite marks, he began licking the tiny wounds, reveling in her shiver as she sank further into him. The gesture shifted something in his heart, revealing a possessive streak he'd never felt before. By the goddess, he wanted to hold this woman forever and never let her go.

"You okay, honey?" he asked, making sure the wounds closed.

"So okay," she said, eyes closed as she smiled, head thrown back on his shoulder. "I'm never moving again. You were onto something with that. I just want you inside me forever."

The words sent a jolt of insane joy through his body. "Same," he murmured against her skin.

Sadly, reality crept in, and Heden's release began to seep down their thighs. Sighing, he placed a kiss on her temple and gently urged her to stand. Rising on wobbly feet, he strode to the table in the center of the room and grabbed the tissues. Trailing back to her, he crouched down and began wiping the evidence of their loving from her thighs.

She sifted her fingers through his hair, sending spikes of pleasure through his sated body, and he grinned up at her, humbled by the emotion swimming in her gorgeous eyes. For someone used to casual flings, he didn't normally experience deep connection with his lovers. But there was nothing casual about Sofia, and he understood she didn't often open herself to men. He was incredibly humbled by her trust and vowed to be worthy of it.

And, if he was honest, he was feeling some pretty intense affection toward her too. Casual was second nature to him, but it was impossible to feel that way toward Sofia. Although it had only been a short while, they were a match in so many ways. Perhaps that was why he felt so close to her even though it didn't make a ton of logical sense. Logic was rarely effective in matters of the heart, and Sofia had bewitched him with her adorable, stubborn personality and voracious intellect.

Tossing the tissues in the wastebasket, Heden stood and grabbed a few more to clean himself. Once finished, he pulled her close and rested his forehead against hers. "Want to take a shower with me before we show the program to the docs?"

Biting her lip, she nodded. "That sounds...functional. I'm in."

"Functional?" he scoffed. "I'll show you functional, woman." Bending his knees, he slipped his hands under her bottom and lifted her, loving how her legs encircled his waist almost by instinct. Placing a peck on her lips, he said, "This is going to be the best shower of your life."

Her dark brow arched. "Well, don't keep me waiting."

Heeding her words, he carried his naked human to his large bathroom, confident in his abilities to prove his statement true.

* * * *

Once dressed, they summoned Nolan and Sadie to the tech room to show them the program. After a brief tutorial, Sofia and Heden promised to help the physicians use the software over the coming weeks. The docs were extremely thankful, and Sadie gave them both a smothering hug before she and Nolan boarded the train home to Uteria.

Night settled in, and Sofia raided the kitchen, devouring the leftovers Glarys had stocked in the fridge. Heden sat with her, drinking Slayer blood as they recounted stories from their pasts. Afterward, Heden led her downstairs to his room, remarking that he wanted her to move her stuff in so she would have everything on hand. After a few minutes of protest, his little human conceded and stuffed her scant belongings in his vacant drawers.

They brushed their teeth side by side, Heden sensing her nervousness as she scraped the bristles over her teeth.

"What's wrong, Sof?" he asked, spitting in the sink. "Don't close up on me now. I just got you here."

She eyed him in the reflection. "It's just moving kind of fast, don't you think? Are we going to crash and burn?"

Finished with his dental ritual, he slid behind her and cupped her shoulders while she finished flossing. "Do you overthink everything, little human?"

She shrugged and leaned down to rinse. "Pretty much. Do you ever weigh the consequences of anything?"

Chuckling, he led her to bed, urging her out of her clothes so she could wrap her naked body around him. Clicking off the lamp, he held her close, loving how she snuggled into him. "I'll let you worry about everything for both of us. I'm a fan of doing what feels right in the moment. After all, you only get one shot at life. Might as well take full advantage."

"That's especially true for a human," she mumbled against his chest.

"Then that's all the more reason for you to relax and enjoy the moment, Sof. The way I look at it, I thoroughly enjoy spending time with you, and since our time is temporary, I want to do it as much as possible. Who cares about anything else?"

"I enjoy spending time with you too," she said, yawning. "You make me laugh. I didn't realize how much I needed that."

"I want to make you happy, sweetheart," he said, running his lips over her springy hair. "For whatever time we have. Don't analyze it to death, okay?"

"Okay," she murmured. "Do you want to have sex? I'm beat."

He breathed a laugh. "I'm not really into banging half-conscious chicks, but thanks. You're almost passed out. I'm fine just holding you, honey."

And he was. Heden, who enjoyed a good cuddle but made sure to extricate himself from romantic situations that were in any way profound, had essentially begged the human to move into his room. That in itself was a major departure from his normal behavior. Contemplating, he wondered why it didn't scare the shit out of him. After all, he'd always been so confident he didn't want a commitment and didn't do "serious."

But his thoughts on the matter had changed somewhat recently, and he'd slowly opened up to the possibility of more. Letting his thoughts wander, he imagined creating all the things he'd deemed too traditional with Sofia. A home of their own. Marriage. Children. Strangely, the idea of building those things with her didn't elicit any doubt or hesitation in his heart. Although they could never have those things together, he did find it encouraging that he was evolving. He'd have to make sure to tell Miranda so she'd stop making fun of him for being a serial dater. Maybe, after a thousand years, he was maturing after all.

"What are you laughing at?" Sofia whispered, her voice heavy with sleep.

"I think I'm excited at the possibility of adulting. Miranda's going to be thrilled."

She chuckled. "Welcome to the world of responsibility and accountability. Nice of you to stop by."

"If you live here, I'm never moving." He kissed her temple.

Marveling at his acceptance of something more, the wheels churned in his brain as his woman fell asleep in his arms.

Chapter 26

The newly cemented couple fell into a pattern, working together to program software that would improve the kingdom. Sofia absolutely adored Sadie and Nolan and enjoyed helping them with the new technology. Heden focused on improving the military communication devices, and after a week, he was ready to install the updated patches that would allow them to communicate through the ether.

Sofia also worked with Heden to create an electronic medical records system for Nolan and Sadie, so they could migrate away from paper charts. The EMRs were an extensive project, but with their combined skills, they plowed through it at a breakneck pace.

Three weeks into Sofia's stay at Astaria, her phone buzzed as she sat in the tech room writing code. Heden was at Takelia, doing a routine security system check at the Deamon prison with Kenden, and Sofia squinted at the unfamiliar number.

"Hey there," an upbeat voice chimed. "Not sure if Heden programmed my number, but it's Miranda. What are you doing right now?"

"I, um..." Sofia rubbed her neck, wondering what the Slayer queen needed. "I'm just working on the EMRs. Are you looking for Heden? He's at Takelia."

"Oh, I know, and he'll be occupied for several more hours. We're kidnapping you, Sofia. It's time we get to know the woman who's stolen our resident bachelor's heart."

"Kidnapping me?"

The door to the tech room swung open, and Sadie and Arderin burst in. "Yep. Arderin brought Callie for a checkup with Sadie, and she's here for the night. The kids are with the nannies, and we need a mom's night out. Also, we just want to grill you. Arderin and Sadie will walk you to the bar—it's not far from the castle. See you there soon."

The phone clicked, and Sofia stared at the two women who had huge smiles plastered over their faces. "Come on, Sofia," Arderin said. "We didn't get off on the right foot, but you've somehow smitten my immature-as-hell brother, and I'd like to set things right. Let's go."

Sofia sat back in her chair, wary. She wasn't really a spontaneous person and had absolutely nothing in common with these immortals. Her purpose in their world was clear, and she didn't want anything to detract from it. "I have a lot of work to do on the EMRs..." she said, hating how lame the excuse sounded.

"Nope," Arderin said, marching over and grabbing her wrist. "I'm pretty sure I can pick you up and carry you over my shoulder, although I'd rather not have to do that since I'm about a million months pregnant. It would be great if you just concede and accompany us willingly." She tugged Sofia's wrist.

"Please, Sofia," Sadie said in her sweet voice. "I can answer all your questions about my pregnancy, and we can have a few drinks. What you've created for us so far is amazing, and I think you deserve a few hours of fun."

Sofia's gaze trailed between them. "Will Evie be there?"

"Yes," Arderin said, giving her a compassionate smile. "You don't have to hang with her if it's too uncomfortable. She really wants to make things right, but I understand if you're not ready."

"I might never be ready," Sofia mumbled.

"And that's okay. But I will remind you that you staked out my house, contemplating my eventual murder, and I've completely let it go." Looking to the ceiling and pursing her lips, Arderin said, "Damn, I'm so evolved. It's pretty fucking awesome."

Sadie laughed and trailed over to Sofia. "Come on," she said, extending her stubbed hand.

Inhaling a breath, Sofia encircled the kind woman's hand, hoping she wasn't setting them all up for disaster. There were some pretty complex dynamics in their group, and a fallout wouldn't be pretty.

"Wow, Heden was right. You're a worrier. That's probably good because he hasn't worried about one damn thing in his life. Let's go, ladies. I hear a virgin daiquiri calling my name." Flipping her long hair over her shoulder, Arderin trailed from the room.

"This is probably a terrible idea," Sofia said.

Sadie shrugged. "Then let's get it over with."

Sighing, Sofia followed the immortals to the bar.

* * * *

Three hours later, Sofia was pleasantly surprised at how much she was enjoying herself. They sat at a high-top table munching appetizers as the server supplied them with endless rounds of beer, wine and virgin drinks for Arderin, Evie and Moira, who'd informed them earlier she was pregnant, followed by a round of raucous cheers. Sofia figured the restaurant wanted to take exceptional care of the queen and her family, so the doting service made sense.

Flanked by Sadie and Lila, Sofia enjoyed getting to know them as they told stories of how they each fell in love with their husbands. Miranda and Arderin sat across from her, Moira and Evie at opposite ends of the long wooden slab. So far, Evie had been pleasant and unassuming, and Sofia wasn't as uncomfortable around her as she'd anticipated. Perhaps it was due to the red wine, which Miranda kept surreptitiously pouring into her glass each time it was low.

"Are you trying to get me drunk, Miranda?" Sofia asked, hiccupping.

Laughing, Miranda nodded. "Oh, hell yes. We want you to spill the beans, Sofia. How in the hell did you get Heden to commit to spending two months with you? I'm used to him running away from most women after two hours."

"I don't know," she said, shrugging. "I told him I wasn't interested and to leave me the hell alone, but I think he just saw it as a challenge or something."

"Brilliant," Miranda said, lifting her glass in the air. "I get so excited when our men are thrown off-balance. Great job, human. Cheers!" They clinked their glasses, sharing smiles as they sipped.

"I mean, it won't last forever. I eventually have to go back to the human world, and I also want to have kids. I'm not getting any younger. But for now, I'm really happy. He says I worry too much and need to live in the moment, so that's what I'm focused on doing."

"Good for you," Arderin said. "And you never know how things will work out. Every one of us was sure we'd never find a mate, and we're all stuck with one for better or worse at this point."

Evie rolled her eyes. "True story."

"Come on, sis," Miranda said. "You love Ken so much. You're not fooling anyone."

"I have to maintain my nefarious reputation, Miranda. Chill." Munching a fry, she winked at her half-sister.

"Have you considered artificial insemination with Heden?" Sadie asked. "It was a perfect option for me and Nolan."

"Yes, but Nolan is immortal, and I'm not. I wouldn't want to sign Heden up for having kids with me and watching all of us eventually grow old and die while he lives on. That's way too heavy to contemplate. And our relationship is still so new anyway. I'm sure he'll get tired of me eventually. We'll both move on, and I'll live out my days in the human world."

"Well, I know my brother, and he's never conveyed interest for a female on a level remotely close to what he expresses for you. Watch out, human. I'm not sure he's going to let you go so easily." Arderin reached over and grabbed a fry from Evie's plate, grinning at her sister-in-law's scowl.

"So, let's get to the topic we all really want to discuss," Miranda said, placing her palms on the table. "How's the sex? Is it incredible?"

Arderin plugged her fingers into her ears. "Gross," she said, eyes squeezed shut.

"It's so damn good," Sofia said, sighing like the lovesick sap she'd convinced herself she'd never become. "It's always been hard for me to open up with men, but I'm so comfortable with him. It's strange and awesome, all at the same time."

"Damn straight," Miranda said. "Our boy's doing you right. Well done, Heden."

They shared a companionable laugh and settled into conversation, Sofia reminding herself to take it easy on the wine. Finally, after several hours, Darkrip materialized at Arderin's side.

"Not to be a downer, ladies, but my wife made me promise I'd show up here if she wasn't home by eleven. You ready, princess?"

"Yes," Arderin said, her lips forming a pout. "Although, I was having so much fun. We have to do this again, ladies."

"Absolutely," Miranda said, gesturing to the server for the bill. "Sofia, I think I speak for the group when I say you're really cool, and we're in awe you accomplished what so many others couldn't. You've turned Heden into an adult. We all owe you a debt of gratitude."

Drunk from the multiple glasses of cabernet, Sofia giggled. "Thanks, guys. I really like you too. Thanks so much for dragging me out tonight. I think I really needed it."

"Anytime."

They all hugged goodbye, and Arderin disappeared with Darkrip. Evie offered to transport everyone else home and whisked them away one by one before reappearing again. Finally, Sofia was left alone in the empty bar with the woman who'd murdered her grandfather.

"I can walk to the castle," Sofia said, kicking the wooden floor with her sandaled toe. "It's not that far, and we walked here."

Evie's green eyes traveled over her face. "Can we sit for a second?"

"Sure." Sofia slid onto the stool as Evie did the same.

Evie spoke, her tone contrite and thoughtful. "I was trying to think of something I could give you, since I took so much from you."

Sofia squirmed, feeling uncomfortable. "Evie—"

"Wait," she said, holding up a hand. "I know this is awkward, but I'd like to finish if you'll hear me out."

"Okay."

Her gaze fell to her lap. "I can't change the past. I'm pretty damn powerful, but even the daughter of the evil Deamon king has her limits." Lips forming a repentant smile, she shrugged. "But I did spend some wonderful years with Francesco when he was young, and I have so many stories from our time together. I'd like to share them with you, to help you remember him and maybe get to know a side of him you never experienced. If and when you're ready. I know you might never be, but I wanted to at least offer."

Sofia studied this woman whose past was comprised of such terrible deeds but who also seemed to have genuinely turned over a new leaf.

"I know," Evie said, rolling her eyes. "It's almost too good to be true. Sometimes, I wake up in a cold sweat and think I'm right back in the Deamon caves and that bastard is torturing me and my mother. Other times, I get lost in nightmares where I'm murdering someone who hurt me, usually a man, and I'm reveling in the pleasure. It's hard to comprehend that I've changed—certainly for you, but even more for me. Ken is my rock, and I couldn't do it without his love. It...*shifted* something in me. I know that sounds corny, but it's the only explanation I have, so I'm going with it."

"How long did Crimeous torture you?" Sofia asked softly.

Evie's gaze was clear and strong. "Several centuries, until I realized I needed to seize control and power for myself. I did it through the only methods I understood. It took a hundred lifetimes for me to learn another way. Francesco saw a glimmer of goodness in me, and it broke me until I snapped. My final action toward him was reprehensible and uncharacteristic of the time we shared together, but it also was the catalyst that set me down this new path. That probably sounds ridiculous to you, but it's true."

"He used to talk about you all the time," Sofia said, the sting of emotion causing a rasp in her voice.

"Yeah? That's nice to hear. I cared about him very much. So much that when he pushed me to be better, I wanted so badly to listen, but I wasn't ready, and he paid dearly for that."

"How bad was his cancer? I wish I could've helped him."

"I know," Evie said, nodding as compassion washed over her stunning features. "He was riddled with the disease in several of his major organs. I knew that if you found out, you'd traipse him all over the world to find a cure. I honestly wasn't sure he'd want that, so I convinced myself there was a humaneness in my actions."

"You knew about me?"

"Of course. I kept up with Francesco over the years and would observe you two together. Your love for him is so pure. It's really beautiful, Sofia. He's the only person you've ever loved in your entire life besides your parents. Maybe you're on your way with Heden. It would be great for you to experience that. Take it from me, love is pretty damn powerful."

Sofia's fingers fidgeted atop her thighs. "We don't have a future, so I hope I don't fall in love with him. I'm not really in the market for a broken heart."

"Unfortunately, broken hearts usually find someone when they least expect it. Regardless, it's nice to see you happy. I'm so sorry I caused you so much pain. My offer stands, and you can redeem it anytime you're ready. Just let me know."

"Okay," Sofia said, standing and stifling a yawn. "Thank you, Evie."

"Let me transport you. You're buzzed, and it's dark as hell outside. Heden would kill me if I let you walk home alone."

"All right."

Evie instructed her to slide her arms around her neck, and in a moment, they were outside Heden's closed bedroom door. "Give him hell, Sofia. Goodnight." Closing her eyes, she vanished.

Heden swung open the door, fangs glistening in the nearby lamplight as he smiled. "Did you have fun, honey?"

Biting her lip, Sofia nodded. "I actually did. Everyone is so cool. How did the prison security systems check out?"

Encircling her wrist, he drew her into the room and closed the door behind them. "Do you think for one moment that I'm going to talk about prison security systems with you when you've just appeared at my door tipsy and adorable as hell?"

Chuckling, she glided her palms up his chest and linked her hands behind his neck. "Did you want to discuss something else?"

Growling, he lifted her and devoured her mouth. Carrying her to the bed, he sprawled them over the green comforter. Smiling down at her, he waggled his eyebrows.

"What I have in mind doesn't require talking."

Overcome with emotion and desire for her handsome Vampyre, she let him show her that his mouth was quite useful, and it was indeed occupied with many other activities besides talking for the next several hours.

* * * *

Bakari entered the lobby of the office building and showed his credentials to the night guard. Verifying his false name on the visitor list, the guard gave him a pass and instructed him to head to the back warehouse. Black shoes clicked on the cold floor as he walked under the fluorescent lights. Arriving at a metal door, he rang the bell.

Several moments later, a man in a white lab coat pulled the door open. "Hello, Bakari. Right on time as usual."

"Hello, Dr. Tyson."

Waving him through the door, he asked, "The guard didn't give you any trouble?"

"No," Bakari said, following him into the warehouse. "I was on the list as you instructed. My car is parked at the loading dock."

"Perfect. The last two canisters are ready for transport. This batch is particularly potent. It's an extremely rare combination. Finding an antidote would require extensive cataloguing by a very advanced software program."

"Two of my enemies are expert hackers, but hopefully, the different combinations will overwhelm any analytic software they create. I appreciate your attention to detail."

"You have my payment?"

"Yes." Reaching in his pocket, Bakari pulled out the vial of Crimeous's cloned blood.

"Excellent," Dr. Tyson said, holding it up to inspect it against the stark ceiling light. "There are so many formulas I can create with this."

"Should I even ask what you have in mind?"

"That wasn't our deal, Bakari, and besides, you'll know soon enough. After all, you weren't the only immortal raised in the human world." Dr. Tyson's incisors glistened behind his slightly sinister smile, relaying the Vampyre portion of his heritage.

"I'll leave you to it then. I wish you the best, Quaygon."

"Dr. Tyson is fine," he murmured. "Can't have anyone overhearing my immortal name."

"Thank you, Dr. Tyson."

They shook hands, the chemist instructing several of the warehouse employees to help Bakari load his car.

Once the containers were loaded, Bakari left the St. Louis warehouse, wondering when he would see Dr. Tyson again. Bakari would most likely need his help to assume his rightful place as sovereign over Etherya's realm. For now, he was content to let Dr. Tyson stew in the human world, which was insignificant—but if he chose to enter the immortal world without Bakari's permission, there would be consequences.

Quaygon, son of Letheria, was a hybrid and therefore an abomination. If he knew what was good for him, he'd live out the rest of his days with the heathen humans. Otherwise, he was doomed.

Chapter 27

Latimus and Kenden worked around the clock to secure the realm while Heden and Sofia completed their tasks. The royal family worried the Secret Society would launch a surprise attack, most likely by poisoning or attempting to spring the prisoners from the Deamon prison at Takelia, but so far, things had been relatively quiet. Besides the chemicals found in Adelyn's lunchboxes and Aron's garden, nothing else had been uncovered.

A week after her ladies' night out, Sofia was in Heden's bathroom securing her hair into a bun when she heard him enter the bedroom. Giving her reflection one last check, she headed to greet him.

"Hey, sweetheart," he said, bending down and giving her a gentle kiss. "You ready for dinner?"

"Yep," she said, excited for the meal she'd prepared. She'd come downstairs half an hour earlier, while the sauce simmered, to quickly shower and tame her hair. "I hope everyone likes Grandfather's sauce."

"They're going to love it," he said, gliding his hand over her shoulder. "You look pretty."

"Thank you," she said softly, humbled he was attracted to her even though she wasn't one of those women who gobbed makeup all over their face. Heden seemed to genuinely think she was beautiful, and it softened something inside her austere heart. "You know, if we were a couple in the human world, people would think I was your sugar mama."

"How so?"

"Because I'm years older than you—in appearance anyway. How old were you when you went through your change?"

"Twenty-eight," he said, grinning. "Yeah, I was going to buy you some Depends pretty soon. You're ancient."

She whacked his chest. "Don't give me a complex. I'm already worried you're going to wake up one day and think I look like Betty White."

"Dude, Betty is hot. All the Golden Girls are. Blanche? Man, I'd be all over that in a second."

Sofia snickered. "I bet you would. She was pretty feisty."

Inching closer, he gently traced the skin of her face. "I think you're gorgeous, Sof. I look at these tiny lines," he said, rubbing the tender skin at the edge of her

150

eye, "and I know they were formed by each laugh you had in your past. I hope I contributed at least partly to forming them. It's a small mark to remind you of our time together."

"Wow," she said, basking in his praise. "I've never heard wrinkles described so eloquently."

Fangs flashed as he grinned. "I adore every part of you, even the wrinkles, although you can barely see them. I get a close-up view because I get to kiss you every day."

Heart pounding from his words, she stepped toward him and placed her palms on his pecs. "Every day for another month. I can't believe I've already been here four weeks."

A slight sadness pervaded his expression. "Me neither. It feels like longer."

"Does that mean you're ready to get rid of me?"

"That's something I can't even joke about, Sof. Not even if I wanted to. I'm not ready to think about you leaving me."

It was a discussion they needed to have, but they had a few weeks to let it simmer. Thankful for the reprieve, she slid her arms around his neck. "But I'm here now."

"Thank the goddess." Leaning down, he enveloped her in a smothering kiss. Afterward, he stared deeply into her eyes...into her *soul*. "Let's get this dinner over with so I can seduce you. I'm determined to make you addicted to my body so you can't ever leave."

"Does it work that way?" she teased, squinting at the ceiling.

"I sure fucking hope so. Come on." Sliding his palm over hers, he led her up the stairs and to the kitchen.

Sofia worked with Glarys to prepare the noodles and garlic bread while the sauce simmered. Tasting it, Sofia closed her eyes in ecstasy. It was perfect.

She and Glarys carried everything into the large dining room. The family was settling around the table: Latimus, Lila and their three children; Miranda, Sathan and Tordor; Evie and Kenden. Once everyone was seated, Sathan said a prayer to Etherya, asking her to watch over Arderin, Darkrip and Callie in the human world. Acknowledging Sofia, he also mentioned her Catholic god in his prayer, the inclusion of her beliefs making her feel so accepted.

Everyone dug in—even Heden, who announced he was going to try the sauce even though he wasn't a fan of human food. Sofia watched him out of the corner of her eye, wanting so badly for him to enjoy it.

"This is amazing, Sofia," Jack said. "Holy crap. I might eat the whole pot."

"Thank you, Jack," she said, feeling her cheeks warm. "I'm glad you like it."

"It's really good, honey," Heden said, squeezing her hand after he swallowed his first bite. "Thick and flavorful. I'm impressed. You might make me a food lover after all."

Thrilled he liked it along with everyone else, the dinner went on with lots of laughter and wine. Once Glarys served dessert and the kids left the table to play in the sitting room, the mood grew a bit more solemn.

"How were the rounds today, guys?" Miranda asked Kenden and Latimus. "Anything we should be concerned about?"

"It's strange," Kenden said, shaking his head as he toyed with his coffee mug. "There are four people plotting to attack us, but they haven't yet. Of course, the Secret Society knows we've beefed up security, but they also have extraordinary powers. I'm wondering why they're waiting."

"Do you think we should consider bringing Melania in for questioning?" Miranda asked.

"Lila has a soft spot for Camron and doesn't want to call attention to Melania's previous dealings unless completely necessary," Latimus said, squeezing Lila's shoulder.

"I know you all probably think it's weak," Lila said, compassion in her stunning features, "but it will break Camron's heart if he discovers her treachery. As we've discussed, it seems she's defected from the Secret Society. Her whereabouts over the past few weeks has been transparent and conspicuous. It's as if she's sending us a message she's no longer plotting against us. I don't want to out her if that's the case."

"Isn't Camron the one who treated you like shit after my father maimed you?" Evie asked.

"Yes, but we made amends, and I don't want to hold a grudge. He's one of my oldest friends, and I'd like to shield him from any pain if I can. Of course, if you think you need to question her, I trust you." She smiled at Latimus. "But I can't imagine she possesses any more knowledge than we already have."

Evie arched a brow. "One day, I need you teach me how to be a saint, Lila. Good lord. It's vomit-inducing."

Lila bit her lip, her fangs squishing the soft flesh. "Thank you?" she said, her tone teasing and hesitant.

"Okay, stop torturing Lila," Miranda said. "Moving on from Melania, where are we with the four remaining members of the society?"

"They're impossible to trace since they have the ability to dematerialize," Kenden said. "The best we can do now is to monitor every inch of the kingdom and ensure the troops are alert. I wish I had a better plan, Miranda. It's hard to fight an enemy who's waiting in the wings to attack. Latimus and I would love to take the offensive, but it's been impossible to capture any of the society members so far."

"You both are doing a great job," Sathan said. "The enhanced security at the compounds, the kids' schools and the Deamon prison is phenomenal. So far, we've thwarted any catastrophes. We'll continue to do our best and stay alert."

"Sadie and Nolan have created several antidotes from the data they've analyzed through our program," Sofia chimed in. "If there is a chemical attack, I'm confident we've identified the chemical combinations they're most likely to use."

"Good," Sathan said. "You two created that program in record time. How are the EMRs coming?"

"That's a much more extensive project," Heden said. "We anticipate being done with it in about three weeks, give or take."

"Perfect timing. I know you're with us for another month, Sofia. We appreciate you helping Heden bring our realm into the twenty-first century."

"And thanks for the amazing pasta," Miranda said, lifting her glass. "I'm going to have seconds, so don't you all even think of making fun of me."

They toasted Sofia as Heden gave her a wet smack on the cheek.

"Thank you all for having me at your family dinner. I still feel terrible I aligned with Bakari in the beginning. It means a lot that you can forgive me."

"You've more than made up for your past transgressions, Sofia," Sathan said, "and we really like who Heden is around you. Hopefully, you'll come visit us after your two months are up. We need you to keep him in check."

"They love me," Heden said, rolling his eyes. "Don't listen to a word my idiot brother says."

They settled into their post-meal food comas, the night eventually winding down as everyone started to head home. Sofia helped Glarys clean the kitchen before Heden led her downstairs. They played video games for a while in the tech room, Sofia loving every minute of their competitive jibing, until they could no longer stifle their yawns. Once they were in bed, she slid over him in the darkness.

"Push into me," she whispered, straddling him as she sprawled atop his body.

Grasping her hips, he inched his shaft into her wet sheath. Anchored on her outstretched arms, she stared into his eyes, so clear even though the room was dark.

"How am I going to let you go?" he whispered, breath heavy as he undulated into her.

"Don't," she said, lowering her lips to his. "Let's pretend a few weeks longer."

"That's the problem, sweetheart," he murmured against her lips. "I'm not pretending."

Sentiment swelled in her chest. "Neither am I."

His broad hand fisted in her hair, cementing her lips to his. Their tongues collided, wet and silky, as they loved each other. As she moved atop his trembling body, she rubbed her sensitive nub against the base of his shaft, bursts of pleasure igniting throughout her body as he filled her. Succumbing to desire and emotion, she exploded, writhing over his large frame as he cried her name.

After they were spent, she lay against his cooling skin, tears prickling her eyes. Thankful for the shadow of night, she willed them away, not wanting him to see. Crying had no place in their predicament and would only make their separation harder. Twirling the coarse hairs of his chest under her fingers, she memorized the texture...counted the cadence of his breaths...inhaled the musky scent of his skin...

Once she was alone in the human world and decades without him stretched before her, she would recall these memories and hope they brought her peace.

Chapter 28

Sofia was in the tech room two weeks later, programming one of the modules on the EMR, when Latimus stormed in.

"I can't believe I'm going to say this but I need your help, human."

Sofia turned in her chair, wondering how in the world she could help the colossal soldier. "Sure. What's up?"

"One of our soldiers' weapons discharged when he was putting it back in the barracks, and it tripped the security system. Heden won't be home from Uteria for another hour, and I can't turn the damn alarm off."

"Yikes," she said, rising. "I'm not familiar with the system but should probably be able to figure it out. Lead the way."

She followed Latimus up the stairs, through the foyer and down a long hallway before he turned a sharp left instead of heading to the barracks.

"Isn't it through there?"

"This way," he commanded with his deep baritone.

Pushing open two wooden doors, Sofia followed him into a large, dark room.

Suddenly, the lights illuminated, and several people yelled, "Surprise!"

Sofia froze, not understanding what the hell was going on. Eyes searching the room, she located Heden standing on a platform in the corner that looked to be a DJ booth. He gave her a wave and a goofy grin.

"Am I being punked?" Sofia asked.

"Welcome to your belated birthday party, Sofia," Miranda said, walking toward her. "We love to throw a party around here, and things have been really tense, so when Heden told us your birthday was a few weeks ago, we thought we'd throw you a bash."

Stunned, Sofia looked at the faces of the royal family as they smiled back. Guilt flooded her that people she'd put in so much danger would go out of their way to celebrate her. "Wow. This is really nice, guys, but I don't need a party. I told Heden I don't really celebrate my birthday."

"Which is all the more reason why you should," Lila said, walking over and drawing her into a warm embrace. Whispering in her ear, she said, "I know you've been alone for your past several birthdays since your grandfather passed. Let us celebrate you."

Sentiment flooded her. "You all do understand I'm ancient for a human, right?" She smiled up a Lila and looked around the room for confirmation.

"Your whole life is ahead of you, Sof," Heden said from the DJ booth, his voice amplified by the microphone attached to the headphones he wore over one ear. "Plus, you get to hear my awesome DJ skills. I'll play the Jonas Brothers if you're lucky. Let's get this party started, people!" Spinning the record with his thick arm, music began to blare from the speakers, and the lights in the room dimmed.

"He's the self-proclaimed best DJ in the immortal world," Miranda said over the music, affectionately rolling her eyes. "Most of the time, we can't get him to stop once he gets going. He won't admit this to you, but he's so freaking excited to show you his 'skills.'" She made quotation marks with her fingers. "It's the same excitement I see in Tordor's eyes when he plays me a new song on the piano. He wants to impress you, Sofia. It's so cute."

Sofia bit her lip. "It is pretty cute."

"Come on," Lila said, drawing her onto the dance floor. "Adelyn loves this song."

Letting her hesitation go, Sofia relaxed and began dancing with Lila, Adelyn, Miranda and Tordor. She thought the children so cute as they jumped and moved to the music. Glancing at the wall, she noticed Latimus standing, arms crossed as he chatted with Sathan.

"Your husbands don't dance?"

"Sathan will dance slow ones with me. He's actually a great dancer. But Latimus is an old fuddy-duddy."

"I can usually coax him onto the dance floor if I promise him favors in return," Lila said. "You know, like giving the kids a bath when it's supposed to be his night. Things like that."

"Bullshit, Lila," Miranda said, laughing. "We know *exactly* what kind of favors you offer him. She's too proper to say it out loud."

Even under the strobe lights, Sofia noticed her blush. "A lady never tells."

Thoroughly enjoying the exchange, Sofia glanced toward the DJ booth. Heden was in his element, bumping along to the beat as he held one earphone to his ear. Gaze lifting to hers, he winked, causing her knees to quake. Holy hell. He was so fucking gorgeous. Sometimes, it baffled her that he even spoke to her, much less wanted her.

"Uh-oh," Miranda said. "Sofia's drooling. Heden's going to be thrilled."

"Sorry, but he's hot," Sofia said, shrugging as she danced. "The hottest guy I've ever been with."

"Keep it in your pants, Morelli," Miranda teased. "There are children around."

They danced for an hour, taking breaks in between to grab drinks and attempt to pull the reluctant dancers onto the floor. After some serious pleading, Miranda was able to get Heden to turn up the lights and step away from the DJ booth so they could sing Sofia "Happy Birthday" and eat the cake.

Sitting at the long folding table on the side of the room, Sofia ingested the most amazing cake of her life, courtesy of Glarys. She'd finished her work in the kitchen and was now seated with them at the table, the close-knit family lost in conversation, teasing and good cheer.

"Evie wanted to come but she wasn't feeling so hot," Miranda said, sitting to her left. "She said you guys had a nice talk though."

Sofia nodded, swallowing the last bite of the scrumptious cake. "I hated her for so long and might never be able to forgive her, but the hate has dissipated into a dull ache. I don't want to despise her. My religion teaches forgiveness and atonement. But it's so hard because she took someone away from me whom I loved very much."

"I know," Miranda said, squeezing her hand. "It's such a fucked-up situation. Welcome to our family, Sofia. When I first met Evie, she instigated some things that caused me to lose my first child when I was several weeks pregnant."

"Oh, Miranda," Sofia said, feeling her heart splinter in her chest. "I'm so sorry."

"Me too. It was devastating. But I agree with forgiveness and atonement too. I can't even imagine the level of torture Evie experienced in her early life. I truly believe, if she'd learned another way, her Slayer side would've shown through. Sadly, it took her a really long time to figure it out."

"I'm trying, Miranda. I really am. I don't have time to live with hate in my heart. I want to have my own child—or children, if I'm lucky—and there's no place for lingering animosity in the next chapter of my life."

"Have you and Heden spoken about what will happen when your two months is over?"

Sofia sighed, surreptitiously glancing at Heden where he sat a few seats away, chatting with Lila. "I have to make a clean break after we part. I've thought about it a lot. Maintaining a connection with him will be too hard and will make me want things I can't have. It will prevent us both from moving on and having a full life."

"Is he on board with that?"

Sofia chewed her bottom lip. "I know he's into casual, so I honestly have no idea how he sees this thing with me. He'll probably be ready for some space once I head back home."

"I'm not so sure," Miranda murmured. "I think he's pretty crazy about you, Sofia."

"It hasn't been that long. He has centuries to find someone else."

"An eternity does him no good if he's already found his soulmate."

Sofia wrinkled her nose. "You believe in that stuff?"

Miranda arched a brow. "I didn't until I met Sathan. I think I fell in love with him when he knocked me unconscious with the butt of his knife."

"Sounds romantic," Sofia said, snickering.

"Right? So fucking weird, but there you have it. My feelings for him were pretty much there from the beginning. I think when you know, you just know. I'm not really sure length of time matters when there's a powerful connection."

Sofia pondered her words, wondering how Heden saw their relationship deep down. From her perspective, there was no doubt: it was the most intense of her life. Sure, she'd dated a few men for a year or two, but that was before she began her quest for vengeance, and she hadn't felt one tenth the desire she felt for Heden. But more than the sexual connection, which was incredible, she enjoyed their banter and similar interests.

His intelligence didn't hurt either. Although she teased him about being a terrible hacker, he was magnificent with everything tech. An impressive feat since he lived in a world where computers were still anomalies. The fact he'd taught himself to be so proficient and that he used those skills to protect his people was exceedingly admirable.

There was something else that tethered them together too. A shared understanding of what it felt like to be alone even when surrounded by others. Heden's stories of how he sometimes felt like an outsider even though he and his siblings loved each other deeply resonated with Sofia. They'd both learned to function as independent, sometimes isolated beings in a world where others didn't quite understand them.

Heden would occasionally tell her of his frustration at being misunderstood by his family. Although his demeanor was jovial, he took the safety and security of the realm seriously and strove to support his family. His siblings, who were all more serious and stoic, didn't understand he'd developed his own way to cope with the world; his own path to functioning the best way he knew how. Sofia had expended the same effort, attempting to live in a world where she just didn't *fit* sometimes. In a way, they both coped with their aloofness and disconnectedness similarly, and she felt that led to a deep, unspoken understanding between them.

He must've noticed her watching him because his gaze drifted to hers, and he gave her a toe-curling grin. Narrowing his eyes, he mouthed, "I want you," and she shuddered. Would she ever feel arousal this consuming for another man? It was unlikely. Their chemistry was undeniable.

The party wound down, Lila and Latimus gathering the children to head home while everyone dispersed. Once they were alone, Heden tugged her toward the empty dance floor.

"Stay here," he said, rushing to the DJ booth and dimming the lights. He pushed some buttons on the console and stalked back over to her. Pulling her into his arms, she laughed when she heard the song.

"'When You Look Me in the Eyes,'" she said, unable to contain her smile. "It's one of my favorite Jo Bros songs."

"I'm not a huge fan, but it's pretty catchy." Sliding his arms around her waist, he held her until there was no space between them. Encircling his neck, she laid her head on his chest. They swayed, his firm heartbeat under her ear, and Sofia began to feel the slide. Into heaven. Into happiness. Into love.

Regardless of whether it made sense or not, she was falling in love with this Vampyre she had no future with. The result of the deep emotion would leave her brokenhearted and shattered, but in this moment, aligned with his strong body, she just couldn't bring herself to give a damn. There would be time for heartache and tears later. For now, she just wanted to enjoy the overwhelming feeling.

When the song ended, Heden turned off the equipment, and they headed downstairs. Beside his bed, he kissed her, slowly removing their clothes until their burning skin was exposed. Lying on his back, he dragged her over his body so she straddled his broad shoulders, facing the foot of the bed. Drawing her core to his lips, he began making love to her with his tongue.

Sofia purred, stretching out over his frame, sliding down to grasp his shaft. Drunk from the sensation of his ardent tongue upon her sensitive folds, she took him in her mouth, hoping to give him even half the intense pleasure he was bestowing upon her.

"Yeah, honey," he moaned, flicking her engorged clit with his tongue. "That feels amazing."

Sucking his thick shaft, her hand worked in tandem on the base as her lips milked him. Reveling in his tremors beneath her, she opened her legs wider, spreading herself so he could spear her with his tongue.

Their groans became frantic, and Sofia cupped the sack below his cock, his hips undulating in response. "I'm so close, honey. Pull away if you don't want me to come in your mouth."

Not on your fucking life, she thought, increasing the pace of her hand as she hollowed out her cheeks, creating suction.

He growled her name and placed his fingers on her clit, rubbing furiously as he licked her sweet juices.

The orgasm blinded her, causing her to splinter atop his body as he buried his face in her core. Moments later, he exploded in her mouth, his release pulsing against the back of her throat as her lips drained it from his straining shaft. Swallowing, she collapsed over his body, cheek resting on his thigh as she struggled to breathe normally.

"Good grief, Sofia," he murmured into her slick folds, causing her body to quake. "That was insane. I could drink every drop of you."

"Mmmm..." she purred against his skin. "So good."

Chuckling, he softly caressed her bottom as they floated back to Earth. Content to lay there forever, Sofia uttered a frustrated grunt when he shifted and contorted her body in his arms.

"I need to brush my teeth," she mumbled against his chest, wriggling into him.

"In the morning," he murmured, hand trailing over her back. "Can't move."

"You're my favorite body pillow," she said, unable to keep her eyes open.

"You're my favorite everything, Sof."

Sofia clutched onto the poignant words as sleep hauled her to the other side of consciousness.

Chapter 29

With one week left in the immortal world, Sofia felt the looming departure settle in her bones as she tried to stay upbeat. After all, there would be so many years to mourn the loss of her Vampyre lover, and she wanted to enjoy the time they had left together.

Heden had texted her earlier, the missive causing her to snicker as his texts usually did.

Heden: Surprise date tonight. Will pick you up at six p.m. outside Chez Heden (aka, my room, duh!). Wear comfy shoes, not because we're going to bang (I mean, obviously we'll do that later) but because we're going to walk a bit. And maybe wear a dress if you brought one. Will make said banging easier later. Mwah.

Biting her lip to contain her smile, she texted him back that she would be ready.

She'd brought exactly one dress, dark blue and flowing above her knees. It was comfortable and paired perfectly with her sandals, which were extremely comfortable. She even applied some makeup from the one scant palette she'd brought. Eye shadow and mascara, but it was something. This would most likely be their last private date, as they would spend Sofia's last week in the realm teaching Nolan and Sadie how to use the EMRs—an extensive task since neither was very tech-savvy.

A knock sounded on the door, and Heden walked in, his eyes lighting up when he saw her.

"Hey," she said, sliding her earring through the tiny hole in her ear. "You look nice." He was wearing a collared button-down shirt instead of his normal t-shirt, along with jeans, a black belt and loafers.

"Yeah, I took it up a notch when I woke up early this morning and got ready before heading to Takelia. How did the programming go today?"

"Amazing. I tested everything, and the EMRs are ready. We'll roll it out to Sadie and Nolan next week."

"Can't wait," he said, encircling her wrist and tugging her close. "Did you put on makeup?"

"Yeah," she said, suddenly feeling like an idiot. "Does it look bad?"

The corner of his lip turned up as he slowly shook his head. "It looks awesome. Sometimes, I look at you, Sof..." The words trailed off as he brushed a tendril of hair behind her ear. "You're just so pretty. I'm really honored to be with you."

Tears stung her eyes as a flush of desire flooded her core. "Thank you," she whispered, swallowing thickly. She would've liked to say more, but her throat was suddenly choked with emotion.

"Ready to go?"

Smiling, she nodded. "Where are you taking me?"

He arched a brow. "What part of 'surprise' didn't you understand when I texted you earlier? Come on, woman. Let's go."

Sliding her palm over his, she squeezed for dear life as he led her from the room.

* * * *

Sofia's hair whipped in the wind as Heden drove them from Astaria, across the open fields for several miles until they entered a clearing. Pulling up to a sprawling home with a red-tiled roof, he helped her from the four-wheeler, and they approached the front door.

"Hello, Prince Heden," a man said, opening the door. He had white hair and sparkling light green eyes. "You are right on time."

"What's up, Genarro?" Heden asked, shaking his hand. "And seriously, chill with the 'Prince' stuff. I think you're the only one in the kingdom who calls me that."

"I have reverence for your family," Genarro said, bowing gracefully. "I would never disparage your title."

"If it impresses the lady, I'm fine with it." Glancing down at Sofia, he muttered, "Are you impressed?"

She giggled. "Sure. I'm always impressed with *Prince Heden*."

"Oh, brother," he said, rolling his eyes. "Something else she can tease me about. Great." Grinning, he asked, "Is everything ready, Genarro?"

"Yes, your highness. This way."

Genarro led them through the house until they came to a sprawling back patio. Gasping, Sofia walked toward the balcony's edge, eyes wide as she gazed over the sloping hills. "It's a vineyard," she whispered.

"I thought it might be similar to the one your grandfather owned."

Sofia inhaled the vibrant air, overcome with the songs of the birds and aromas of something so familiar to home. "It's magnificent." Staring up at him, she basked in his thoughtfulness. "Thank you."

"Come on," he said, extending his hand. "Let's explore."

They strode down the stone stairs from the balcony, Sofia's sandals landing on the soft ground. Navigating the vines at a slow, reverent pace, she explained to him the inner workings of being a vintner, which she'd learned from Francesco all those years ago. She'd spent so much time with him between the vines, learning and laughing, and the memories flooded her as they strolled. Plucking one of the grapes from the stem, she placed it on her tongue, flavor saturating her taste buds as she chewed.

"Let me taste," Heden said, waggling his eyebrows as he touched his lips to hers. Swirling his tongue in her mouth, he groaned, her knees buckling at the primal sound. "Mmmm... Tastes so good."

Sofia beamed, swallowing the tart fruit. "I think you ate more of me than the grape."

"Now you're catching on," he said, winking.

Hand in his, they trailed to the end of the vines, and Sofia noticed the table set for two under the setting sun.

"Wow," she said, almost in awe of the romantic setting. "You really went all-out."

Turning to face her, he cupped her cheek. "You're leaving me in a week, unless you want to stay longer..." The words trailed off, and Sofia remained silent, heart pounding in her chest, not wanting to sully the beautiful moment with hard discussions and melancholy realities. "Well, anyway," he continued, shrugging, "I figured you deserved a romantic dinner. You haven't strangled me yet, so I figured you kind of liked me."

"You're okay."

Fangs glistened as he flashed her a gorgeous smile. Pulling out a chair, he gestured for her to sit and then took his place across from her.

A brown-haired woman appeared, bottle in hand. "Would you like to taste, Ms. Sofia?"

"This is Genarro's daughter. She married a Slayer a few years ago and loves to cook for him. Tonight, I've hired her to cook for us." Lifting his gaze, he said, "Luciana, your husband tells me you're a natural chef. Pretty impressive for a Vampyre."

"I love it," she said, lowering the wine to Sofia's glass, a question in her expression. Sofia nodded, and Luciana poured her a taste.

Swirling the red liquid, Sofia took a sip, eyes closing in ecstasy. "It's fantastic. A blend of...let me see..." Taking another sip, Sofia said, "Cabernet Franc, Merlot and Montepulciano?"

"Yes," Luciana said, eyebrows lifting in wonder. "That's impressive."

"I love wine," Sofia said. "It's excellent. I'll take a glass, thank you."

Luciana poured them both a glass and scuttled away, telling them she'd return with a salad and the main course after sunset.

Reaching over, Heden offered his hand, and Sofia slipped hers into his warm grasp, contentment filling her every pore.

"Are you happy?" he asked, his thumb moving back and forth across the smooth skin of her hand, the caress mesmerizing.

"So happy," she said, voice gravelly from emotion. "This brings back so many memories of Grandfather. Thank you, Heden. It's so incredibly thoughtful."

"Tell me about him. I'd love to hear your stories."

So, she did. Under the setting sun, she told him how Francesco had held her when her parents died, promising to love her with all his heart and raise her as his own. He'd taught her to dance and how to cultivate wine and had let her cry upon his shoulder when the first boy she'd ever kissed told her she was ugly when they ended their brief teenage relationship.

"Was he blind?" Heden asked.

Sofia breathed a laugh. "No, he was just awkward, and so was I. Young love is messy. I look back on those years and think of all the life I've lived in between. I'm at least a third of the way through, if you look at it mathematically. So strange it will all be over one day. My father's grandfather lived to be one hundred and ten, so at least I've got some good genes."

"I bet you'd be even hotter than Blanche at one hundred and ten," he said, sentiment glowing in his eyes, reverent and sad. "I'd love to see it, Sof. We could have a huge party for you."

Her eyes darted between his, communicating with her gaze what she wouldn't with her words. There would be no more shared birthday celebrations once she returned home. There couldn't be.

Thankfully, Luciana appeared, salads in hand, and they commenced eating, the conversating traveling to safer subjects.

"Do you like the salad?" Sofia asked, ingesting another forkful.

He nodded. "I've come to appreciate eating since it's one of the things I get to do with you. Food is pretty good. You humans and the Slayers might be onto something."

They ate under the newly risen moon, Heden recounting his own stories of growing up after the Awakening. He spoke of his bond with his siblings and Lila, love evident in his tone but also a latent twinge of loneliness.

"It must've been difficult being the youngest," she said sympathetically.

"Yeah," he said, sipping his wine. "It's so hard to explain because I love my family so much. I'd die to save any of them from pain or danger. But they're all really intense. I've always been pretty chill, and I think it's hard for them to understand me sometimes, and vice versa."

"I get it," she said, finishing the last of the amazing gnocchi Luciana had prepared. "Sometimes, I have trouble making connections with people since I'm an only child. I learned how to function on my own and actually think that's pretty awesome. Humans always want to paint some sad story about women living alone, especially at my age, but I actually kind of dig it. I get to do what the hell I want, when I want, and I don't have to confer with anyone else. It kind of rocks."

Heden chuckled. "You are pretty independent, although we've managed to get along pretty well."

"We have. I think we're pretty compatible."

"It's probably just the bangin' sex."

Sofia snickered. "The bangin' banging."

Throwing back his head, Heden laughed, looking so handsome in the moonlight. "Yep, the bangin' banging. Speaking of, your dress is pretty. Once we have dessert, I want to worm my way under it."

"Well, folks, he's not a subtle man," she murmured into her glass.

"No one would ever accuse me of being subtle," he said, arching a brow.

Dessert arrived, and they devoured the tiramisu, Sofia commenting it was some of the best she'd ever had. Finished with the meal, they slowly traversed the rolling hills, Heden tugging her toward the thick trees that lined the vineyard.

Gliding her toward one of the trees, he gently pushed her back into the bark. Lowering his lips to hers, he kissed her softly, sweetly, until their desire began to smolder. Sofia reached for his belt, unclasping it and sliding the zipper down, urging his clothes from his hips. His hands trailed down her sides, bunching the fabric of her dress, baring her to him.

When he lifted her with his strong arms, she encircled his waist with her legs, panting with longing as she looked into his ice-blue eyes. Pushing the slip of fabric that covered her mound aside, he aligned the head of his cock with her dripping opening.

"Sofia," he whispered, staring into her soul. "You're mine."

She nodded, clenching her hands behind his neck. "Always."

Cementing his lips to hers, he thrust into her, the movement filled with an urgency that conveyed their impending separation. Groaning in ecstasy, she threw her head back against the tree, his hips pumping into hers as he murmured words of love against her neck. As his thick shaft slid along the engorged folds of her core, he licked her nape, preparing it for his invasion. Pointed fangs dragged across her pulsing vein, and he impaled her, hand clenching in her hair as he fucked her, deep and thorough.

Sofia felt every inch of him inside her, his cock and his fangs spearing her as he clutched her close. The moment was so intimate, she felt raw...wrung out...so open she barely retained her grasp on reality. But her beautiful Vampyre supported her, held her when she might've floated away, loved her as she fell apart in his arms. Never had she felt so safe.

I love you.

The words flitted through her frazzled brain, true on the most visceral level. She wouldn't speak them aloud—that wouldn't be fair to either of them—but she would clutch them as tightly as she held her lover's shoulders, knowing with all her heart they were true.

The base of Heden's shaft stroked her swollen clit as he hammered her, the action so pleasurable her eyes rolled back under closed lids as she moaned his name.

"Don't forget this, baby," he said, unlatching from her neck and bringing his lips to the shell of her ear. "I need you to remember how good we are together."

"I won't," she cried, fingers fisting in his thick hair. "Oh, god, it's heaven."

"Come all over me, baby," he commanded. "Fuck, you're so tight. It feels so good, Sofie."

Stars exploded behind her eyes as she began to come, mouth open in a silent wail as he pounded her. Her walls convulsed around him as he jutted into her, drawing out his pleasure as she came. Burying his face in her neck, he began to spurt into her core, seeds of his release pulsing inside her as he claimed her for one of the last times.

Overcome with sadness, her arms clasped him so tightly the muscles spasmed. There, against the rugged tree trunk, they held each other as they struggled to reclaim their breath.

Eventually, he slipped from her warmth, drawing a handkerchief from his pocket to wipe away his release.

"Since when do you carry a handkerchief?" she asked, one eyebrow arched as he slyly grinned.

"Since I decided I was going to fuck you against a tree in a vineyard a few days ago."

"Hmm." Her features maneuvered into a mask of mock consideration. "Good lookin' out."

Their sated laughter permeated the sloping valley as they cleaned up and headed back through the vines, slow and unhurried. Heden eventually drove them home, looking adorable as hell when he asked her if she'd had a good time once they reached Astaria.

"I had an amazing time. Thank you, Heden."

"You're welcome, honey. I like making you smile."

It just so happened he was in luck, because Sofia rewarded him with what was possibly the most brilliant smile of her life before he led her inside the castle.

Chapter 30

Heden and Sofia spent the next week training Nolan and Sadie. Since neither was proficient at technology, the training required immense patience and lots of demonstration. Thankfully, the physicians eventually felt comfortable enough to implement the program, and their era of using paper charts came to an end.

Proud of the "Dinosaur Doctors," as he lovingly called them, Heden suggested they go out to celebrate, and they ended up at the bustling pub in Uteria's main square. As they chatted over beers and wings, Sadie asked Sofia when she would head back to the human world.

"I...well, probably in a few days," Sofia said, eyeing Heden as he sat silently beside her. "The EMRs were my last project. Between that, the chemical analyzation program and the updated military comm devices, Heden and I accomplished a lot. I guess it's time I get back to my own life though."

"I'm really sad to see you go," Sadie said, reaching over to grasp her hand. "Promise you'll contact me if you need anything, especially if you decide to go forward with insemination. I'd love to be a resource for you."

"I will." Sofia squeezed her hand, so thankful for such genuine friendship over their short acquaintance. "I'm going to miss you guys so much."

"Sofia has promised to show me the sunset in Positano," Heden said, sliding his arm over her shoulders. "She's got another thing coming if she thinks I'm letting her off the hook with that one." Grinning, he winked at her.

Sofia smiled back, although the action was forced. Of course he would remember the conversation they'd had in the forest all those weeks ago, before their discussion with Tatiana. She had indeed promised to show him the blazing sunset she adored but realized now, she could never keep that promise. Their relationship had evolved so rapidly yet so organically, she feared she'd already lost herself.

The past weeks had been filled with deep reflection. Sofia understood the possibility of finding a partner as remotely compatible as Heden was unlikely. They were almost too perfect for each other, and that terrified Sofia because it made her want to give up every single dream she'd ever had and beg him to let her stay.

But to what end? Yes, she could stay in the immortal realm and have a few good decades with him before she truly began to age, but what about when she turned sixty? Seventy? Eighty? He would still be locked in his immortality, young and vibrant, while her body began to fail. He would feel obligated to care for her, perhaps through illness or dementia, and then he would watch her body grow frail until she eventually passed.

And what of their children? Heden had floated a few comments over the past few weeks, commending Sadie and Nolan's choice to have children through artificial insemination. Sofia understood he was testing the waters, judging her reaction to see if she was open to discussing the possibility. So far, she'd shied away. In her dreams, she was able to bear his child, a boy or girl with ice-blue eyes and thick hair, with his jovial disposition and accepting nature. But her dreams were impossible, and her only option was to have a human child. One that would also grow old and wither before his eyes, dying decades after she did, leaving him alone in grief or pain.

Sofia cared about Heden too much to let him make those choices. So, she would make the hard decisions for them both. He was the optimist between them, the one who pushed her to see possibilities when a solution seemed bleak. Understanding this, she knew he would fight her on the decision. Her strong and compassionate Vampyre would most likely ask her for more time, wanting to nurture their connection. The sentiment was moving, but Sofia was a realist. She comprehended that as she aged, their happiness would wane. Unwilling to set them both up for heartache, she stood firm in her resolve to go home in a few days, and with great difficulty and remorse, she would ask him for a permanent end to their relationship.

It would be too hard to see each other over the years. Too many memories tied up in what they could never have and the differences that would always keep them separate. Although Sofia longed to show him the sunset from the cliffs of the Amalfi Coast, she would bury that dream deep inside. Maintaining any sort of contact with him after they parted wouldn't be fair to either of them.

"Dang, Sof," Heden said, yanking her from her musings. "You got all serious there. You okay?"

"Yeah," she said, waving her hand. "Sorry. Let's chug these beers. I want to meet Daphne before we head home."

Emitting a positivity she certainly didn't feel, she focused on enjoying the time she had left with the wonderful people she'd come to love in the immortal world.

* * * *

Heden observed Sofia as she cooed to Daphne, joy evident on his little human's face. He'd driven them to Sadie and Nolan's home at Uteria, which they'd purchased from Kenden when he moved to Takelia, and his woman had gravitated toward the baby immediately.

As he watched, she rubbed her nose against the little girl's, her gaze reverent. It was a poignant moment showcasing Sofia's intense desire to become a mother herself. Heden had dropped hints over the past few weeks that he was open to discussing different possibilities of how they could have children together, but so far, she hadn't taken the bait. He understood why. That discussion led down a rabbit hole neither of them were ready to traverse. But their two-month window was rapidly closing, and they would have to tackle the issues eventually. Realizing he didn't want to draw it out any longer, Heden decided he'd bring it up tonight and wouldn't let Sofia dodge the conversation any longer. It was time to discuss their future—or lack thereof—and make some hard decisions.

They said goodnight to the new parents, Sofia reluctant to release Daphne until the last moments, and hopped into the four-wheeler to head to Astaria. Under the full moon, silence stretched between them, both of them quietly acknowledging the impending discussion. Once back at Astaria, Heden led her to the soft grass that lined the meadow beside the castle. Smiling down at her, he tucked a wayward strand of her springy hair behind her ear.

"You looked pretty damn awesome with that baby in your arms tonight, Sof," he said, hoping to keep the tone light.

"Yeah? She's so freaking cute. I didn't want to let her go."

His gaze roved over her face. "I'm not sure I'm ready for kids yet, but I'm willing to discuss it with you. I think it's time we did."

Inhaling deeply, she nodded. "We're at different places in our lives, Heden. You have so much time. It's unbelievable. I wish with all my heart I had more. But I don't, and unfortunately, I can't change that. I'm ready for the next chapter of my life. I'm ready to be a mother."

A cold wave of anxiety coursed through him. Although he'd toyed with the idea of having kids with Sofia through insemination, the idea still seemed so faraway. For someone who'd been a proclaimed bachelor for centuries, the stark change was daunting.

"I know," she said, shrugging under the moonlight. "It's scary. I don't expect you to be ready for such a drastic change. I'm pretty sure you entered into this thing with me intending for it to be casual. That's your M.O., and I always understood that."

"It was, for so long," he said, realizing he'd changed so much since meeting her. "But I don't think it was ever really casual with you, even if I convinced myself in the beginning. It certainly isn't casual now."

Her lips formed a sad smile. "Well, I'll wear that on my sleeve. I tamed the immortal world's resident bachelor."

Heden chuckled. "You've done that and so much more. Is there any way we can at least try to make this work? I'm willing to put in the effort if you are."

"It's not about effort," she said, shaking her head. "I wish it was that easy. But there are fundamental differences between us we can't change. I'll always be human, and you'll always be immortal. I won't sign you up for a temporary lifetime of unknowns and heartache. I care about you too much, Heden."

His heart slammed in his chest. "I care about you too. So much, Sofie."

"I know," she whispered, placing a palm over his chest. "Please, don't make this harder than it already is. I want to remember our time together fondly."

"I'll still come visit you in the human world."

"No," she said, eyebrows drawing together. "That's impossible, Heden."

"What are you talking about?" he asked, confusion and fear twining together in his gut. "Of course I'll come and see you. You still have to show me the sunset at Positano."

Her chin warbled as those magnificent eyes flooded with tears, glistening as she struggled to speak. "We can't. I know it seems harmless now, but it will end up causing us so much pain if we clutch onto something that isn't real."

"Something that isn't real?" he asked, her words causing a sharp pang in his solar plexus. "Are you fucking serious? How can you say that?"

"Don't curse at me," she said, lowering her hand and glaring up at him. "We both knew what would happen here, Heden. I won't let you disparage me for making hard choices we both know deep down are right."

"So, what? You're just going to leave and never see me, never talk to me again? How can you walk away so easily?"

"This isn't easy for me!" she cried, arms slicing through the air as she stared at him in disbelief. "Don't you think I want to stay? I've almost caved a hundred times and asked you if I could stay longer."

"Yes," he said, reaching for her hand. "You can stay as long as you want. Months. Years. Decades. Please, Sof, don't give up on us. We need more time. Can't you see that?"

"I don't have time," she said, swiping away an errant tear. "It's so damn frustrating you can't understand that. I keep telling myself it's impossible for an immortal to comprehend things like aging and death, but it's maddening you refuse to see it."

"Oh, I refuse to see it? I understand death and loss more than you'll ever know. My parents were taken from me before I ever got to know them. I grew up searching for bonds I never truly understood. Alone. Aloof. Disconnected from everyone, even my family, in so many ways. I love them so much, but they all had a purpose, while I floundered, struggling to find my place. It's pretty much how I've functioned my entire life. You're the only person outside my family I've even considered opening my heart to, and you toss it away like it's nothing."

"Well, I'm sorry the first person you decided to be an adult with came with her own set of fucked-up issues. That's life, Heden. It's really intense and hurts a hell of a lot. Sorry I couldn't be some immortal princess who could wait forever for you to decide when you're ready to have a family. I'll never be that person. I hope you find her one day. For now, it's better if we end this on the best note possible."

170

"I didn't even contemplate I'd never see you again after you left Astaria," he said, overwhelmed at the thought of losing her. "I always entered into this with the hope we'd at least be friends."

"For how long? Until one of us marries? Until I have a child and focus on raising her? We're worlds apart, Heden. It will never work. We have to let each other go."

"How?" he asked, stepping forward and cupping her face. "How can I let you go? I won't do it, Sof."

"I'm so sorry," she whispered, nostrils flaring as her eyes shimmered. "I wish it didn't have to be this way. It has to end."

"Sofie," he whispered, lowering his lips to hers. "I can't."

"Please don't hate me. This is already so hard for both of us." Lifting to her toes, she spoke against his lips. "Make love to me. Once more, so we can remember. *Please*, Heden."

Feeling the sting of tears behind his own lids, he captured her lips in a passionate kiss as he swept her into his arms. Carrying her through the darkened castle, he entered the room where they'd spent so many weeks laughing and loving. Frantically, they tore at each other's clothes, aching to connect in the most primal way. Spreading her legs, he slipped inside her, needing to show her how much he cared for her...how much he...*loved* her.

Threading his fingers through her hair as it fanned across the pillow, he stared into her soul as he undulated his quivering body into hers. She gazed back, regret and sadness lurking in the depths of her luminous eyes.

"Sofie," he whispered, emotion threatening to choke him.

"Don't say it," she said, covering his lips with her fingers as she shook her head upon the pillow. "Please. You'll break my heart."

But instead, his own shattered deep in his chest as she rejected the words he'd never even thought to say to another. Overcome with pain and sadness, he loved her with every movement of his hips, every kiss upon her silken skin, every moan that escaped his lips as her velvet walls squeezed him tight.

And when he could take no more, he emptied everything into her. His pain and heartache and longing that they could change their impossible circumstances. Afterward, as he stroked her cooling skin, he felt the drop of a single tear upon his chest. Cursing every god who'd created them to be so different, he stewed in the unfairness of life in general.

In the morning, he woke, reaching for her and finding the bed empty. Searching the room, he noticed her stuffing the last of her things into her pack.

With a gentle smile, she sat on the bed. "We've finished all our programming tasks, so there's really no reason for me to stay," she said, smoothing a hand over his cheek. "I'm going to head through the ether. Please tell everyone I said goodbye. It was so amazing getting to know your family. I wanted so badly to tell them myself, but I realize now, it's time to go. Drawing this out any longer will just lead to more heartache. I don't want that for us, Heden."

Heden swallowed thickly. "This can't be goodbye, Sof. You're shredding my heart over here. Please stay a little longer. Give me another week at least. Then you can give everyone a proper goodbye."

She pursed her lips and gazed toward the ceiling, chin trembling as she fought off tears. "I can't. I want to so badly, but I can't. Every day I stay, my feelings for you grow exponentially." Locking her gaze with his, she rubbed her thumb over his lips. "Thank you for seeing the best in me. I'm so thankful for you. Be happy, Heden. Please. I can't do this if I know you won't be happy."

"How can I be happy without you?" he whispered, clutching her wrist.

"You'll find a way, little immortal," she said, smiling through her tears as she replicated the affectionate nickname. "I know you will. Goodbye." Leaning down, she gave him a reverent kiss as he caressed her hair for the last time.

And then, she was gone, sure as the wind that whipped through the leaves of the old oak trees on the edge of Astaria.

Cupping his face in his hands, Heden began the long, arduous task of letting her go.

Chapter 31

Heden arose that morning, numb and listless, wondering how he would carry on without her. After barely a few months, Sofia had bewitched him so thoroughly he thought his heart might never recover. He threw himself into helping Sathan, Kenden and Latimus, spending much of his time testing the security systems on the train, at the prison and on their servers. The tasks were mundane but time-consuming and kept him from thinking about Sofia every second of the day.

But at night, when he crawled into the bed he now thought of as theirs, he yearned for the softness of her body against his. For the way she would nuzzle into his side and throw her silken leg over his thighs.

Sometimes, as he sat in the tech room, he would reverently gaze at the chair where she'd sat for so many hours, programming beside him as they worked to improve and protect the kingdom. She'd had nothing to gain besides helping them, and he remembered this whenever the anger surfaced.

With snake-like precision, it would seethe into his veins, making him queasy as he inwardly railed at her for leaving. For not even attempting to give them a chance. But after a while, the bouts of anger would always dissipate, and he would see their situation from her point of view. If the tables were turned, he would never want her to watch him grow old as she stayed locked in immortal youth. He could imagine her gazing at him with pity as his body became withered and brittle before he eventually passed on. It was a terrible sentence to impose on anyone.

He would often wonder if she'd decided to move forward with a donor, wishing with all his heart he could give her children. The idea had seemed so daunting when they'd spoken under the moonlight, but now, as he lived in the agony of her absence, he would give anything to have a child with her.

As the weeks dragged on, he thought the pain might lessen, but strangely, it continued to grow—into something pulsing and latent and ever-present, deep inside his heart. Recalling the words he'd almost uttered to Sofia the last time they made love, Heden accepted that he'd fallen in love with a woman for the first time in his long, connection-free life. How fitting it had been with her, a woman so much like him in so many ways but so fundamentally different in others. At times, the irony would overwhelm him, and he would recall the memories they'd created during their short but passionate affair. They helped him navigate the pain, and he was truly thankful for them.

Sometimes, he would walk to the spot where they'd had their last impassioned argument, on the soft grass under the stars, and gaze up at the moon, wondering if she was doing the same in her world. Did she miss him? Did she think of him even half as much as he obsessively thought of her?

One night, several weeks after her departure, Heden stood in that very spot under the moonlight. Breathing a laugh, he rubbed his hand over his heart as he remembered how furious she'd been when he was belting pop songs outside her door in Louisiana. It was nights like this, when he felt so lonely without her, he would steep himself in the memories of her fiery spirit.

And it was there, as he lowered to sit upon the grassy knoll, he realized something very important: He had to find a way to be with Sofia.

The realization was intense because it entailed a plethora of unknowns and even more terrifying realities. The loss of his bachelorhood. Building a life with someone. Shifting focus from himself to a unit they would form together.

The possibility was daunting and yet it felt...right. Natural. True.

Heden understood Sofia's concerns about their seemingly insurmountable obstacles and differences and knew he had to figure out a way to overcome them. It would be difficult, but for the goddess's sake, he was an extremely intelligent person. With his intellect and skills, there had to be a way for him and Sofia to build a life together, where they could have biological children and an immortal future. The possibility had to exist if he just tried hard enough, didn't it? Wracking his brain, different possibilities began to churn in his mind.

Lost in thought, he didn't hear his brother behind him until he squeezed his shoulder.

"Hey, Sathan," he said, turning. "Is everything okay?"

"There's an outbreak at Uteria. Fifteen Slayers sick and vomiting. It's possible the attack has begun."

Standing, he cupped his brother's arm. "What do you need from me?"

"We're heading there in a four-wheeler in fifteen minutes. I'd like you to come if possible. We need all hands on deck."

"Okay," Heden said. "I'll be ready."

Sathan studied him with his dark eyes. "Are you okay, Heden?"

Sighing, he rubbed his neck. "Not really, but I want to help. I've got a lot of shit to figure out, Sathan."

"I'm so sorry, brother," he said, concern lining his angular features. "She was special. I wish things had been different for you both."

"Me too."

Silence ticked between them. "Did you fall in love with her?"

Heden's lips curved. "Yep. I sure did."

"Damn. That's rough, bro. Is there anything I can do?"

"Let me help you at Uteria," Heden said, patting him on the back as they began to trek toward the castle. "We can't let those bastards hurt our people."

They strolled in silence until they were at the barracks. Before Heden could head inside to prepare, Sathan clutched his forearm. "Heden?"

"Yeah?"

"I'm really proud of you. You've turned into such an amazing man. I'm honored to be your brother."

Heden felt his nostrils flare, and pride swelled in his chest from the heartfelt words. His oldest brother was a father figure to him in so many ways, and the assurance gave him strength. "Thank you, Sathan. That means a lot."

His brother gave a nod. "Go on. We're rolling out in ten."

Heeding his directive, Heden headed inside to prepare to help his people.

* * * *

The sickness spread across the kingdom, vicious and vile, leaving destruction in its wake. Armed with the antidotes they created, Nolan and Sadie did their best to test the patients for the exact combinations in their blood and supply the appropriate cures. Their success rate was eighty-five percent in the first week, thanks mostly to the software Sofia and Heden had created that allowed them to work so quickly. The other fifteen percent were Slayers with compromised immune systems who would've most likely succumbed to other viruses or flus if exposed.

Vampyres' self-healing bodies were immune to the toxins, allowing an influx of soldiers to sign up for the army. Years removed from war, many of the troops had been transitioned to law enforcement positions and would need to be retrained. Although the chemical warfare required a different type of soldier, Sathan and Miranda felt it was only a matter of time before Bakari and Vadik decided to employ some type of ground offensive. Preparation was essential.

Along with helping Sathan and Miranda try to curb the pandemic, Heden threw himself into researching everything he could about immortality, Etherya's history of granting requests to immortals and even old wives' tales that circulated throughout the kingdom. He spent countless hours examining the archives at Astaria, Valeria and Uteria, meticulously searching for evidence Etherya had granted immortality to anyone other than Nolan. There were no other instances in the age-old scrolls and manuals, but Heden remained determined. If there was a way to solve their conundrum, he would find it.

Two weeks into the pandemic, Heden was at the Deamon prison at Takelia, implementing some enhanced security measures on the server. Evie had come up with the idea of implementing call buttons throughout the prison, connected to a pager she wore at all times. Heden, Kenden and Latimus thought it brilliant since, upon being paged, she could transport inside and essentially freeze the inmates in place. Although the Secret Society had the power of dematerialization, Evie had the ability to control people's movements with a thought.

Finishing up, Heden completed his last item on the checklist, confirming each call button was wired properly. Pleased everything was online, he began walking from the room that housed the main servers.

Out of nowhere, a man appeared in his path, blocking the doorway, holding an eight-shooter aimed at Heden's chest.

"You must be Vadik," Heden said, lifting his hands, palms facing forward as he attempted to stay calm. "Man, you Deamons are all really fucking pasty. Crimeous could've at least given you some self-tanner, being that you lived in the caves for all those centuries—"

"Shut up!" Vadik spat. "Disable the security system now, or I'll lodge eight pellets in each chamber of your heart so fast you'll be dead in seconds."

"Uh, yeah, not gonna do that," Heden said, his jibing tone unrepresentative of the fear coursing through his veins. With his mind, he called to Evie, having no idea if she'd hear him since she was at the governor's mansion—but it was worth a shot. Then, he sent a quick prayer to Etherya, asking for protection, and reached for his phone in his back pocket.

Vadik cocked the eight-shooter, causing Heden to freeze again. Shit. The guy looked like he meant business.

"There are two guards in the hallway—"

"They're dead," Vadik interrupted. "That's what happens when you're ill-prepared to fight an enemy who can materialize out of thin air. No one will hear you if you scream. Disarm the security system."

"Look, dude, I'm not going to disable the system. You can try yourself, but it's encrypted in about a thousand ways I'm pretty sure you'll never understand. What's your objective here?"

"To distract you so I could gain the upper hand, of course," a deep voice said behind him.

Pivoting, Heden looked into his brother's eyes as he sneered back. His face was a mask of hatred and arrogance, cold and unyielding. Steeling himself, he said, "I don't understand, Bakari. Why do you hate us so much? I wasn't even born when you were abandoned in the human world. I'm sorry it happened, brother, but it doesn't have to be this way. We can start over."

"Start over?" Bakari scoffed. "This world has devolved into chaos, filled with hybrids and weaklings. It's appalling. None of you can be saved. I must exterminate you and start anew." Lifting an eight-shooter, he aimed it at Heden's heart. "Look at you, in love with a human, for the goddess's sake. You're an *abomination*."

"I'm not going to help you, Bakari," Heden said, refusing to rise to the bait. "So, you can shoot me or you can leave, but it's not fucking happening."

"There is another who could disarm the system," Bakari said, arching a brow. "If you force me to bring her here, I will."

Heden shook his head. "You'll never find Sofia. We spoke about her post-immortal world plans extensively. She always planned to go off the grid once she went home. I'm confident you have no idea where she is."

"Is that so?" Bakari asked, his tone chilling. "Diabolos, bring in the human."

Heden whirled, his heart leaping in his throat at the thought of them holding Sofia hostage. A Slayer entered the room, a squirming woman in his arms, head covered by a brown cloth. Jumping into action, Heden lurched for the newly minted call button against the wall. Depressing it, he rushed toward the Slayer, intent on rescuing Sofia, but a million shards of pain exploded in his chest, and he gasped for air.

Sofia's beautiful face flashed through his pain-riddled mind, the last thing he saw before everything turned to darkness...

* * * *

Ananda pulled the cover from her head, her lips forming a cruel smile as she watched Heden bleed out on the floor. "He bought it. He thought I was Sofia."

"Yes," Bakari said, pleased his plan had worked. "He has no idea we haven't been able to find any traces of her in the human world. We must hurry. If the four of us work together, we can each transport twenty-five Deamons per minute to the cave."

They closed their eyes and began to chant, dematerializing from the main security room to the cell block that held the prisoners. Vadik and Bakari systematically shot each Vampyre guard with their eight-shooters until all nine were dead. Then, they began extracting the prisoners.

In a relentless cycle, they chanted the spell, transported a prisoner to the designated cave near the Purges of Methesda and returned to grab another. Two full minutes passed before Evie materialized into the cell block, Latimus and Ken running in behind her, soldiers flanking them.

Evie stared at them, palm held high, frustration lining her expression.

"Tatiana gave me a potion that prevents your freezing spells, Evie. Your powers are useless here." Yelling toward Ananda and Diabolos, Bakari said, "Keep transporting the prisoners. Vadik and I will fight them off."

"You can fucking try!" Latimus snarled, running toward Bakari, an SSW in his hand.

Bakari lifted the eight-shooter, and Latimus knocked it to the ground as if it were a feather. Reaching for his SSW, Bakari extended the glowing blade. "Okay, brother. Let's see how strong you really are."

They began to spar, blade crushing against blade, as Kenden and Evie rushed Vadik, weapons drawn. The immortal troops backed them, battling the wayward Deamon prisoners who were fighting with their bare hands. Now free of their cells, they fought for their lives.

The skirmish escalated as Ananda and Diabolos appeared and vanished in the background, transporting an inmate each time they disappeared.

"We have to stop them from freeing the prisoners!" Kenden yelled above the scuffle.

Pushing against Bakari's wide body, Latimus plunged his shoulder into his brother's chest, causing him to gasp and fall back. Seizing the opportunity, Latimus sprinted toward Diabolos, who was clutching a Deamon in his arms, about to dematerialize. Lifting his Glock, he shot the Slayer between the eyes.

Diabolos wheezed, eyes growing wide, before falling to the ground in a heap.

"Should I use the healing serum?" Ananda asked Bakari.

"No," Bakari said, recovering. "We don't have time. Grab one more prisoner and retreat!"

Evie approached, encircling Bakari's neck with her hand. "You son of a bitch," she said, squeezing. "It wasn't enough for you to have unlimited riches in the human world? Why are you intent on attacking us?"

Bakari grabbed her back, squeezing her throat as they stared each other down, both gasping for air. "I am the true sovereign, Evie," he said through clenched teeth. "We'll never waiver in our efforts to exterminate you. You've all become complacent, and it gives us ample opportunity to strike. You know this to be true. Until we meet again, good luck with your nightmares. I know they haunt you, and that brings me great joy." Closing his eyes and beginning the chant, he vanished into thin air.

Lifting his lids, Bakrai observed the musty cave. Ananda and Vadik appeared, a Deamon in each of their grasps. Taking a mental headcount, he tallied their efforts.

"We extricated almost two hundred," Bakari said, mulling as he struggled to catch his breath. "It's a good start."

Vadik nodded. "We'll begin to clone more soldiers using Crimeous's blood. I'm confident we can figure out the process, especially with Dr. Tyson's help."

"Yes," Dr. Tyson said, stepping from the shadows. "I don't really like the immortal world, but I'm interested in the science. I will help you in exchange for the terms we discussed. I look forward to partnering with you all."

"Should we at least try to extricate Diabolos' body and bring him back to life?" Ananda asked.

"No," Bakari said. "It's too dangerous. May his soul find peace in the Passage."

"I doubt he'll end up there," Ananda muttered.

"Shall we begin the next phase?" Vadik asked.

"Yes," Bakari said. "We will blaze this next chapter with thought and care. We must plan small attacks to divide them, and large ones when we are sure we cannot fail."

"Then we'd best get to work," Dr. Tyson said. "Vadik, please show me where you've stored the equipment you stole from the human world."

Vadik led the hybrid immortal down the long chamber as Ananda eyed Bakari. "Your disdain for the hybrid is palpable."

"He is necessary for now. Once he's served his purpose, he can return to the human world or die."

"We're all expendable to you, aren't we, Bakari?"

"Yes," he said, unwilling to waste the effort to lie. "But you've always known this."

"I have," she said, one eyebrow arching. "I find it rather...entrancing, in a way. At least we have no illusions about who you are. Excuse me, but I feel I need to rest for a few moments. That was a lot of action for my old, withered heart." Shuffling away, she ambled toward one of the chambers of the cave.

Lifting his arms, he addressed the Deamons. "Children of Crimeous, I am your leader now. In exchange for your freedom, we will begin a new war. One we will not lose. I, Bakari, son of Markdor, ask for your allegiance!"

The former prisoners cheered in assent, the sound invading every cell in Bakari's body, causing him to feel like the king he would one day be. Reveling in the glory, he silently thanked Etherya for today's victory.

* * * *

Evie transported to Heden's side immediately after the battle, leaving Kenden and Latimus to deal with the released inmates. Crouching down beside him in the security room, she felt his pulse. Nothing. Flipping him over, she noted the extensive damage. Eight small wounds fractured the skin above the eight chambers of his heart, bleeding and open. Pulling her shirt over her head, she covered the wounds, hoping to stop the gushing, and placed her hands over his chest. With precise movements, she began performing CPR.

"It won't work," a voice said beside her. "There's too much damage."

Evie looked up at the stunning woman. "I'm open to suggestions, Tatiana."

Bending her knees, Tatiana placed her hand above Heden's chest, palm open. Closing her eyes, she inhaled a deep breath. Slowly circling her hand over his body, she assessed.

"The bullets were infused with a poison Crimeous used to employ for his weapons. It won't allow his body to self-heal. Several of the bullets missed a direct heart chamber, but without combatting the poison, he's doomed."

"Do you have a potion?" Evie asked.

Tatiana pulled a vial from the pocket of her flowing dress. "It isn't specific to this poison, so I don't know if it will work, but I think we must try."

"Do it," Evie said.

Tatiana sprinkled drops over Heden's face and chest. "Transport him to the infirmary at Uteria. It is the most advanced. If he doesn't regain consciousness in a few days, you must employ other methods."

"Such as?"

"He loves the human, perhaps more than he realizes. You know that has the power to heal. Good luck, daughter of Rina. You must transport him now."

"Why are you helping us, and why in the hell are you helping Bakari? It seems like a waste of effort to help both sides."

Tatiana's eyebrows lifted. "So you will owe me. I always need favors from one as powerful as you, and it is imperative I have things of value to offer Bakari. You will understand one day. Now, go."

Gathering Heden in her arms, Evie whisked him to Uteria.

Chapter 32

Sofia stood on the balcony of her rented home overlooking the magnificence of the Tyrrhenian Sea. It had been an act of wistful spontaneity to move into a home that overlooked the sunset she'd wanted so badly to show Heden. It was quite uncharacteristic of Sofia's stoic demeanor, but she'd changed so much in the past few months, she barely recognized herself. Perhaps she wasn't so stoic after all.

Lost in nostalgic memories of her romantic, sometimes infuriating, always amusing Vampyre, she counted the days since she left him. Eighty-seven days, four hours and thirty-three minutes. Check that. Lifting her wrist, she noted the time. *Thirty-four minutes.* Sighing, she watched the waves crash upon the shore, contemplating if there would ever come a time when she didn't feel so empty.

When she'd first returned home, she'd sold her flats in New York and Florence along with most of her possessions. Wanting to start fresh, she'd moved to Positano, hoping the lovely seaside town would refresh her spirit. Needing to stay inconspicuous, on the off chance Bakari came for revenge, she searched available rentals. Since she spoke fluent Italian, she'd charmed the owner of the small home she now occupied, agreeing to pay him a year up front if he took cash. The man smiled with glee and gladly took her euros. Afterward, she was set; ready to resume her life and have children.

She met with a gynecologist in town who recommended some highly regarded sperm banks in Naples. Instructing Sofia she could browse through anonymous profiles online, she set about looking for a donor. Many of the profiles were outstanding: men with doctorates and PhDs, semi-professional athletes, CEOs of large corporations. But none of them had what she truly wanted: sky-blue eyes with a killer sense of humor and a brilliant intellect. Sadly, none of them were Heden.

Of course, she could never have Heden's child, but that didn't stop her from wishing. For things she couldn't have and dreams that would never come true. After almost three months of filtering through profiles, Sofia decided to put looking for a donor on hold. The gynecologist had given her a thorough exam, and her egg count was excellent for a thirty-nine-year-old. The kind physician thought her prognosis favorable to get pregnant into her forties, although she did offer to help Sofia with fertility treatments if needed. It was all so daunting to someone whose heart was a shattered, broken mess, and she realized she needed to take some time to mourn the loss of the love of her life.

How had it happened? Sofia had no idea. Not so long ago, Heden had been the hacker she was determined to beat, an enemy she wanted to destroy. Now, almost half a year later, he was the person who consumed her every thought. Gaze drifting to the moon, which sat low on the horizon as the sun set miles away, she wondered if he ever did the same. Did he look at the celestial satellite and think of her, hoping she was gazing back?

Sofia wasn't sure, but she hoped he missed her terribly. It was what he got for being so damn charming and making her fall madly in love with him. Jerk. Breathing a laugh, she realized he would think her inner rantings hilarious. He'd peck her on the cheek and tell her how cute she was when she was mad at him. Oh, how she'd give anything to be mad at him one more time, so they could make up and whisper words of forgiveness as they loved each other.

A rustling sounded to her left, and she gasped. Evie appeared from nothingness, a determined look on her face.

"Evie?"

"I'm sorry if I startled you," she said, holding up a hand. "But it's been a week, and Heden hasn't regained consciousness. I've been searching for you for three days. Nice job, by the way. I'm impressed at your ability to disappear off the face of the damn planet."

Sofia's heart leapt into her throat. "Heden's unconscious?"

Evie nodded, lips drawn into a firm line. "The Secret Society attacked the prison while he was updating the security systems. They killed the two guards outside and shot him with an eight-shooter. The bullets were also poisoned. He's on life support."

Sofia covered her mouth with both hands, heaving in breaths. "Oh, my god. I have to go to him."

"Yes," she said, nodding. "That's why I'm here. We hope having you near might help him wake up. Grab whatever you need, and I'll transport you."

Flinging open the sliding glass door, Sofia stuffed items in a bag, barely even registering what she was packing. Overcome with fear that he would die, she slung the bag over her shoulder. "Let's go."

Threading her arms around Evie's neck, they dematerialized to Uteria.

* * * *

Heden swam in the murky waters, the liquid dark and stifling. Sofia was yelling at him, and he wondered what he'd done to piss her off. Was she still mad he was singing outside her door? Wait...that wasn't it. Maybe she was upset about him telling Kenden they were together. Wading through the water, he remembered her forgiving him for that rather quickly. What in the heck had he done? He wanted so badly to figure it out, but his brain was incredibly fuzzy, and he was having a hard time stringing thoughts together.

"*I mean it, Heden,*" her voice called, filled with passion and...fear? "*You'd better wake the hell up. There's no way I broke my heart into a million pieces so you could die first. Wake the fuck up! Now!*"

Heden wanted to laugh at how bossy she was. He was extremely comfortable, thank you very much, and didn't quite feel like leaving the water yet. No, it was inviting and warm, and he felt himself slipping further into the shadowy depths...

An eternity later, her voice returned, stubborn and commanding as ever. "*If you don't come back to me, I'll never see you again. Never get to hold you. Please, Heden. Come back to me. I'll stay here forever. I don't care anymore. Just, please, don't die.*"

The words registered in the far reaches of his mind, and he ached to hold her. He hated when his Sofie cried, although she was beautiful when tears streamed down the smooth skin of her cheeks. Wanting to comfort her, he tried to reach for her, but his arms wouldn't move.

"Sofie?" he called, drowning in confusion as to why his body wasn't functioning. "Where are you, honey?"

Sobs surrounded him, and he fought against the invisible confines, clenching his teeth as he thrashed to escape. It was no use. His muscles felt like liquid and air, heavy and light, all at the same time. Frustrated at his inability to reach her so he could hold her and kiss away her tears, he succumbed to the darkness once more.

* * * *

Sofia sat beside Heden's bed, clutching his hand as she prayed. Eyes raw from crying, there were no tears left to shed. After three days, his prognosis was the same: he couldn't survive without life support.

Eyeing the tube that fed into his lungs, she watched the machine pump air. Once. Twice. Again. Over and over. The monotony was grating to her nerves, and she gritted her molars together in frustration.

"Any change?" Nolan asked, approaching her and sliding a supportive hand over her shoulder.

She shook her head. "I don't understand. He was supposed to live forever. If I had known..." Emotion clogged her throat as she struggled to speak. "I never should've left."

"There's nothing you could've done, Sofia," he said, compassion lacing his British accent. "Sometimes, these things just happen."

"I wish there was something I could do."

"Me too. In the meantime, Glarys sent lasagna over. I've been instructed we're both meant to eat it for lunch, or she'll come looking for us."

Sofia's lips formed their first tentative smile in days. "Did she send along fresh grated parmesan to put on top?"

"She wouldn't be Glarys if she didn't. Let's go to the break room and eat. I think you need a few minutes away from this stuffy room."

Nodding, she grasped the hand of the only other human in the realm. Together, they warmed up the dish the kind mother figure had prepared.

* * * *

Heden hiked in the woods, tickled by how much fun he was having with Sofia. Who knew a human could be so damn adorable and engaging? Turning to pick her up and lift her over the log, his eyebrows drew together. Where was she? She was behind him a moment ago.

"She's not here, my friend," a female voice called to his right.

Pivoting, he smiled at Tatiana. "Hey, super confusing riddle lady. How's it going?"

She gave a good-natured shrug. "Fine for me, but you've seen better days."

Glancing around, he searched the forest. "Is that why Sofia disappeared? I swear, she was right beside me."

"You're lost in the memory of the hike you took before you met me in the woods," Tatiana said. "It's a pleasant memory for you, and you find it safe. But it's time for you to return home, son of Markdor. Your time in Etherya's realm isn't yet over."

The words were perplexing. "Am I in the Passage?"

She shook her head. "You're in the in-between. It's a paradoxical place, tough to understand even for one as bright as you. You seem to be stuck here, and I think you know the reason why."

Heden's eyebrows drew together. "I can't imagine why I'd want to be stuck here. I'd much rather be at home with my family. And with Sofia."

"Ah, but you have no home with Sofia. It is an unfortunate but unwavering truth. This causes you much pain and hiding here is as good a place as any."

Resting his hands on his hips, he plopped his foot on a nearby log, contemplating. "Are you saying I'm stuck here because I don't want to go home and accept reality?"

Tatiana's head tilted to the side. "Perhaps. What do you think?"

Heden inhaled the fragrant air, mulling her words. It was true that here, in this place, the agony of Sofia's absence didn't hurt so much. He didn't have to suffer with the knowledge they were forced to live separate lives due to factors beyond their control. Instead, he was just...numb. It was a welcome reprieve from the pain he'd experienced over the past few months.

"I know it feels better," she said, "but that is an illusion. You are stronger than the shell of the person you are here. Running from your pain won't heal you. It will only create more for the ones you leave behind."

He toyed with his bottom lip with his fangs. "Living in that world is so damn hard. I don't understand how to live without her."

"Then don't."

He sighed. "She's adamant she doesn't want me to witness her grow old. That it's better we part."

"I think she is correct in that assertion."

"But you're telling me to go back," he said, frustration curling in his gut. "So she can just leave me again? Sounds pretty shitty to me."

Tatiana crept forward, leaves crunching under her sandaled feet. When her face was inches from his, she grinned and tapped his forehead with her finger. "For someone so smart, you are blind to so much. Go home, Heden. You have lived your life without purpose for so long. Although you do much to help your people, you shy away from hard choices. This has to change for you to realize your full potential."

Heden chuckled. "Are you telling me I need to 'adult'? Because I'm pretty terrible at it."

Throwing back her head, she gave one of the deep throated laughs he was beginning to expect from her. "Yes," she said, amber eyes glowing. "You need to 'adult.' It baffles me how each new generation of humans denigrates their languages. Wait until you see the millennials' children's children. You will think them insane."

"You can see the future?" he asked, awed by the prospect. Not even Evie was that powerful.

"I function differently in the world than most creatures. Time is not a constant for me. You will discover soon enough. For now, go home. Each moment you stay here increases your family's suffering along with Sofia's."

"I don't want that," he said, kicking the leaves at his feet with his sneaker. "How do I go back?"

"Can't you hear?" Tatiana asked, pointing to the sky. "She's calling you. All you have to do is answer."

Sofia's voice filtered through the clouds, soft but vibrant. "*Heden. Please come back to me.*"

Closing his eyes, he concentrated, focusing on her words in the dark void.

"Good," Tatiana said, sounding a million miles away. "Tell Miranda to pull the loose brick along the soothsayer chamber far wall."

"What?" Heden asked, lost in another one of her riddles. He fought to open his eyes, but they were cemented closed. Directing all his energy to Sofia's muffled voice, he swam toward it through the obscure dimness. Feeling as if he might suffocate, he struggled to reach her.

* * * *

Sofia felt something brush against her cheek and batted it away. When the nagging jolt persisted, she rose from her slumber to tell whoever it was to cut it out. Rapidly blinking her eyes, she immediately understood she'd fallen asleep beside Heden, face planted on the hospital stretcher. After imploring him for several hours to wake up, she'd laid her cheek against the soft sheet beside his abdomen to rest for only a minute…

His fingers twitched, and she gasped, shooting from the chair. Eyes still closed, he lifted lethargic arms to the tubes at his throat, trying to pull them free.

"Nolan!" she screamed.

Both physicians rushed in, Sadie immediately reaching for the tubes while Heden gulped for air and Nolan held down his flailing arms. Terrified, Sofia waited.

Sadie removed the hoses and gently slapped her fingers on Heden's face. "Heden! Heden!" she called. "It's okay. I need you to breathe on your own. You can do it."

Her massive Vampyre sucked in a huge breath, eyes flying open as he searched the room.

"Oh, my god," Sofia cried, rushing to stand beside Sadie. "You're awake. You came back to me." Making the sign of the cross, she looked to the sky. "Thank you."

"She's a heathen," he almost whispered, his voice raspy from the tube. "Thinks heaven is real."

Sadie laughed. "Does she now?"

Sofia sat on the bed and leaned over him, throwing her arms around him as she placed ardent kisses over his face. "How can you already be making fun of me? Oh, Heden, I was so worried for you."

"I'm here, Sof," he murmured, running his hand over her hair. "I missed you so much."

"I'm never leaving again. Screw the consequences. I can't do this without you."

"Sofia," he said softly, caressing her face with his fingers. "I think you look more and more like Blanche every day. It's so hot."

Head falling forward, she laughed upon his chest, overcome with joy that he'd returned to her. Holding him tight, she resigned herself to their future—whatever it may hold. The alternative was now unthinkable.

* * * *

Two days later, Heden sat in Sadie's office holding Sofia's hand as the physician discussed his prognosis.

"The poison from the bullets somehow wormed into the vessels around your heart, Heden. It's created a strange phenomenon where your arteries carry the poison away but the veins transport it right back. After consulting with Nolan, we think you're going to have to do some old-school rehabilitation."

"What does that entail?" Heden asked.

"Five hours each day on the treadmill, spread out intermittently. This will cause your heartbeat to accelerate, and the arteries will be able to flush the poison from the area around your heart to your kidneys and liver so they can filter it from your body. If you follow the regimen for three months, we think your body will be completely decontaminated and back to normal."

"Okay," he said, feeling weak as he ran his thumb over Sofia's soft skin. "I'll do whatever I have to do to recover."

"Can I help him?" Sofia asked.

"That's up to Heden. I'm sure he'd love moral support, but that's for you two to decide."

Sofia nodded and helped him stand. Since his heart wasn't functioning at full capacity, the most mundane task drained his recovering body. "Lean on me," she said, lifting his arm and placing it across her shoulders. They shuffled back to the infirmary bed, which Heden was thankful he would be discharged from tomorrow.

Lowering onto the bed, he struggled to catch his breath as he caressed Sofia's face. "You're the sexiest nurse I've ever had."

She grinned. "Damn straight. I'm going to help you kick your recovery's ass. I almost lost you, and I want that poison out of your body as soon as possible."

Heden studied her, his irises roving over her face. "Does that mean you're staying?"

"Yes." Her tone was unwavering. "I'm here and I'm not going anywhere. We'll get you better and then we'll forge ahead with what we've got. I thought about it a lot while I prayed over the past few days, and honestly, we have a lot of challenges others will never face, but almost losing you changed everything. I have no ties in the human world, and I can have a human child just as easily here as I can there. We can figure out how to make this work."

While his heart swelled from her desire to stay with him, something felt...*off.* She'd been so sure of her decision to leave before his injury, and he didn't want that to be the only reason she decided to stay.

Licking his lips, he said, "Are you sure, Sof? There are still so many obstacles for us."

His little human palmed his cheeks and began to piece together his shattered heart. "I love you," she whispered, eyes clear and brimming with emotion. "I don't give a damn about the obstacles right now. This is all that matters." Lowering her hand, she covered his heart.

"Sofia," he breathed, drawing her close so he could thread his fingers through her hair. "I love you so much. I wanted to tell you before you left."

"I know," she said, her smile so bright. "You don't have to say the words for them to be true, Heden. I feel it. It's so amazing."

Brushing her lips with his, he gazed into her blue-green eyes. "Is love going to be enough?"

"Yes," she said, capturing his lips with hers. "It has to be."

There, in the staid, sterile room, he kissed her, overjoyed at being in her arms once more. But a nagging fear lingered in the far reaches of his mind: they hadn't yet overcome the tremendous issues that led to their separation. Pushing it away, he clutched onto the moment, thrilled his beloved human had returned.

Chapter 33

Sofia threw herself into Heden's recovery, ensuring he stayed on schedule with his workout sessions so the ominous toxins would exit his body. He was a fun patient, albeit rather annoying, as he would attempt to pull her onto the treadmill, stating he'd rather exercise with her—naked. She loved his jibing but also urged him to take his rehabilitation seriously. Almost losing him had shaken her to her core, and his complete recovery was her ultimate goal.

They fell back into their seamless pattern, settling into the life they were only supposed to share for two months. Although Sofia was infinitely happier with Heden, concerns lingered in the back of her mind. She'd committed to stay with him for the long haul, and that was easy, for she now accepted she loved him, body and soul. But that promise also led to a multitude of unknowns.

Since having biological children together was impossible, they decided once Heden was healthy, they would search for a human donor. She'd always been fine with artificial insemination when she was single, but for some reason, it didn't sit well with her now they'd cemented their relationship. Sighing as she sat in the green grass under the moonlight one evening, she acknowledged the truth: she wanted Heden's babies. With sky-blue eyes and thick, black hair, they would be beautiful. In her dreams, they inherited his buoyant personality and her practical common sense. She could almost see their faces when she closed her eyes and concentrated.

They'd discussed adopting immortal children, but Sofia had always longed for biological children. Ones that would have Francesco's features and sparkling eyes. Heden understood that desire, and they decided having human children was their best alternative. She knew Heden would love them with all his heart for the finite lives they would live. He would raise them with her and be there for them when she passed on, until they eventually left the Earth as well. Would their children ever fall in love? How would that be possible if they lived in the immortal world?

There were other challenges too. Bakari's presence in the immortal world was a chilling perplexity, and he was a menacing nemesis who loomed in the backs of all their minds. Their mortal children would be vulnerable, and she and Heden discussed various methods to keep them safe. With their skills, Sofia knew they could create several kick-ass security systems that would protect their family and others in the realm, but the Secret Society still posed a serious threat.

Blowing a breath through her puffed cheeks, she pushed away the unknowns. They were just too overwhelming. Once Heden was healthy, they would sit down and discuss all the complexities and heartache that came with their future predicament. For now, it was best to soldier on and focus on his rehabilitation.

"Hey, sweetheart," Heden said, approaching from behind and sitting next to her. "You look like you're pondering the mysteries of the universe. Did you figure them out?"

"Nope," she said, pasting on a smile, determined to stay the course. "I just really like it out here. There's something peaceful about this spot."

"I came here so many times when you were gone," he said, taking her hand and lacing their fingers. "I'd look at the moon and wonder if you were doing the same and possibly thinking of me."

Swallowing thickly, she remembered her desolate loneliness without him. No obstacles were insurmountable enough to cause her to want to feel that despondent again...were they? "I did the same," she whispered, clenching her fingers over his. "Living without you was awful."

"Yeah," he said, tucking a strand of hair behind her ear. "It pretty much sucked."

Reminding herself to be thankful for what she had, and that Heden had survived his attack, she rested her head on his shoulder. Together, they would discern how to navigate their complicated future, for their connection was too pure and their love was too magnificent to squander.

* * * *

Heden strode atop the treadmill, his body growing stronger each day. Sofia had been home for weeks, helping his heart heal infinitely more than any exercise could. Each day, he would send a prayer of thanks to Etherya for bringing his love back to his life.

But Heden read people well, and he understood Sofia still had reservations. Hell, he had them too. They had discussed various possibilities for their future: living in the immortal realm versus the human world, having human children, how they would raise human kids in a world tailored to Slayers and Vampyres. There were just so many challenges they would have to navigate. But Heden loved his little human and knew he would be miserable without her by his side for as long as they had. Unable to set her free, he let her resume their life, telling himself it was the only option.

One day after his rehab session, he sought out Nolan. Sitting in the infirmary, they chatted about the choice Etherya had given him when she granted his immortality.

"She seemed quite thankful I trudged through the ether in an attempt to save Sathan," Nolan said. "She warned it took great effort for her to offer me immortality, but she seemed...curious. Afterward, she informed me I am the only creature in her expansive lifetime she's ever manipulated mortality for. I got the sense she was...*intrigued* in some way and wanted to observe the results of such a massive transformation."

Heden nodded, contemplating. "I want so badly to ask her to do the same for Sofia. Since you have firsthand experience with the goddess and the enormity of her decision to grant immortality, what do you think my chances are?"

Nolan inhaled a deep breath as he pondered. "Etherya warned me something so expansive requires great effort and sacrifice. Remember, she offered me two choices: immortality, or death. It wasn't a 'wine and roses' scenario," Nolan said, making quotation marks with his fingers. "Lost to terror, I chose immortality and regretted that decision for almost three hundred years. A condition of her offer was that I could never enter the human world again. Once I realized I would never see my family again, I became despondent and extremely unhappy. Thank goodness Sadie came along, or I fear my future would've been almost unlivable."

"I'm so glad you found her, man," Heden said, patting his shoulder. "You two are so damn cute together."

Nolan beamed. "I love her so much. Sometimes, I'm still baffled I have a family. It's more than I ever hoped for during those long, lonely centuries."

Looking to the ceiling, Heden rubbed his beard. "I wonder what sacrifices she would require of us if we requested she turn Sofia immortal."

"I don't know," Nolan said, "but I hesitate to offer you hope, Heden. As I said, I'm the only being she's ever manipulated mortality for. When my transformation was complete, she was ravaged and spent. She fell to the ground and wept, and the sky opened up to a magnificent storm filled with black clouds and torrential rain. I was petrified, but Sathan led me to Astaria and took me in, thank goodness. It was all quite extraordinary. I'm not sure she was supposed to change me, if that makes sense. It seemed the forces of nature were quite angry at her choice to turn me."

Heden nodded, hands on his hips as he stared dejectedly at the floor. "It sounds daunting, but I have to try."

"Well, there's no worthier cause than love, my friend," Nolan said, cupping his shoulder. "I wish you the best of luck."

That evening, Heden approached Sathan as he sat in his office. Lowering into one of the broad-backed leather chairs facing his desk, Heden implored him to speak to Etherya on his behalf.

"I know she used to converse with you by the river," Heden said. "You're the only immortal she's ever appeared to on a regular basis. I've never seen her in the flesh and have sent her a thousand pleas over the last few weeks, to no avail. I think she's ignoring me," he said, scowling.

"The goddess is fickle, brother," Sathan said, leaning back in his chair. "She hasn't appeared to me for years now. She prefers to observe from afar and stay out of our affairs. Several times over the centuries, she told me the Universe becomes displeased when she interferes in our free will. Each time she does it, she suffers. Now that Crimeous is gone, I think she's content to watch over us and let us be."

"Well, that pretty much sucks since I've fallen in love with a mortal. Damn it, Sathan. I wish I could change our predicament."

"I thought you and Sofia had decided to build a life here."

"We have, but it's not ideal. I'm so bummed I can't give her biological children, and raising mortal children here is going to present a ton of problems. I just..." He rubbed his forehead, frustrated. "It just fucking sucks."

"I will try to summon the goddess," Sathan said. "Let me see if I can attempt to sway her."

"Thanks, bro," Heden said, feeling a tiny swell of hope in his heart. "I'll continue to do the same, although I think she'll appear to you before me. Let me know."

The weeks wore on as Heden completed his physical therapy. Each night, as Sofia snuggled into his side, he reminded himself he was extremely fortunate to have found a woman who was so damn amazing. His little human was a coding whiz, a video game lover, funny as hell and absolutely gorgeous. Even with their obstacles, finding her had been exceedingly fortuitous. Vowing to focus on the strengths of their magnificent connection, he reveled in her smell and the softness of her smooth skin.

Until the day his brother approached him as he was climbing down from the treadmill. Wiping his brow with his towel, his eyebrows drew together at Sathan's downcast expression.

"What's wrong, Sathan?"

His brother slid his broad hand over his shoulder. "I'm sorry, brother. Etherya finally appeared to me. She was quite angry I summoned her and told me she's also heard your prayers. They won't do any good, Heden. She's immovable on offering Sofia immortality. She warned me not to ask her again, or there would be consequences. I'm so damn sorry."

A long breath left Heden's body as he collapsed on the workout bench, running his hand through his hair. The news was deflating and heavy.

After Sathan consoled him, Heden headed to shower, contemplating his next move. Perhaps there were other creatures with Etherya's powers on the Earth, possibly living in the human world. It wasn't likely, but Bakari, Evie and Tatiana had all resided there, so it wasn't impossible. Could there be some other being or force who could grant his request? Unwilling to be deterred, he toweled himself dry and plodded to the kitchen to find his love.

She was cooking chicken marsala in a large pan and smiled at him as he entered the expansive kitchen. The jolt in his solar plexus was palpable. Sofia's broad grin was the most beautiful thing he'd ever seen. Vowing to be worthy of the innumerable sacrifices she was making to live with him in the immortal realm—until he could hopefully figure out a better solution—he lifted her in his arms and twirled her in time with her melodious laughter.

Chapter 34

Bakari sat in the darkened cave flipping through the withered book. The spine had long ago begun to fray, and he was careful with the pages lest he damage them. The journal archived his history in a way, and for someone who had no ties—who had no family—it gave him purpose on a planet he wasn't meant to inhabit for more than a few hours.

The first pages had been written by Zala, centuries ago, when she'd exhumed his small body and resuscitated him. The ancient witch had been quite powerful and had raised him to comprehend they both were different...separate...alone. Later, she taught him separateness led to fear, and if fear was exploited properly, it was a powerful motivator. In those early decades of his life, Bakari understood he could wield much power and cause much pain by manipulating people's anxieties and phobias.

Tracing the faded parchment, Bakari read the words Zala had scrawled, detailing the extensive spells she'd cast upon him when he was just a babe. When he'd first read them at the tender age of ten, he was overcome with curiosity.

"What spells did you cast on me, Zala?"

"Ones that made you able to survive on the blood of creatures like me instead of the others."

"What others?"

"They don't deserve you, my boy," she'd said, caressing his cheek. "It's no matter now. You're here, and you shall never know of them. Not so long as I exist."

Thus had ended the cryptic conversation, which, strangely, he still recalled to this day. Zala had also trained him to eat food, so his thirst for blood became an anomaly that added to his separateness along with his severely pointed incisors, which were quite different from the scant others he came into contact with during his formative years.

Once Zala passed on, Bakari entered many new phases of life. In some, he was kind. In others, he was murderous. He loved many beautiful women, amassed great wealth, which he squandered and regained, and had a thirst for blood, both for nourishment and for taste.

He could never discern why he craved drinking from people's veins, for humans had long ago lost their thirst for cannibalism. But he ached for it all the same and would sate his thirst by draining others and disposing of them like the meals they were. Only when he met Xen did he truly begin to understand.

Xen practiced medicine in a small rural town outside of Yangzhou, China in the 1600s. Bakari had long ago accepted he would never age, nor grow ill, and he dedicated this portion of his endless life to researching Eastern medicine in the hopes of finding the reasons why. He thought perhaps the doctrine would hold some clues as to why he wasn't quite...human.

When he walked into the medicine woman's tent, Xen stood beside the crackling fire and gasped. Pointing at him, she exclaimed, "Xīxuèguǐ! Jiangshi!" He would later learn they both translated to "bloodsucker" and "vampire." Desperate for information, Bakari befriended the woman, hoping she could explain his strange heritage.

He was charming when he expended the effort and soon seduced Xen under his spell. Deep in love, she gladly imparted her knowledge to him as he held her each night, softly stroking her skin. She informed him of the ether and the immortal world beyond and the stories it held. When pressed on how she'd come to possess this knowledge, she explained it had been passed down her family line through generations by song and folklore. She didn't know which one of her grandfathers' grandfather originated the tales but knew they'd generated many centuries ago. Bakari realized yet another dead end in his life, as he would never know how Xen's ancestors discovered the immortal world so very long ago.

Once his time with Xen was over, Bakari relocated to the Transylvanian region of Romania. There, he made use of the vast libraries built during the European Renaissance and tirelessly researched any mentions of the immortal world. The progress was slow, leading him down a spiral of frustration and anger, and he killed and drained many during this time of his life. It was here the legend of Count Dracula was born, most likely from his murderous actions.

Eventually, through painstaking efforts, Bakari found others like him. Others who were from the world humans couldn't even fathom. Some of them shared their knowledge, and Bakari realized his true heritage as the child of the revered Vampyre royals. Once he learned to generate the ether, he stepped through to observe the realm that had cast him out so long ago. To his dismay, they were embroiled in a bloody war he wanted no part of, for he'd seen enough human war to last a hundred lifetimes. Deciding he'd return once the species eradicated each other, he returned to his comfortable life in the human world.

But over time, vile seeds planted over his entire life began to grow and curl in his mind. He was akin to a god in the human world, massively wealthy as all human gods were, and he felt he deserved the same in the realm of his birth. After all, he was the son of Markdor and Calla. How dare the immortals not even acknowledge his presence upon the Earth? How dare they not respect him as the humans did?

As his rage grew, so did his quest for vengeance. Convinced the immortals were weak creatures who needed to be curbed by an intelligent and omnipotent leader, he decided he would let Crimeous defeat them and then murder the Deamon king himself, understanding he burned in the sunlight. Frustrated his siblings, who were king and commander of the Vampyre army, hadn't discerned that yet, he convinced himself they were too stupid to rule the realm. They must be exterminated so he, the true sovereign, with his centuries of acquired knowledge and intellect, could reign.

Of course, his plan failed, as his siblings actually defeated Crimeous with the help of his powerful spawns. Bakari hated Evie with a passion he couldn't explain, and he'd been convinced she would fail. But no, she had prevailed along with the others, and they had proceeded to denigrate the kingdom into one of hybrid spawns and a false utopia. It went against everything Bakari had been taught. Everything he believed deep in his soul.

Zala had ingrained in his young mind all those centuries ago that there was a pureness to remaining separate. A natural order that must be maintained. When Bakari learned of Etherya, he understood she created the species that way. After all, if there was no value in separateness, his entire life was a lie. It was his difference that made him special. There was a systematic order that made the planet churn. Without those mechanisms in place, the world would devolve into chaos, and his presence upon it would mean nothing.

Dedicating his life to Etherya and what he believed was her true vision, he determined only he could save her realm. He must exterminate the immortal royals and their vapid spawns before they denigrated all that was right and holy. His mind was crazed with the potential successes he would attain. He would now be preeminent in two worlds, unstoppable in his quest to make things function on a higher level than others could ever begin to see.

And then, he would look out upon his planet and bask in his moment of exaltation. The moment where he was no longer separate but the one they all aspired to be. By the goddess, it would be *glorious*.

There would be many steps along the way. Bakari was slowly realizing Callie might be more integral to his scheme than he'd originally anticipated. It was no matter. He could convince her to fight with him—of that, he was sure. Crimeous's blood and dark tendencies ran through her quite vehemently, even if Darkrip and Arderin chose not to see it. Once she aligned with him and they succeeded, he would murder her, of course, but it would be nice to exploit her potency while he could.

Pondering the possibilities, he closed the withered archive and sat back in his chair. Lifting the goblet, he drank the human blood Zala had ensured he would thrive on for his long life. Stewing in the vast possibilities of victory, he resumed plotting his next moves.

Chapter 35

Heden and Lila sat on the park bench as Sofia rolled in the grass with Symon and Adelyn. His woman's laugh was infectious as she lifted Symon in the air, holding him high as he giggled with mirth.

"She's so wonderful with children," Lila said, fangs slightly squishing her lower lip as she smiled.

"She's fucking amazing. She's going to be an incredible mother."

Lila chewed her lip, her eyebrows drawing together as she stared ahead. "So, you are going to choose a human donor?"

"It's the best choice we have," he said, arm stretched over the bench as it surrounded her shoulders. "Now that I'm completely recovered, we're ready to move forward."

Lila nodded, her expression thoughtful.

"Okay, buttercup, what's the deal? I thought you of all people would be on board with making a family from non-traditional methods."

"It's not that," she said, her words thoughtful. "It's just..."

"Go on."

Lifting her stunning lavender eyes to his, he felt them bore into his soul. "She's stuck in a world that isn't hers, Heden. A world where she's going to eventually age, and her body will break down. You'll still be healthy and vibrant as she deteriorates, and then you'll have to do it all over again with your human children. I know it doesn't seem so bad now, but what about the future? I fear you're not allowing yourself to see how difficult this is going to be. For both of you."

The images flashed in Heden's mind. Of Sofia becoming ill and him having to nurse her, possibly for decades, before she perished. Of their human children growing up in an immortal world, so different from everyone else, continuing to age as their friends lived in immortality. Then, having to care for them before they died. It was extremely overwhelming.

"We've discussed so many possibilities for our future. I offered to live in the human world with her, but she doesn't have any family there, and all of you are here. Plus, we'd have to move every few years or live in hiding, so people wouldn't wonder why I never age. Eventually, I'd have to start telling people she's my mother, or my grandmother, whenever we move to a new place. Kinda creepy. Here, everyone knows our situation."

"But can she really be happy with that, Heden? Deep inside? She already told you the first time she left what her true wishes were. She only pushed them aside because you almost died. Do you really think they've changed?"

Heden studied Sofia as she played a game of tag with the kids next to the swings. "Probably not. But what the hell are we supposed to do, Lila? We love each other."

She scrunched her nose and gave him a contrite arch of her blond eyebrow. "Can I say something kind of harsh?"

"Yikes," he said, grimacing. "I don't think I'm going to like this."

Laughing, she shook her head. "You might not."

"Okay, lay it on me."

Inhaling deeply, she said, "I think if you truly love her, you have to let her go. There's a selfishness in molding your love to this future you've decided to make. I understand the need to be with someone desperately, believe me, but sometimes, you just have to have the fortitude to walk away when you know in your gut it isn't right. I had the strength to walk away from Latimus, and our relationship became something so much better in return. When you act in fear, you limit your possibilities."

Sighing, Heden squeezed her shoulder. "So, you're telling me I'm a selfish prick? Low blow, buttercup."

"Oh, Heden, you know I love you," she said, her tone so genuine.

"Chill, Lila, I'm joking." Pulling her into his side, he placed an affectionate kiss on her hair. "I know you'll always secretly love me more than Latimus."

Chuckling, she smiled. "Be glad he's not here to hear you say that. He might murder you."

Heden chomped his gum as he grinned. "I can take him."

Lila snickered. "Okay," she said, rolling her eyes.

They sat in silence, letting her words sink in. "Honestly, Lila, you're right. About everything. Living here and raising mortal children while I live on is going to be really tough. I just don't see another scenario."

"Have you asked her what she wants?" Lila's irises searched his. "Deep down in the far reaches of her heart? I think you should."

He rubbed the back of his neck, pondering. "I think I'm afraid to ask her," he murmured.

"All the more reason you should."

"Damn, Lila, why are you so smart? It's exceedingly unfair considering how gorgeous you are. Most people barely get one or the other."

"You're the smartest person I know, Heden," she said, resting her head on his shoulder, "and that's why I know you understand this scenario won't make either of you happy. If you choose to go forward, I'll support you, of course, but I think it's a mistake. I'm so sorry to say it. I truly am."

"Thanks, buttercup," he said, resting his cheek on her head.

Lost in silence, they observed their loved ones play as the gravity of future choices loomed in the air.

* * * *

That night, as Sofia was prepping for bed, Heden gently cupped her shoulders. "Can we talk for a minute?"

"Whoa," she said, eyeing him in the reflection. "You're never this serious. Did someone die?"

"I just want to chat, Sof. Come on." Grabbing her hand, he led her to the tech room.

"In here?" she asked.

"Yeah," he said, sitting on the edge of the large table in the middle of the room. Drawing her between his legs, he ran his finger over her collarbone. "If we talk near a bed, we'll probably just end up boning before we finish two sentences."

Her eyebrow arched. "In case you've forgotten, we've done quite a bit of boning in this room as well."

Chuckling, he squeezed her wrists. "That we have. So, now that I'm back to one hundred percent, we need to talk about the future. I know we've discussed different options these last few months, but I think it's time to nail down exactly what we want."

Wary eyes darted over his face as her expression grew more somber. "Okay. You start."

He took a moment to consider his words. "When you left all those months ago, it was because you felt it best we part forever rather than leading lives that would ultimately cause us both to suffer. I'm wondering why you changed your mind."

Blowing air through her extended bottom lip, it fluttered the hair above her brow. Extricating from his touch, she stepped back, easing to perch on the edge of the computer desk. Crossing her arms over her chest, she said, "Because you were hurt and almost died. That put a lot of things into perspective for me."

Heden also crossed his arms, tapping his foot as he studied her. "There's a difference between changing perspectives and changing your mind, Sof. I'm wondering if you still feel the same about our situation but you're pushing it aside because of what happened."

White teeth gnawed her lip. "I almost lost you. It made me realize I had to spend whatever time I had left with you, no matter what the cost."

"And what would be the cost?"

Annoyance pervaded her features. "Why are you interrogating me?"

"Because we never truly discussed this, and I think that was a huge oversight for both of us. We just headed straight back into the life we were only supposed to have for two months."

"So, are you saying you want it to end? Wow, I didn't see that coming."

"Of course I don't want it to end. I want it to stay just like this forever."

Realization entered her eyes. "But it won't be like this forever," she said softly.

He shook his head. "We've probably got three, maybe four more decades before things begin to drastically change. I need to know if you're okay with that."

She lifted her hands in a shrug. "What do you want me to say?"

"I want you to be honest."

Her gaze fell to the floor, and Heden could see the wheels churning in her mind.

After a fitful bout of silence, he said, "The thing is, I don't think you really changed your mind, Sof. I think you just compromised your beliefs because you love me."

"I do love you," she said, those stunning eyes blazing with emotion. "That requires sacrifice. I have no problem with that."

Standing, he strode toward her and cupped her face. "But I have a problem with it, little human. I would be some piece of shit if I let you choose a life with me when you truly didn't feel it was the right path. And honestly, as much as I hate to say it, I'm not sure it's the right path either."

"I don't know what to think." Her frustration was palpable. "I don't want to live a life without you, but I also don't want to saddle you with my death and our children's deaths. The thought tears me apart. It's maddening."

"So, you haven't really changed your mind."

A single tear slid down her cheek, and he wiped it away as she whispered the words that sealed their fate. "I haven't really changed my mind."

Inhaling deeply, he caressed her face, committing it to memory so it would live there for centuries to come. "I have to let you go, Sofia," he said, placing his forehead against hers. "I didn't get it before, but I do now. Maybe it's because I almost died. Just thinking how much you suffered for three days while you watched over me and begged me not to leave you...I can't imagine how painful that was."

"It almost broke me," she said, shaking her head. "It was awful."

"And you want to save me from the same pain. From suffering while I watch you slip away, knowing I can never save you."

"Bingo," she said, shoulders lifting. "I don't want you to have to watch me die. To watch our children die. To raise children in a world where they can never find love. What if our mortal children fall in love with an immortal? We've relegated them to the same predicament we're in now, but I might not be around to help you navigate it with them. There are so many disasters I want to shield us both from, Heden." She cupped his jaw, tender and reverent. "I love you so much, I'd live without you to prevent that heartache for you. For us."

Heden finally understood. After all his consternation and anger and pain from her leaving all those months ago, he finally comprehended she had done it for love.

It was such a magnificent gift, and he was humbled she had the foresight to see what he couldn't.

"You're so amazing, Sof. I wish I could change things for us."

"I know. It fucking sucks."

Placing a sweet kiss on her lips, he pondered their next move. As the idea formed, he knew in his heart it was right. "I have a proposal."

"I think we just decided I have to say no to any proposal."

Heden chuckled. "Were you this funny when we met? I don't remember you being this funny."

"You rubbed off on me. It's a nice side effect of dating a self-proclaimed comedian."

Smiling, he ran his thumb over her lips. "Let's spend a week at your home in Positano. You promised me a sunset, and I'm not letting you renege. We'll spend seven more sunsets together, and then we'll say goodbye properly. Something worthy we can hold onto once you're old and I'm still incredibly handsome."

Tears streamed down her face as she warbled a laugh. "That sounds perfect."

"Okay, little human. We'll make the rounds this week so you can hug everyone here one last time, and then we'll head to Italy. I'm excited to see your home."

"Italy was always home for me until I met you. Now, I want to live here, even if I'm not physically with you." She tapped his chest over his slowly breaking heart. "If you'll have me."

"You'll always live here, Sof," he said, covering her hand as her palm rested over his heart. "I love you with all my soul."

"I love you too." Standing on her toes, she kissed him.

Heden drew her close, burying his face in her neck so she didn't see his own tears swimming in his eyes.

Chapter 36

The week in Italy was the absolute best of Sofia's life. After saying some heartfelt goodbyes to the people she'd come to love in the immortal world, Heden accompanied her through the ether to Positano. He'd been awed by the quaint seaside town, bustling yet charming with its cliffside buildings and gorgeous scenery.

They set off to enjoy all Sofia's favorite things: Italian wine, delicious pasta, walks across the pebbly beaches. The balcony of her secluded rental home sat high on the cliffs in a perfect location to watch the sunset each evening. The first night, they held each other on the balcony, Sofia gazing at Heden while he gaped, open-mouthed at the glory of the setting sun.

"You were right, Sof," he said, his eyes slightly glassy. "It's so damn gorgeous. I'll never see a sunset again without picturing this one with you. Thank you."

Locked in a gentle embrace, they stood, heads resting against each other, silent and content above the ocean.

Sofia introduced him to some of the local merchants. One of them, who passersby seemed to lovingly address as "Uncle Tony," helped Sofia identify which of the gigantic lemons would make the best lemonade. Once they trekked home, Heden drank her homemade concoction, surprised by how much he enjoyed it.

"I think I'm officially a food and drink lover," he said, toasting Sofia with the glass. "It's fantastic, honey."

Their days were filled with laughter and teasing, their nights with poignant passion. Each evening, after they made love, they would get lost in deep conversation, agreeing it wouldn't hurt to dream just a little bit longer.

"I like Bianca or Isabella," she said late one night as her body cooled upon the bed, fresh from their heated lovemaking session.

Tracing his finger over her cheek as his head rested on his palm, he squinted. "Bianca is good. I don't think I'm a fan of Isabella. What about Marcus for a boy? I've always liked that name for some reason."

"We'd name a boy Francesco," she said, her gaze questioning. "Wouldn't we?"

He feigned contemplation, squeezing one eye shut. "I think we should just go with Screech. We can carry on my family tradition of prematurely blowing my load."

Sofia burst into laughter, overcome by his teasing. "Please, tell me you're kidding."

"I'm kidding," he said, kissing her softly on the lips. "I would be honored to have a boy named Francesco with you, honey."

Sofia swallowed, lost in the sentiment in his eyes. Her nostrils flared as the tears began to well.

"Don't cry, sweetheart," he said, his face a mask of pain. "You promised if we discussed this stuff, you wouldn't get sad. Maybe we should stop."

"I'm okay," she said, shaking her head on the pillow. "I just wish so badly it was true."

"Everything about our love is true, Sof. Please don't forget that. I need you to hold onto it."

"I will," she whispered, drawing his lips to hers. "Love me again before we fall asleep."

Lost in the promises of a tomorrow that would never come, they loved each other until exhaustion overtook their ravaged bodies.

Finally, the last night arrived. Sofia awoke solemn and cranky, but her jovial Vampyre would have none of it. Urging her to don her bathing suit, they walked to the ocean and swam in the warm summer water. Somehow, Heden managed to loosen her bikini top and threatened to feed it to the fish. Sofia pleaded for it back, mortified, until he assured her no one was around to give a damn.

A slight fear shot down her spine at the notion Bakari could be lurking in the distance, waiting for the opportunity to attack them while they were unaware. But Heden convinced her they were safe, enveloping her in his strong embrace, reminding her how protected she felt in his arms. Observing the private pebbled beach that bordered the stairs leading up the hill to her home, she accepted their solace and relaxed. He somehow lost his shorts a few moments later—which Sofia was pretty damn convinced was intentional—and their squeals of laughter echoed off the cliffs as they skinny-dipped.

As the sun began to inch toward the horizon, Sofia emerged from her shower, throwing on a light yellow dress to combat the summer stickiness. Joining Heden on the balcony, she maneuvered in front of him to watch the sunset.

His front bracketed her back as his arms encircled her waist. Silent and thoughtful, they watched the ocean consume the glowing orb. Warm breaths caressed her neck as he inhaled behind her, calm and sure. As the ember-red half-circle eased into the void, he rested his lips against the shell of her ear.

"I love you."

Tears streamed down her face, free and unabetted, as she clutched onto the words. The coarse hairs of his beard caressed her neck as he nuzzled the delicate skin of her nape. "By the goddess, Sof, it's more than I ever hoped for. These feelings I have for you, they're so encompassing. You make me so happy. I'll never be sorry."

Her body shook in his arms, words impossible due to her sobbing. Sinking into him, she drew upon his strength, thankful he was there to support her inconsolable tears.

"It's okay, little human," he murmured, hands gently gathering her dress and lifting it. Sounds of clothes rustling registered in her ears, and she felt him searching, finding her wetness. He slipped inside her, joining them as the rays of the dying sunset illuminated their skin. Turning her head, she searched for his lips, kissing him with all her ardor as he pumped into her most intimate place.

"Look at me, Sofia," he said against her lips.

Opening her wet eyes, she stared into his soul.

"Please don't be sad," he said, undulating against her quivering body. "There's so much time for that later. Please, just focus on loving me."

"I love you so much," she cried, gliding her hands to fist in his hair. "I'm so sorry."

"No, baby," he said, his breathing harsh and labored. "No apologies. You're perfect." His fingers found the place between their bodies that drove her wild and brought her to the edge of sanity.

"My beautiful Sofia," he whispered.

"Heden," she cried.

Together, they shattered, their bodies depleting against one another as they both rejoiced and mourned their love. Trembling, they held each other, murmuring words that had no meaning except in the far reaches of their hearts. Heden surrounded her with his arms, carrying her to bed and pulling her into his cooling frame.

The bedroom curtain whipped, lazy and sluggish, from the nighttime breeze as she spread herself over every inch of his body. Slumber engulfed her for a while until he roused beneath her. Unable to move, lethargic with sorrow, she watched him dress. Once his things were gathered, he sat upon the bed.

His thumb traced over her cheek as they memorized each other one more time. Silently, he nodded, acknowledging her pain. She nodded back and reached up to catch the lone tear that trailed down his cheek. Smoothing the wetness over his skin, she smiled as much as her trembling lips would allow. He grinned back, reverent and sad.

Lowering, he kissed her, sweet and soft.

Sofia's heart leapt when he stood, most likely attempting to follow the man who'd stolen it.

From the doorway, he gazed at her for an eternity that only lasted a moment.

And then, he pivoted and returned to the immortality that made their love impossible.

Burying her face in the pillow, Sofia cried the tears she'd promised him wouldn't fall when he left her to resume his infinite future without her.

Chapter 37

Miranda grunted as she pulled at the brick that slightly jutted out from the wall. Frustrated it wouldn't budge, she flattened her foot along the wall as leverage and tugged again. Nothing. Annoyed at the stubborn rock, she collapsed on the floor in a huff, contemplating what tools she could use to move the damn thing.

"You still trying to find the loose brick?" Kenden asked, striding into the soothsayer chamber.

"Yeah," she said, angrily rubbing her forehead. "Every time I think I find one that sticks out, I look at it five minutes later and it seems even with the others. My eyes are going to cross soon."

"Hmm..." Kenden said, approaching her and extending his hand. He pulled her up and rubbed his chin as he contemplated the wall. "What exactly did Tatiana say to Heden again?"

"From what he remembers, she said, 'Pull the loose brick along the soothsayer chamber far wall.' This seems to be the far wall," Miranda said, gesturing to the open doorway across the room. "Do you see a stone that sticks out?"

"No," Kenden murmured, eyes narrowed. "They all seem pretty uniform. This chamber hasn't been used in centuries. It's possible any loose brick cemented to the ones around it over time."

"Maybe," Miranda said. "From what we know of Tatiana, she knows some pretty weird and important stuff. I'd really like to chase this rabbit hole and figure it out."

Kenden smiled. "Then I have no doubt you'll find it, Randi. When you're determined, nothing will get in your way."

Miranda nodded, running her hand along the cold wall. After a moment, Kenden said, "We could always check the abandoned soothsayer chamber at Restia. Tatiana didn't specify which compound, did she?"

"No, but that chamber was much smaller and only held copies of the most significant main scrolls in case something happened to this chamber. This is where the goods were kept."

"I vaguely remember the head soothsayer at Restia. He was young and quite zealous about his role in preserving our history. Sadly, he passed in the Awakening, but I remember his fervor for maintaining the soothsayer chamber there." Shrugging, he said, "I mean, it's worth a shot."

Miranda pursed her lips. "Okay. Want to come with me?"

"Sure. I'm up for an adventure. I'll drive us in a four-wheeler."

They set out through the open fields, catching up on their families and the state of the kingdom. Kenden and Latimus had been exhaustively rebuilding the army, and Evie and Larkin had been leading missions to far reaches of the realm in search of caves or natural structures where Bakari and his team of escaped prisoners and associates were hiding. So far, they'd found nothing. Perhaps the Secret Society had created a cloaking spell to hide their location from the naked eye. Perhaps they were in an uncharted part of the kingdom near the Purges of Methesda. Regardless, the immortal world was now on alert and involved in a conflict with unpredictable foes. Miranda was determined to keep her people safe and unharmed.

"Sadie informed me there haven't been any new cases of chemical poisoning in three weeks," Miranda said. "What do you think Bakari is waiting for?"

"I can't say for certain, but he's now got a battalion of soldiers as well as chemical weapons and magical powers. If it were me, I'd study the enemy and remain patient until I figured out the most effective ways to attack. He's most likely building his army, perhaps even cloning more."

"We have to find him, Ken. We can't let that happen."

"I know," Kenden said, squeezing her hand atop the leather seat. "Latimus and I will be done with the current round of training next week, and we're going to join the search. Jack is going to lead the next training round, and I'm confident he'll do a great job. Darkrip has offered to help, but he's stretched thin now Creigen's here. Evie has been relentless in tracking the unmapped land at the outer stretches of the kingdom, although I'm worried she's putting herself in danger."

"Evie's the toughest amongst us all," Miranda said, wanting to assure him. "She'll be fine."

"I hope so."

"You're going to be a father," she said, thrilled for her cousin. "I'm so happy for you, Ken."

His lips curved as he gave her a loving grin. "Remember when it was just you and me all those years ago? Things have changed so much."

"But you're still my ride or die, Ken."

"You're still mine too, even if you continue to listen to that human heavy metal garbage."

"Shut up," she said, swatting his arm. "You *will* come to appreciate Metallica one day. When that day comes, I'm going to do a freaking dance of joy. Just you wait."

Kenden pulled up to a sloping green-thatched hill housing a wooden door. Hopping from the vehicle, Miranda pulled the key she kept in her safe at Uteria, inserted it and turned the lock. The door clicked open, and Kenden illuminated his flashlight so they could step inside.

"Yuck," Miranda said, fanning her hand in front of her face. "It's so musty in here."

"I don't think anyone's been in here for centuries," Kenden said, slowly illuminating the chamber with the flashlight. Scrolls aligned the dusty tables and shelves that permeated the room. Clicking her phone, Miranda turned on the flashlight app.

"Wow," she said, fingers trailing over the felt that housed some of the scrolls on the center table. "These are ancient." Setting her phone down, she began to extricate some of the parchments from the felt bags.

They poured over them for half an hour, reading about the history of Etherya's Earth and the goddess's two beloved species. After categorizing them more efficiently in the chamber, Miranda began examining the far wall.

"I don't see any loose stones," she said, running her palm over the smooth surface.

"Me neither," Kenden said, crouching to examine the lower part of the structure.

Suddenly, Miranda gasped. "This one's loose!"

Kenden stood, grabbing the brick and helping her jerk it back and forth. Suddenly, it popped free and dropped to the ground. Eyes wide, Miranda grabbed Kenden's flashlight and shone it through the small hole.

"Holy shit," she breathed, maneuvering the flashlight. "There's a whole room filled with more scrolls."

Kenden's eyebrows narrowed. "There was only supposed to be one soothsayer chamber room at each compound."

"Well, someone built another one, and it looks like they went out of their way to keep it secret. I'll bet there's a hidden one at Uteria too."

"Damn," Kenden said, grasping onto one of the bricks by the hole. "Let's see if we can make a big enough opening to crawl through."

After grabbing some tools from the four-wheeler, they began to demolish the wall. Finally, they created an opening large enough to squeeze through.

Miranda began opening the parchments, careful not to damage them. Her heart began to pound as she realized their significance. "They all have 'Hidden Prophecy' in their titles. Like this one," she said, showing it to him and reading aloud.

"*Addition to the Restian Hidden Prophecy Soothsayer Scrolls by Ethu, the Youngest Soothsayer.*

Enclosed, please find the hidden prophecy of the Vampyre Prince Bakari. The Eldest Soothsayer did not sanction this scroll as he will not sanction my others. He does not concur with my choice to keep a separate secret archive, but I believe our children will need to know the history of the realm, even the history others deem too dangerous or insignificant. If the scrolls at Uteria are destroyed, my hope is that these scrolls will preserve our chronicles. If I am punished for my deeds, I will consider it a worthy retribution.

Peace be to all of Etherya's creatures."

"Well," Miranda said, arching a sardonic brow, "guess somebody tried to tell us about Bakari after all."

Kenden scanned the scrolls, awe in his features. "How many more warnings are in these hidden prophecies? My god, Miranda, we could have so many enemies we know nothing about."

Inhaling a deep breath, she nodded. "Let's get to cataloguing them. The more we know, the better."

They collected the scrolls with care, wanting to preserve the withered parchments so they could analyze them at Uteria. When they'd almost finished gathering them, she lifted a scroll that had a strange symbol on it.

"Have you ever seen this mark?" she asked.

"No. It doesn't look like any of Etherya's creatures' written languages."

"I want to open it."

Kenden nodded. "Gently."

With careful movements, she broke the wax seal and unrolled the paper. Reading aloud, her tone became more concerned as she advanced.

"Addition to the Restian Hidden Prophecy Soothsayer Scrolls by Ethu, the Youngest Soothsayer.

Be it known that the Elves have all but perished from the land. They were not Etherya's creatures, and we did not revere them, but they were a simple people, and we wished them no harm. Our magnificent King Valktor visited their realm, hoping to abet them, but it was too late. He returned with their prophecy scrolls, which we have catalogued.

The Eldest Soothsayer deemed some of the prophecies impossible, and they were discarded, but I believe all divinations must be catalogued for historical purposes. Below, you will find the hidden Elven prophecies, listed in the order I deem most important.

Peace be to all of Etherya's creatures.

Elven Prophecy #1

A lone Elf will survive our kingdom's destruction. He will evolve into a powerful being, castigated by the goddess Etherya. Embroiled in his hate, he will spawn children upon the Earth who will cause great devastation. The firstborn spawn of his firstborn spawn will align with the marked Vampyre prince to destroy Etherya's realm as we know it, and it will exist no more..."

Swallowing thickly, Miranda gazed up at Kenden. "The firstborn spawn of Crimeous's firstborn spawn," she said softly.

"Callie," he murmured.

Miranda nodded. "We have to show this to Darkrip as soon as possible."

Kenden nodded, his expression pensive. "Come on. Let's get everything in the four-wheeler and head to Uteria. There's so much to categorize, and this might only be the beginning."

Consumed with a latent foreboding, they collected the secret prophecies, intent on identifying the new threats they most assuredly held.

Chapter 38

Heden sat at the Bourbon Street coffee shop attempting to focus on his research. Difficult, since his eyes kept darting to the door every five seconds. He hoped the handwritten note he'd left on Tatiana's door would implore her to show. Nervous, he tapped on the keypad, awaiting her arrival.

The bell above the door rang, and she breezed in, the airy skirt of her long dress flowing behind her. Her smile was kind as she approached the table. "May I?" she asked, gesturing to the vacant seat across from him.

Nodding, he rubbed his damp palms on his thighs. "I wasn't sure you'd show. I stopped by your house multiple times before I realized you weren't really living there anymore."

"I've been spending time at some other places I enjoy upon the Earth. But your note did intrigue me."

The server came over, and Tatiana ordered an herbal tea before continuing. "So, you didn't return to the immortal world after leaving Italy?"

He shook his head. "I figured it was worth a shot to see if you could use your super-potion powers to create something that could turn Sofia immortal and allow us to have biological children together." Breathing a laugh, he ran his fingers through his hair. "When I say it out loud, it sounds insane."

Tatiana slowly stirred the steaming liquid the waitress set in front of her with the tiny metal spoon that accompanied it. "You both had a magnificent goodbye. Is that not enough?"

"I said goodbye because our relationship in our current form won't make either of us happy. It took me a while to get that, but I get it now. Even with that knowledge, I'm determined to figure out another way."

Amber irises studied him as she blew steam from the tea. "And what makes you think I know of another way?"

"The conversation we had in the in-between. You seemed to indicate there was hope."

Her eyes narrowed. "Hope for happiness between a mortal and an immortal is futile."

"I know," he said, running a frustrated hand over his face. "I was hoping you have some potion or knowledge to help me figure out how to grant Sofia immortality."

Setting the cup in the saucer, she slid a hand over his wrist. "I'm so very sorry, son of Markdor. Truly, I am. Your love for her is palpable. There is only one on the planet who can grant immortality."

"Etherya," he said, clenching his jaw.

"Yes."

"I've prayed and pleaded to her so many times, but she won't appear to me. She finally appeared to Sathan and told him she won't even consider it."

"The Universe was extremely displeased with her when she granted Nolan immortality. I understand her decision."

Defeated, Heden sat back in his chair. "I've researched every human library and every archive and soothsayer manual in the immortal world. I just don't know what to do, Tatiana. How can I give up?"

Her lips compressed as she looked out the window, contemplative and pensive. Finally, she trained her gaze upon him. "Although time is your enemy, I think you must take some. Time to think. Time to truly process your emotions and the gravity of the choices you face. Only then will you find the remote possibility of a solution."

"So, you think there's hope? I'm so afraid of losing faith, Tatiana."

"There is a beauty in your love. Both of you were two solo puzzle pieces searching to be whole. You're extremely close to locking in place, but like any puzzle, if the edges are bent, the pieces remain unconnected."

"Wow," he said, rubbing his beard. "I need to write this stuff down. Your riddles are insane, lady."

Her rich laughter washed over them, and she sipped the last of her tea before standing. "Take some time, Heden. You will know how much you need. I truly wish for all your dreams to come true. Until we meet again, know that I am sending you positive vibes through the ether." Giving him a nod, she exited the shop, the bell ringing solemnly behind her.

Frustrated and sad he still had no discernable solution, Heden packed up his laptop and headed back to the immortal world.

* * * *

Several weeks later...

Heden gritted his teeth, punching the hanging bag with his bare fists. Sweat dripped down his brow as he unleashed every unwanted emotion on the lifeless target. He'd been frequenting the gym at Astaria often since his return from the human world, hoping the uptick in energy would help spur his brain into solving the conundrum of building a sustainable life with Sofia.

So far, no such luck.

Latimus stalked in, his face an unreadable mask as usual. Normally, Heden would make fun of him for his perma-scowl, but he just didn't feel like jibing with him today. Or any day, really. He'd become so sullen and withdrawn since his return, he knew his family was worried. Unfortunately, he just couldn't seem to shake the funk.

"How was your visit to the Slayer military hospital?" Heden asked.

"Fine," Latimus said, although frustration emanated from his massive frame. "This new batch of chemicals has a twenty-five percent mortality rate in Slayers. Bakari's becoming more effective even with the program you and Sofia created."

"Damn," Heden said, sighing. "I can try to make some tweaks, but I'm pretty sure the software is already functioning at its highest capacity."

"I'll let you know if we need you to reconfigure anything. For now, we're on top of it." Latimus grabbed the punching bag. "Throw some stationary punches. I'll hold it steady."

Complying, Heden began a series of rapid-fire jabs, the resulting pain upon his knuckles a welcome distraction from his completely fragmented heart. After a few minutes, he began to wheeze.

"All right," Latimus said in his deep baritone. "That's enough. Take a break. Here." His brother thrust a canister at him.

"Thanks," Heden said, gulping the water as if his life depended on it. "Whew, that's good." He wiped his brow with his forearm.

Latimus crossed his arms and regarded him, foot tapping on the blue mat. "You look like shit, Heden."

A laugh escaped his throat. "Thanks, bro. You're pretty fucking hideous too."

Latimus scowled. "I mean it. You must've lost twenty pounds since you returned from the human world. You're chiseled because you spend hours in here every day, but you still look thin."

"Sadie said I might have some lingering health effects from my wound. If I keep working out, I'll be fine."

"It's not from your injury, and we both know it."

Sighing, Heden sat on the nearby workout bench. "What do you want me to say, Latimus? That I miss her? That I'm a fucking shell of a person without her? Even if it's true, I just can't figure out how to change our impossible situation."

His brother stood stoic, the mindless tapping of his foot driving Heden insane. "Dude, if you're just going to stare at me all day, I'm out."

Latimus's eyes narrowed. "I'm just remembering a conversation we had many years ago, when I was distraught after Lila's maiming. I was so sure there was no way we could be together. There were so many obstacles in our way. But you convinced me anything was possible if I wanted badly enough to make it happen."

"That was true," Heden said, shrugging. "You guys certainly had some struggles, but there was always a way forward if you fought hard enough. I'm glad you figured it out."

"I'm wondering why the same doesn't hold true for you."

"Um, because I'm immortal, and Sofia is human. A future together is impossible for us. Every scenario we imagined is ultimately filled with so much heartache and pain. Until I can find a way around that, we just can't be together, Latimus. It breaks my heart, but I won't put Sofia through that. I can't put either of us through that. It's just fucking awful."

Latimus stood firm, contemplating.

"Dude, you're annoying the hell out of me."

"If I recall," Latimus said, eyes searching the ceiling as he placed his hands on his hips, "you said something to the effect of 'If I ever meet someone for whom I feel half the emotion you and Lila feel for each other, I'll never let her go.'" Piercing him with his gaze, he asked, "I think that was it, right?"

"Yes, but our situation is different—"

"Bullshit," Latimus interrupted. "I don't think it's different at all."

Heden scoffed. "Okay, awesome. Tell me how in the hell I'm supposed to build a life with a mortal. Can't wait to hear it."

His brother shook his head, disappointment in his eyes. "You've always been afraid of committing one hundred percent, Heden. For the goddess's sake, I think you seduced over half the women in the kingdom. To what end? What was the purpose? It's time for you to truly commit to something. It's going to require sacrifice and hard choices. That's what people do when they love each other. They throw it all on the line and never accept defeat."

Heden stood, palms exposed as he slashed his hands in frustration. "I've made a thousand hard choices—"

"No, you haven't," Latimus said, stepping forward. "You're amazing at helping us with the weapons and the tech, but that's easy for you, Heden. Finding a way to be with Sofia is going to be extremely difficult. It's time you put that brain of yours to good use and figure out a way to make sacrifices to be with her."

"Sacrifices? I'd make a million sacrifices to be with her if I could."

"How? What methods have you truly employed?"

"I prayed to Etherya a thousand times, asking her to bestow immortality on Sofia. When she finally appeared to Sathan, she basically told him to tell me to fuck off. I approached Tatiana, and she just spouted her usual riddles, so that didn't help. I researched every immortal archive and human library I could. I'm not sure what else you want me to do here, bro."

"So that's it?" Latimus said, lifting his hands. "A few prayers, some rejections, some research and you're done? If someone told me I'd have to live without Lila for an eternity, I'd blaze the damn planet until I found a way to be with her."

Heden opened his mouth to speak and promptly closed it. What was he missing? Was there something else he could've tried? Tatiana had told him to take time to digest things, but he'd come up with absolute shit. Maybe there was still something he hadn't considered...

"Now you're getting it," Latimus said. "Finding a way to be with Sofia is going to be *hard*, Heden. You want to sit around and mope all day? Fine with me. But I have a feeling you'd rather discern a way to be with the love of your damn life. So, figure it out. We live in a world of magical creatures and potions that can bring people back to life, for the goddess's sake. There has to be a way you can figure out how to live with a mortal."

Heden's eyebrows drew together as he contemplated.

"You always tell me how damn brilliant you are. Use your intellect and find a solution."

"Damn it," Heden said, lowering back to the bench. Gripping the sides, he clenched his fists. "I have no idea what else I can do."

"Did you talk to Evie? She shares Etherya's blood. Maybe she can help you."

Heden nodded. "Yeah, but that was before I did the bulk of my research. I learned a lot about human rituals from lots of different cultures. There are some really fascinating stories of otherworldly things that happen over there. I wouldn't be surprised if there were more immortals who have frequented the human realm over the centuries than we even know."

Latimus's lips drew into a thin line as he contemplated. "Maybe Evie could use her powers along with some ancient human spell or something to try and bestow immortality on Sofia. I don't know, Heden, but I think you're giving up too easily."

Feeling his heartbeat accelerate as numerous possibilities began to filter through his mind, Heden stood and approached his brother. Grabbing Latimus's face, he tried to place a walloping smack on his forehead. Latimus shoved him away, causing Heden to laugh.

"Damn, Latimus, I really needed that kick in the ass," he said, smiling for the first time in the goddess knows how long. "It's nice to see your surly personality put to good use. Now, tell me I'm your favorite brother and that you love me."

"Get the hell out of here so you can figure out a way to bond with the human and leave me alone."

"Oh, I'm going to figure it out," Heden said, excitement coursing through his veins as he gathered his sweat-soaked towel and slung it around his neck. Trailing to the door, he continued. "And then I'm going to bond with Sofia, and we're going to build a huge house right next to yours and Lila's, and you'll get to see me every second of every day. You're gonna love it!"

"I'm banning you from Lynia!" Latimus called after him.

"No way, bro! You're stuck with me."

Chuckling as he trekked to his chambers, he swore his heard his brother mutter a curse before he was out of earshot.

Heden recommitted himself to the task of finding some way, any way, to create a sustainable future with Sofia. The next day, he approached Evie armed with the knowledge he'd gained from months of meticulous research. Although she was sympathetic to his cause, she was adamant no amount of effort would allow her to bestow immortality upon Sofia. Even with her potency, there was no entity besides Etherya who had the capacity to render someone immortal.

"Are you absolutely sure?" he asked as they sat in front of her mahogany desk at Takelia.

"I share Etherya's blood, and that gives me a certain...*insight* into her powers," Evie said. "You can choose to believe me or not but trust me when I say, Etherya is the only one on the planet powerful enough to manipulate mortality or immortality."

Heden sighed and ran his hand through his hair, frustrated at his inability to elucidate the situation. He had always been able to find a solution to even the most indiscernible problem, and his inability to build a sustainable future for him and Sofia was maddening.

Evie encircled his wrist, squeezing as empathy welled in her green eyes. "You're trying so hard, but sometimes, you just need to take the simplest path."

His eyes darted between hers. "I'm open to suggestions."

"I *feel* your love for her, Heden. It's amazing. I think you need to speak to Etherya directly. I think she'll be swayed by the sentiment in your heart."

"I called upon her so many times, Evie," he said, shrugging. "She wouldn't appear to me. And when she finally spoke to Sathan, she was clear it was a no-go."

Evie grinned. "My advice? Try again. And don't stop trying until she appears to you. I mean, what the hell have you got to lose? And lord knows, you've got nothing but time."

Heden bit his lip. "Are you telling me to piss off the goddess who can decimate me with a snap of her fingers?"

Her scarlet eyebrow arched. "I think that's exactly what I'm telling you. She'll either grant your request or disintegrate you on the spot for driving her insane. Either way, you'll get a dramatic conclusion."

Laughing, Heden stood and embraced her. "Okay, I'm down. But remember to hide my porn if she murders me. I'll text you a picture of my stash so you know where I keep it."

"Ohhhh," Evie said, pulling back and waggling her brows. "I'll put it to good use." Cupping his jaw, she smiled reverently. "I wish you luck, my friend. You and Sofia deserve all the happiness in the world."

Since Evie was one of the most omniscient people he knew, he chose to heed her advice and forged ahead. That evening and each night after, he trekked to the river, standing upon the spot where he knew the goddess spoke to Sathan. For hours, he would call to Etherya, begging her to appear, to no avail. Undeterred, he continued the ritual, firm in his belief if he summoned her long enough, she would surface. As Evie had pointed out, he had nothing if not time.

One night, as the gurgling river kept him company, Heden sat on the soft grass, silently praying to the goddess, begging her to materialize. So far, hours had ticked by, and his pleas had gone unanswered. Unwavering in his palpable desire to build a life with his beloved, he sat patiently, eyes closed as his fingers twined together.

Suddenly, a rustling sounded to his right, and he lurched to his feet, hoping this would be the night she finally emerged. Bright light materialized from nothingness until her image appeared, floating and airy. Long, blood-red curls flowed down her back above her white, ethereal dress.

"Hello, son of Markdor," she said, the anger in her tone sending a jolt of fear down his spine. "I have heard your pleas, and they disturb my peace immensely. I implore you to stop your prayers. They are wasted and fruitless."

"My goddess," he said, bowing on one knee. "I am honored with your presence."

"Rise and tell me why you insist on pleading for something you know I will never grant."

Standing to his full height, he contemplated his words, wanting to make sure his appeal was seamless so it enhanced her chances of changing her mind. "My goddess Etherya, you must be able to sense I love the human with my entire soul. I beg you to take pity on us and grant us the ability to have a future."

The goddess's eyes narrowed. "Sofia Morelli is destined to remain human, and this cannot be changed. I find your entreaty a nuisance."

Licking his dry lips, he forged ahead. "I understand you made the human physician Nolan immortal. Why can you not bestow the same gift on Sofia?"

The goddess's beady eyes bore into him, her figure floating above the grass. "Nolan acted honorably when he followed King Sathan through the ether in an attempt to save him. I conferred immortality on him in return for his deeds."

"Sofia has done so much to help our kingdom, Goddess," he pleaded. "To help your people and mine." He detailed all Sofia's efforts, making his case for her worthiness. Once finished, he asked, "Knowing all that, doesn't she deserve immortality?"

Etherya blinked, slow and thoughtful, the silence threating to choke him. Then, she opened her mouth and said firmly, "No."

Heden's heart lurched to his knees. "No? How can you say that, Etherya? I can't think of anyone who deserves immortality more."

"Quiet!" she said, slicing her hand through the air. "Do not anger me, son of Markdor, or I will vanish and leave you to your heartache."

"I'm sorry, Goddess," he said, bowing his head in contrition. "I just want so badly to build a life with her. She's...the love of my life."

He thought the goddess might have sighed. "The Universe was displeased when I bestowed immortality upon Nolan. It was a rash decision but one I do not regret. Unfortunately, an imbalance was created when I granted him immortality. I do not want to displease the Universe further."

Heden stayed silent, wracking his brain for stronger arguments he could make to change her mind.

"But my heart is intrigued by your persistence. You must truly love the human to beg so passionately."

"I do, Goddess. With all my heart."

Silence stretched as she studied him. "Then, perhaps you could help me."

"Help you?" he said, lifting his gaze to hers.

"Yes," she said with a nod. "Help me restore balance and relieve the Universe's displeasure."

Heden's irises darted between hers. "How?"

Lifting her chin, she said, "You could choose to become human."

Heden's eyelids fluttered in quick succession, unsure he'd heard her correctly. "Become human?"

"Yes. I would extricate your immortality and render you human. You would function as a human, requiring food and water, and would eventually die as all humans do."

A thousand emotions ran through Heden's body as he deliberated. Locking his gaze with hers, he asked, "Would I be able to have human children?"

"Yes." She tilted her head. "You would be able to impregnate human females. You would be human in every sense of the word. Your body would resume aging from the day you went through your immortal change and advance in years until its eventual end."

Running his fingers through his thick hair, Heden struggled to catch his breath. The possibility was overwhelming.

"I will give you one day to consider. It is a formidable task for me to undertake, but I will do it to rebalance the Universe and to thank you for your efforts across the kingdom. You have done much to help my people. If you wish to accept my offer, meet me here tomorrow under the waxing moon. I will not make this proffer again. Choose wisely, Heden, son of Markdor." Lifting her hands, palms facing the sky, she closed her eyes and vanished.

Heden expelled a huge breath through puffed cheeks, the gravity of the choice before him enormous. Lifting his phone from his back pocket, he called Sathan.

"What's up, Heden?"

"I need to have a video call with you, Latimus and Arderin tomorrow morning. It's important."

"Are you okay?"

"Yes. I think I'm actually more okay than I've been in a long time. Can you coordinate the call? I'll need at least an hour, and I feel like everyone will take it seriously if you schedule it."

"I'll do it as soon as I hang up. Are you sure you don't need anything? Miranda and I are at Uteria, but I can come to you."

"I'm good, bro," he said, beginning his trek back to Astaria. "Actually, I'm really fucking good. Talk to you tomorrow."

Stuffing his phone in his back pocket, Heden headed toward the darkened castle, his heart so full with possibility he damn near skipped home.

Chapter 39

Sofia sat in the coffee shop, scrolling the wheel of her wireless mouse as her chin rested on her fist, elbow propped on the table. She was spending her fortieth birthday filtering through endless sperm donor profiles. *Happy birthday to me*, she sang sarcastically in her mind.

She'd put off searching for a donor after Heden left because her heart was a heap of broken mush that would most likely never recover. But time had a way of kicking your ass, and she decided she'd resume on her fortieth birthday. So, here she was, in the Italian coffee shop with great Wi-Fi and amazing cappuccino, deciding which man's sperm she wanted shoot up her vagina. *Happy birthday, indeed.*

As she continued to absently scroll, a text window suddenly popped up on her screen. Three words appeared from the blinking curser: **I see you.**

Sofia gasped, immediately searching the coffee shop. They were the first words Heden had written when he'd hacked into her laptop in L.A.

Thick heartbeats threatened to close her throat as she placed her fingers on the keyboard. **Heden?**

The curser blinked. Once. Again. Several times, driving her insane. Struggling to breathe, she waited.

Finally, a message appeared: **40.874240, 14.656890.**

"What the hell?" she murmured, struggling to decipher the numbers. Dragging the curser, she copied the digits and pasted them in the internet search bar.

"They're coordinates," she whispered, striving to understand what was happening. Plugging them into a map application, she noted the longitude and latitude coordinates corresponded to a town called Moschiano, which was about a two-hour drive away. Contemplating, she chewed her lip. What did the mysterious coordinates represent? Had Heden sent them to her?

Pulling out her phone, she dialed his number. They'd promised each other they would never make contact even in emergencies, but she didn't give a damn. Each ring of the phone frazzled her shattered nerves until his voicemail picked up.

"Of course you let it go to voicemail. Bastard." Huffing with frustration, she pondered a moment longer and then gathered her things and headed to the rental car office a few blocks away.

Several hours later, she slowly navigated a gravel driveway that opened up to an expansive property. Acres of open land stretched in the background as she pulled up to a green-shingled house. Stepping out of the car, she closed the door and approached the archway. Opening the metal gate, she stepped through, hesitant and unsure.

"Heden?" she called, tentatively walking over the flat stone patio. "Hello? Is anyone here?"

Advancing forward, she saw the edge of the balcony and approached the flat surface of the balcony's edge. Peering over it, she broke into a huge smile.

"Hey, little human," Heden said, waving up at her from the ground below. "Took you long enough. I've been waiting forever."

"Heden!" Squealing, she vaulted down the stairs and ran to him, leaping into his arms, causing him to emit an "oomph" when he caught her. Wrapping her legs around his waist, she rained kisses all over his face, his beard tickling her lips.

"Damn, Sof, you almost knocked me over. I hope that means you're happy to see me."

"You're so thin," she said, concern smothering her as she ran her hands over his shoulders. "Are you okay? Is it something from your injury?"

He smiled, his gaze reverent as it roved over her face. "I've been pretty fucked-up and haven't really been drinking a lot of Slayer blood. It's hard to nourish yourself when you're not sure how the hell you're going to make it through another day."

"Oh, Heden," she said, his face blurring from the tears in her eyes. "I missed you so much too. Can you stay for a while? Maybe I can try to fatten you up with some pasta."

His eyebrow lifted. "That statement might prove truer than you think," he murmured.

"Huh?"

He kissed her and set her gently on her feet. Reaching behind his back, he pulled a single red rose from the back pocket of his jeans. "Happy Birthday."

"Thank you," she said, taking the flower and inhaling the fragrant scent. "I think I'm supposed to be washed up now, but I feel pretty good."

His irises raked over her. "Did you move forward with a donor?"

Sighing, she shook her head. "I only started looking again today. Told myself I'd resume on my fortieth birthday. Whether I like it or not, time's a tickin'."

Extending his hand, he urged her to take it. "Walk with me."

Sliding her palm in his, she squeezed. "Did you bring me to an abandoned winery to bang me against a tree again? I'm open, but I think this place has seen better days."

Throwing back his head, he laughed, loud and deep. The sound sent thrills of pleasure through her body. Although he'd lost weight, he still towered over her and looked delicious in his jeans and black polo shirt. "I brought you here because this place is for sale."

"Okaaaay," she said, glancing up at him as they strolled between the deadened vines. "I didn't realize Vampyres were into deserted human wineries, but I've been wrong before."

"Actually, I find I'm not really invested in Vampyre interests these days. I've become much more enthralled with human interests."

"Heden," she said, stopping short and facing him. "What in the ever-loving hell are you talking about? You're not making any sense. Why are you here?"

He licked his lips, and Sofia realized he looked incredibly nervous. When he opened his mouth to speak, she thought something was different but couldn't put her finger on it.

"I finally made a choice, Sof," he said, a reverence in his tone. "A commitment that required sacrifice and deep reflection."

"Well, I'm proud of you. What was the choice?"

He struggled to speak as he pushed a strand of hair behind her ear. Licking his lips again, she noticed his teeth. "Where are your fangs?" she asked, squinting at the strange image. His incisors didn't form the points they had in the past. "Did you...shave them down?" Looking around, she felt off-balance. "Am I stuck in one of Tatiana's weird visions or something?"

He gently grasped her upper arms, rubbing them in a soothing caress. "I didn't shave them down, Sof. They disappeared."

"Disappeared," she repeated, wondering if the bizarre conversation was ever going to make sense. "When?"

"When I accepted Etherya's offer."

Blood pulsed through every vein in her body as she whispered, "What offer?"

His chest heaved with labored breaths as he beamed down at her. "Her offer to become human."

Sofia sucked in a breath, exhaling it slowly as she stared up at him. "That's impossible."

"No, little human," he said, shaking his head, "it's extremely possible and it's already been done, so I hope you still kinda like me because reversing it actually *is* impossible."

The forgotten rose slipped from her fingers as disbelief coursed through every cell in her trembling frame. Tentatively, she laid her palms against his cheeks. As wetness pervaded her eyes, she stroked his face, searching for evidence he spoke the truth.

"You're human?"

He nodded, eyes closing as he nuzzled into her hands. "God, Sofie, I missed your touch. It's amazing to feel your soft skin again."

"How did you convince her to turn you human? What does that mean? Are you mortal now?"

Lifting his lids, he placed his hand over hers upon his cheek. "Yes, sweetheart. I'm human in every way. I'm going to start aging from twenty-eight and advance just like you."

Puffs of air jetted from her lungs as her chin trembled. "Does that mean you can give me babies?"

"As many as you want, Sof," he said, elation encompassing his every feature. "I mean, within reason. I just came around to the notion of this whole wife and kids thing, so let's not go overboard."

Giving a jubilant laugh, she gazed at him with wonder. "But what about your family? How could they agree to this?"

"I love them so much, Sof, but they have families of their own now. Something they've created that's so magnificent for each of them. I want to create that with you."

Overwhelmed by how much he'd given up so he could build something with her, the tears that had been threatening to fall slid down her cheeks. "Heden, how could you do this? It's such a huge sacrifice. You're forfeiting eternity to be with me for less than a century in the best of scenarios."

"I'm relinquishing an infinity of loneliness to spend a lifetime with you. There's no contest, honey. I'd choose that option every day and twice on Sunday."

"I can't even imagine how you made this decision," she said, caressing his face. "It's such a gift."

"You know what's awesome? I've got a lifetime to make you understand how simple it was to make this choice. Nothing has ever felt truer than deciding to spend the rest of my life with you, Sof."

"Come here," she cried, pulling him close and devouring his lips, lost in the splendor of his astonishing decision. Their tongues slid over each other, familiar and passionate, until she thought her knees might buckle. "I'm so humbled by you," she whispered, brushing his lips with hers. "I don't even know how to begin to thank you. My god, Heden. We're going to have a future together. It's amazing. I'm overwhelmed."

"I mean, we could still bang against one of the trees," he said, jerking his head toward the nearby forest. "You kinda owe me one here."

Her laughter erupted over the sloping hills as she held him close. "I'll bang you anywhere. Everywhere. If that's what I have to do to even this out, I'm in." Caressing his cheek, she said, "I love you so much."

"I love you too," he said, placing his forehead against hers. "And I can't wait to build our life together. It's going to be fucking awesome, Sof."

"Does this winery have something to do with it?"

Lifting his head, he gazed over the withered vines. "It's just a thought, but I know you love to make wine, and you're great at it. Also, you're loaded, and I have no money except Vampyre lira, which is only good in the immortal world. I thought we could maybe buy this place and spruce it up and bring it into the twenty-first century. We could create the first virtual winery, where people could see 3D renderings of each glass on an app and order various tastes or quantities. I don't know, I'm spitballing here."

"I love it," she said, wheels already churning in her mind. "And we could create a rewards system through the app where they accrue points to win trips to visit the winery. And we could develop a virtual hub where people can log on from across the world and drink wine together while connecting online."

"Like Facebook for wine."

"Exactly."

"Damn, that's a great idea. Let's look around. I want to see the whole property. The owner lives a few miles away and said we could have free rein of the place."

"Does that include the woods over there?"

"Sofia," he said, his grin so sexy she felt a rush of moisture between her thighs. "You've brought this up a few times now. If you want to ravish my body, you have to ask me nicely."

Standing on her tiptoes, she softly pecked his lips. "Heden, will you please let me ravish your body?"

Reaching down, he grabbed her hips, lifting her over his shoulder as he proceeded to march toward the forest. "Little human, I thought you'd never ask."

Her blissful giggles radiated across the gentle slopes and rows of vines as her beloved granted her request.

Epilogue

Heden heard the euphoric sounds of children playing as soon as he stepped onto the soft grass. Trailing through the vines, thick with ripe grapes, he broke into a huge grin as the little girl ran toward him.

"Papa!" she said, arms outstretched as love washed over his skin. Crouching down, he picked her up and balanced her on his hip, pretending to eat her ear.

"Yum! An ear all for me. It's so scrumptious."

Her high-pitched giggles expanded his heart so much he thought it might burst. "You can't eat my ear. Ew!"

"Sure can. Just you wait. Were you a good girl for Mama?"

"She was a really good girl," Sofia said, walking toward them, their son perched on her own hip. "Bianca is a big girl now, and I'm so proud of her."

"I'm big too," Francesco said, his tiny lips forming a pout.

"You're big too, Frankie," Heden said, leaning over to kiss his cheek and then Sofia's lips. "Hey, honey."

"How was the drive back from Rome?"

"Not bad. I only sped a little," he said, winking. "After two days with stuffy investors, I was ready to get home."

"I'm so excited the venture capitalists love our virtual wine club idea," she said, excitement lacing her stunning features. "I can't believe we're fully funded for launch. Great job with the meetings. Wish we could've gone with you, but it would've been too much. Someone had to take care of the wonder twins here."

"Thanks for taking one for the team. I definitely owe you unlimited babysitting breaks for a month. And maybe unlimited banging breaks too."

"What's banging?" Bianca asked.

"That's when you hit something hard, like a wall or a tree," Sofia said, shooting Heden a stern glare.

"Really hard," Heden said, waggling his brows. "And over and over—"

"Okay, Papa's really tired and needs to stop talking right now. Good thing Mama made some pasta. Who's hungry?"

The twins cheered as their parents set them on the ground and ran to the house, breaking into a sprint to see who was faster.

Closing her eyes, Sofia sighed. "I'm exhausted."

Chuckling, he pulled her into a warm embrace. "They have way too much energy, that's for damn sure." Palming her cheeks, he stared into her blue-green eyes. "I missed you, Sofie. Damn, you look so pretty right now. Even with dried food on your shirt," he finished, snickering.

Her features scrunched. "I think there's a compliment in there somewhere?"

Laughing, he consumed her lips in a passionate kiss. Resting his forehead on hers, he said, "I picked up the new virtual reality game with the awesome reviews. I thought we could play it once the kids are asleep. Naked, of course."

"Mmmm..." she said, arms squeezing around his neck. "That sounds naughty. I'm so in."

Brushing one more sweet kiss over her lips, he straightened and threaded his fingers through hers. Together, they strode to the home they'd built under the glow of the late afternoon sun.

"Miranda called today," Sofia said. "Everything's set for Tordor's birthday party at Uteria next weekend. I told her I'd help cook, but she said Glarys and Jana have it covered."

"I can't wait to see everyone. We haven't been there since Christmas."

"It's so awesome of your family to celebrate Christmas with me even if they don't believe."

"You're family now, honey. It's an important holiday for you, and it's really fun to celebrate because it brings everyone together."

"Maybe we can have everyone come here next Christmas. I'd love to decorate the house and get a tree and host."

"Let's bring it up at Tordor's party. I'm sure they'd love that. Did Miranda have any updates on Bakari when you spoke?"

Sofia shook her head. "After the last attack three months ago, he's been quiet. Latimus estimated he lost a hundred Deamon soldiers in that attack, so Miranda thinks he's cloning more. They still have no idea where he's hiding. She thinks it's in the immortal world, but he could also have a base here. It's terrifying," she said, worry crossing her features as she glanced toward their children in the distance.

"I've got you, sweetheart," he said, clenching her hand, his tone reassuring. "I have the utmost faith in Latimus and Ken. They'll be ready for the next attack. And we're armed here with weapons and the kick-ass security system we programmed. We're smarter than the Secret Society. I won't let anything happen to our family."

Their children called to them, beckoning them inside, and Sofia clutched his hand. Gazing up at him, she whispered, "Thank you. For loving me and protecting us and for our babies. I love you all so much."

Turning to face her, he tucked a black curl behind her ear. "Thanks for being a terrible hacker. Otherwise, I never would've had to correct all your work, and we never would've fallen in love."

Chuckling, she shook her head. "You're still jealous I'm better than you. When will you let it go? Just accept it, buddy."

"Give me a few decades. Maybe I'll get over it then."

"That I can do," she said, tugging him toward the house. "If we're lucky, I can give you many more decades."

"I think we're pretty damn lucky, Sof, so I like our chances."

Full lips curved into a poignant smile, she whispered, "So do I."

Rejoining their children, they headed inside to enjoy the magnificently mundane task of eating family dinner.

Before You Go...

*Wow, readers, we waited a LONG time for this one. I hope you felt Heden and Sofia's happy ending was as perfect as I did. To me, there's something so romantic about giving up an infinite loneliness to spend a lifetime with the love of your life, and I hope you felt the same! Ready to continue reading about our awesome immortals? I wrote a sweet, steamy novella called **Two Souls United**, which follows Jack's Uncle Sam and lovely Glarys as they find their own happy ending.*

*After **Two Souls United**, you can dive right into **The Cryptic Prophecy**, Etherya's Earth Book 6! This is the first book in the next generation of our favorite immortals and it's steamy and action-packed. We finally get a resolution with Bakari as we see Darkrip and Arderin's daughter, Callie, fall in love!*

* * * *

Please consider leaving a review on Amazon, Goodreads and/or BookBub. Indie authors survive on reviews and they are so appreciated. Your friendly neighborhood author thanks you from the bottom of her heart!

* * * *

Books by Rebecca Hefner

Etherya's Earth Series (Fantasy/Paranormal Romance)
Book 1: The End of Hatred
Book 2: The Elusive Sun
Book 3: The Darkness Within
Book 4: The Reluctant Savior
Book 5: The Impassioned Choice
Book 5.5: Two Souls United
Book 6: The Cryptic Prophecy
Book 6.5: Garridan's Mate (in the Hearts Unleashed anthology)
Book 7: Coming Soon!

Prevent the Past Series (Sci-Fi Time Travel Romance)
Book 1: A Paradox of Fates
Book 2: A Destiny Reborn
Book 3: A Timeline Restored

Books also available in Audiobook and eBook format!

Acknowledgments

Thanks so much to everyone who's waited *almost* a year for this book! I felt it was important to take some time and launch a new series to keep things fresh. Although I love writing my new books, Etherya's world and the complex, funny, amazing characters who inhabit it will always be my first love because it was, well, first! Rest assured I'm not done with this world and will keep writing books for our amazing immortals (and humans!) until the stories no longer appear in my head. Can you guess which characters are next? I planted a few *very* vague seeds in this book, but you'll have to wait to see! I hope to publish at least one Etherya's Earth book per year (more if they flow faster) along with the new series that I'm currently writing (and some that only exist in my head right now!). Thank you all for being on this journey with me, and I'll see you in the next book.

Special thanks to Sharan D. for her unwavering support. She's always one of the first to read my books and leave a review, and I think I forgot to mention her in the acknowledgments of my last book, which was a huge oversight. You're awesome, friend. Thank you!

Thanks to Jaime who let me use her awesome line about hiding the porn. Ha! It was a perfect line for our sexy jokester, Heden, and you did him justice!

And thanks to all of you who read these books and get lost in these worlds with me. You'll never know how much it means to have you along for the ride. Until next time, stay well and don't forget to seize your dreams!

About the Author

Rebecca Hefner grew up in Western NC and now calls the Hudson River of NYC home. In her youth, she would sneak into her mother's bedroom and read the romance novels stashed on the bookshelf, cementing her love of HEAs. A huge Buffy and Star Wars fan, she loves an epic fantasy and a surprise twist (Luke, he IS your father).

Before becoming an author, Rebecca had a successful twelve-year medical device sales career. After launching her own indie publishing company, she is now a full-time author who loves writing strong, complex characters who find their HEAs. She would be thrilled to hear from you anytime at rebecca@rebeccahefner.com.

Follow Rebecca Here:

www.rebeccahefner.com

Made in the USA
Columbia, SC
22 October 2021